李淑玲 著
Li Shuling

仪式与女性自我
当代美国女剧作家研究

Ritual and Female Self

A Study of Contemporary American Women Playwrights

南京大学出版社

序

　　李淑玲曾就读于南京大学外国语学院英语系,并获得英语语言文学博士学位。淑玲对美国文学,尤其是美国现当代戏剧进行了系统学习和研究。作为她的导师,我见证了她在学术道路上的成长与进步。她的学术专著《仪式与女性自我——当代美国女剧作家研究》即将付梓,我感到非常欣慰。

　　戏剧与仪式的关系源远流长且错综复杂。西方戏剧脱胎于古希腊的酒神节祭祀仪式,早期戏剧与仪式大致相同,包括装扮、动作、对话、歌唱、舞蹈等表演元素。维克多·特纳认为,戏剧与仪式都具有阈限性和表演性,是对日常生活的逃避和象征性颠覆。耶日·格洛托夫斯基将自己的戏剧看作一种过渡仪式,力图在剧场表演中获得仪式般的交融、疗愈和改变效果。理查德·谢克纳在《仪式的未来》和《表演研究》中深入探讨了仪式与戏剧的动态关系,提出了从仪式到戏剧的实效-娱乐二元关系结构。施旭升认为,"仪式""节日"和"狂欢"构成了戏剧艺术真正的精神原型。作为人类活动的重要组成部分,仪式也经常被剧作家写进剧本,搬上舞台。古希腊悲剧《安提戈涅》主要围绕是否为战死的波吕涅克斯举行葬礼和哀悼仪式展开。莎士比亚戏剧中更是不乏对求爱仪式、婚礼仪式、宗教仪式、政治仪式的描写与呈现。现当代剧作家让·热内、彼得·谢弗、爱德华·阿尔比、奥古斯特·威尔逊等也将形形色色的仪式融入戏剧作品,借以架构情节、塑造人物、表达主题。

　　20世纪70年代在美国女性主义运动第二次浪潮中,仪式和戏剧都成为女性反抗性别不平等、宣传女性主义思想的策略。一方面,女权人士在社区组织妇女参加"意识提高""哀悼与愤怒"等具有强烈政治斗争色彩的仪式;另一方面,女剧作家将神话、宗教及生活中的仪式进行女性化书写,邀请现场观众参与,形成了独具特色的女性主义仪式剧。这些表演实践启发和影响了很多成长于那个时期的女性剧作家,如玛丽娅·福尼斯、玛莎·诺曼、温迪·华瑟斯坦、恩托扎克·香格、保拉·沃格尔等,她们巧妙地把仪式嵌入戏剧结构中,或直接展演女性仪式,或从女性视角化用、颠覆以男性为中心的传统仪式,形成了一种独特的艺术风格。然而,学术界对这一现象的关注和研究却远远不够。淑玲撰写的这本专著以玛莎·诺曼、温迪·华瑟斯坦和保拉·沃格尔的九部代表戏剧作为阐释文本,深入研究仪式与女性自我、女性成长的复杂关系。

与已有研究相比,本研究具有三个突出特点:一是跨学科性。借用人类学、社会学和政治学中关于仪式的研究成果,从象征性、表演性和微观权力政治三个层面分析戏剧作品中表演的仪式,阐释女性自我的阈限性和生成性,考察性别、家庭及社会权力之间的关系,为女性主义戏剧研究提供了新的视角和路径。二是兼顾戏剧的内容与形式研究。本书从两个层面研究了仪式的功能:一方面,仪式是剧中女性人物的生存和斗争策略,通过表演、戏仿,甚至错误表演各种仪式,女性人物颠覆男权话语,巩固姐妹情谊,克服身份危机,完成自我的赋权、改变与重塑;另一方面,仪式也是诺曼、华瑟斯坦、沃格尔等女性剧作家共同采用的艺术技巧,仪式的时间、空间和表演过程与戏剧行动的发展相呼应,与戏剧结构形成完美融合。三是理论性强,且善于将理论概念应用于文本分析。本书围绕表演性这一核心概念,探讨了戏剧文本内部仪式的表演性、作为行动和事件的戏剧文本以及女性性别身份的表演性,关注女性主义运动和女性戏剧表演实践。

本书对从事欧美戏剧研究、女性主义研究、表演性理论研究的学者,以及对相关研究感兴趣的大众读者有着较大的启发意义,特此为序。

何成洲

2022 年 10 月 6 日

前　言

　　20世纪60—80年代，女性主义运动第二次浪潮席卷美国，促成了众多女性戏剧团体的成立，鼓舞了一大批知识妇女投身戏剧创作，产出了大量以女性经验为基础、女性问题为主题的戏剧作品。梅根·特里是二战后第一位影响巨大的女剧作家，她既是导演、演员和剧作家，也是积极的女性主义活动家，被称为"美国女性主义戏剧之母"。特里不仅创作了《让母亲镇定下来》《来来去去》《走进西蒙娜》等60余部戏剧，而且联合玛丽娅·福尼斯、阿德里娜·肯尼迪等五位女剧作家于1972年组建了妇女戏剧委员会，支持女剧作家的戏剧创作与演出。与特里一样，玛丽娅·福尼斯、恩托扎克·香格、蒂娜·豪、艾米丽·曼等剧作家都具有强烈的女性意识，在大胆实验新的戏剧手法以展演复杂的女性经验方面，取得了不菲成就。1981年，作为美国主流戏剧"风向标"的普利策戏剧奖颁发给了贝斯·亨利。随后，玛莎·诺曼、温迪·华瑟斯坦、保拉·沃格尔和玛格丽特·艾德森分别获得1983、1989、1998和1999年普利策戏剧奖，创造了二十年内五位女剧作家获得该奖的历史纪录。自此，女剧作家逐渐从戏剧领域边缘向主流和中心靠近，成为当代美国戏剧的一股强劲力量。

　　战后成长起来的女剧作家们深受当时社会动荡与文化思潮变化的影响，其戏剧作品涉及政治、经济、种族、性别、战争等丰富主题，博采音乐、舞蹈、民间仪式等不同技巧，在思想性和艺术性上都有所突破和超越。在各种社会运动中，女性主义运动第二次浪潮的潮起潮落对她们戏剧创作的影响最大。一方面,她们汲取女性主义新思想,利用舞台讲述女性故事,揭示性别压迫,塑造处于深刻变化中的女性形象;另一方面,她们也通过再现女性主义运动对其进行见证、反思和批判,以文学形式参与这一运动的历史进程。

女性主义运动与女性剧场互相影响渗透的一个典型例子是仪式的运用。为了唤醒妇女的女性意识,构建女性共同体,女性主义活动者创造性地组织表演了各种各样的仪式。例如,"意识提高"仪式将女性组织起来,通过轮流讲述、互相拥抱、集体唱歌跳舞等形式鼓励女性走出封闭的自我,联合起来,共同斗争;"少女初潮"仪式颂扬女性力量;"月经魔杖"仪式保护女性免遭强奸;女性受害者祭奠仪式表达女性的痛苦、愤怒和反抗的决心。受到这些仪式活动的启发,很多女剧作家尝试将仪式融入戏剧表演,开创了一种被巴蒂亚·帕德斯称为女性主义仪式戏剧的新形式。20世纪70年代比较著名的女性主义仪式剧团有"做女人挺好剧团""女性实验剧团""新周期剧团"等,它们上演了《魔鬼盗日》《珀耳塞福涅归来》《女儿们的周期》等典型的仪式戏剧。这些戏剧的仪式特征表现在三个方面:首先,将神话传说、宗教典仪和民间节庆中与母系、女性相关的仪式融入戏剧文本中,构成戏剧故事和框架,通过表演这些仪式歌颂女性精神和力量;其次,在表演中,邀请观众直接参与,打破虚构与现实、演员与观众之间的界限;最后,强调戏剧的改变力量,希望通过仪式戏剧的表演改变参与者的思想,并鼓动她们去采取行动。

虽然女性主义仪式戏剧随着女性主义运动第二次浪潮的退却而逐渐衰落,但是仪式作为一种有效的戏剧策略经常被女剧作家们使用。特里的《走进西蒙娜》以仪式开始,也以仪式结束,中间还穿插了酒神精神、西蒙娜死亡与重生以及基督附体等仪式场景。福尼斯的《费芙和她的朋友们》像是一场1935年版的"意识提高"仪式,而华瑟斯坦在《海蒂编年史》中直接呈现了她参加过的"意识提高"仪式。帕克斯的《爱情花园信徒》围绕各种求爱和婚姻仪式展开。在香格的《献给要自杀的黑人姑娘》和《第七号魔咒》中,黑人女性通过集体仪式找

前　言

到姐妹情谊，实现自我成长。诺曼、华瑟斯坦、沃格尔的戏剧不但包含了很多日常生活和互动仪式，还将一些具有特殊意义的仪式巧妙地融进戏剧结构，她们的剧作如《晚安，妈妈》《非凡女性及其他》《我如何学会了驾驶》等都运用仪式塑造人物，推动情节，展示权力关系，表达女性主义思想，形成了独特的艺术特色。

为了更深入、更系统地考察仪式与女性戏剧的关系，本书从诺曼、华瑟斯坦和沃格尔戏剧中选取九部作品，以人类学和表演研究中关于仪式的理论为指导，分析这些作品中仪式的象征意义、表演效力和政治寓意，考察在仪式过程中改变和重构的女性身份，阐释仪式与女性自我之间错综复杂的关系。在此基础上，运用社会学和文学研究中的表演性理论解读仪式表演与性别身份的关系。

本书由六部分组成。第一部分是绪论。首先从作品人物、主题、思想等方面阐述了诺曼、华瑟斯坦和沃格尔戏剧中蕴含的强烈女性意识；然后梳理了国内外已有的研究文献，指出仪式研究的独特价值；最后从仪式的象征性、表演性和政治性三个层面建构了本研究的理论框架，为本书的主体分析奠定了基础。

第一章聚焦于玛莎·诺曼的三部戏剧，分析剧中底层妇女表演的死亡仪式以及在仪式表演中摧毁和生成的女性自我。诺曼戏剧中的女性主角是沉默的群体，处于社会边缘，地位卑微，被男性凝视、操控和剥削，但她们并不屈服，努力寻求克服存在危机的途径。通过表演死亡仪式，她们摧毁之前的自我，在阈限时空中经历象征性死亡，并以不同的自我呈现在观众面前，从而获得新的自我身份。《出狱》中的阿丽/阿琳通过驱魔仪式和重新命名仪式，将自己从一个邪恶、暴力、令人憎恨的前犯人转变成了品行端正、自食其力、平和内敛的公民。《晚安，妈妈》是杰西为自己设计并亲自表演的安魂弥撒，其事件性不是发生在杰西自杀的时刻，而是在她宣布将要自杀的时刻。她的语言、动作、行为兼具象征性和表演性，在摧毁自己的身体之前生成了一个健谈、理智、坚决、自主、强大的新自我。《僵局》中的莉莉指导了亨利的葬礼、逃犯的死亡与复活仪式以及阿奇的成人礼。在仪式过程中，莉莉由前妓女变成男性的精神导师，由男性欲望的客体变成了经济独立、拥有人生智慧和精神力量的主体。诺曼将这些边缘女性置于兼具毁灭与生成力量的仪式中，展示了她们身份变化的过程。

第二章以温迪·华瑟斯坦的三部戏剧作为阐释对象，研究中产阶级白人女性如何被传统仪式建构，又如何通过策略性表演进行抵抗和自我重构。华瑟斯坦将受过高等教育的职业女性置于她的舞台中心，观察和记录处于变革时期的女性生活。在其剧作中，仪式是一个政治场域，各种社会力量在这里相遇、对抗与协商，服从与反抗共存，女性身份不断被重新定义。在《非凡女性及其他》中，落伍的大学社交仪式表演传统女性气质，灌输父权思想，女大学生们则通过将其狂欢化打破刻板的性别定式，抵制仪式的控制，建构了其"非凡女性"身份。《海蒂编年史》中的"意识提高活动"是独具女权主义特色的集体仪式。在以弗兰为代表的激进女权主义者满腔热情地表演时，以海蒂为代表的人文主义者却表现了疏远与质疑。仪式的歌曲、语言、动作和程序既富有象征意义，又充满表演效力。经过对抗与斗争，海蒂被仪式改变，成为一个真正的女权主义者。在《罗森韦格姊妹》中，当格尔吉斯虔诚地举行犹太安息日日落仪式时，她的姐姐萨拉冷漠地抵制，妹妹裴夫妮好奇地观看，这暴露了她们不同的身份认同，引起了关于自我的辩论和反思。最终，她们与过去达成和解，彼此认同，形成了新的姐妹共同体。

第三章转向保拉·沃格尔的戏剧作品，解读戏仿仪式与女性自我赋权的关系。沃格尔的戏剧更加关注两性间的权力斗争，展现叛逆的、具有颠覆和僭越精神的女性。对沃格尔和她的女性人物来说，仪式既是可以模仿的象征结构，也是可以戏仿和挑战的文化符号。她们用戏仿的、讽刺的方式调用仪式，嘲弄僵化的性别规范，解构压迫性的父权制和异性恋话语，反转男女间的权力结构。在戏仿的仪式中，她们表演变化的、兼具两性气质的性别身份，为自己赋权，成为欲望主体。《七口之家》中的女同性恋夫妻戏仿各种经典戏剧中的死亡场景，为她们想象中的儿子表演死亡仪式，同时扮演父亲角色和母亲角色，在男性气质、女性气质之间自由切换,成功挫败了皮特想要篡夺父亲地位的企图。《巴尔的摩华尔兹》被称为驱爱仪式和纪念仪式,是对弗洛伊德哀悼模式的戏仿。安娜与同性恋且患有艾滋病的哥哥互换身份,使男性与女性、异性恋与同性恋、自我与他者互为认同,用荒诞的戏仿表达了爱与哀悼。《我如何学会了驾驶》戏仿了男孩的成人礼和传统的求爱仪式,女主人公丽儿从一个模仿传统女性气质的小女孩变成了一个男性气质十足的驾驶员,从被男性凝视、虐待和控制的欲望客体变成了主体,从受害人变成了幸存者,超越成长的痛苦与危机,实现了女性的自我赋权。

第四章跳出具体文本,从历史和理论层面探讨仪式与女性自我的表演性。在女性主义第二次浪潮中,激进的女权主义者不仅在现实活动中创造和组织各种专属于女性的仪式,还将仪式与戏剧表演结合起来,开创了一种独特的女性主义仪式戏剧,利用仪式表演影响和改变女性。诺曼、华瑟斯坦和沃格尔的剧作产生于这一历史语境,虽然不属于女性主义团体创作的仪式戏剧,但也呈现出明显的仪式特征。这些戏剧中的仪式既是剧中女性人物表演的社会行为,也是将戏剧与其文化背景、观众和意图关联在一起的文本策略,兼具再现与表演两种特性,在虚构和真实两个世界里都引起了某种改变。在虚构的戏剧世界,其表演结果为:建构新的身份、实现女性赋权、巩固女性共同体。而对于真实世界,其表演性体现在四个方面:见证了女性为反抗父权制压迫和性别歧视所做的斗争;塑造了新的、处于阈限与改变过程中的女性形象;表达并具形化了女性主义思想和精神;在当代美国女性剧场中形成了一种新的戏剧美学特征。另外,诺曼、华瑟斯坦和沃格尔戏剧中女性自我的不断改变与重构也揭示了女性身份认同的表演性,表明自我认同并不是本质的、固定不变的存在。父权制话语通过仪式控制女性身体,迫使她们按照性别规范表演女性气质。同样,女性主义话语也可以运用仪式中的女性身体抵抗操控,实现重新意指和身份重构。在这个过程中,尽管主导意识形态的话语很强大,主体能动性还是可以发挥作用,对准则和文化符号进行重新意指,产生转变性效果。

　　最后一部分为结论。在诺曼、华瑟斯坦和沃格尔的剧作中,仪式是剧中女性人物为克服身份危机、实现自我赋权而采取的一种实践策略,也是剧作家组织戏剧行动、表现女性主义思想的戏剧技巧。作为活跃于美国当代戏剧舞台的女性剧作家,诺曼、华瑟斯坦和沃格尔透过仪式展示了女性自我的转变与生成过程,塑造了不同阶层的女性主义者形象,形成了独具特色的戏剧风格。

Contents

Introduction / 001

I   Woman-Conscious Drama: The Œuvre of Norman, Wasserstein and Vogel / 005

II Literature Review / 019

III Ritual, Liminal Female Self and Performativity / 033

Chapter One   Destruction and Resurrection: Marginalized Women Reborn from Death Ritual and Ritual Death / 049

I   An Ex-con's Self-Reformation Through Rites of Affliction and Renaming / 054

II An Epileptic's Self-Empowerment by Performing Her Own "Requiem Mass" / 081

III A Whore's Elevation to Spiritual Guide in Initiating a Few Rituals / 105

Chapter Two   Compliance and Resistance: Educated Women Redefined by (Mis)performing Rituals / 129

I   Becoming "Uncommon Women" by Carnivalizing College Rituals / 134

II A Humanist's Conversion to Feminist by Participating in a CR Ritual / 163

Ⅲ Three Sisters' Self-Renewal after a Jewish Ritual of
Sabbath Sundown / 187

**Chapter Three   Subversion and Reconstruction: Transgressive
Women Empowered Through Parodied Rituals** / 213

Ⅰ Negotiating Gender Roles in Playacting Rituals of "Dying"
and "Service" / 217
Ⅱ Identifying with the Other Through Fantasized "Rite of
Loving Exorcism" / 240
Ⅲ Shifting Power Through Parodied Rites of Initiation and
Courtship/ 264

**Chapter Four   The Performativity of Ritual and Identity in
Contemporary American Women's Drama** / 287

Ⅰ Ritual in the Women's Movement and the Feminist Ritual
Theater / 290
Ⅱ The Performativity of Ritual / 300
Ⅲ The Performativity of Female Self / 313

Conclusion / 326

References / 334

Introduction

Since the first American female dramatist Mercy Otis Warren created her only play *The Group* in 1775, women playwrights had been silent and invisible in the history of American drama and theater. Although the first wave of feminism promoted the development of women's theater, women's dramatic works did not gain enough recognition. During the years from 1921 to 1958, only five plays by women were awarded the Pulitzer Prize.[①] Women did not become an influential force in the dramatic world until the second wave of feminism swept across America in the 1970s. Promoted by the women's movement, numerous avant-garde, alternative women's theater companies were established and a number of significant women dramatists appeared. In his article "What Do Women Playwrights Want?" published in 1992, Robert Brustein pointed out, "The spate of plays by, for, and about women have multiplied in the last decade[...]In terms of numbers, if not in broadness of theme, American women playwrights now represent a significant movement that is surely unprecedented in history." (28) With the boom of feminist theater, a group of talented young women playwrights came to the forefront and made outstanding achievements. From 1981 to

---

[①] The five plays are Zona Gale's *Miss Lulu Bett* (1921), Susan Glaspell's *Alison's House* (1931), Zoë Akins's *The Old Maid* (1935), Coyle Chase's *Harvey* (1945), and Ketti Frings's *Look Homeward, Angel* (1958).

1999, five women playwrights won the Pulitzer Prize,[①] the same number of Pulitzers awarded to women for the previous sixty years. The present author would like to select three of the Pulitzer winners, Marsha Norman, Wendy Wasserstein and Paula Vogel,[②] as examples to examine how women playwrights deploy ritual or ritualization to dramatize the transformation and constitution of female self.

Born in 1947, 1950 and 1951 respectively and awarded the Pulitzer Prize for Drama in 1983, 1989 and 1998 one after another, Marsha Norman, Wendy Wasserstein and Paula Vogel are three of the most original playwrights emerging in the 1980s and 1990s, and have become representative female voices in contemporary American drama. All three belong to the baby-boomer generation of Americans. They have been nurtured by the second-wave of women's movement and encouraged by their forerunners such as Zona Gale, Susan Glaspell and Lillian Hellman. Devoted to playwriting, they have used theater to represent women's experiences and issues with implicit or explicit woman consciousness and feminist commitment, trying their best to articulate different female voices in the male-dominated theater.

Since her first play *Getting Out* premiered in 1977, Norman has produced twelve original plays, six adaptations, eleven screenplays and one novel until 2020, which win her numerous awards. Her masterpiece, *'night, Mother* has been translated into twenty-three

---

① The five plays are Beth Henley's *Crimes of the Heart* (1981), Marsha Norman's *'night, Mother* (1983), Wendy Wasserstein's *The Heidi Chronicles* (1989), Paula Vogel's *How I Learned to Drive* (1998), and Margaret Edson's *Wit* (1999).

② They are also three of the five women playwrights studied by Christopher Bigsby in his monograph *Contemporary American Playwrights* (2004), in which ten contemporary playwrights (five men and five women) are included because Bigsby think they "for different reasons, seem to merit greater attention or whose public reputation has attached itself to certain plays at the expense of others (Viii)".

languages and performed all over the world. Janet Brown acclaims that Norman is "the most successful author of serious feminist drama working in the U. S. today"(60). In contrast to Norman's serious "she-tragedies"(Spencer 147), Wasserstein devotes herself to comedy and avows to write "serious plays that are funny"(Bryer 258). In 1989, her play *The Heidi Chronicles* enjoyed a long-running Broadway and regional theater success, winning her the Triple Crown: the Pulitzer Prize, the Tony and the Critics' Circle Award. From the first play *Uncommon Women and Others*(1977) to the last *Third*(2005), all her eleven plays have been staged on Broadway or Off-Broadway, making her commercial success and a highly-exposed celebrity in American mainstream theater. Though starting to write plays earlier than Norman and Wasserstein, Vogel had not gained public recognition until *The Baltimore Waltz* won her the Obie Award for Best Play in 1992 and *How I Learned to Drive* brought her six national prizes in 1998, including the Pulitzer Prize, the Lortel Prize, the Drama Desk Award, and the Obie Award. Both a playwright and a professor, Vogel has created more than twenty plays, among which eleven have been produced and ten published. Vogel is still active in American theater now. Her new play *Don Juan Comes Home from Iraq*(2014) is a powerful anti-war play about America's twenty-first-century war experience. Her latest work *Indecent* won a finalist for the 2016 Edward M. Kennedy Prize for Drama and was nominated for the 2019 Equity Joseph Jefferson Award for Large Play Production.

Norman, Wasserstein and Vogel have distinct characteristics of their own in terms of dramatic genre, style, character and theme. Norman is famous for her tragedies about ordinary and invisible women who struggle desperately for the right and power to control their destinies. She employs classical realism and climatic structure in a new and creative way.① Wasserstein wins fame and popularity by her comedies about the stories of upper-middle-class women who are entrapped between family and career. Except *The Sisters Rosensweig*, all her other plays apply episodic structure. Vogel fuses comedy with tragedy, places all walks of women center stage and addresses contemporary concerns such as domestic violence, pornography, pedophilia, and AIDS in a defamiliarized and burlesque style.

Though addressing women's issues with different stories and various dramatic forms, Norman, Wasserstein and Vogel share common grounds in at least two things. Thematically, all of them are concerned about the awakening and growing process of girls/women in terms of body, sexuality and psychology. One focus of their dramas is the female identity in transition and transformation, that is, how women seek, perform and realize themselves in the feminist and post-feminist era. Formally, they have been constantly experimenting new dramaturgical techniques to convey their women-conscious stories and explore unique aesthetics that belong to them. Ritual is one of the devices used by all of them.

Norman, Wasserstein and Vogel have attracted considerable critical attention since the 1980s. Critics have studied their dramas from various perspectives, among which feminist, psychological, cultural, ethical, stylistic and comparative readings are the most important approaches. However, ritual, one phenomenon that exists in almost every play of them and often plays an essential role in character development and dramatic structure, has not got enough

---

① There is a debate on the realism in Norman's plays, especially *'night, Mother*. Feminist critics such as Dolan (1988) and Forte (1989) criticize the realistic format as not feminist. Demastes (1993) argues that Norman's realism is different from traditional one and can be called "post-Beckettian realism" or "anti-classic realism"(113). Begley (2012) contends that *'night, Mother* is "a work of hyperrealism", a fusion of realism and symbolism (339 - 347).

exploration that it rightly deserves. In fact, ritual is not only a strategy that female characters deploy to deal with crisis in life and change in social status, but also an important device that the women playwrights employ to address the feminist theme and organize dramatic action.

This book focuses on the rituals that female characters perform in the representative plays of Norman, Wasserstein and Vogel, and explores the functions of ritual performance as a strategy of self-transformation for female characters and as an effective dramatic device for these women playwrights. A few specific questions will be addressed: What rituals do female characters perform in the selected plays? What kind of female selves do they construct by performing these rituals? What is the relationship between ritual and dramatic action in terms of time, space, structure and acting body? How do Norman, Wasserstein and Vogel use ritual to accommodate women's experiences and issues? What is the performativity of ritual and identity in contemporary American feminist theater?

I Woman-Conscious Drama: The Œuvre of Norman, Wasserstein and Vogel

Judged from theme, characterization and style, the plays of Norman, Wasserstein and Vogel can be categorized as woman-conscious drama. Woman-conscious drama, coined by Rosemary K. Curb, refers to "all drama by and about women that is characterized by multiple interior reflections of women's lives and perceptions" (302). Curb argues that this term is more inclusive than feminist, lesbian or post-modern drama because it may cover all of them. What she emphasizes is not a specific political stance or dramatic form, but a collective identity, a kind of consciousness of being a woman.

According to Curb's interpretation, woman-conscious theater presents "a multi-dimensional unravelling of women's collective imagination in a psychic replay of myth and history" (302). It is polymorphous and anti-hierarchical, representing "many layers of women's experiences which have been hidden, silenced, ridiculed, trivialized, and erased" (Curb 302). The central issue of woman-conscious drama is the female identity, that is, the discovery, recognition, formation, construction, and realization of female self.

Nannerl O. Keohane, Michelle Rosaldo and Barbara C. Gelpi distinguish three levels of women's self-consciousness: feminine, female, and feminist. Feminine consciousness looks upon female body as the object of men, being "the woman as defined by male gaze, construct, and desire" (ix). Female consciousness is less inert and passive but still serves patriarchy, regarding woman as the other, the second sex. Its typical image in theater is virgin mother or Mother Earth, whose function is "giving and preserving life, nurturing and sustaining" (Keohane, Rosaldo, Gelpi ix). Only feminist consciousness is entirely self-defined and subversive, reflecting the oppressive situation of women on the one hand, and trying to seek alternative, non-oppressive ways of living for women on the other hand. Although woman's consciousness exists on all three levels simultaneously, Curb points out that woman-conscious drama primarily mirrors female and feminist consciousness, and it emerges with the development of the women's movement in the 1970s (303).

Belonging to the baby-boomer generation, Norman, Wasserstein and Vogel have witnessed and participated in some of the momentous social changes in the country's history, such as the Cold War, the Civil Rights Movement, the Anti-Vietnam War Movement, and the women's movement. The drastic social shifts, especially the new feminist movement have shaped their cognition and conception. They are educated by traditional mothers at home as little girls yet enlightened by feminist books like *The Second Sex*, *The Feminine Mystique* and *Sexual Politics* at school, and inspired by feminist activities such as protest march, consciousness-raising, and bra-burnings in communities. These experiences have not only awoken their woman consciousness but also influenced their playwriting.

Marsha Norman's woman consciousness was rooted in her rebellion against her mother, a Methodist fundamentalist, who excluded radio and television from the home and forbade Marsha Norman to play with other children. Recalling her childhood, Norman said, "I was born into a family to which I did not belong. If I was to survive, I knew that I had to find another group to support me ... and even see who I was." (Craig 166) She turned to other women whom she regarded as a matriarchy family and who were more kindred in mind and spirit. The first was her Great Aunt Bubbie, an unmarried old lady who took Marsha Norman in her house as her own little kid. The second was Norman's piano teacher, Olga, who was always demanding and strict with her. Her most enduring mentor, Martha Ellison, was her English teacher who discovered her writing talent and introduced her to the works of Lillian Hellman. Reading Hellman's plays since middle school, Norman confessed that she considered Hellman as her role model and precursor who "are willing to share their lives as well as their work, make it possible for those who come after them to survive" (Norman 7). In order to get out of the isolation and alienation she suffered in her immediate family, Marsha connected herself to the world beyond family and set up a social community where women from different families can "sit around and talk to each other about their memories of devastating events in their lives" (Bigsby, "Contemporary" 210).

Once entering theatrical world, Marsha Norman gained access to a broader perspective and started out a tough journey to search for self and tell women's stories. When being interviewed by Linda Ginter-Brown, Norman said firmly:

> Clearly, women in our culture feel invisible. I feel invisible. I felt invisible as a girl. That's why I have said so often, you know. I write about people you would never see, like me. This has got to change! We have got to have our stories told! ... We just have to fight this, and the stories of women are wonderful ways, the stories I love best ... So I think that what I can do, in looking at this, is to see that women's stories survive. (176 – 177)

Therefore, whatever genre Norman resorts to, tragedy, comedy or musical, all her plays are primarily about and for women, giving women their voices in theater.

Mother/daughter relationship and women's escape from old traps—family, marriage, prison or former selves—are two major themes in Norman's early works. In *Getting out* (1977), Arlene, a girl once sexually abused by her father, emotionally ignored by her mother, economically exploited by a pimp, and spiritually disciplined by prison guards, struggles to escape from her painful past by using a new name and resisting her earlier self, hoping to survive through honest work. The daughter in *'night, Mother* (1983), Jessie, is also an entrapped woman who has to get free from her mother's control by taking extreme measures and gains autonomy by destroying herself. Mothers in both plays are unconscious victims of patriarchal society. They cannot protect their daughters from hurt, nor can they understand the desperate struggles that their daughters make. In her one-act play *Third and Oak: The Laundromat* (1978), the motherlike

Albert and the daughterlike Deedee encounter in a laundromat and make a hesitant yet fruitful conversation, revealing their sadness, loneliness and sympathy to each other. In these plays, Norman finds "in dialogue between women a way of opening up channels to emotional needs and anxieties"(Bigsby, "Contemporary" 210). This demonstrates Norman's effort to bridge a mutuality of women that cuts across class and age.

Though being praised as a tragedy queen of contemporary American drama, Norman has created a series of comedies such as *Circus Valentine* (1979), *The Holdup* (1987), *Sarah and Abraham* (1988), and *Loving Daniel Boone* (1992), in which the pure women relationship gives way to complicated male-female relationship. Instead of focusing on women's loss, predicament and plight, Norman attempts to explore how patriarchal culture constitutes men and women's social roles, mutual relationships and power politics. In *Sarah and Abraham*, Norman reshapes biblical myth to focus on women in fresh ways and reclaims women's matriarchal role in a patriarchal world. She goes back to the past and the west frontier in *The Holdup* and *Loving Daniel Boone* to retrospect the historical myth and redefine heroism from feminist perspective, expressing her new ideas of what a heroic act should be and how to achieve a balanced male-female relationship.

The response to Norman's comedy is cold and harsh. Some critics even express their disappointment because they think Norman has quitted her fight for women.[1] In fact, Norman does not abandon her original goal of writing about serious women's issues. She just turns to a different strategy. She contends that laugh is "one of the primary

---

[1] Norman talked about the negative reviews on *Circus Valentine* and *The Holdup* when being interviewed by Linda Ginter-Brown in 1993, and defended her comic works.

methods of dealing with pain"(Savran, "In Their Own Words" 184), and that her comic plays are not simple entertainment. What she wants to do is to make the audience have a good time as well as a strong experience at the theater. Just as what she and Linda Ginter-Brown discussed in their 1993 interview, Norman is a very positive writer who sees the possibilities instead of the doom. In her comedies, women are not depicted as victims as before. They become high priestess, brave explorer or female initiator. Therefore, Norman's sense of humor and comic spirit, similar to that of Wasserstein and Vogel, is an alternative optimistic strategy to deal with women's problems, providing a way out for them.

In the 1990s, Norman met her own trap in dramatic art. She once said from her home in the New York City area: "I realize I am not going to do better than *'night, Mother*. I'd explored that vein and I was ready to step down from being the queen of serious drama. So okay—I was ready to write in another form."(Noth 120) Her new form is musical. Since the success of *The Secret Garden* in 1991, Norman has written six musicals: *The Red Shoes*(1993), *The Color Purple*(2005), *The Master Butchers Singing Club*(2010), *The Trumpet of the Swan*(2011), and *The Bridges of Madison County* (2014), which bring her more prizes and make her a leading book and libretto pioneer in the modern world of musicals. Even in such an entertaining dramatic form, Norman still shows her concerns about women's fate. In *The Color Purple*, poor black women are abused not just by society but also by their husbands and fathers. Having noticed the persistent theme through all Norman's plays, Noth comments,

> Themes of importance to mankind, such as midlife passion, family relationships, sensitivity among species, treatment of workers run through her

musical output just as the aftermath of prison and the consequences of suicide ran through her serious plays. (124)

In other words, Norman, by giving women's issues priority, becomes more universal by addressing general human experiences.

Wendy Wasserstein's woman consciousness was ignited by her mother too, especially the double standards her mother imposed on her and her brother. When his brother received books about traveling around the world, she was given girls' tales like *Eloise* and *Madeline*. When her brother played all kinds of sports, her mother forced her to attend dance school and learn feminine etiquette. What was worse, when she went to school with work shirt, the headmistress would call her mother to tell her that Wasserstein should get dressed up and wear pink (Bennetts 5). Wasserstein was bothered and angered by these ridiculous conventions for girls.

The college education Wasserstein got at Mount Holyoke was also confusing and problematic. According to her reminiscence, at the beginning girls were told to graduate and get married to lawyers, then they were encouraged to compete with men and become lawyers by themselves, but at the moment of their graduation, the rules changed and women were called on to turn back to families again. On the one hand, the conventional notions of being a mother and wife had been shattered by feminists like Betty Friedan, Kate Millet and Germaine Greer. On the other hand, college girls were required to perform traditional rituals like Tea Hour, Milk and Crackers, and Father-Daughter Weekend which reinforce feminine manners. Wasserstein, similar to other girls who studied on campus and attended feminist consciousness-raising meetings off campus, was caught between the two conflicting sets of values.

When Wendy Wasserstein enrolled at the Yale School of Drama

in 1973, she was shocked by the voicelessness of women in theater. The plays she had to read and watch were all written and directed by males. She discovered that theatrical representation of women was very stereotypical and distorted. When interviewed by Carolyn Casey Craig, Wasserstein said,

> It amazed me in terms of the perception of women ... we were reading a lot of Jacobean drama; and, excuse me, but it seemed that men were basically kissing the skulls of women and dropping dead from the poison. And I thought ... "I don't identify with this. This doesn't happen to any of my friends." So I decided as an almost political act ... that I would write a play for the Yale School of Drama in which there was an all-woman curtain call. (188)

She realized that the message about women delivered by these plays was totally untrue and harmful. This did not represent anyone she knew. Such uncomfortable experiences stimulated her strong determination to write women-centered plays in which women's happiness and pain would be displayed with equal weight with that of men.

Czekay once pointed out, "Wasserstein's plays do not necessarily focus on explicitly feminist topics, but they are woman-conscious in their consistent treatment of women's conflicts." (17) Wasserstein started her playwriting with an all-women drama *Uncommon Women and Others*(1977). This play initiates her long journey of chronicling baby boomers' dilemma between personal lives and professional fulfillment from the 1960s to the 1990s, even into the beginning of the 21st century. The college girls in *Uncommon Women and Others* are young, energetic and rebellious, risking at new things and dreaming of "have-it-all" in the future. Janie and Harriet in *Isn't Romantic*(1983), seven years older and more career-oriented, have been sent into "the jungle of New York to seek fulfillment, self-respect, and romance and take-out food" (Gussow C11). In her Pulitzer drama *The Heidi Chronicles* (1988), Wasserstein biographizes Heidi Holland's self-development from a middle school student to a college professor, interweaving her private ups and downs with the social transformations in the 1970s.

In the 1990s, Wasserstein entered into her midlife. She created a Chekhovian play *The Sisters Rosensweig* (1991), in which three sisters were facing different middle-aged crises. Similarly, Lyssa, the successful doctor in *An American Daughter* (1997), and Professor Laurie Jameson in *Third* (2005), are both more than fifties, holding important positions in institutions yet still struggling as veteran feminists. Having noticed this characteristic, Czekay comments,

> Wasserstein historicizes each play's present by integrating references from contemporary cultural, political, and feminist history ... This dramaturgy allows her to frame the personal with the larger context of the political and, thus, offers gendered experience as a historical category. (20)

Michael Feingold concurs that Wasserstein's project is "to dramatize the female life of America in her time without scanting its complexity, its inconveniences, or its lapses into the absurd" ("Wendy Wasserstein").

Female characters in Wasserstein's dramatic works are not rigid, conservative or traditionally feminine but intelligently humorous, intellectually self-reflective and spiritually optimistic. They are not only active in social movements but also adventurous in sexual and political life, expressing genuine sexuality and desires. Wasserstein prefers to portray women's trouble and sadness in a comic way. Such representation once invited much critique and disparagement from feminists who were annoyed by the "un-seriousness" of her comic female characters (Chen 12 – 14). This, in fact, is a misunderstanding of Wasserstein's philosophy. For Wasserstein, humor can not only entertain but also deflect, "it helps you deal with things which are overwhelmingly tragic"(Cohen 265). She once refuted, "My work is often thought of as lightweight commercial comedy, and I have always thought, no, you don't understand: this is a political act." (Winder 172) Craig admits that Wasserstein uses comedy as "a balancing act, a way to hide the pain, but also to reveal it … to explore it. And to break it too"(197). In fact, Wasserstein's feminist consciousness lies in her female characters' pursuit of true self with comic spirit.

Wasserstein had devoted her life to writing plays about women's issues until her untimely death from cancer in 2006. Having earned her fame in commercial, popular mainstream American theater, she is praised as "the beloved playwright widely regarded as the official poet of both a generation and a sex"(Jones 16). She is not only a true believer of feminist spirit but also a realistic chronicler of feminist movement. In Homes' words, Wasserstein "has been among our chief theatrical witnesses, capturing the essential elements of contemporary women's lives, infusing them with a decidedly female sensibility and returning them to us as theater"(34).

Paula Vogel also has a mother who inflamed her woman consciousness but in a very different way from both Norman's and Wasserstein's mothers. Suffering from a turbulent marriage, Vogel's mother got divorced and raised up her offspring by herself. Her painful and hostile relationship with her husband frightened little Paula and let her see gender battle at an early age. However, the mother's strong will, rebellious spirit and humorous personality set a good example to the little girl who would grow up to be a feminist playwright. When Paula Vogel entered the drama world, she was, as Norman and Wasserstein once were, shocked and angered by the western theatrical tradition that "all drama by definition from Aristotle is about finding a male protagonist" (Craig 217). Vogel says, "Women have been trained to empathize with male subjects, so we are always translating our personal response from one gender to the other. Men have not learned how to empathize directly with a female character." (Savran, "Playwright's Voice" 272) Therefore, Vogel has struggled against this sexist tradition from the beginning of her play writing by finding female protagonists for her dramas.

What Vogel represents in her drama is neither feminine nor female consciousness but real feminist consciousness. In her first experimental play *Desdemona: A Play about a Handkerchief* (1973), Vogel rewrites Shakespeare's *Othello* from a startling feminist perspective. Desdemona, Emilia and Bianca, the three voiceless female characters in the original play are situated at stage center and no male character appears through the action. The protagonists in *The Oldest Profession* (1981) are five old prostitutes who are struck by poverty due to Reaganomics and die one by one with each blackout. In *And Baby Makes Seven* (1986), the protagonists are two lesbians who get married and live with their three imaginary sons. The main characters of *The Mineola Twins* (1996) are sister twins who represent two sides of America, one conservative, and the other radical. Vogel persists in representing women's experiences in her drama and reversing male discourse into female one.

Vogel's plays are highly political. She intends to establish a counter discourse by making dialogues with famous male playwrights. Her strategy, as David Savran points out, is "responding to, critiquing and dismantling someone else's work" ("Loose Screws" x). Except for *The Baltimore Waltz*, all her works until now are an act of retaliation to an early male-authored canonical text. *Meg* (1977) is a revision of Robert Bolt's *A Man for All Seasons*, elevating Meg, Thomas More's daughter, to the subject of her own life as well as history. *And Baby Makes Seven* talks back to Albee's *Who's Afraid of Virginia Woolf*, re-imagining fantasy and family values in homosexual marriage. *The Oldest Profession* responds to David Mamet's *The Duck Variations* in both structure and theme, celebrating the sensual delight of old women instead of men. Her Pulitzer Prize-winning play *How I Learned to Drive* is a *Lolita* story that narrates from the point of view of the female, shifting the position of victim and victimizer. In this way, Vogel re-examines and re-visions patriarchal playwrights, opening up a dialogue between traditional and feminist theater. She deconstructs the male discourse and defamiliarizes the accepted dramatic stories so that spectators can see the characters and their situations in a new light.

Female protagonists in Vogel's plays are never obedient, chaste or nice in the traditional notion, "never reduced to their functions as wives, mothers, and daughters" (Pellegrini 479). They, in fact, are eager to express their desires, dare to say no to men's manipulation and want to be active makers or unmakers of their destinies. Desdemona is not drawn as an innocent wife and Bianca becomes a new woman who is free and independent. They are not the passive victims who are manipulated by Othello and Iago, but full-blown and willful rebels against the roles that men have forced upon them. The over seventy grannies in *The Oldest Profession* are still involved in the business of prostitution. They manage to make a living and hold their dignity and self-esteem until the last moment of life. Anna in *The Baltimore Waltz* imagines that she travels to Europe to cure her ATD (a euphemism for AIDS) but ends with making love with any man she meets in her fantasy. The lesbian couple in *And Baby Makes Seven* invites a gay to join them in order to have a child. Overcoming all difficulties, the two women get their real baby and create a new mode of family. Charlene in *Hot 'N' Throbbing* is a pornographer who writes stories about women's erotica and becomes collusive of her own death. She is one of the "female characters who are as flawed as male characters" (Bigsby, "Contemporary" 314). These subversive female characters are so complicated and ambiguous that the audience would feel difficult to identify with. However, they are more articulate than their male antagonists and can free the audience from the traditional binary mode of gender. Just as Vogel remarks,

> Feminism means being politically incorrect. It means avoiding the easy answer—that isn't really an answer at all—in favor of posing the question in the right way. It means refusing to construct an exemplary feminist hero. (Savran, "Loose Screws" xii)

These estranged female images, in fact, are much truer than "good" or "virtuous" angels in the room. Even if they are bad, they are as bad as man.

Vogel often tackles subtle and controversial social issues that hurt women, such as sexual abuse, domestic violence, prostitution and pedophilia. However, she also realizes that women should not pity themselves as tragic victims. They must learn how to survive traumas and get a way out. The best example comes from *How I Learned to Drive*. A little girl named Li'l Bit is molested by her uncle Peck from eleven years old. She, as an innocent victim, is vulnerable at the beginning. But she learns how to protect herself from being hurt more by drawing a line between them and playing the game according to her rules. During the process of learning how to drive, Li'l Bit grows up and masters the skill of controlling the car as well as her life. She finally takes full responsibility of her life by forgiving her uncle and reconciling with her past. Not being victimized but empowered by her traumatic experiences, she becomes the subject rather an object. When talking about Vogel's feminist strategy, Savran comments,

> All of her work is devoted to exposing not just how women are entrapped and oppressed, but the possibilities that figures like Desdemona or the oldest professionals have to contest, subvert, and redefine the roles they have been assigned. ("Loose Screws" xi)

Nowadays, Vogel is even more active and concerned about current social affairs. In her recent works *The Long Christmas Ride Home* (2003), *Civil War Christmas* (2008), *Don Juan Comes Home from Iraq* (2014), and *Indecent* (2015), Vogel addresses more ambivalent social and cultural issues like dysfunctional marriage, the fragility of human connection, the impact and ethics of Iraq war, lesbian romance, and so on. Vogel's theater is the one that meets life in a head-on collision. She is never afraid of revealing hidden problems and penetrating controversial topics. She argues,

> Wherever there is confusion or double, triple, and quadruple standards, that is the realm of theater. [And that] drama lives in paradoxes and contradictions. (Interview)

Vogel is still on her way to explore the ambivalent dilemmas that modern society confronts.

The three levels of woman's self-consciousness that Keohane classifies can be seen through the kaleidoscope of Norman, Wasserstein and Vogel's dramatic works. With a strong sense of being women, Norman, Wasserstein and Vogel have displayed women's laughs and tears on stage successfully, reversing the biased assumption that "the pain in the world is a man's pain"(Betsko and Koenig 426) and proving that women's issues deserve dramatic efforts. By portraying various female characters—oppressed victims, struggling professionals and rebellious feminists, they present women as central subjects who suffer from existential angst, identity crisis and metaphysical pain which have long been regarded as men's privileges. Just as Marsha Norman said, they, together with their peers like Tina Howe, Beth Henley, Ntozake Shange and Suzan-Lori Parks, have opened a door for women theater and must work hard not to "let the door close ... because it's a very difficult door to get open again"(J. Brown 190). As representative women playwrights of the baby boomer generation, they have demonstrated the transformative process of female identities in transitional American history by dramatizing women's exterior experiences in life and interior reflections on self. Their woman-conscious drama has become a valuable legacy in American literature and has imposed considerable influence upon the younger generation of playwrights such as Margaret Edson, Lynn Nottage, Quiara Alegria Hudes and Annie Baker.

II Literature Review

Since they started their playwriting in the 1970s, Norman, Wasserstein and Vogel have gradually been accepted by audience as well as critics and some of their masterpieces have been acclaimed as feminist classics. However, the road to canonical status is not smooth and criticisms of their dramatic works have gone through ups and downs, ranging from praise, welcome, doubt to disparagement, and even personal attack. Although very different in terms of quantity, topics and methodology, criticisms of Norman, Wasserstein and Vogel have manifested a few common features. First, the performance and success of their plays not only arouse debates among conservative male critics, but also arguments inside of feminist camp. Most of the debates revolve around two issues: whether their works are feminist, and whether they deserve canonical status. Second, academic researches on their plays fall far behind performance reviews. Although there are numerous newspaper and journal articles, academic monographs are still few. Third, much critical attention is paid to their representative plays, *Getting out* and *'night, Mother* for Norman, *Uncommon Women and Others* and *The Heidi Chronicles* for Wasserstein, and *How I Learned to Drive* for Vogel, with other works being ignored more or less.

Regarded as "one of the most impressive debuts of an American playwright" (Bigsby, "Contemporary" 214), Norman's first play *Getting Out* attracted much public attention[①] when it was staged at Lucille Lortel Theater. Since then critics have analyzed the mother-daughter relationship, split female self, past and present, and psychopolitics in it (Ginter-Brown 1991; K. Foster 1994; Cline 1996; Wang 2014). It is considered as "the most feminist of Norman's plays. Not only does it focus on woman's struggle for self-determination in the face of powerful patriarchal forces; it documents the social construction of gender" (Murphy 203). Norman's second play *Third and Oak: The Laundromat* has enjoyed similar feminist reception although only one

---

[①] Important reviews include: Eder, "Stage '*Getting Out*' by Marsha Norman"(1979); Klemesrud, "She Had Her Own '*Getting Out*' to Do"(1979); Kroll, "Before and After Meet in a Girl"(1979); Simon, "Kopit, Norman, and Shepard"(1979), etc.

academic article focusing on it can be found until now. ①

However, her masterpiece *'night, Mother* invited controversial critical responses after being awarded the 1983 Pulitzer Prize. The debate among the mainstream critics is about the play's universality. Some critics dismiss it as "female hysteria and paranoia" or "suspense melodrama". The influential media like *Variety*, *Daily News*, and *Newsday* deny its tragic value and universal appeal. ② Other critics such as Robert Brustein and Trudy Scott defend its universal significance by resorting to Aristotle's standards, and claim it as "an authentically American play but with the stark inevitability of Greek tragedy" (Dolan, "Feminist Spectator" 22). There are also two opposite attitudes towards *'night, Mother* in feminist camp. While some feminists applaud Norman's success in male-dominated theater, radical feminist critics feel disappointed with its defeatist female characters, suicide theme and realistic form (Dolan, " *'night, Mother* "; Case, "Personal is not Political"; Forte, "Realism Narrative"). They condemn its subordination to male dramatic structure and patriarchal ideology, and even call it "a form of anti-feminist backlash"(Dolan, " *'night, Mother* "). As time goes by, the above critical ambivalence has been cleared up. The feminist and canonical status of *'night, Mother* has been reinforced with continuous scholarly efforts in recent years. Besides feminist studies, critics have analyzed *'night, Mother* from psychological,

---

① This play is usually discussed together with other plays of Norman. The only one that focuses on it I could find is Grace Epstein's "At the Intersection: Configuring Women's Difference through Narrative in Norman's *Third and Oak: The Laundromat*"(1996).

② Jill Dolan summarizes the negative review on *'night, Mother* in details in her influential book *The Feminist Spectator as Critic*. Ann Arbor: University of Michigan Press, 1988, 27 – 34.

philosophical and aesthetic perspectives.①

The sole monograph on Norman's play in America up to today is *Marsha Norman: A Case Book*, which is edited by Linda Ginter-Brown and published in 1996. This book consists of eleven essays focusing on the entire range of Norman's works and two interviews with Norman by the editor. Kundert-Gibbs, Linda Ginter-Brown and Drew's essays analyze the mother-daughter pairs, hunger as metaphor and time philosophy in *'night, Mother* respectively by comparing it to Samuel Beckett's *Footfalls* and Lillian Hellman's *Days to Come*. Norman's less-known plays like *The Holdup*, *Traveler in the Dark*, *Sarah and Abraham*, and *The Secret Garden* are also examined from historical, symbolical, mythological and psychological perspectives. In spite of Brown's efforts to cover Norman's non-major works and to change their fate of being ignored, these plays have not attracted enough academic attention.

Though being popular and successful in Broadway, Wasserstein's plays received little scholarly attention at the beginning and then got negative, even unfair evaluations from feminist critics. Charges against her *Uncommon Women and Others* include: elitism, stereotypes of female images and the conservative comedic form.② The faults that critics find in *The Heidi Chronicles* include: "Its failure to provide feminist role models, its critique to the feminist movement, its omission of low-income women and women of color,

---

① For more details see S. Brown, "I Thought You Were Mine: Marsha Norman's *'night, Mother*"(1989); Burkman, "The Demeter Myth and Doubling in Marsha Norman's *'night, Mother*"(1990) ; Spencer, "Norman's *'night, Mother*, Psycho-drama of the Female Identity" (1987); Demastes, "Jessie and Thelma Revisited: Marsha Norman's Conceptual Challenge in *'night, Mother*"(1993); Begley, "Objects of Realism: Bertolt Brecht, Roland Barthes, and Marsha Norman"(2012).

② These three charges are made by Helene Keyssar in her *Feminist Theater: An Introduction to Plays of Contemporary British and American Women*. New York: Grove Press, Inc. , 1984.

its colorful male characters, its engaging use of language, humor, and song, its linear (nonfeminist) structure, and its surprising ending."(Barnett xii)① Such critical delay and repudiations are caused partly by the theatrical prejudice against women playwrights and partly by the dogmatic feminist approach that evaluates literary works. When being asked why critics have treated her works, especially *The Heidi Chronicles*, so unkindly, Wasserstein replied, "I think because there aren't enough plays by women—by and about women—. So that you have this one play supposedly standing for all women's plays."(Barnett 185) Wasserstein never intends to represent all women, nor tries to be ideological or didactic, so "critics looking for a straightforward feminist point of view are likely to be disappointed by her complex vision of life"(Barnett, fly page).

With the coming of the post-feminist age, critics have abandoned the previous radical paradigm and affirmed Wasserstein's contributions to feminist theater by reevaluating her plays in a broader social and historical context. Gail Ciociola published her book *Wendy Wasserstein: Dramatizing Women, Their Choices and Their Boundaries* in 1998, in which she invented a new terminology "fem-en(act)ment" to designate the feminist disposition recurring

---

① Claudia Barnett sums up the charges against *The Heidi Chronicles* in the Introduction to *Wendy Wasserstein: A Casebook*. The examples of negative reviews are as follows: Jill Dolan. *Presence & Desire: Essays on Gender, Sexuality, Performance*. Ann Arbor: University of Michigan Press, 1993. Karen Malpede. "Interview of *The Heidi Chronicles*." *Plymouth Theater*, (42. 3)1990: 464 - 465. Phyllis Jane Rose. "An Open Letter to Dr. Holland." *American Theater*, Oct. 1989: 26 - 29. Laurie Stone. "The Women's Movement Carried off My Baby in a Flying Saucer." Review of *The Heidi Chronicles*, Plymouth Theater, Village Voice, 13 June 1989:36.

through Wasserstein's major plays.① In order to reverse the critical hostility that Wasserstein's drama aroused, Claudia Barnett organized a group of critics to analyze Wasserstein's writing from a variety of ways and published it as *Wendy Wasserstein: A Casebook* in 1999. In this collection of essays, Wasserstein's plays are contextualized in her life experiences, American and Jewish culture and theatrical tradition. They are explored from biographical, historical, feminist and aesthetical perspectives in comparison with plays of Ibsen, Rachel Crothers, Caryl Churchill, Charlotte Keatley and Chekhov,② which enriches and expands the criticism of Wasserstein.

The death of Wasserstein in 2006 prompts the revival of her plays in American theater and the reassessment of her works among critics. Sue Donaldson (2006) reads *An American Daughter* by relating it to women's political reality in today's America, revealing the double pressure and unfairness that professional women suffer from. In 2007, *The Heidi Chronicles* was staged in China. Andrew Kimbrough records this theatrical event and demonstrates that "the

---

① According to Ciociola, "fem" for female perspective and feminist intent; "(act)" for stage drama; and "en(act)ment" for the revelation and successful execution of one's overall motifs and motives. As a whole, "fem-en(act)ment" is textual or performance drama that, guided by a feminist disposition, thematically and stylistically enacts situations of interest to women, the psychological and social effects of which form the core of that drama.

② The nine essays in this book are: Bette Mandy, "Women's Movement: The Personal as Political in the Plays of Wendy Wasserstein"; Stephanie Hammer, "Bachelor Machine: Postmodern Travels, Female Communities, Melancholy and the Market in Bachelor Girls"; Robert F. Gross, "Generations of Nora: Self-Realization and the Comedies of Rachel Crothers and Wendy Wasserstein"; William C. Boles, "We've All Come a Long Way: The Role of Women in *Uncommon Women*, *Top Girls*, and *My Mother Said I Never Should*"; Miriam M. Chirico, "Female Laughter and Comic Possibilities: *Uncommon Women and Others*"; Deborah Brewer, "Building the Gift: Creating a Character in Wasserstein's *The Sisters Rosensweig*"; Gaylord Brewer, "Wendy Wasserstein's Three Sisters: Squandered Privilege"; Helene Keyssar, "When Wendy Isn't Trendy: Wendy Wasserstein's *The Heidi Chronicles* and *An American Daughter*"; Glenda Frank, "Three American Daughters: Wendy Wasserstein Critiques Success".

play resonated with its Chinese audience", especially "relevant to a new generation of women" (152). Jill Dolan (2008) reconsiders feminist performance criticism by looking back at her critique of *The Heidi Chronicles* and acknowledges that "Wasserstein's aim had never been revolution, but instead, to show women in some of their complex humanity, to create 'universal meanings' on the basis of women's experiences"("Reviewing Wendy" 434). Cortney C. Barko (2008) examines the female artists and paintings in *The Heidi Chronicles* and asserts that Wasserstein revives forgotten female artists, by doing so, giving these women voices. In "After Chekhov", Foster(2013) expounds why women playwrights rewrite *The Three Sisters* by drawing on contemporary theories of adaptation. Two significant monographs have been published. Jan Balakian (2010) studies seven of Wasserstein's plays by locating them in the specific social backgrounds and focusing on their creative process in *Reading the Plays of Wendy Wasserstein*, which reemphasizes Wasserstein's contributions to feminist theater. In *Wendy Wasserstein*, Jill Dolan (2017) makes an extensive analysis on Wasserstein's major plays through today's feminist critical lens and proves that Wasserstein's dramatic works continue to matter in American culture. Therefore, Wasserstein's canonical status as a feminist playwright has been reconfirmed.

　　Less fortunate than Norman and Wasserstein, Vogel's early plays have been rejected by theater, let alone attract academic attention. Her *Desdemona*, written in 1977, has not got staged until 1993. *The Oldest Profession* is only performed after eight years of its birth. The early critical books like *Feminist Theater* (1984), *The Feminist Spectator as Critic* (1988), *Feminine Focus: The New Women Playwrights* (1989), even *The Cambridge Companion to American Women Playwrights* (1999), do not mention the name of Paula

Vogel. The slow burn of her career, as Bigsby points out, can be attributed to the fact that the gender issues and other aspects of her sensibility make "her work seem tangential to the interests of mainstream theater"("Contemporary" 391). Her identity as a self-declared lesbian excludes her from mainstream values. However, Vogel refuses to make any compromise to the conventional ideology.

Vogel's radical feminist plays did not get receptive critical response until 1998, the year she won the Pulitzer Prize. Bigsby devotes one chapter to commenting on her works in his *Contemporary American Playwrights* (1999), praising highly of Vogel's feminist gesture, defamilliarisation strategy and painfully comedic style. Craig also uses one chapter to introduce Vogel and her major plays in her book *Women Pulitzer Playwrights* (2004), giving a detailed analysis on the structure, characters and theme of *How I Learned to Drive*. In *A Companion to Twentieth Century American Drama* (2007), Ann Pellegrini summarizes five features of Vogel's play: ghost of the past, scrapbook dramaturgy, strange ordinary, being a "bad" feminist, and time pulse. New historical books on American drama such as C. W. E. Bigsby's *Modern American Drama: 1945—2000* (2001) include Vogel as a significant contemporary playwright and provide a comprehensive introduction of her dramas.

The present scholarship on Vogel's plays mainly focuses on sexual and gender issues, exploring the feminist implications and aesthetics in her works with psychoanalytical, cultural, ethical or stylistic approaches. In "The Sexual World of Paula Vogel", Robert M. Post (2001) studies the characters' sexual orientations and relationships in seven plays of Vogel and concludes that "different-sex and same-sex relationships appear relatively equal in the need for the participants to cope with problems [...] They are equal in normality and abnormality"(42). Taking *How I Learned to Drive* as sample, Andrea J. Nouryeh(1999), Mary K. DeShazer (2002) and Graley Herren(2010) concentrate on trauma of sexual abuse in the play, analyzing the psychological hurt it causes, the difficult healing process the female character undergoes, and the dramaturgical strategy that shifts the position of abuser/victim successfully. Contextualizing *How I Learned to Drive* in the absurd public discourse on child sexual abuse, Andrew Kimbrough examines the ethics of the play, arguing that it "offers a model of community that is profoundly ethical and operable because it is radically understanding and inclusive of those whom we identify as different and undesirable" (49). The sexual politics embodied in *How I Learned to Drive*, *Desdemona* and *Hot 'N' Throbbing* is also a heated topic. David Savran regards Vogel as a male impersonator, pointing out that she "has learned how, as a feminist, to write like a man" ("Paula Vogel" 191). Sharon Friedman(1999) and Marianne Novy(1999) compare *Desdemona* with that of Shakespeare and Ann-Marie MacDonald, affirming that Vogel's Desdemona is more subversive and her play marks an important shift in the feminist critical perspective in drama, that is, "from discovering and creating positive images of women [...] to analyzing and disrupting the ideological codes embedded in the inherited structure of dramatic representation" (Friedman 132).

Some critics are fascinated with Vogel's style of theater. Christopher Bigsby (2004) and Brian Richardson(2001) link Vogel to Beckett and appreciate her sense of absurdity. David Savran(1996), Ann Linden(2002) and Shannon Hammermeister(2000) emphasize Brecht and Shklovsky's influence on Vogel and pay more attention to her Alienation Effect. Joanna Mansbridge designates Vogel's dramaturgical style as "performative burlesque", foregrounding the performativity of social and sexual body in Vogel's theater.① In her recent book *Paula Vogel* (2014), Mansbridge uses "an embodied aesthetics" to show how Vogel integrates defamiliarization and camp humor to embody female characters and highlight the performativity of gender. She analyzes gender, family, fantasy, history and memory in nine plays of Vogel, arguing that "to see a Paula Vogel play is to participate in a three-way dialogue with the dramatic canon, social history, and contemporary American Culture"(1).

The perspectives and arguments of PhD dissertations and MA theses on the works of Norman, Wasserstein and Vogel are similar to that of journal essays. However, one prominent feature of these studies is that they often link Norman, Wasserstein and Vogel to other playwrights and analyze their works in a specific discourse. For example, D. Janardanan (2007) offers an analysis of image of loss in plays by Williams, Miller, Norman and Vogel. C. L. Wimmer (2001) elucidates women's anger in the plays of Hellman, Shange, Norman, Henley and Vogel. E. R. Thompson (2010) contextualizes Norman and Vogel in southern incest writing tradition and argues that contemporary women change incest narrative from victimizing to surviving. Carolyn Cope (2005) contends that there is a woman's aesthetic in the dramas of contemporary American women playwrights after studying plays of Fornes, Hughes, Wasserstein, Norman and Parks. Such comparative study is popular and fruitful in American academy.

Norman, Wasserstein and Vogel have been introduced to

---

① Joanna Mansbridge discusses this style in her journal article "Popular Bodies, Canonical Voices: Paula Vogel's *Hot 'N' Throbbing* as Performative Burlesque"(2009). She makes a further study in her PhD Diss. "Camp, the Canon, and a Performative Burlesque: Paula Vogel's Plays as Literary and Cultural Revision"(2010), extending this concept to the analysis of Vogel's all major plays.

Chinese readers as Pulitzer Prize winners and feminist playwrights. Domestic studies on them usually focus on their prize-winning plays and take a feminist perspective, resulting in, according to CNKI database, seven PhD dissertations, more than ten MA theses, and about fifty journal essays. The PhD dissertations usually have a wide scope, trying to analyze more plays with diversified critical theories. Cen Wei(2009) makes a comparative study on the plays of Lillian Hellman and Marsh Norman, exploring the evolution of female identity in their plays. Wang Li (2014) examines the past and memory in Norman's seven plays, demonstrating the dynamics of the past and the present. He Anfang (2006) studies five major plays of Wasserstein and traces the process of self-search and identity construction of her female characters. Chen Lin (2011) focuses on Wasserstein's comedic form and spirit, exploring the relation between comic form and feminist issues like female self and identity. Zuo Jin (2010) and Zhang Jinliang (2007) put a few American women playwrights together, including Norman and Wasserstein, to search for the unique linguistic features of women playwrights. Jin Lili(2013) contextualizes Vogel's four plays in the dramatic tradition and analyzes them in the perspectives of feminist and intertextualization.

The scope of journal essays at home is still limited. Most of the present studies of Norman are about *Getting out* and *'night, Mother*. Critics have discussed female subjectivity, mother-daughter relationship and patriarchal oppression in the two plays with feminist, existential, space and semiotic theories (Liu 2008; Cen 2010; He Anfang 2013; Bai 2014). Among the five academic essays on Wasserstein's plays, three analyze the female characters, especially on the female identity crisis and feminist dilemma they confront, two are about the comic spirit of Wasserstein's plays.① Except for Fan Yisong's introductory article "Paula Vogel and Her Plays", all other ten articles about Vogel's drama focus on *How I Learned to Drive*, exploring the trauma, discourse power, alienation effect, cultural, feminist and ethical implications of the play.② Vogel's other plays have not gained any critical attention until now.

Rituals in the plays of Norman, Wasserstein and Vogel have been noticed by some critics. Murphy(2001) points out that Arlie's renaming and self-killing in *Getting Out* is symbolic, marking her identity transformation in a ritualistic way (202 - 203). When introducing *'night, Mother*, Bigsby (2004) realizes that "Norman has also seen the play as a ritual, a requiem mass for the soul of the departed"("Contemporary" 238), and that the domestic items she assembles are part of the ritual and are charged with significance. The pity is that Bigsby turns to other issues without expounding it as a ritual. Comparing the marriage rite and initiation rite in *The Holdup* with the traditional male-centered rites, Wattenberg(1990) argues that Norman redefines the categories and feminizes the traditional initiation rite(515). But his focus is still on the male characters rather than on the heroine Lily.

Both Murphy (2001) and Craig (2004) have discussed the rituals in *Uncommon Women and Others* in their books. Murphy thinks that

---

① The three articles on female identity are: Wu Qinghong, "On the Feminist Plays of Wendy Wasserstein"(2007); He Anfang, "A Quest of Self: A Review of Works of Wendy Wasserstein"(2006); Wang Lei, "On the Female Identity Crisis in Wendy Wasserstein's Plays" (2013). The two on comic style are: He Anfang, Fei Chunfang, "On the Comic Spirit of Wendy Wasserstein's Plays" (2015); He Anfang, "The Atmosphere of Sadness in Wendy Wasserstein's Comedy"(2015).

② Three articles published in core journals are: Liang Chaoqun, Zhang E, "*How I Learned to Drive*: A Successful Seduction"(2014); Zhang Shengzhen, "Growing up Through Trauma: A Study on *How I Learned to Drive*"(2012); Li Shuling, "Seduction of Alienation Effect: Narrating and Performing Strategy in *How I Learned to Drive*"(2016).

rituals like Gracious Living represent the dated traditions of women's colleges and cause the girls' confusion (217). Craig points out that the teas and other rituals of Gracious Living are useless because they "do not prepare them for the options and obstacles they face"(189). But both of them neglect the performativity of the rituals. Craig also analyzes the consciousness-raising in *The Heidi Chronicles* and claims that "the ritual is funny in its effusiveness, but it marks the key moment of Heidi's initiation into the movement"(199). Tracing the origin of consciousness-raising ritual, Balakian (2010) examines its significance in the context of American feminist movement. But neither of them explores the role that this ritual plays in forging Heidi's identity or in developing the dramatic action. Critics like Bigsby (2004), Balakian(2010) and V. A. Foster (2013) have been impressed by the Jewish ritual in *The Sisters Rosensweig*, suggesting that the ritual embodies Jewish culture that Sara rejects. However, none of them gives further explanation on it.

Only some fragmented discussion on ritual in Vogel's plays can be found. When reviewing *The Baltimore Waltz* in 1992, Robert Brustein comments, "it is a touching rite of loving exorcism, personal yet transcendent." (29) Savran (2003) argues that the parodied funeral services in *And Baby Makes Seven* are comparable to those in Albee's *Who is Afraid of Virginia Woolf?* ("Paula Vogel" 39). Bigsby (2004) has noted the scene "Initiation into a Boy's First Love" in *How I learned to Drive*, arguing that the play depicts the transformative process of Li'l Bit from adolescence to adulthood, from innocence to experience as well as from "girl" to "boy" ("Modern" 417). However, no one has explored these rituals theoretically. Their features and functions remain to be unearthed.

One paper that inspires the present study is Carolyn Cope's (2005) doctoral dissertation "The Women's Aesthetic in Selected

Plays of Maria Irene Fornes, Holly Hughes, Wendy Wasserstein, Marsha Norman and Suzan-Lori Parks". Regarding ritual as one of the special dramatic devices that women playwrights use, Cope analyzes consciousness-raising in *Fefu and Her Friends* and *The Heidi Chronicles*, college rituals in *Uncommon Women and Others*, family rituals in *'night, Mother*, and rituals of courtship and marriage in *Devotees in the Garden of Love*. But his four-page discussion just describes the rituals in these plays without making deeper exploration.

The literature review shows that ritual in Norman, Wasserstein and Vogel's plays has not been given enough critical attention. Although female identity and gender politics have been explored extensively by feminist scholars, few have touched upon the dynamic relation between ritual and the formation/transformation of female self. Such insufficiency is probably due to the fact that ritual is so ubiquitous and familiar in daily life as well as in drama that they are taken for granted or undervalued by critics. The other possible reason is that most previous studies focus on "what" rather than "how", that is, what trauma, confusion and oppression the female protagonists are entrapped in and what female self they search for, rather than how they perform thereby constitute their identities and how the self-metamorphosis take place. Therefore, the performative and structural function of ritual has been overlooked. Another insufficiency of the scholarship is that ritual in Norman, Wasserstein and Vogel's plays has been discussed in separation and fragmentation. It has not been examined as a unique strategy shared by their female characters, nor as a dramatic technique shared by these women playwrights. Based on these observations, the present book will explore the intricacies between ritual performance and female identity as well as the aesthetic function of ritual in these women playwrights' dramas, which will complement and enrich the current scholarship.

III Ritual, Liminal Female Self and Performativity

Ritual exists in every known culture and is performed by people every day. It is "a key domain of the inquiry and analysis of central human issues such as identity, culture, heritage, media, and power" (Brosius ix). However, to define ritual is "a notoriously problematic task" (Snoek 3) and a "lost cause from the outset" (Kapferer 36), because there are endless definitions proposed by theologians, anthropologists and sociologists who can recognize a ritual when they see one but hold very diverse criteria for what ritual is. According to the 1771 edition of the *Encyclopedia Britannica*, ritual is a "book directing the order and manner to be observed in celebrating religious ceremonies, and performing divine service in a particular church, diocese, order, or the like" (329). This meaning has in fact disappeared in modern society.

In modern sense, ritual is a type of behavior or practice, a series of enacted symbols that represent or embody myths, beliefs and social relations. Since rituals are usually divided into the sacred and the secular, there are two orientations in defining it. Some scholars emphasize its religious qualifier, regarding it as "prescribed formal behavior for occasions not given over to technological routine, having reference to beliefs in mystical beings or powers" (V. Turner & E. Turner, "Image and Pilgrimage" 243).[①] Others prefer to

---

[①] There are a few similar definitions. For example, rituals are "conscious and voluntary, repetitious and stylized symbolic bodily actions that are centered on cosmic structures and/or sacred presences" by Evan M. Zusse (1987); "Religious ritual ... are those religious actions whose structural descriptions include a logical object and appeal to a culturally postulated superman agent's action somewhere within their overall structural description" by Thomas Lawson and Robert McCauley (1990).

foreground its cultural and constitutive features. For example, Stanley J. Tambiah defines ritual as,

> [A] culturally constructed system of symbolic communication. It is constituted of patterned and ordered sequences of words and acts, often expressed in multiple media, whose content and arrangement are characterized in varying degree by formality (conventionality), stereotype (rigidity), condensation (fusion), and redundancy (repetition). (128) ①

Both of the two kinds of definitions attempt to give a clear demarcation between ritual and other social actions by listing some so-called essential features of ritual such as symbolic, formal, repetitive, structured and conventional.

However, the above traditional dichotomous division of rituals and definitional squabbles have been deconstructed and abandoned by contemporary ritual scholars. Schechner argues that mixing the secular with the sacred is very common in today's observances, celebrations and life-passage events(53). He extends the notion of ritual to "collective memories encoded into actions"(52), which is very general and inclusive. Snoek even proposes to give ritual a polythetic and fuzzy definition to replace the traditional monothetic, non-fuzzy one(6). He lists twenty-four characteristics of ritual such as "culturally constructed; traditionally sanctioned", "liminal", "purposeful", and suggests people to construct their own definition according to their aim of study. Rejecting formality, fixity, repetition as intrinsic qualities of ritual, Bell and Grimes have

---

① Similar definitions include: "[Ritual] is the performance of more or less invariant sequences of formal acts and utterances not entirely encoded by the performers" by Roy Rappaport (1999); "[Ritual is] patterned, repetitive, and symbolic enactment of a cultural belief or value; its primary purpose is alignment of the belief system of the individual with that of society" by Robbie Davis-Floyd (1992).

pointed out that ritual can be dynamic, singular, innovative, and improvisational. Therefore, they give up defining ritual and propose to use another term—ritualization—"a way of acting that specially establishes a privileged contrast, differentiating itself as more important or powerful"(Bell, "Ritual Theory" 90). They believe that it is more fruitful to discuss kinds and degrees of ritualization in technologically advanced societies since "all human behavior is to some degree ritualized"(Grimes, "Ritual, Media, and Conflict" 13). Such a broader notion of ritual can also be seen in Erving Goffman and Randall Collins' study of interaction rituals in daily life.

Some of the rituals in this study are easy to be recognized according to the traditional definition and characteristics. Among them are the rite of initiation and funeral in *The Holdup*, Gracious Living and Milk 'n Crackers in *Uncommon Women and Others*, Ritual of consciousness-raising in *The Heidi Chronicles*, the Sabbath Sundown in *The Sisters Rosensweig*, and Children's Service in *And Baby Makes Seven*. While some behaviors or events initiated by characters themselves are not rituals at first sight, but can be categorized as ritual or at least ritualized actions according to Bell and Grimes. Bell regards ritual as "a type of social strategy", and asserts "that is intrinsic to ritualization are strategies for differentiating itself—to various degrees and in various ways—from other ways of acting within any particular culture"("Ritual Theory" 90). In order to judge whether one action can become ritualized or not, Grimes makes a list of family characteristics which include traditionalizing, elevating, repeating, singularizing, and stylizing them or entering them with a non-ordinary attitude ("Craft of Ritual" 194). Both Bell and Grimes situate ritual and ritualization in a larger spectrum of social and cultural practice, emphasizing their differentiation from other daily, routinized forms of practice. In light of their theory, the last night of Jessie with her mother is not only a farewell ritual but also a Requiem Mass designed and performed by Jessie, which is rich in symbolic meaning that needs to explore. So are Arlene's renaming and "self-killing" in *Getting Out*, drive teaching and learning in *How I Learned to Drive*, and the imaginary European travel in *The Baltimore Waltz*. These actions are performed by the characters with special intention and symbolic signification. They are elevated, singularized, empowered, and thereby ritualized simultaneously.

Though there are countless rituals in the world and none of them is identical with each other, they do share some basic elements: ritual space, ritual time, ritual object, ritual language, ritual body, and ritual action. Ritual action refers to the whole plot of the rite as it moves from beginning through middle to end. Ritual body is the body of the ritual actors who enact or participate in the ritual in a special or sacred time and place. Usually all objects, alive or dead, and all utterances, linguistic or nonlinguistic, are believed symbolically meaningful in rituals. Among these elements, ritual body is the most fundamental and essential one because the body "mediates all action: it is the medium for the internalization and reproduction of social values and for the simultaneous constitution of both the self and the world of social relations" (Comaroff 124). Bell's study shows that ritual body is always conditioned by and responsive to ritualized environment, in which it is molded and restructured ("Ritual Theory" 100). In most cases, ritual body is the locus for the play of all kinds of social power and can demonstrate the conflicts of self, culture and society.

As early as 1909 Gennep had noticed that people everywhere had to go through an intermediate stage and perform special rituals whenever they passed from the profane to the sacred, from one group or occupation to another, or even from one age to another. He named such rituals as *rites of passage*, which usually include ceremonies of birth, coming-of-age initiations for boys and girls, ceremonies for marriage, funeral, initiation into religious or political societies, rites of social advancement and job specialization, and so on. Since they are usually performed by people when they meet personal or social crisis, these rituals are also called "life-crisis" rites. After further analysis on rites of passage, Gennep discovered that all such rites move through three phases: the preliminal, liminal, and postliminal. The liminal stage, also named as the rite of transition, is a period of time when ritual subject "wavers between two worlds" (Gennep 18), or as Turner reaffirms, "liminal entities are neither here nor there; they are betwixt and between the positions assigned and arrayed by law, custom, convention, and ceremonial."(Turner, "Ritual Process" 95) The liminal phase has fascinated Turner because he recognizes in it a possibility for ritual to "be creative, to make new situations, identities, and social realities"(Schechner 66). It is a time-place where ritual subjects could be transformed from one social self to another, being inscribed with new identities and new powers. Ritual, in Turner's eyes, is a process of becoming.

　　Inspired by Gennep and Turner's ritual theories, the present author argues that the female protagonists in the selected nine plays by Norman, Wasserstein and Vogel are in a transitional or liminal stage of life. Confronted with various life crises, these women stand in-between two worlds, two identities or two kinds of lives. They doubt, negate, or even hate their earlier self, and are eager to seek a new self. For example, Arlene in *Getting Out* has to choose what kind of person she wants to be and what kind of future life she prefers to lead at the moment she steps out of the prison gate. Jessie in *'night, Mother* determines to become a totally different woman by killing herself after ten years' hesitation between life and death. Her last night turns to be the liminal time between two worlds as well as her two identities. College girls in *Uncommon Women and Others* have to go through a long self-search journey before they know who they are and what they really want. Heidi Holland wanders outside of the Consciousness Raising activity before her final conversion to feminism. Anna in *The Baltimore Waltz* suffers from the split of self when the news of her brother's death comes and reincorporates the loss into her new self after roaming across Europe in her fantasy. Li'l Bit in *How I Learned to Drive* gets empowered and becomes a girl with masculine traits through the parodied rite of initiation enacted by her uncle. In order to deal with life crises and find a way out, these women have resorted to ritual as a special strategy to express their thoughts, negotiate power relations and reconstruct their identities. Sometimes, they take initiatives in designing, directing and performing these rituals, and sometimes they are forced to get involved in by others. As ritual subjects, they are situated in a state of confusion, ambiguity and wavering, but at the same time, they are active, subversive and determined, full of transformative potentials and possibilities. In other words, their selves are liminal, waiting to be transformed by the rituals they perform.

In order to understand the meaning, nature and function of ritual, scholars have approached the concept from various perspectives and provided a number of different even contradictory theories. There have existed many debates on some basic questions concerning ritual. For example, how to interpret ritual language, ritual body and ritual act? Why can ritual embody and reinforce cultural values, ideals and models yet at the same time enable people to modify and challenge them? What is the dynamic between ritual, culture and politics? It is not possible or necessary to introduce all the debates and theories, but it will help to look into some of the basic notions of ritual and the newest insights that ritual scholarship has achieved.

One fundamental and well-accepted notion is that ritual is thought in action. Rituals are symbolic behaviors that express and represent the beliefs, ideas, values and social relations of society. The early ritual theorists like Durkheim argue that ritual itself is not thought or idea, it just enacts or embodies them. It displays the ultimate values of a community or refers to a sacred or transcendental reality. Individuals perform rituals according to prescribed norms and experience the collective ethos together. In this way, their sense of self and community is formed or reinforced. With the cultural turn in humanities in the 1970s, scholars begin to regard ritual as a cultural phenomenon and a system of symbols whose meaning depends on its relationship to other symbols within the system. Scholars such as Edmund Leach, Clifford Geertz, Nancy Munn and Victor Turner focus their study on interpreting the meaning of ritual statements, activities and events, trying to find out the rules that govern the ritual orchestration and the interaction of cultural symbols and social experience. They contend that ritual not only expresses social experience but also models or shapes social order. In Turner's term, ritual facilitates both the continuity and the redressive transformation of social structures.[①] Similarly, clothes, decorations, language, actions of ritual participants and other elements of ritual are all analyzed as cultural signs that symbolize something else. One typical example is death and rebirth of novices in initiation ritual. Gennep, Turner, Eliade and many other anthropologists have noticed one universal pattern: the novices are weakened physically and mentally,

---

① Catherine Bell makes a detailed introduction to the theoretical development of ritual in her book *Ritual: Perspectives and Dimensions* (1997). Some of the information used here is from this book, pages 61 – 67.

dispossessed of all secular things, or humiliated with extreme measures, in other words, they remain "dead" for a period; then they are welcome back and get a new status or identity. Their death and rebirth certainly are symbolic, representing a destruction of the previous status and the formation of a new self. These theses and the method of semantic and symbolic interpretation have always been illuminating and useful in ritual study.

The second essential notion is that ritual is performative, which means, as Rappaport points out, "Ritual not only communicate something but is taken by those performing it to be 'doing something' as well." ("Ecology" 177) The performative dimension of ritual can be understood in three dimensions. First, speeches uttered in ritual are performative. Influenced by J. L. Austin's performative theory, scholars like Ruth Finnegan and Benjamin Ray begin to analyze what words in ritual do and accomplish, demonstrating that ritual speech can perform social transactions and create certain social states (Bell, "Ritual: Perspectives" 69). Second, ritual activity is believed to be a social act that is analogous to speech act, which contains locutionary, illocutionary and perlocutionary force. Scholars like Leach, Tambiah and Bloch are fascinated by the performative efficacy of ritual act. Applying Searle's speech act theory to the analysis of rituals like baptizing, naming a ship, wedding, Ndembu circumcision rites and Catholic Mass, they conclude that ritual act is productive, creative and constitutive. Third, ritual is regarded as cultural performance, an event "that does not simply express cultural values or enact symbolic scripts but actually effects changes in people's perceptions and interpretations"(Bell, "Ritual: Perspectives" 74). Having noticed ritual's connection to drama, music, folklore and dance, scholars give more attention to its performative aspect and turn to study how ritual empowers people to change and reshape cultural ideals and values. They find that ritual participants are not passive but active performers who often reinterpret and reorient value-laden symbols. Therefore, "ritual as a performative medium for social change emphasizes human creativity and physicality"(Bell, "Ritual: Perspectives" 73). This performative approach to ritual pays more attention to what ritual does rather than what ritual expresses, which marks a turning point in ritual study.

Without denying the semantic, symbolic and performative dimensions of ritual, recent scholars like Catherine Bell, Clifford Geertz and Bruce Kapferer provide an alternative understanding of ritual by contextualizing it in power politics theories of Lukes, Bourdieu and Foucault. They conceive ritual as a kind of cultural practice, emphasizing its productive and political aspects. Focusing on the ritual acts themselves, they argue for the dynamics of ritual process in two ways. Kapferer believes that ritual itself forms a virtuality—a different model of reality, in his words, "a really real, a complete and filled-out existential reality"(47), in which people can break free from their everyday constraints and determinations, and realize their constructive agency. This internal dynamic can be constitutive as well as subversive or revolutionary. While Bell, Bloch and Comaroff have explored the external dynamics of ritual, discovering that neither culture structure nor ritual performance is static, they, in fact, change and accommodate themselves to each other according to specific historical situations. The deployment of ritualization, Bell points out, is "the deployment of a particular construction of power relationships, a particular relationship of domination, consent and resistance" ("Ritual Theory" 206). The most important element during this process is the lived body, which may at first appear to be controlled by its projection and embodiment of cultural schemes, but in fact can be empowered by its misuse, resistance or personal re-appropriation of the hegemonic order. Just as Jean Comaroff asserts, ritual is "a struggle for the possession of the sign" (196). The internal together with the external dynamics of ritual shows that ritual is not only a process of cultural reproduction but also an arena of power politics.

The complicated relation of ritual and drama is manifested in three aspects. First, it has long been believed that drama originates from ritual. Western drama can be traced back to the Athenian festivals of Dionysus in the sixth and fifth centuries BC. Nietzsche announces that "Greek tragedy in its oldest form dealt only with the sufferings of Dionysus"(51). The Cambridge anthropologists such as Gilbert Murray, Jane Harrison and Francis Cornford perpetuate this view, arguing that "tragedy is in origin a Ritual Dance, a Sacer Ludus ... originally or centrally that of Dionysus, performed at his feast ..." (Murray 341). The western notions of drama can be said to stem from the Greek festivals, rites and ceremonies. According to Wang Xiaoyun, Xi Qu in China(Chinese Opera) originates from an ancient rite of exorcism called *nuo yi*, which is similar to the fete ceremony of Dionysus (111 – 119).

Second, all kinds of rituals, sacred or secular, private or public, individual or collective, have been described, accounted and performed in dramatic works throughout history. They play an indispensable role in representing culture, developing character and organizing plot. The rite of burial for Polynices performed by Antigone is the central event of Sophocles' tragedy *Antigone*. Rituals like courtship, wedding, funeral and religious ceremony are commonplace in Shakespeare's plays and the power of ritual languages to create and transform are culturally reverenced(Hansen 111). Rituals are also abundant in modern drama by Jean Genet, Peter Shaffer, Harold Pinter, Edward Albee, and so on. Various rituals could be found in many women playwrights' works. For example, Megan Terry's Obie Award play *Approaching Simone* begins with a ritual and ends in a return to the spectacle. Beth Henley's *The Miss Firecracker Contest* critiques beauty pageants and other institutionalized rituals which offer women up as commodities for consumption. Maria Irene Fornes' *Fefu and Her Friends* contains a 1935 version of a consciousness-raising group. Suzan-Lori Parks' *Devotees in the Garden of Love* is built around the combined rituals of courtship and marriage. In a word, dramatic texts are permeated with various rituals.

Finally, ritual and drama, both as performance, share much common ground in terms of form and function. Victor Turner argues that both of them are "public liminality" and "socially framed guided doings", sharing important characteristics such as "subjectivity", "escape from the classification of everyday life", and "symbolic reversals"("Frame" 465 - 492). Jerzy Grotowski regards his theater as a type of *rite de passage*, an initiation rite for modern man, proposing to "abolish the distance between actor and audience by eliminating the stage, removing all frontiers"(189). Taking Tadeusz Kantor's work as example, Hans-Thies Lehmann illustrates that "postdramatic theater is the replacement of dramatic action with ceremony"(69), highlighting the aesthetic quality of ceremony and the ritualistic element of theater. Emphasizing the continuum of "the efficacy/ritual-entertainment/aesthetic performance dyad", Schechner points out that the distinction between ritual and theater is not clear-cut and contends "whether one calls a specific performance 'ritual' or 'theater' depends mostly on context and function"(79 - 80).

This study will analyze the rituals in the dramatic works by Norman, Wasserstein and Vogel rather than live performance in theater. Textual analysis is the major methodology. Since ritual is a kind of cultural performance and all the rituals under consideration are performed by the female characters as a strategy to negotiate power and recreate identity, the theory of performativity is particularly illuminating and helpful for this research. Performativity is such a complicated concept that it means different things when being used in different fields. This author will apply J. L. Austin's ideas of linguistic performatives to interpret the speeches delivered by ritual subjects. Judith Butler's theory of gender performativity is invoked when discussing the formation of female identity. Taking literary text as action, the study also explores what Norman, Wasserstein and Vogel's dramatic works do and perform in American feminist theater by referring to the performativity of literature formulated by Jonathan Culler, J. Hillis Miller, Eva Hettner Aurelius and He Chengzhou.

Inspired by the utterances such as "I do" and "I name this ship the Queen Elizabeth" spoken on different rituals, J. L. Austin argues that language use is not just constative or descriptive, but also performative, which means to say is to do, "the issuing of the utterance is the performing of an action"(Austin 6). Speaking as an act can change or create reality by doing something. According to Austin, the function of speech act can be analyzed in three dimensions: the locution (the semantic and referential function of language), the illocution (what the utterance actually is doing, such as promising, warning, threatening), and the perlocution (what effect the utterance produces in the recipient). Performative utterances cannot be assessed as true or false, but instead either felicitous or infelicitous, depending on the situation in which they are uttered. Whereas the work of the illocutionary can be accomplished in the saying of whatever is said, that of the perlocutionary might or might not follow the issuing of a speech act. Austin's theory highlights the changing and making power of language. It is "in itself a critique of language-as-representation"(Aurelius and He 13).

Austin excludes fictional performatives on the stage or in a poem from his consideration because he thinks that they are not spoken seriously, but "in ways parasitic upon its normal use"(22), implying that utterances in fictional texts are quotations of original performatives, and that they mimic the form but lack the illocutionary force of that which they cite. Such distinction is exploded by Jacques Derrida, who argues that a fundamental characteristic of language is its iterability since a sign or a mark that is not repeatable could not be an element in a language. He asks, "Isn't it true that what Austin excludes as anomaly, exception, 'nonserious', citation(on stage, in a poem, or a soliloquy) is the determined modification of a general citationality ... without which there would not even be a 'successful' performative?"(17-18) Since all speech acts are constituted on the basis of iterability and citationality, it cannot make sense to call fictional utterance non-serious or parasitic.

Judith Butler further develops Austin's theory of performativity and Derrida's point about the citationality and iterability of language in her study of feminism and gender identity. According to Butler, there is no innate or stable gender identity that precedes gender attributes and norms. Gender is the effect of bodily acts, gestures, movements and styles of various kinds. It is "tenuously constituted in time, instituted in an exterior space through the stylized repetition of acts" ("Gender Trouble" 179). The iteration of gender norms operates like a performative speech act where the discursive repetition of norms acts to constitute the illusion of a gendered self. However, Butler argues, one cannot perform this or that identity at will. The performative norm is a form of compulsion, which implies that the iteration of norms actually compels bodies to act, gesture and behave in a rigid regulatory way that constantly attempts to embody the fantasy of a natural gender core. Gender is always doing, always performing, repeated acts, and in this way "congeal over time to produce the appearance of a substance, of a natural sort of being" ("Gender Trouble" 43).

Theorists have not only explored what language and act can do but also asked what literary text as action and event can do, which constitutes another aspect of performativity theory. Jonathan Culler asserts that "like the performative, the literary utterance does not refer to a prior state of affairs", it "too creates the state of affairs to which it refers", it first "brings into being characters and their actions" and second "brings into being ideas, concepts, which they deploy"(96). J. Hillis Miller regards literature as a speech act or conduct which "does something that may do other things in its turn" ("Literature as conduct" 2). He applies performativity to interpreting the novels of Henry James and Holocaust literature, arguing that literature can effect change in its readers and bear witness to what happened in the past.[①] Terry Eagleton also discusses the nature of fiction in light of performativity, claiming that "literary speech acts belong to the larger class of verbal acts known as performatives, which do not describe the world but accomplish something in the act of saying"(132). Focusing on the effect or the desired effect of literary text, *Performativity in Literature* (2016) edited by Eva Hettner Aurelius, He Chengzhou and Jon Helgason have illustrated how identity is formed through textual acts and how literature influences and changes reality. They argue that three issues

---

　① For more details, see J. Hillis Miller, *Speech Act in Literature* (2001); *Literature as Conduct: Speech Acts in Henry James* (2005); and *The Conflagration of Community: Fiction Before and After Auschwitz* (2011).

are central in the application of the theory of performativity in literary studies, they are action, event, and textuality (19).

Incorporating the theories of ritual and performativity, this book studies not only what ritual does within the dramatic text but also what the dramatic text as action does in contemporary American theater. On the one hand, it explores the symbolic meaning and performative force of ritual as well as the power relation negotiated through it in order to elaborate the transformative and constitutive process of women's self-identity. Ritual time and ritual space will be analyzed in relation to ritual body's movement. The objects, songs and music appearing on ritual will be interpreted symbolically. The utterances and gestures made by ritual body will be investigated through the lens of performativity. On the other hand, it goes beyond the stories and turns to the performativity of the dramatic texts to examine how Norman, Wasserstein and Vogel as women playwrights create new female images and bring change to American feminist theater. Its examination on the relation of ritual performance and gender identity sheds new light on the theoretical discussion of ritual, identity and performativity.

As women playwrights with different concerns and styles, Norman, Wasserstein and Vogel have devoted their dramas to portraying women from different social strata and with various individual pursuits. Norman's protagonists are usually the poor, forgotten and marginalized women who have been entrapped in life-death crisis and have to undergo self-destruction in order to survive and become the self they dream of. Wasserstein's characters are often college-educated, professional women who are shaped by both patriarchal gender norms and feminist ideals and struggling between compliance and resistance. They have to constantly search for who they are and what self they want to be. Women in Vogel's plays are inherently rebellious and transgressive regardless of their social status. Concerned with gender politics and female sexuality, they subvert any oppressive gender norms and patriarchal discourse to get self-empowered. Although all the female characters in this study have deployed the strategy of ritual and ritualization to deal with their crisis and construct their new selves, the specific rituals they enact are diverse, the ways they perform them are distinctive, and the effects they achieve are quite different.

In order to highlight each playwright's characteristics and at the same time give a panoramic view of their individual dramatic worlds, this author studies each of the playwrights one by one in the first three chapters. Chapter one investigates how marginalized women get rebirth and construct new identities by performing the rite of affliction, renaming, the Requiem Mass, funeral, the dying and resurrection and the initiation rite in Norman's most influential plays *Getting Out*, *'night, Mother* and *The Holdup*. Chapter two examines how educated women negotiate with various discourses and constitute their different identities by performing or mis-performing college, feminist and religious rituals in Wasserstein's three representative comedies *Uncommon Women and Others*, *The Heidi Chronicles* and *The Sisters Rosensweig*. Chapter three explores how transgressive women subvert gender norms, shift power structures and reconstruct gender identities by parodying various rituals in Vogel's *And Baby Makes Seven*, *The Baltimore Waltz* and *How I Learned to Drive*. After the analyses on the specific rituals, the study moves to a theoretical discussion on the performativity of ritual and identity in Chapter four.

Chapter One

Destruction and Resurrection:
Marginalized Women Reborn from
Death Ritual and Ritual Death

As a woman playwright, Marsha Norman prefers to dramatize "the personal crises of ordinary women struggling to have a self and be a self"(Kane 256). Most of the female characters in her plays are from lower rank of society and victims of patriarchal oppression. Frank Rich points out, "Marsha Norman's profound achievement is that she brings both understanding and dignity to forgotten and tragic American lives." (3) These marginalized women are usually entrapped in critical situations from which they attempt to escape and survive. Norman once said, "What interests me is survival, what it takes to survive. I find people very compelling who are at that moment of choice. Will they die or go on? If they go on, in what direction or for what purpose."(Beard 17) Standing on the crossroad of life and struggling in the dilemma "to die or to go on", these dispossessed, dependent and humble women are on the way to get independence, self-esteem and self-determination. They have to discard their old self and find a way out to forge a new self.

One important strategy that Norman's female protagonists deploy to deal with their crisis and survive is ritual or ritualization, which, as Schechner argues, can "help people deal with difficult transitions, ambivalent relationships, hierarchies, and desires that trouble, exceed, or violate the norms of daily life" (52). Various rituals can be found in Norman's plays: the rite of affliction and renaming in *Getting Out*, funeral in *Traveler in the Dark*, moon worship and sacred wedding in *Sarah and Abraham*, funeral and the rite of initiation in *The Holdup*, weekly manicure and the Requiem Mass in *'night, Mother*, ritual farewell to her imaginary self and funeral fantasy in *Trudy Blue*, to name but a few. One prominent and significant phenomenon is that most of the female protagonists have performed one or two kinds of death rituals such as Mass and funeral and undergone a symbolic or ritual death in physical, emotional or spiritual form. It seems that they have to get resurrection from destroying themselves or something outdated. Norman not only represents these women's tragic past to her audience but also demonstrates their transformative process from the past to the future and from crisis to rebirth.

Death is believed as a natural part of the life cycle in most cultures across the world. People have created various rites to perform on the occasions of death and during the process of funeral and mourning. Such death rituals are common in all societies and are necessary social practices to incorporate the deceased into another world and to reintegrate their relatives into society. As Derek Morgan and Robert Lee argue, "The story of the practices and rituals of death tells us as much about the living as the dead or dying."(x) Death rituals are not only important for the dead and their relatives but also for anthropologists who attempt to study indigenous customs and traditions. Anthropologists have discovered that death rituals may be "intimately connected with culturally specific notions concerning rebirth, fertility, ancestral spirits, or the immortality of the soul" (Salamone 107). Death rituals such as rites of funeral, burial, Mass, Service, praying and mourning, have been portrayed in ancient Greek plays, Shakespearean plays as well as modern dramas by Edward Albee, Eugene O'Neill, August Wilson, and so on.

Chapter One Destruction and Resurrection

Ritual death, which does not mean an actual but symbolic death, recurs in ancient mythology, folklores and many indigenous rituals. It is usually the first phase of the dying-and-rising archetypical pattern, which is prevalent in religions around the world, such as Jesus Christ's crucifixion and resurrection in Christianity, death and reincarnation in Hinduism, Samsara in Buddhism. In his seminal book *The Golden Bough*, James Fraser analyzes the dying-and-rising of Dionysus, Osiris, Adonis, and Attis in Greek mythology and associates this motif with fertility rites and calendrical rites, in which an ever-renewing cycle of nature and time is created and displayed (908-1123). During the cycle, suffering and death, similar to winter of the seasons, is the necessary condition for future rebirth. As Van Gennep demonstrates in *The Rite of Passage*, ritual death also plays an important role in social and political life. A semi-civilized king has to go through ordeals and humiliations, pretending to be dead before being elevated to throne. The Brahman must undergo initiation ceremonies which "enact[ing] death in previous world and birth in the new one" before he can be incorporated into higher caste or position (Gennep 104 - 105). Such kind of "dying" and "twice-born" is recurrent in Baptism of Sabians, the Ordination of Bishop and the Initiation of magician. It is clear that ritual death always takes place in the liminal stage of rites of passage which echoes Turner's assertion that "liminality is frequently likened to death, to being in the womb, and to invisibility, to darkness"("Ritual Process" 96). Therefore, it is a symbolic and preparatory state for a new identity to come into being.

This chapter studies Norman's three plays, namely, *Getting Out*, *'night, Mother*, and *The Holdup*, to explore how female characters express their voices, embody their ideals, and reconstruct their identities by performing death rituals and undergoing ritual death. Arlene gets control on her body and renews her self by killing her alter ego Arlie symbolically in the rite of affliction. She also confirms her new identity by declaring her new name to the outside world repeatedly. Jessie empowers herself by designing and performing her own Requiem Mass at her last ritualized night, and constitutes her autonomous, determined and free self through her performative language and acts. Her death cannot be understood physically or literally. It should be interpreted as a spiritual or symbolic one. Lily directs, organizes and participates in the funeral of Henry, the dying and resurrection of the Outlaw, and the initiation rite of Archie, leading the Outlaw and Archie to a new stage of life and elevating herself to the status of men's life nurturer as well as spiritual guide. All these women, like Phoenix in Greek mythology, obtain a new self by destroying their former self or an old world symbolically. They express and embody the feminist ideals that Norman believes and advocates.

I. An Ex-con's Self-Reformation Through Rites of Affliction and Renaming

The title of Norman's first play *Getting Out* implies that it is about a transitional moment of the heroine's life. Arlene, a girl who had been in prison for eight years, comes out on her first day of parole and faces a new yet precarious world. She is eager to turn over a new leaf of her life. However, her life is haunted by a prison guard, her mother, her former pimp, and especially her earlier evil self. All people and memories in the past reappear and persist in controlling her present and future life as she crosses the threshold of her apartment. Arlene has to escape from them and re-create herself if she wants to reintegrate into the society successfully. There are at least three implications by naming the play as *Getting Out*. Literally, it refers to Arlene's release from prison, getting out of the jail walls physically. It also connotes Arlene's "cutting ties" of family and institutions, her attempting to break through the invisible siege built by the old acquaintances and former prison guards. In addition, Arlene is entrapped in another "prison", that is, the psychological pain, shame and loss symbolized by her hateful alter ego, Arlie. Arlene and Arlie's hidden yet painful conflicts restrict Arlene's progress into the new stage of life. She has to fight internally against her own former self and find a path out of this psychological "prison".

Most of the scholarship of the play revolves around how patriarchal institutions abuse and exploit Arlie/Arlene's body, thereby destroying her spirit and sense of self. Two opposite attitudes coexist as to the question whether Arlene could "get out" or not. Gretchen Cline's "The Impossibility of Getting Out" represents the pessimistic interpretation, which believes that there is no way for Arlene to get out because she has been subjugated and scapegoated by male dominated family, society and institutions.[①] Some critics argue that men, including her father, pimp, prison guards, and even the priest, form a patriarchal panopticon where Arlene is surveilled, punished and locked. She is always in their gaze and control no matter she is inside or outside of prison.[②] They take Arlene as a shattered victim of patriarchal system and see no hope for her

---

[①] Gretchen Cline, "The Impossibility of Getting Out: The Psychopolitics of the Family in Marsha Norman's *Getting Out*," in *Marsha Norman: A Case Book*. ed. Linda Ginter-Brown. New York & London: Garland Publishing, Inc., 1996.

[②] Timothy Murray. "Patriarchal Panopticism, or the Seduction of a Bad Joke: 'Getting Out' in Theory." *Theater Journal*, 1983, 35(3): 376 – 388; Patricia R. Schroeder. "Locked Behind the Proscenium: Feminist Strategies in *Getting Out* and *My Sister in This House*." *Modern Drama*, 1989, 32: 104 – 114.

recovery or future prosperity. Such pessimistic discourse pays all attention to the tragic dark side of the play and puts much effort to attack the evil patriarchal society, ignoring the agency of Arlene and the potential force in her struggles.

Other critics hold a more optimistic view. Kane contends that Norman "offers the possibility of hope to a struggling Arlene in the character of Ruby" who befriends and encourages Arlene to find her path to survival(261). Murphy finds Arlene's power in her inner reconciliation with Arlie because "by integrating Arlie into her present life, Arlene will learn to mother herself"(203). Without denying the damage that male authority figures do to Arlene, Bigsby stops blaming the evil environment and turns his eyes beyond victimization of women. He points out that "interpretations of the play which see it as an assault on patriarchy seem wayward" ("Contemporary" 218). Arlene is presented as someone "whose principal struggle is to resist the pathological role in which she is cast, who needs to see herself as something more than a victim, more than the deterministic product of environment and heredity"(Bigsby, "Contemporary" 218). He even argues that Arlene has got out when she decides to transform Arlie into Arlene by stabbing herself in prison and accepting a new name. All the above interpretations are insightful. However, Kane finds hope in sisterhood rather than in Arlene herself, Murphy reaches his conclusion without providing detailed text analysis, and Bigsby does not explore Arlene's stabbing and renaming from the perspective of ritual. They fail to reveal the rituals' symbolic and performative significations, let alone the complicated power relations between Arlene and other characters.

The present author argues that Arlene's "getting out" has been embodied and realized in her performance of rituals. Two critical ritual events take place in the transformation from Arlie to Arlene:

Chapter One   Destruction and Resurrection

one is Arlie's self-affliction in prison, and the other is her persistence in naming herself as Arlene instead of Arlie on her first day out of prison. The first ritual, the rite of affliction, elicited by a Christian priest, changes a violent, vindictive and hateful second-degree murderer into a meek, self-disciplined and diligent prisoner, or as Kane calls her, a "born-again Christian"(257). The second one, the rite of renaming, is Arlene's declaration of autonomy and independence, marking her change from a prisoner to a self-supporting citizen. In both rituals, Arlie/Arlene is the one who initiates the action and performs it with clear purposes. She wants to drive off the evil side of herself by stabbing her body and letting blood flow out in order to get purified, and then she determines to defend and maintain her new identity when others threaten to push her back to the old state. She is not, as many critics believed, a totally passive victim of patriarchal oppression but an awakened woman who takes actions to survive and thrive.

Arlie/Arlene's self-affliction is one case of the rites of affliction. Originally, the rites of affliction are performed to "mitigate the influence of spirits thought to be afflicting human beings with misfortune" and its function is to "rectify a state of affairs that has been disturbed or disordered; they heal, exorcise, protect, and purify" (Bell, "Ritual: Perspectives" 115). Gradually, the rite broadens to include other kinds of affliction such as sin, karma, pollution of childbearing, and death. People in different times and cultures adopt various ritual forms to get rid of the evil and restore health or the body-mind holism. For example, Ndembu perform elaborate rituals to appease and dismiss the spirits of the dead who bring diseases to their tribe. In Korea, shamans dance around the patient and burn a straw doll wearing the sick person's clothing to drive the evil spirit out. For Christians, confession and penance are the most common means to free themselves from demonic possession, original sin, and personal faults and problems. According to Bell, the major theme of rites of affliction is purification: to purify physically and spiritually. People use water, fire, milk, and even drugs to cleanse their body and shake off their sins ("Ritual: Perspectives" 118–119). Modern psychologists have proved that such rituals can provide emotional catharsis and effect psychotherapy to people who suffer from mental pressure and psychological problems.

Arlie/Arlene's self-affliction is not performed bodily on stage. It is narrated by her to Ruby. Arlene recalls her vague memory and relates it in a broken language:

> They tol' me ... after I's out an it was all over ... they said after the Chaplain got transferred ... I didn't know why he didn't come no more till after ... they said it was three whole nights at first, me screamin' to God to come git Arlie an kill her. They give me this medicine an thought I's better ... then that night, it happened, the office was in the dorm doin' count ... an they didn't hear nuthin' but they come back out where I was an I'm standin' there tellin' them to come see, real quiet I'm tellin' them, but there's all this blood all over my shirt an I got this fork I'm holdin' real tight in my hand ... an there's all these holes all over me where I been stabbin' myself an I'm sayin' Arlie is dead for what she done to me, Arlie is dead an it's God will ... I didn't scream it, I was jus' sayin' it over and over ... Arlie is dead, Arlie is dead ... they couldn't git that fork outta my hand till ... I woke up in the infirmary an they said I almost died. (53)

It is such a painful experience that Arlene cannot retell it without feeling hurt again after so many years. Two figures are mentioned in her narration: one is the Chaplain, the other is Arlie. Chaplain, although absent from this event, plays a critical role in triggering

Chapter One Destruction and Resurrection

Arlene's extreme behavior. Arlie, the one who is announced "dead" here, represents Arlene's old "hateful self". Why does Arlene have to stab her own body to kill Arlie? What do fork, blood and body symbolize in this rite of affliction? And what does Arlene achieve through this bloody ritual?

Arlie once was an "unpredictable and incorrigible" girl (53). Sexually abused by her alcoholic father and neglected by a mean and self-hated mother, Arlie grew up in pain, shame and envy, which led to her aggressive, resistant and foul-mouthed personality. In order to protect herself from being hurt further, she was always ready to take revenge against anyone who had done wrong to her. She flung a boy's pet frogs into the street just to see them get squashed by cars because the boy did not allow her to watch his pets. She peed in all her Mama's shoes when her sister locked her up in Mama's closet. She even made bologna and toothpaste sandwiches for her father, attempting to kill him. She fought, stole, got expelled from school, and at last sent herself to correctional institutions for forgery, prostitution and second-degree murder, three years in Lakewood State Prison and eight years in Pine Ridge Correctional Institute respectively. However, imprisonment did not change Arlie. She continued to behave wildly and viciously. She screamed, refused to eat, threw everything she got, and beat up other inmates. She even started a fire to burn herself in order to threaten guards to let her out of her cell. What she did resulted in nothing but long lonely segregation, which made her more desperate and violent. It seems that Arlie's life has reached an impasse. She cannot make a living as a citizen in society, nor can she adjust herself to prison life to get survival as an inmate.

It is at this critical moment that the prison Chaplain appears in Arlie's life. Though Arlie rejected to see the Chaplain in the beginning, she gradually accepted him and looked forward to his regular visits on every Tuesday. No direct description about what the Chaplain did to her is given in the play, but it indicates that he is not only kind to Arlie but also respects her. According to C. Bigsby's interpretation, it is the Chaplain's kindness and respect that triggers Arlie's process of recovery ("Contemporary" 219). Disagreeing to Cline's willful comment that "the priest commits a metaphorical rape" on Arlie (14), Bigsby points out that the Chaplain offers her such hope as she has. Arlie's change is obvious. She started to read the Bible that the Chaplain gave her and promised "won't scream or nuthin'" (46) if they move her from lockup to TV room. She began to do what the Bible told her, "depart from evil and do good" (46), and behaved so well that she got out of segregation. Every week she waited for the Chaplain's visit with "starry-eyed" eagerness (45). The most important is that the Chaplain gave her a formal and elegant new name—Arlene, and wrote it on the front page of the Bible, which provided her a sense of self-esteem and dignity. When the warden and guards called her "wildcat" "girlie" "honey" (37) and abused her as a sexual object, the Chaplain assured her that "animal is wild, not people" (9), bringing her back into human community. In Arlie's eyes, at least in these days, the Chaplain is her light, her God, the one who will save her from previous guilt and guide her into a brighter future.

However, Arlie/Arlene's attachment to the Chaplain is fatal to her because when he transferred to other place and left without saying goodbye to her, she felt being cheated and deserted by him as well as by God. She was lost again and soon returned to her old self: depressed, angry and hysterical. She raised hell in the prison and screamed for three whole nights. It seems that the wild animal-like Arlie came back to life again. But the truth is that the present Arlie/

Arlene is different from the old one. On the one hand, she has been converted to Christianity by the Chaplain, following God and hoping to get salvation by leading a moral and normal life. On the other hand, her past experiences are still haunting her body and mind, disturbing her peace and undermining her determination frequently. She is so weak that she has to depend on external force to overcome her inner conflicts and past evils. Believing the Chaplain's words that "Arlie was my hateful self, and she was hurtin' me and God would find some way to take her away"(52), Arlie/Arlene firstly relies on the Chaplain, dreaming that his talks and preaches would take Arlie away from her forever. When the Chaplain betrays his promise and abandons her, she turns to God, praying loudly and desperately day and night, and begs God to "come git Arlie and kill her" (52). Again, God does nothing to help her. It is at this moment that Arlie/Arlene realizes that nobody but herself can redeem her.

The only way that Arlie/Arlene knows to get a new life, as what the Chaplain teaches her, is to get rid of Arlie, and the single person she can depend on at that moment is herself. Therefore, at that decisive night, Arlie/Arlene picked up a folk and stabbed her body until holes were all her body and blood soaked her shirt. She did this quietly, and then calmly asked all the officers to come and see. She did not scream as before but murmured "Arlie is dead" (53) to herself and others again and again. It is explicit that Arlene does not want to commit suicide. Her intention is to exorcise Arlie out of herself by torturing her body. Ironically, the fork, a tool to sustain life, is used by her as a weapon of self-destruction.

Wang Li interprets Arlene's action as a ritual of sacrifice, implying that it marks her conversion to Christianity (40). This interpretation echoes Cline's blame that Arlie's self-mutilation is the result of the Priest's metaphorical rape on her psychology, and that her internalization of self-loathing and abnegation symbolizes her scapegoating in patriarchal society (14). It is true that the Priest's inculcation changes Arlene's self-concept, leading her to the belief that Arlie is her hateful self. However, the Chaplain never makes clear to her how God would take Arlie away. Also, as Bigsby argues, the play is "not simply a study of the pathology of child abuse ... nor does conversion have anything to do with religion" ("Contemporary" 219). Arlene does not afflict herself to please God, nor is she controlled by the Chaplain. She, in fact, takes action after she realizes that she is deserted by the Chaplain and God. Therefore, it is a misunderstanding to see the play just as a complaint of male oppression or the hysteria of female criminal. Arlene's self-killing is a ritual she performs to exorcise her evil self and get salvation through self-destruction.

Arlie/Arlene is converted to a Christian by the Chaplain and learns to read the Bible, which enlightens her moral sense on the one hand, but imposes some false Christian beliefs on her on the other hand. The Chaplain asks her to follow the doctrine "depart from evil and do good" (46) and lectures her to believe that her earlier self is evil and hateful, which is like a ghost dwelling in her body. What the Bible tells her is that "For the Lord forsaketh not his saints, but the seed of the wicked shall be cut off" (50). These words should be understood metaphorically, but Arlie/Arlene is so simple-minded that she interprets them literally and uses a fork to "cut off" Arlie. Although misled by the Chaplain, Arlene's action is brave and self-determined. Her rite of affliction is a strategy to wash away her sinful past and get purified. Performing this ritual is the first step she takes to control her own body and declares her new identity.

The body that Arlie dwells in and Arlene destroys has never belonged to her. Foucault has argued that the body is the medium of

Chapter One Destruction and Resurrection

the play of power. Arlie/Arlene's body has been a locus where male forces inscribe their desires, maneuver their power and implement their control of females. Her own father is the first man who batters her body. Arlene's memory implies that she was sexually abused by her father, but she lied to her mother that she got hurt by riding bike. Her father beat her up severely when he suspected that she told truth to her mother. He then controlled Arlie's body by offering the little girl chewing gum and pocket money. Carl, her so-called boyfriend, cheated her and induced her to work for him as a prostitute. Arlie's body became a commodity which was consumed by "dude""old droolers""sicko"and "drunk"(26) and sometimes tortured by them. Her complaint that "they tying me to the bed"(26) clearly illustrates her entrapped situation as a sexual object. In the prison, her body suffers more subjugation and exploitation. As the "exhaustive disciplinary apparatus", prison "gives almost total power over the prisoners; it has its internal mechanisms of repression and punishment"(Foucault 235-236). Arlie is not only confined and disciplined by usual institutional means, but also gazed and exploited by male wardens and guards as a female convict. They even put a two-way mirror in the shower room and watched her body when she had a bath. Her father, mother, the guards and Bennie all complained about her skinny body and tried to feed her with more food. What they are concerned about is not Arlie's health or happiness. In fact, they attempt to control Arlie by manipulating her body.

Arlie has resisted such patriarchal oppression constantly by fighting, screaming, and refusing to eat. Barbara Brook argues that our bodies frequently resist when we attempt to adapt our bodies to the ideas of self, and the most dramatic example of this in western society is dieting and eating disorder (10). When the patriarchal institutions abject Arlie's self by sexualizing and objectifying her body, Arlie also takes her body as a weapon to resist. She rebelled against her father by refusing to eat. She dumped food and plates on the floor when guards forced her to eat. In order to get out of the cell, she once set the fire to burn herself. However, all her attempts are in vain because she is too weak compared with the patriarchal forces. One dialogue between Arlie and a guard demonstrates her weak position. When the guard tells Arlie, "You gotta eat." Arlie retorts, "Says who?" The guard replies, "Says me. Says the warden. Says the Department of Corrections." (12) Explicitly Arlie is disadvantageous in terms of power. She is powerless and helpless when confronted with omnipresent oppression.

Arlie/Arlene must control her body if she wants to get autonomy. However, at this moment, her body has become the abject to be cast out, and her self has been split into two: one is the old repulsive and hateful Arlie, the other is Arlene, the rational, moral and spiritual self. For Arlie/Arlene, the abject self that is formed and deformed with shame, trauma and repression equals the body which has been gazed, battered and conquered by men. To destroy the body means to kill Arlie symbolically. And to kill Arlie signifies her triumph over patriarchal subjugation. Brook contends, "Abjection is a liminal state, and it is this positioning of women, on the threshold, or 'in-between'."(45) Arlie/Arlene is just in such a fluid and transitional state, waiting for a ritual to elevate her to a new state. Julia Kristeva emphasizes abjection as dynamics rather than as stasis. She suggests that the abject can be re-appropriated for women instead of being used against them (85). If cultures work through regulations and rituals to contain the abject, women certainly can create rituals to reverse this course. In this sense, Arlene's performance of the ritual of affliction does not mean her surrender to patriarchal institutions. On the contrary, it symbolizes her fight for the right of controlling her own body. Instead of relying on the Chaplain or God, Arlene performs the ritual by herself and for herself.

The blood in Arlie/Arlene's ritual is symbolic too. Representing the essence of life, blood is believed globally to have magic power. There are many rituals that involve the intentional release of blood in both western and eastern cultures. Blood symbolizes deep commitment in the blood brother ritual and rituals of pledges, vows, alliances, contract, and so on, in which blood will be mingled, poured or consumed. In rituals like body piercing and sacrifice, blood is the symbol of death and rebirth, owning the power of purification and redemption. The extreme example is the Sacred Blood of the Christ that is shed to save the entire human being. In rites of affliction, blood is believed unclean or contaminated, with close tie to evil or guilt, therefore, it must be let out and get recycled so as to exorcise the evil and renew the self. [1]

The blood in Arlie/Arlene's ritual could be interpreted in two dimensions. First, when she intentionally stabs her body with the fork and watches her blood flow out, blood is dirty and contaminated in her mind, symbolizing her old self, the battered, hateful and guilty one she wants to exorcise from her. The bloodletting signifies the death of Arlie. However, when she is immersed in the red blood and feels the pain of dying, blood becomes pure and fresh, symbolizing the life force. She is purified and redeemed by it. Therefore, the bloodletting also symbolizes the birth of Arlene, a different and new self.

---

[1] For detailed information, please refer to *Encyclopedia of Religious Rites, Rituals and Festivals*. Ed. by Frank A. Salamone. New York: Routledge, 2004; "Blood Ritual" in *Wikipedia*, https://en.wikipedia.org/wiki/Blood ritual.

The repeated "Arlie is dead" uttered by Arlene during the ritual is a typical speech act. According to the theory of performativity, the function of a speech act embraces three dimensions: "locution, the semantic and referential functions of language; illocution, the kind of act I was accomplishing or attempting to accomplish in saying these words; and perlocution, the effect I produce by issuing the utterance"(Loxley 18). The semantic meaning of the sentence is to describe an event, to report that Arlie dies. Clearly, the statement is false since Arlie is not dead in terms of physiology. In fact, its significance does not lie in what Arlene says but in what she does by saying it. The first act she performs is to announce the death of Arlie to the public, thereby to express her determination to cut off from her past life and to start a new one. The second act she performs is to declare and confirm the birth of Arlene, showing her inner identification with a new self. By saying the words and doing the acts, the female protagonist accomplishes her identity transformation from Arlie to Arlene. In addition, by declaring her own death and rebirth, Arlene now is not a passive object but an active subject who dominates in the power play with men and determines her own destiny. Therefore, the perlocution of her utterance is to empower Arlene and entitle her the right to control her own body, mind and future for the first time.

This ritual of affliction changes Arlie/Arlene absolutely. She calmed down and began to behave well soon. Arlene recalls, "Officers was sayin' they's seein' such a change in me an givin' me yarn to knit sweaters."(53) Arlene tries to adapt herself to prison life and learn how to work and cooperate. When she tells Ruby that "they said things ain't never been as clean as when I's doin' the housekeepi' at the dorm"(53), she still feels very proud. The most important is that Arlene "got in the honor cottage an nobody was

Chapter One Destruction and Resurrection 067

foolin' with me no more or nuthin"(53). Her change not only brings her manual skills and peaceful life, but also gives her honor, respect and dignity. She survives from the tough confining days and succeeds in getting herself out of the prison by winning the opportunity of parole after eight years.

However, when Arlene gets out from the prison, she finds that nobody outside recognizes her new identity, and she is still the "same hateful brat"(24) in their eyes. Her old acquaintances, including her mother, call her "Arlie girl" and see her as "wildcat" "liar" and "prostitute" (14 – 24). Their doubt, prejudice and threat besiege Arlene again and form a social "prison" which is more difficult for her to escape from. At the same time, meeting and talking with these people bring back all her traumatic memories. She realizes that Arlie has always lived in her mind although she has repressed her deliberately. Arlie can be called up by "fears, needs, and even simple word cues"(5), and disturbs her at any moment. She is entrapped again in the conflicts of her split selves. Arlie is too aggressive, violent and rebellious, while Arlene is too meek, withdrawn and obedient. If Arlene/Arlie wants to survive and starts a new life, she has to build up her new identity in front of the public and "kill" Arlie again, which means to reconcile her two selves in her mind and integrate her into the outside community. Therefore, whenever others call her "Arlie", Arlene immediately rebuts them angrily and tells them firmly that her name is "Arlene" now. The entire action of the play is structured on the alternating scenes of her being called "Arlie" and her correcting them into calling her "Arlene". Such scenes are repeated for nine times throughout her dialogues with Bennie, Mother, Carl and Ruby. Norman ritualizes this renaming process to emphasize Arlene's struggle and determination to change her identity.

Personal names are not only signs that distinguish individuals but also powerful symbols that represent one's present status and future expectations. They manifest one's identity and exert some mystical influence over their bearers. There are various ceremonies to name or rename a person across the world. As a kind of common ritual, naming or renaming has "an important and powerful force that grants newborns and older people alike the gift of an identity"(Salamone, 272). Lucile H. Charles argues that "naming gives one existence and makes him part of the world of men"(21). In *Naming and Identity*, Richard Alford contends that names symbolize identities and naming has two functions, "First, they provide messages to the members of the society at large about who an individual is; Second, they provide messages to the named individual about who he or she is or is expected to be."(51) According to Alford, people may get new names when they enter adulthood, marriage or parenthood in order to underscore the transformations they are undergoing. Also when an individual wishes to abandon an unwanted identity, he or she may abandon his or her old name and assume a new one. He points out further, "Just as the constancy of personal names can reflect and reinforce a constancy of identity, so, too, changes of personal names, both formal and informal, can reflect and reinforce identity changes."(81–82)

The two personal names of the female protagonist, Arlene and Arlie, as demonstrated earlier, represent her two different identities. Arlie represents her past evil self, the identity she wants to abandon, while Arlene represents her future ideal self, a new identity she desires. Although Arlene has identified with her new name and new identity in her mind since her ritual of affliction, she has not gained recognition from people around her, especially those who hold stereotypical notion of her. She has to announce, defend and confirm

Chapter One Destruction and Resurrection

her new name repeatedly in front of them, thereby, reinforce her new identity again and again. Changing her name means to change her identity and to declare her determination to break from the past. It is a liminal phase that will lead to a new life, yet it is also a tough battle between her and the outside world. Arlene's insistence is confronted with other people's resistance, which embodies the complicated power relations among them.

The naming battle between Arlene and Bennie runs through the entire play and demonstrates their see-saw power struggle clearly. The first dialogue of the play is Bennie and Arlene's argument over how to address her, which is also Arlene's first announcement of becoming a new individual in outside world. Arlene's determination to change and Bennie's doubt is expressed vividly in their dialogue:

> Bennie(*from outside*): Arlie?
> Arlene: Arlene.
> Bennie: Arlene? (*Bringing the trunk just inside the door*)
> Arlene: Leave it. I'll get it later.
> Bennie: Oh, now, let me bring it for you. You ain't as strong as you was.
> Arlene: I ain't as mean as I was. I'm strong as ever. You go on now. (*Beginning to walk around the room*)
> Bennie (*Scoots the trunk into the room a little further*): Go on where, Arlie?
> Arlene: I don't know where. How'd I know where you'd be goin'?
> ...
> Bennie: Nobody to take care of you.
> Arlene: I kin take care of myself. I been doin' it long enough.
> Bennie: Sure you have, an you landed yourself in prison doin't it, Arlie girl.
> Arlene(*Wheels around*): Arlie girl landed herself in prison. Arlene is out, Okay? (17 – 18)

As Arlene's former prison guard, Bennie is used to seeing her as a weak incorrigible girl, who is unable to take care of herself and will potentially commit crimes again. Therefore, he still calls her "Arlie" when they arrive at Arlene's apartment. When Arlene corrects him, he is surprised and shows strong doubt. He has not realized that Arlene is not an inmate but a free person now, and their relationship has been totally different. As Arlene assures him that she is independent and capable enough of taking care of herself, Bennie retorts sarcastically by mentioning her guilty past. Bennie's prejudice and stereotypical attitude hurt and anger Arlene so much that she wheels around and claims firmly that "Arlie girl landed herself in prison. Arlene is out"(8).

Bigsby has noticed Arlene's emphasis on the two names' difference and contends that the "distinction which is without meaning when she utters it at the beginning of the play but which acquires meaning as it proceeds" ("Contemporary" 214). In fact, Arlene's statement, as a performative act, is meaningful since the beginning. It firstly expresses the big difference between Arlie and Arlene. Secondly, it is a performative utterance that declares her new identity signified by the new name. She becomes Arlene through the act of saying she is. Thirdly, Arlene's response and action indicate that she is doing her best to escape from Bennie's control and to gain the right to decide her future life, which symbolizes the start of her persistent fight for self-independence.

Norman dramatizes Arlene and Bennie's power conflicts through their struggle for naming. At the beginning, Bennie does not take Arlene's words seriously and continues to call her "Arlie" during their talk, especially when he mentions Arlie's wild behaviors in prison. His purpose is to bring Arlene back under his control. However, Arlene is very serious and firm. When Bennie says, "But you got

Chapter One Destruction and Resurrection

grit, Arlie," Arlene immediately reminds him "I have said for you to call me Arlene"(9). This time, Bennie begins to catch Arlene's real intention and makes a compromise by consoling her that "Don't git riled. You want me to call you Arlene, then Arlene it is"(9). It seems that Arlene has gained the upper hand in this round. However, Bennie often makes slip of tongue and has to correct himself after he calls her Arlie again. Such repeated mistakes, according to Freud, are not accidental. It implies that Bennie has not accepted Arlene's new identity and still regards her as Arlie unconsciously. This is explicit when Bennie attempts to rape Arlene. When Arlene struggles and shouts, "I could mess you up good," Bennie says, "Now, Arlie. You ain't had a man in a long time."(32) This enrages Arlene and recalls Arlie back to life. She goes "into a violent rage, hitting and kicking him" and screams "I'll kill you, you creep"(32). This is a typical state of Arlie, which ironically proves that Bennie is right. Bennie sarcastically asks, "You will? You'll kill ol' Bennie ... kill ol' Bennie like you done that cab driver?"(32) According to Bennie's logic, Arlene will return to Arlie if she resorts to violence. This cruel reminder stuns and hurts Arlene, she "looks as though she has been bit" and becomes "passive, cold and bitter"(32). Bennie takes advantage of Arlene's weakness and plots to make love with her. Without any weapon to protect herself, Arlene begins to call Bennie's action as "rape" and describes the usual procedure of raping, which shocks and stops Bennie suddenly. Norman makes full use of the power of naming and vividly shows the climax of their struggle in the following dialogue.

> Bennie: Don't you call me no rapist. (*Pause, then insistent*) No, I ain't no rapist, Arlie. (*Gets up, begins to tuck his shirt back in and zip up his pants*)

>   Arlene: And I ain't Arlie.
>
>   Bennie: No I guess you ain't.
>
>   Arlene (*Quietly and painfully*): Arlie coulda killed you. (32-33)

Being called a rapist is out of Bennie's expectation because he does not want to destroy Arlene; he is just "motivated by confused feelings of sexual aggression and romantic need"(Bigsby, "Contemporary" 218). By naming Bennie's action as rape and implying that he is a rapist, Arlene successfully awakens Bennie's conscience and forces him to reflect upon his actions. When Bennie asks Arlene not to call him rapist, Arlene warns him again that she is not Arlie either. This time, Bennie realizes that the girl before him is not the old Arlie anymore. He begins to accept her new identity and show respect to her.

However, Arlene's efforts to rename herself meet more resistance from her mother. Her naming battle with Mother reveals their unbridgeable gap and mutual indifference. Mother's first voice on stage is to shout repeatedly: "Arlie? Arlie girl you in there?" "Arlie?""Arlie? I know you're in there"(14), which brings Arlene as well as the audience back to her childhood trauma that she was violated by her own father. During their talk, Arlene is eager to learn about the present conditions of her family, but her mother mumbles about trivial affairs in their old days, ignoring Arlene's questions. When Arlene tentatively tells her mother that "they don't call me Arlie no more. It's Arlene now"(17), she actually wants to indicate that she has become a new person, not the foul-mouthed violent little girl. However, her mother pretends not to hear it and continues to complain about Arlene's ugly hair, skinny figure and inability to work. After a long delay, Mother casually starts an interrogating dialogue.

Chapter One Destruction and Resurrection   073

>   Mother(*Continuing to sweep*): So, you're callin' yourself Arlene, now?
>
>   Arlene: Yes.
>
>   Mother: Don't want your girlie name no more?
>
>   Arlene: Somehin' like that.
>
>   Mother: They call you Arlene in prison?
>
>   Arlene: Not at first when I was bein' hateful. Just my number then.
>
>   Mother: You always been hateful.
>
>   Arlene: There was this Chaplain, he called me Arlene from the first day he come to talk to me.
>
>   ...
>
>   Mother: Since when? (*Arlene backs off*)
>
>   ...
>
>   Mother: That your picture?
>
>   Arlene: That Chaplain give it to me.
>
>   Mother: The one give you your "new name". (20)

It seems that Mother is interested in her daughter's new name now. However, she does not take it seriously or change her attitude even after she learns the story between Arlene and the Chaplain. Mother insists on addressing her daughter as "Arlie", so Arlene has to remind her repeatedly in vain. When Mother suspects that Arlene earns money in prison by serving guards, she expresses her contempt by shouting "you play, Arlie? ... Makes me sick. You got family, Arlie, what you want with that playing"(21). Mother jumps such conclusion and hurls insults at Arlene based on imagination rather than facts, believing her daughter must have used the body to get money just because she once did so as a little girl. In her mother's eyes, Arlene is still the old "Arlie", who would never change.

The only time Mother calls her daughter "Arlene" is when she discovers Bennie's hat and doubts that Arlene has been "screwing a goddamn guard" (23). Uttering the word "Arlene" with an emphasized sarcastic tone, Mother in fact shows her distrust, disappointment and disgust to her daughter. No matter how hard Arlene tries to convince her mother that she and Bennie do not sleep together, and that she is not the earlier Arlie, her mother still holds a stereotyped opinion of her. Depressed and angered by her mother's attitude, Arlene asks wearily that [you think I am the] "same hateful brat, right?" Mother confirms with a reply, "Same hateful brat. Right."(25) Believing that "I'm your mother. I know what you'll do"(24), Mother does not believe that her daughter will become a good decent woman. Her prejudice against Arlene is not eliminated, but reinforced by this unhappy meeting. On the surface, Norman dramatizes the argument between Arlene and her mother over two names. What is behind the argument is the conflicts of mother and daughter, past and present, and the old and new selves. Arlene is eager to forget her past, free from mother's control and get her new identity being recognized. But Mother fixes Arlene in the past and rejects her new name, which symbolizes the denial of her new identity.

Similar to Mother, Carl, Arlene's former boyfriend and pimp, also regards Arlene as the same girl he used to know by calling her Arlie or other nicknames. Carl addresses Arlene with various names, which indicates their special and complicated relationship. By calling her "mama", "my lady", he suggests that Arlene is still a prostitute who works for him. By using "baby", "girlie", "sugar", "sweetheart", and "doll", he wants to show their intimacy as former lovers. In both relationships, Carl is the one who controls and exploits Arlene's body.

The various names that Carl addresses Arlene drags her back into her former social position and relives her traumatic memories of being a teenage prostitute and an unmarried mother. When discussing the force of a name, Butler points out that it "depends not only on its iterability, but on a form of repetition that is linked to trauma, on what is not remembered, but relived, and relived in and through the linguistic substitution for the traumatic event" ("Excitable Speech" 36). Carl's repetition of the old address of Arlene not only relives her traumatic experiences, but also anticipates her dark future. When Carl mentions Birmingham and suggests that they go to New York together to start their business again. Arlene's former self, Arlie, immediately appears on the stage and complains bitterly that she has been sexually abused by repulsive clients. Such traumatic memories triggered in Arlene's mind haunt and threaten her new self as well as her choice of future. At this moment, Bennie's voice from outside "Arlene? Arlene" awakens her illusion and brings her back to the present.

> Bennie's Voice: Arlene? Arlene?
> Carl: Arlene? (*Jumping up*) Well, la-de-da.
> Arlene: Bennie, this here's Carl.
> Carl: You're interruptin', Jack, Me an Arlie got business.
> Bennie: She's callin' herself Arlene.
> Carl: I call my ladies what I feel like, chicken man, an you call yourself "gone". (28)

The two names here not only represent her two selves, but also predict two different kinds of life paths in front of her. Carl and Bennie's dialogue demonstrates explicitly that Arlene has to make choice between two lives. It is clear that Carl's purpose of addressing Arlene as Arlie is to delimit and fix her identity as his girl who serves him and earns money for him. Bennie's defense of her new name suggests that she is a free and autonomous individual now. Choosing to be Arlie means going to New York with Carl and earning a lot of money quickly as a prostitute, but perhaps putting her into prison again. Choosing to be Arlene, as Carl describes, means she has to work hard with long hours every day yet gets very low salary, possibly being confined to her prison-like apartment for the rest of life. Facing the seduction from Carl on one hand and worried about her future fate as an unskilled laborer on the other, Arlene becomes puzzled and hesitant because neither is the life she desires. She wonders for the first time whether the price of freedom is enduring poverty and financial imprisonment.

Arlene's self-redefinition and self-reformation is not a smooth journey. Bennie's sexual harassment, Mother's misunderstanding and Carl's enticement show that Arlene is still locked in the sexist male-dominated society that will not recognize her as an autonomous individual. All of them imprison her in the patriarchal structure as a sexual object and deny her right to be master of her own life, which undermine Arlene's will and power. Arlene in fact wavers at some moments and sways between her two different selves. She invokes violence that Arlie used when Bennie attempts to rape her. As Mother slams the door and shouts at her "don't you touch me"(25), the image of Arlie jumps out from her mind and she almost does something malicious to fight against Mother. She has to repress such impulsion by telling herself "no, don't touch Mama, Arlie"(25). She keeps the colored matchbook Carl gives her and deliberates whether she should meet him in the bar and go to New York the next day or not. Norman seems to imply that it is possible for Arlene to return to her old way of life if nobody provides help and support. Bigsby comments correctly that Arlene's seedy apartment is "either her destination or the limbo through which she will pass on her way to further degradation" ("Contemporary" 213). Therefore, Arlene needs someone who sympathize with her and guide her life to a bright future. In this sense, Ruby, her upstairs neighbor plays a critical role in Arlene's metamorphosis.

The importance of Ruby has attracted some critical attention. Cline contends that Ruby embodies Norman's idealized individualism that leads to a hopeful ending (23). Kane reads Ruby as "a benevolent mother surrogate who is sharply contrasted with Arlene's own mother"(261). Wang Li argues that Ruby performs the role of both surrogate mother and sisterly confidante of Arlene by offering care, comfort and aid (48). Though these interpretations are insightful, they are based on the last scene of the play, ignoring some meaningful details in the dramatic text. In fact, Ruby means more than a mother surrogate or a sisterly friend who just provide traditional female tenderness.

As the only person who accepts Arlene's new name immediately without hesitation, Ruby performs both Arlene's role-model and an instructor who helps Arlene to make sensible choice and find her own path to survival. Norman highlights the scene of their first encounter. Mistaking Arlene as Candy, Ruby knocks at the door and yells that she wants to get back her money. When Arlene tells her Candy isn't here, Ruby shouts uncertainly: "Arlie? That Arlie?"(39) As Arlene opens the door, Ruby asks again: "It is Arlie, right?"(39) Without extending her hand or inviting Ruby to come in, Arlene just replies calmly, "It's Arlene," which makes a clear distinction between the two names and displays her present self in front of the stranger. Though surprised a little, Ruby understands at once what Arlene means by using a more formal and elegant name. In fact, Ruby has learned from Candy earlier that her sister was called Arlie, who once was a whore, a forger and a killer, "more like the meanest bitch that ever walked" (41), thus the one she expects to see is a violent, evil and degenerate woman. However, Arlene's image is much better. She is polite, reserved and decent, always ready to defend herself-esteem. After chatting for a few minutes, Ruby realizes that Arlene is totally different from Arlie. She cannot help telling Arlene that "you don't seem like Candy said"(41). From this moment, Ruby calls her Arlene instead of Arlie, embracing her new identity warmly. Ruby's recognition and acceptance marks Arlene's first successful step to enter social community.

Although having named herself in a new way, Arlene in fact is not well-equipped for a new life. On the one hand, she is uncertain about her future fate as an ex-con without any practical skill to make a living. On the other hand, after killing Arlie symbolically, she has been so meek that she even does not know how to deal with bad guys like Bennie and Carl. In these two aspects, Ruby performs a role-model for Arlene. Similar to Arlene, Ruby was also an ex-con and had confronted the same troubles when she got out of prison. After tough struggles, she now earns her living as a cook and enjoys independence, freedom as well as self-dignity. She confesses that she was so crazy on her first day out that she heaved a whole gallon of milk right out the window. When she saw the bottle bounced, she told herself "Ruby, if a gallon of milk can bounce back, so can you" (41). She kept saying it to herself for about a year in order to get self-confidence and power. This story, together with Ruby's words of wisdom, encourages Arlene very much and convinces her that if Ruby can, she can. In addition, Ruby demonstrates bravery and firmness in face of threats from men. When Carl catches Arlene's arm and forces her to go with him violently, Ruby opens the door and stops Carl. Then she quarrels with Carl and rebuts him relentlessly and contemptuously. At last, she drives him away. As Bennie visits

Arlene again to annoy her, it is Ruby who blocks the door and warns that she would call the police or beat him with a watering can. Ruby's manner and behavior set examples to Arlene, illustrating that women must be firm and strong if they want to escape from man's harm, and that their only way of getting out is to fight persistently.

Ruby is also Arlene's helpful instructor who takes the responsibility of guidance when Arlene is disoriented. She plays a key role at two critical moments. On the first occasion, Ruby enlightens Arlene that one can come to terms with one's past and suggests her to reconcile with her former self. Battered by a series of failure in winning her old acquaintances' recognition as a renewed individual, Arlene discovers that Arlie, though killed symbolically and repressed in her mind for a long time, never dies, and that her deliberate denial of her past self in fact causes her psychological split. On the one hand, Arlene becomes furious at people who keep calling her Arlie and disappointed at herself who cannot escape from Arlie's ghost. On the other hand, she realizes that her new self has been subjugated by institutions and is too meek to survive. Arlene, like a lost lamb, "breaks down completely, screaming, crying, falling over into Ruby's lap"(99). At this moment, Ruby holds Arlene tenderly and rocks her as with a baby. Waiting for her to calm down patiently, Ruby tells her that "you can still love people that's gone" (54), which consoles Arlene and helps her to achieve a whole self by reintegrating Arlie with Arlene. Just as Roudane points out, Arlene must "learn to accept her former self, to grant Arlie her presence, and to push beyond the emotional wreckage of her past. And such an insight becomes the master key to her existing and existence"(126). In the final scene of the play, Arlie and Arlene are "enjoyably aware of each other"(56) for the first time and authentically converse with one another happily. Arlene at last gets out of her former psychological prison by merging her two split selves and gains an integrated self. In this sense, the girl on the stage now is neither Arlie nor Arlene but a new autonomous woman with both Arlie's energy and Arlene's self-discipline.

The other critical occasion is when Arlene picks up the matchbook Carl gives her and tries to make her decision. Ruby watches for a moment and intervenes because she "knows that what she says now is very important" (55). With a retrospective tone, Ruby narrates her real story of being put into jail for prostitution by writing her phone number on a matchbook. Hearing Ruby's words quietly, Arlene tears up the matchbook with firm determination, which implies that she completely cut ties off the past and will never return to prostitution. Then Arlene discards her distrust of Ruby and accepts Ruby's invitation to play cards together. This decision is in fact significant for Arlene's self-development because it means she has got out of isolation and connected herself with other females who have similar experiences. They set up a bond that will unite them to fight and survive together. This sisterhood gives hope to all women who suffer from patriarchal oppression and embodies the spirit of the feminist movement.

Ritual is deployed by Norman successfully in portraying the liminal female image. The two rituals that Arlene enacts are symbolic, performative and political. The blood she shed, the body she stabbed and the old name she discarded symbolize the old self-identity she hates and wants to destroy, while the new body purified by blood and the new name she defends symbolize the self she is eager to identify with. Arlene's speech acts and body gestures are not descriptive, but performative, through which her rational, independent and moral self is constituted. In addition, the ritual performance is a process of power struggle between Arlie/Arlene and the oppressive patriarchal system. She uses her body as a weapon and ritual as a strategy to defeat men's manipulation and empower herself. Though with a weak hope of prosperity, Arlene gets out of the traps of family, prison and the past. She at last reintegrates her two selves and determines to face the tough but free outside-prison life bravely.

Ritual is also Norman's dramatic technique to narrate the story and organize the dramatic structure. The rite of renaming starts from the first line of the play and continues through the entire plot. Arlene's repetitive act of renaming is inserted in her conversations with Bennie, Mother, Carl and Ruby. It initiates each of their conversations and constitutes the basic conflict of their confrontation. The rhythm of the play coincides with every conversation as well as each repetition of the ritual, which reveals Norman's mastery of artistic form. The rite of affliction is narrated by Arlene to Ruby at the moment of Arlene's hysteria caused by anger and frustration. As Arlene pours out her traumatic memories and lets out her feelings, the play reaches its climax in emotion and theme. The narration of the ritual is cathartic. It heals Arlene's trauma. It also establishes emotional bond between Arlene and Ruby. After baring her heart to Ruby, Arlene calms down and trusts Ruby completely, which leads to the solid sisterhood that Norman attempts to convey and advocate. Norman interweaves the two narrative lines skillfully and displays a girl's transformative process on the stage.

II. An Epileptic's Self-Empowerment by Performing Her Own "Requiem Mass"

Similar to Arlene in *Getting Out*, Jessie in *'night, Mother* is also entrapped and desperate to find a way out. As a middle-aged divorced epileptic, Jessie is confined to her ill body, isolated house as well as suffocating mother-daughter relationship. Lacking both a sense of self and a sense of existence, Jessie struggles to search for a true self and the ultimate meaning of life. After a long journey of pursuit, Jessie's final decision is to say no to all and kill herself with her father's pistol, which, for her mother, is giving up, but in her opinion, is "the other thing I'm trying" and "how I have my say" (75). Suicide for Jessie is the last effort she makes to control her body and give her life meaning.

Such dual interpretations of Jessie's suicide have troubled audiences as well as critics since its premiere in 1982, resulting in disparate understanding of the play. Critics such as Jill Dolan, Sarah Reuning and Jenny Spencer regard Jessie as a victim of patriarchy and a defeatist, arguing that her suicide is a result of loss, anger and depression and that her choice is "a relinquishing, rather than a regaining, of control"(Reuning 55). Other critics contend that Jessie is a woman who has woken up and taken an action to be "the author of her own fate"(Bigsby, "Contemporary" 232). Her self-destruction is "her way of triumphing over time"(Drew 87), and her death brings "freedom, autonomy, and individualism" (R. H. Smith 279). Norman herself expresses the same idea, "my sense of 'night, Mother is that it is a play of nearly triumph ... this is not a despairing act." (interviews 339) Laurin Porter also believes that "Jessie has resolved the central issue of the play before the curtain rises ... This is a play about female empowerment" (205). The debate shows that the negative side sees an old Jessie who suffers from disease, abandonment and loneliness, while the positive side sees a new Jessie who is firm, autonomous and powerful.

This study argues that 'night, Mother should not be read just as an event of suicide, but also an event of ritual, by which Norman demonstrates the transformative process of Jessie's identity. Jessie, as the ritual subject, is in a liminal state, "betwixt and between social categories or personal identities"(Schechner 66). In the past, she is a defeated woman controlled by others. But since her declaration of self-killing, she has become independent and self-determined. Her personality is necessarily ambiguous and indeterminate during the transitional stage. The words she says and the ritual of Requiem Mass she designs and performs are symbolic and performative, constituting her new identity. Only through her self-destruction and ritual performance could Jessie be redeemed and endow her life with true meaning. The play, as Bigsby correctly points out, is "assuredly not a study of a suicide. It is a study of life"("Contemporary" 233). It is about "contemporary life, and what gives it—or fails to give it— value" (Rich). Jessie empowers herself by designing, instructing, preparing and performing her ritual of Requiem Mass and the play illustrates how this empowerment takes place.

A few critics have noticed the ritualistic characteristics of *'night, Mother*. Carolyn Cope contends that Norman has set up family rituals such as an old custom of making hot cocoa and the ritual of the Saturday night manicure to derail Jessie's plan of suicide (77). Wang Li interprets the ritual of the Saturday night manicure as Jessie's scrupulous care for her mother (127). Analyzing the repetitive routines that Jessie and Mama do in the evening, Kundert-Gibbs argues that "such a daily ritual protects the women, yet at the same time cuts them off from the outside world"(50). However, no one takes the entire play as a ritual of Requiem Mass. In fact, when being interviewed by David Savran, Marsha Norman says,

> The first line of dialogue I wrote for *'night, Mother* was Jessie's line, "We got any old towels?" As soon as I wrote it down, I understood that it

was a ritual piece, that Jessie was coming in to celebrate this Requiem Mass, that she has these stacks of towels; here are the witnesses, the household objects. She comes in as though she is the altar boy. (186)

The playwright regards her work as a ritual of Requiem Mass, in which Jessie plays the role of the altar boy. She believes that the household objects (certainly the audience) are the witness to Jessie's ritual. In his *Contemporary American Playwrights*, Bigsby mentions Norman's idea of Requiem Mass and asserts that it is "a suggestion which reinforces her insistence that Jessie's is not a meaningless death, not a surrender to absurdity"(238). However, Bigsby does not make further exploration on the ritual features of the play. Following Norman, this study will analyze *'night, Mother* as a ritual of Requiem Mass designed and performed by Jessie and participated by her mama Thelma to expound how Jessie ritualizes her last night and reshapes her self-identity successfully.

Requiem Mass, also called Mass of the Resurrection, Mass of Christian Burial or Funeral Mass, is "a Mass in the Catholic Church offered for the repose of the soul or souls of one or more deceased persons" (Salamone 78). Similar to daily Mass, Requiem Mass consists of two parts: the Liturgy of the Word and the Liturgy of the Eucharist, which are made up of a series of rites such as Testament reading, praying, Gospel proclaiming, preaching, presenting gifts of Bread and Wine. As an important part of Christian funeral, it connects the secular grief expression to the praise of Jesus, especially the worship of Jesus' victory over death through the Resurrection. The Eucharist, based on the Last Supper during which Jesus shared bread and wine with his disciples, has been celebrated by Christians to commemorate the life, death and resurrection of Jesus.

In the play, when Thelma threatens Jessie that suicide is a sin and she will go to hell for that, Jessie replies that "Jesus was a suicide, if you ask me" (18), which equals her death to Jesus' martyrdom. There are at least three similarities between Jessie and Jesus' death. Firstly, it is a voluntary action. Secondly, it is endowed with special purpose and meaning by their subjects. Thirdly, it is expected that the death will bring rebirth and immortality to their subjects. It is not accidental for Norman to name her heroine Jessie, which shares a similar pronunciation with Jesus. In this way, Norman sets up connection between them and gives symbolic and holy implications to Jessie's death.

Both time and space in the play have been ritualized by Norman intentionally with her creative dramatic devices. According to Catherine Bell, if an act is performed in a special time and space with a special purpose and gets "privileged distinction" from other ways of acting, then it is ritualized. People can "engage in ritualization as a practical way of dealing with some specific circumstances. Ritual is never simply or solely a matter of routine, habit, or 'the dead weight of tradition'"("Ritual Theory" 92). The Saturday night in the play looks very ordinary and routine at the beginning. Jessie is busy with her daily housework, and Thelma, as usual, is eating her sweet food and waiting for Jessie to manicure her fingernails. Small talk just goes on smoothly between mother and daughter. However, such ordinariness is shattered as soon as Jessie announces that she is going to kill herself in a couple of hours. "This night" suddenly becomes their "last night". Their conversation and hot cocoa making, like the talk and meal of Jesus with his disciples, will be their "Last Supper". The singularity of this night is based on thousands of other routine nights yet transcends them all at the same time. Just like what Jessie explains, "We wouldn't have more talks like tonight, because it's this next part that's made this last part so good."(75)

Norman also highlights the ritualistic sense of Jessie's action by blurring the time in the play and the time in theater. What is more intriguing is the time that Norman sets for the performance of the play. In the stage directions, Norman insists that "the time is the present, with the action beginning about 8:15. Clocks onstage in the kitchen and on a table in the living room should run throughout the performance and be visible to the audience"(3). The beginning of the action in the play is almost the same time of curtain up every night in theater. Therefore, the boundary between real and theatrical time is blurred, so is that between reality and illusion. The audiences are forced to enter the role of witnessing Jessie's ritual performance with full awareness of the running time and the inevitability of her self-killing. With the real clocks clicking on stage, Jessie controls not only the time of her last night but also the time of the audience in theater. As Kane assures, "Jessie has planned an agenda for this evening; the momentum and timetable are hers."(265)

Though the setting of the play is a naturalistic country house filled with real people's clutter and comforts, Norman has transformed the stage into a ritual space by foregrounding the door of Jessie's bedroom where she is going to commit suicide. The stage directions give an elaborate description of the entry.

> One of these bedrooms opens directly onto the hall, and its entry should be visible to everyone in the audience. It should be, in fact, the focal point of the entire set, and the lighting should make it disappear completely at times and draw the entire set into it at others. It is a point of both threat and promise. It is an ordinary door that opens onto absolute nothingness. That door is the point of all the action, and the utmost care should be given to its design and construction. (3)

Chapter One Destruction and Resurrection

As the following diagram shows, the stage is divided into two parts by the door: on one side is the earthly world, while on the other side is the black unknown world of "absolute nothingness". With the change of light, the door is mystified and gilded with magical power, symbolizing "both threat and promise". The hallway and the door here constitute the limen or threshold of rites of passage, functioning as the passageway between two worlds.

Kitchen ⟶ Living room ⟶ hall | Door | bedroom

According to Gennep, the door is "the boundary between the foreign and domestic worlds in the case of an ordinary dwelling, between the profane and sacred worlds in the case of a temple. Therefore, to cross the threshold is to unite oneself with a new world" (20). In rituals, such liminal space can be expanded or minimalized both practically and conceptually. As the site of the action, it retains "its peculiar quality of passageway or temporariness" (Schechner 67). Since the dramatic conflict of 'night, Mother is embodied in Jessie's will to cross the bedroom door and shoot herself and the opposite will of her mother to stop her from doing so, the door becomes the central and pivotal spot of the stage, separating mother and daughter, life and death, old Jessie and new Jessie. In an interview with Savran, Norman even elevates the status of this door to the level of another character by saying, "You have Mama and Jessie and the door behind them," forming an equal triangle (Savran 185). Revolving around the door, Jessie and Thelma get involved in a desperate battle of wills and wits, empowerment and disempowerment, and life and death.

What is the most important in ritual is the ritual body: what the body says, what the body does, and what change is inscribed to the body. In *Ritual Theory, Ritual Practice*, Bell argues, "The strategies of ritualization are particularly rooted in the body, specifically, the interaction of the social body within a symbolically constituted spatial and temporal environment."(93) It is believed that body is "a highly restricted medium of expression and a key to the relationship of self, society, and cosmos"(Douglas 174). Like Arlene in *Getting Out*, Jessie is the ritual body of her Requiem Mass. However, Jessie used to be a woman who cannot control either her body or mind because of physical disease and who has no say in anything because of her dominating mother. Having inherited epilepsy from her father, Jessie often catches fits and loses control of her body. When a fit comes, she will suddenly crumple, slide down, turn blue and jerk like a puppet whose strings are cut and foam like a mad dog. This disease weakens her memory and scares people around her. Consequently, she cannot hold any job and is isolated from outside world. She has to rely on medicine to gain control of her body and mind all the time. Jessie has been trapped in her unreliable body. Norman once comments, "Jessie was told that the door was locked ... 'you have this problem; people don't want to deal with you; you cannot trust your body'. Jessie has lived for a long time imprisoned in a body that would fail her."(Craig 181) Her mother's friend Agnes stops visiting them after seeing Jessie have a fit because she thinks that Jessie is "like a corpse"(42).

Jessie's life has been in the hands of her mother and Jessie's values are based on her relationship with men. In order to find Jessie a husband, her mother invites a carpenter named Cecil to their house to build an unnecessary porch and arranges their marriage. Although Jessie tries her best to be a good wife and uses all her means to please her husband, Cecil does not love her and deserts her for another girl. He leaves home regardless of Jessie's sadness and begging. After

Chapter One Destruction and Resurrection

Jessie's divorce, it is Mama who takes Jessie into her house and lets Jessie do all the housework in order to make her busy and feel useful. Jessie lives like a servant or a parasite in her mother's house. She loses independence, autonomy and rights to make decisions on her life. Jessie loves her father, a quiet man whom she once could talk with and rely on. His early death not only breaks her heart but also takes her only job away because nobody visits their book store after Father is gone. Jessie and Mama depend on Jessie's brother Dawson economically, who never shows care or respect to Jessie, even interferes in her private life by opening her mail-order bra. Jessie's sister-in-law Loretta looks down upon her and shows superiority over her explicitly. Jessie does not have any friend and always locks herself in the house without even going to the front steps. Mama's confession is true, "I didn't tell you things or I married you off to the wrong man or I took you in and let your life get away from you."(72) Mama deprives Jessie of any chance to have her own life in the name of love and protection. That is why Jessie feels that "I'm tired. I'm hurt. I'm sad. I feel used"(28). She never has a truly autonomous self. Just as she complains to Mama, "It's somebody I lost, all right, it's my own self ... I'm what was waiting for and I didn't make it." (76)

Jessie has to make full use of her body in order to get empowered and become the self she pursues since it is the only property she owns now. Norman emphasizes this point in the stage directions, "It is only in the last year that Jessie has gained control of her mind and body, and tonight she is determined to hold on to that control."(2) Just as Jessie argues with her Mama, it is not her sickness that forces her to destroy herself physically. She in fact has not had a seizure for a solid year and she feels as good as she has ever felt in her life. Instead of being controlled by epilepsy, Jessie has a better body and a clearer mind. She insists that what she likes about is that she makes her decision without any external pressure, just following her own will. For her, this is the best way to maintain her control of body and destiny.

As the ritual body, Jessie performs two roles: "the altar boy" and the ritual subject. Set in the ritualized time and space, Jessie enters from her bedroom to the kitchen with a sense of purpose. Carrying a stack of newspapers and asking Mama whether "we got any old towels", she seems busy with a special event. Norman compares her to "the altar boy", the person who helps the clergy to do supporting tasks like fetching and carrying at the altar during a Christian liturgy. If, as has been discussed, Jessie's suicide can be likened to Jesus' sacrifice, then her bedroom is like the altar where blood will be shed. The first thing Jessie does is to prepare the necessary supplies for her sacrifice. When the curtain rises, Jessie is searching everywhere for some old towels, blanket or pillows and newspapers to put on the bedroom floor for her body and blood, which marks the start of the ritual preparation. Then, Jessie asks Mama where Daddy's gun is and finds the pistol in one shoebox in the attic with Mama's unwilling help. When Jessie gets the gun, she sits down to clean and check it with swift and skillful acts like an experienced soldier. She has ordered new bullets for fear that the old ones do not work. Regardless of Mama's curiosity and concern, Jessie finishes her preparation with high efficiency and firm determination. At such moments, Jessie performs the role of "the altar boy" for herself and gets ready for her last act.

However, Norman does not display Jessie's violent shooting act on stage. What she demonstrates to the audience and foregrounds in performance is what Jessie says and how Mama responds before the decisive last moment. Therefore, the eventness of the play lies not in

Jessie's execution of suicide but in her announcement to commit suicide. Slavoj Žižek expounds the importance of narrative to event and contends, "The proper moment of subjective transformation occurs at the moment of declaration, not at the moment of the act." (191) According to He Chengzhou, "Discourse has the transformative power. The speaking subject undergoes a dramatic change in narrative and will act in a totally new way. ("Literature as Event" 6) Taking *The Doll's House* as example, He argues that Nora's transformation takes places at the moment when she tells her husband, "I believe I am first and foremost a human being. I, just as much as you—or at least, that I must try to become."(Ibsen 184) While her act of leaving home at the end of the play is just the result of her transformation.

Similarly, the rupture of Jessie's identity begins from her declaration that "I'm going to kill myself, Mama"(13), which shocks her mother as well as the audience. The first response of Mama is disbelief. She regards it as a funny joke and urges Jessie to take medicine and never say such a thing again. However, Jessie insists calmly and seriously. She uses various ways to express the same idea. "I am", "Shoot myself. In a couple of hours", and "Waited until I felt good enough"(13-14), which at last convinces Mama to take her words seriously. Jessie's declaration is performative. Its illocutionary acts are to announce her decision of suicide and to promise to do so very soon. It brings about at least four perlocutionary effects. First, it threatens and hurts Mama; Second, it marks Jessie's break from her old self; Third, it starts her new self journey; Fourth, it triggers the following dramatic action of the play.

From this moment, Jessie begins to act in a totally new way. Instead of being numb, silent and hesitant, she becomes humorous, communicative and determined. As the ritual subject, Jessie attempts to gain her dignity, autonomy and life value by what she says and does during the ritual process. Language is used by her as both weapon and defense mechanism. Sometimes she argues with Mama, pouring out her pain, anger and existential angst and rationalizing her choice of suicide. Sometimes she ignores what Mama says, redirecting their conversation according to her purpose. She becomes more communicative than Mama and maneuvers language to serve for her purpose. She unearths the past lies and truths about her life, cuts off the bonds between her and Mama, arranges Mama's life and her funeral after her death, and especially expresses her understanding and definition of existence and non-existence. According to the theory of performativity, Jessie's ritual performance is performative: what she says together with what she acts produces what she is.

The first act that Jessie does through performative language is to declare her rights of equality, privacy and ownership. Physical weakness and economic dependence put Jessie in an inferior social position. She cannot get any social recognition, nor could she win affection or respect from people around her. Family members either break into her private territory rudely or treat her indifferently, which insults Jessie and damages her self-esteem. After long-age suffering and obedience, Jessie rebels to protect her human rights and regain her self-dignity. When Thelma says she can ask Loretta, Jessie's sister-in-law, to wash clothes if Jessie is mad about doing the wash. Jessie answers sarcastically that it is impossible because Loretta is so arrogant that "she thinks she's better than we are"(22). Then Jessie tells her mother firmly, "She is not."(22) The locution of this speech act is that Loretta is not superior to Jessie or Mama, while its illocution is to declare Jessie's right of equality with Loretta, and of course with all other human beings. Mama catches Jessie's intention and responds quickly, promising "Loretta doesn't ever have to come over here again"(23), which implies that Jessie wins in this round of battle with Mama, which is the perlocution of her speech act.

　　Then Jessie admits that she is often disturbed by her brother Dawson too. To answer Mama's question "What does Dawson do, that bothers you?"(23) Jessie explains, "He just calls me Jess like he knows who he's talking to. He's always wondering what I do all day. I mean, I wonder that myself, but it's my day, so it's mine to wonder about, not his."(23) Jess is a pet name used by Dawson to address Jessie, suggesting that Dawson regards her as a dependent infant or animal. Jessie refuses such insulting tag and affirms that she is not the person that Dawson takes for granted. Jessie demarcates a clear line between her life and Dawson's by repeatedly emphasizing that her life belongs to herself, not to Dawson. Jessie complains that "they (Loretta and Dawson) know things about you, and they learned it before you had a chance to say whether you wanted them to know or not"(23). By saying these words, Jessie in fact fights against others' interference into her life and protects her privacy and self-esteem as a respectable and independent adult. What she achieves is Mama's assurance that "they're none of them ever setting foot in this house again"(24). Jessie successfully expels people who have interfered in her life out of her territory and defends her basic human rights.

　　Jessie's second act is done by a question-and-answer game, by which she claims her right to know truth by unearthing the mysteries and lies haunting over her life in the past forty years. As Norman remarks, "Knowing is the most profound kind of love, giving someone the gift of knowledge about yourself."(Ginter-Brown 73) Paige also proposes, "A prerequisite for a woman's becoming autonomous—fully realized and independent—is that she must first have a sense of *her own* history ... she must have a sense of *where* she has been."(108-109). Believing that "things don't have to be true to talk about them"(41), Thelma has taken the advantage of narratives to fool Jessie, creating an illusionary world for her daughter. Although Jessie has a lot of doubts and questions, she never dares to ask her mother. In this ritualized last night, Jessie determines to explore the real world she lives in and know where she has been.

 The first person Jessie asks about is Thelma's best friend Agnes, a woman who once visited them often but does not now. At the beginning, Thelma still plays her usual games and refuses to tell Jessie truth. When Jessie asks why Agnes won't come over here, Thelma ignores the question and turns to cocoa making. Then, with Jessie's insistence, their conversation changes to a struggle of power.

> Jessie: It's because of me, isn't it?
>
> Mama: No, Jess.
>
> Jessie: Yes, Mama.
>
> Mama: O.K. Yes, then, but she's crazy. She's as crazy as they come. She's a lunatic.
>
> Jessie: What is it exactly? Did I say something, sometime? Or did she see me have a fit and's afraid I might have another one if she came over, or what?
>
> Mama: I guess.
>
> Jessie: You guess what? What's she ever said? She must've given you some reason. (42)

 Under pressure, Thelma has to admit that Agnes sees Jessie catching fit one time and is so scared that she refuses to visit them, which, for Jessie, is a relief because it is not dislike of her that stops Agnes. Jessie's inquiry shows that most of the stories Mama tells her are not true. The dramatic conflict of Jessie's strong will to know truth and Mama's reluctance reflects their different mindsets and

Chapter One Destruction and Resurrection   095

philosophy of life. Mama accepts the world as it is and never thinks about why. Just as she says, "I don't know what I'm here for, but then I don't think about it."(49) However, as an awakening woman, Jessie is eager to know who she is and what her life is for. She can no longer tolerate her mother's lies as before. Angry with Mama's lies, Jessie blames her, "You lied about setting fire to all those houses and about how many birds she has and how much okra she eats and why she won't come over here. If I have to keep dragging the truth out of you, this is going to take all night."(44) What is significant here is not the facts that Jessie narrates but the gesture she performs. She in fact is fighting for her right to pursue truth by warning Mama that she knows she has been cheated for many years and she would not be a puppet in her mother's hands. Jessie gets the upper hand in their argument and forces Thelma to be honest in their following conversations. When Jessie puts forward her second question: did you love Daddy? Thelma replies "no" immediately, which pleases Jessie because "Mama understands the rules better now"(45).

　　Now that her mother gives in to her determination for the truth, Jessie goes on to raise all kinds of questions she is eager to know. She learns that her father and mother never love each other, that father has tortured Mama by keeping silent all day long until his death, and that her husband Cecil leaves her not because of her smoking or fit but for another girl. She then asks Mama to give her a detailed description of her fits and finally knows what they look like. The biggest secret that Mama keeps is about Jessie's disease. Jessie has always believed that her fit had been caused by a horse-riding accident which was witnessed by Cecil and has felt endless shame. But now Mama tells her that she had fits since she was five years old and it is inherited from her father who also has small fits. Out of fear, shame and guilt, Thelma never lets anybody know about their disease, including Jessie and her father. This information hurts Jessie so much that she almost loses control of her temper. She moans to Mama, "I don't like this. I don't like this one bit."(70) When Thelma insists, "I didn't want anybody to know. Least of all you," Jessie shouts to her, "Least of all me. Oh, right. That was mine to know, Mama, not yours."(70) For Thelma, it is her responsibility to keep the disease as a secret in order to prevent her daughter from feeling like a freak. In her eyes, Jessie is still a helpless little baby who depends on her nursing. She never sets Jessie free to be an autonomous individual. But for Jessie, Mama betrays her and deprives her of the right to know truth, which causes more hurt and damage to her life. Jessie has to rebel to cut off the bond between them. By stating that "that was mine to know, Mama, not yours", Jessie tries to make Thelma understand that she is not Mama's property but an independent person who is entitled to know everything about herself.

Jessie's third act performed by words is to declare her willing separation from Mama and her absolute autonomy. As a victim and an "agent" of patriarchy, Thelma imitates her oppressor and teaches Jessie to be passive and submissive. She manipulates her daughter's life by making all decisions for her. She believes that what she does is in her daughter's best interests. She cannot understand Jessie's quest for autonomy. As Jessie exposes all the lies and mistakes she makes, Thelma admits that "this is all my fault, Jessie, but I don't know what to do about it now"(72). Exasperated by her mother's ignorance, Jessie repeats that her life belongs to her and it does not have anything to do with other people. But Thelma still holds that their lives are bound together. She pleads with Jessie, "Everything you do has to do with me ... You might as well kill me as you, Jessie, it's the same thing."(72) Regarding Jessie as an extension of herself,

Chapter One Destruction and Resurrection

Thelma intends to stop Jessie from committing suicide by underlining their bond. Out of Thelma's expectations, Jessie is not moved, but enraged by Mama's words and goes to the extreme to retort.

> Then what if it does! What if it has everything to do with you! What if you are all I have, and you're not enough? What if I could take all the rest of it if only I didn't have you here? What if the only way I can get away from you for good is to kill myself? What if it is? I can *still* do it! (72)

Here, Jessie's six "what if" sentences are like six bullets, challenging her mother's ideas and defeating her emotionally. These words could be read as Jessie's declaration of independence, a typical speech act too, whose locution is that she knows that they are bound as one, but she hates this bond because Mama cannot satisfy her demands, so she kill herself deliberately to set herself free from Mama. Its illocution is to pour out Jessie's anger to Mama and announce her independent status as a full-fledged individual. By doing this, Jessie tears herself away from Mama's maternal and physical grip and gets back her rights on her body and life from Mama's hands.

As a ritual subject, Jessie has prepared gifts for her family and arranged a gift-giving episode, which itself is an important ritual in social life. The special gifts that Jessie has prepared for each family member convey different meanings and symbolize different things. The gift giving ritual is her unique way to talk back and make reconciliation with important people in her life. The calculator and house slippers she gives to Loretta are in fact gifts Dawson gave to her in the past; Jessie now asks Loretta to keep them in order to express her anger and irony. The calculator, bought by Dawson for himself and transferred to Jessie because he disliked it later, is used to count money, so it symbolizes economic power. It is useless for

Jessie since Loretta and Dawson control every penny of the family and all store accounts are in Dawson's name. What is more ridiculous is that Dawson buys house slippers for Jessie as her Christmas gifts every year, but the size is always Loretta's rather than Jessie's. This insult hurts Jessie so deeply that she never wears any of them. These useless gifts from Dawson not only suggest his superiority to Jessie but also represent patriarchal oppression on her. Jessie re-gifts them to Loretta to revenge Dawson and rebel against patriarchal system. Her revenge climaxes in her letter to Dawson. It is not a gift for him but a list of gifts she wants Dawson to buy for their mother in the next twenty years. As she describes, they will cost him a lot and he will feel like a jerk if he does not do as she demands. In this way, Jessie reverses their positions in the power matrix and accomplishes her vengeance by manipulating Dawson.

Jessie's gifts for her husband and son represent her forgiveness and true love for them. She gives Cecil's phone number to Mama and asks her to call him, telling him that they have talked about him and she has only good things to say about him. The most important is to ask Cecil to find their son, the best gift that Jessie offers to her husband. She has no resentment to Cecil and respects his choice of leaving her. Jessie sends her watch to her son Ricky and does not mind whether he will keep it as remembrance or sell it to buy food or dope. What she wishes is to give him something good, whether it is good memory, good meal or good dope. As the most valuable thing she owns, the watch expresses her love to her son, and as a symbol of time management, it also expresses her hope that Ricky would learn to value time and control his life. The tranquility on her face shows that she has got reconciliation with the two men in her life. Although both of them have deserted her cruelly, she forgives them and leaves without hatred.

Chapter One Destruction and Resurrection

　　Jessie's gifts for Mama seem ordinary and trivial, but full of symbolic meanings. Her re-appropriating and re-gifting acts constitute a refusal of patriarchal devaluation and suppression. The first one is a box of little things that Mama lost, forgot, ignored or even did not know she had, such as old pictures and a free tube of toothpaste hanging on the door. Jessie collects and keeps them for a long time and then gives them to Mama as her last presents. Norman dramatizes Thelma's complicated and ambiguous reaction to the gift. When Thelma sees these things, she is surprised because she cannot believe Jessie did all this in this house but she never noticed. She is pleased by regaining what she has lost and by what Jessie did for her. She is puzzled because she does not know what they mean and why Jessie gives them to her. Then, she refuses to accept them because she is worried that these things will make her think of Jessie. It is not difficult to see that these little things share a similar fate with Jessie, long-ignored and worthless in Mama's eyes. Jessie lifts them from dust and displays them to Mama as gifts, redeeming them in new deployments and significations. Her action shocks Mama and forces her to recognize the values of these old useless things. However, the problem is that Thelma never realizes that her daughter is the most precious thing she has ignored for a long time. By rediscovering the value of forgotten things, Jessie in fact gives her humble life meaning and value. She, like the little things, stands in front of Mama as a gift rather than garbage.

　　The other gift for Thelma is a ring Jessie inherits from Granny. It first symbolizes the bond of women from one generation to another, linking the daughter, mother and grandmother by "nonlinear temporal transmission, a matrilineal symbolism with its own rhythm and specificity" (Begley 353). It is also a symbol of shackles that bind and restrain women in patriarchal society in which women are confined to domestic space, especially the kitchen. Therefore, Jessie's act of re-gifting the ring to her mother expresses her care, love and gratitude to Mama on the one hand, and symbolizes her rejection of patriarchal oppression and escape from family traps on the other hand. Jessie revenges people who hurt her, forgives whom she loves and thanks those who care about her by performing the gift giving ritual. The ritual demonstrates her wit, benevolence and free will as a rational and mature individual.

  The movement of Jessie's body forms the ritual's central action, magnetizing eyes of her mother as well as of the audience. Where she goes not only influence Thelma's emotion but also decides the intensity of the drama. During their conversations, Jessie moves around the kitchen, the living room, the hall and the bedroom, trying to complete the tasks she lists on her note pad one by one. Every movement of Jessie's body affects Thelma's emotion and intensifies the stage atmosphere. As discussed above, Norman has ritualized the stage space with the bedroom as the altar of Jessie's sacrifice and the door as the limen separating two different worlds. Everyone, including Thelma, Jessie and all the audience, is constantly aware of the existence of the door, which "opens onto absolute nothingness"(3). Kundert-Gibbs argues, "This door acts as a magnetic force, growing in intensity as the evening wears on and pulling Jessie and Mama (and us) out of the naturalistic, 'next door' world." (48) As a symbol, the door not only embodies the complexities of mother-daughter relationship, but also incarnates "death, rebirth, nonbeing, silence, peace, heaven, hell, and much more" (Kundert-Gibbs 48). Similarly, Jessie's passing through the door to her bedroom is a symbolic act too, signifying threat to Thelma but promising Jessie kind of renascence and redemption. Norman highlights Jessie's three passing acts, with each marking one

Chapter One Destruction and Resurrection

stage of her ritual of Requiem Mass chronologically and gradually leading to the final act.

The first time that Jessie enters her bedroom is after she has announced the suicide decision to Mama and got all necessaries ready for that. She "takes the gun box, puts it on top of the stack of towels and garbage bags, and takes them into her bedroom" (20). At this moment, Jessie finishes her preparation task patiently and begins to wait for her right time calmly. However, for Thelma, this moment is the beginning of her panic and struggle. She stares at Jessie's back and sneaks to the phone to contact Dawson for help. Norman gives a vivid description of Thelma's behavior: she "picks up the receiver, looks toward the bedroom, starts to dial, and then replaces the receiver in its cradle as Jessie walks back into the room" (20). Worried about her daughter, Thelma is eager to inform his son of Jessie's crazy plan and get help from outside, but at the same time, she must be cautious because Jessie threatens to kill herself before Dawson gets here if Mama calls him. Thelma is entrapped in dilemma and has to face her daughter's death alone. With Jessie coming back to the living room, Thelma as well as the audience gets relaxed for a while and the long antagonistic life-death wrestle between mother and daughter moves on.

The second time that Jessie enters her bedroom is to get the box of gifts after she asks Mama all the questions she wants to know and rebuts Thelma with her "what if" speech. Jessie's interrogation and Thelma's confession have exhausted both of them physically and emotionally. In consequence, as Jessie stands up and turns for the bedroom, Thelma bursts into desperate tears and grabs Jessie's arm tightly, begging "don't leave me, Jessie" (72). However, Jessie carefully takes Mama's arm away and goes into her bedroom resolutely. This time, Thelma breaks down and cannot even pick up the telephone receiver. She stoops to clean up the bottles on the floor like a crazy woman. She does not get up when Jessie returns, "hoping that maybe if she just makes it look nice enough, Jessie will stay" (73). However, it seems that entering the bedroom is nothing special for Jessie. She goes there just to get the gifts she has prepared. But for Thelma, this passage through the door to the bedroom is a horrible journey, representing endless darkness, absolute failure and permanent loss. Though Thelma does not give up and continues to beg Jessie to stay, she is becoming weaker and weaker and gradually realizes that she is unable to stop Jessie from leaving her. When Jessie gives Thelma the gifts and instructs her how to deal with them, Thelma in fact has wilted and entered into a state of hallucination. She accepts everything numbly and feels that the person in front of her is not her daughter, and her Jessie is "already gone" (78). Literally, it means that Jessie has "died" even before her shooting. But metaphorically, it means this Jessie is different from the one that Mama is familiar with. The question Norman wants the audience to think is the change of Jessic's identity. As Thelma wonders, "who am I talking to?" What the audience should ask is: Is this Jessie the docile, dependent, invisible woman?

The answer is explicitly negative. This Jessie who speaks actively and acts with determination, is in sharp contrast to that passive, misery, self-reproached old Jessie whom Thelma has taken for granted. It is the new Jessie that prepares and performs her ritual of Requiem Mass to mourn the "death" of her old self and to celebrate the coming of a new self. What is unique for this Mass is that it is performed by the dead soul before her actual death. Therefore, all would be meaningless without Jessie's last act of crossing the door to kill herself, the promise she declares to accomplish at the beginning of the play. When the right moment arrives and Jessie has "said everything I (she) had to say"(78), she vanishes into her bedroom and locks the door. Regardless of Mama's pounding and screaming out of the door, Jessie shoots herself with her father's gun and answers Mama as well as the world with a sound "like No"(89). Thelma collapses against the door, the limen that separates mother and daughter forever.

There has been a lasting debate on how to interpret Jessie's act of suicide since *'night, Mother* was first produced. Impressed by the play's naturalistic props and realist format, critics like Jill Dolan, Jeanie Forte and Stanley Kauffmann take it as a work of critical realism, focusing on its social conditions and regarding Jessie's suicide as "a real person making a real choice"(Begley 347). Whether they praise it for Norman's revelation of female entrapment in a male-centered ideology or condemn it for its defeatist resolution of suicide to escape that entrapment, they fail to read the play beyond conventional realism. Other critics propose alternative readings by invoking new perspectives. Borrowing Brecht and Barthes' theories, Begley makes a nuanced analysis on signs of food and crafts in the play, arguing that *'night, Mother* is an "uneasy fusion of realism and symbolism" (347), and it is "distinguished by its meticulous evocation of Jessie's life and death as a continuum, one organized around patient, personalized labors ... Her suicide is the last in a series, a final instance of craft" (352). Jessie's shooting, similar to other labors she does, is symbolic and constructive. Both Demastes and Kundert-Gibbs compare *'night, Mother* with Beckett's *Footfalls* and contend that we could look at the set of *'night, Mother* in the same abstracted way as we look at the set of *Waiting for Godot*. Reconsidering the play in a metaphysical perspective, Demastes asserts that it belongs to "anti-realist realism" or "post Beckettian realism" that challenges realist assumptions and Jessie's suicide is the result of her "new thinking" and her free embrace of "a reality that does not exist"(111-118). After comparing the two plays in various aspects, Kundert-Gibbs points out, "In both cases, the 'suicide' of the daughter takes on the religious/ritual significance of a sacrifice for her mother ... a voluntary death infusing within the dead (or nearly dead) a new life."(60)

After analyzing *'night, Mother* as Jessie's ritual of Requiem Mass, this study contends that Jessie's ritualistic suicide is not for her mother, but for herself. Jessie achieves rebirth metaphorically and symbolically through this "revolution of life and death"(Kundert-Gibbs 59). Her last act of crossing the door to shoot herself is just one of the serial acts she plans and performs at this special night. It should not be interpreted as a real action but a symbolic death, which is common in many rituals and leads to rebirth of the subject. The message that Norman wants to convey is not that Jessie "chooses to *die*" but that "she *chooses* to die"(Stone 58). Jessie denies all the causes that Thelma lists and blames no event and no agent in her choice, insisting that it is her free decision to say what happens to her body. The significance of the act of shooting lies not only in itself but also in the role it plays in the process of the ritual of Requiem Mass. On the one hand, it is an extreme means Jessie deploys to revenge the patriarchal society, to free herself from Mama's control, and to have absolute autonomy. On the other hand, although taking place later, it functions as the premise of all the acts that Jessie does through the evening. Without it, they are meaningless crazy behaviors; with it, they become Jessie's purposeful ritual performance. In Jessie's words, "it's this next part that's made this last part so good."(75) As one of her serial acts, it is both the continuity and the rupture of her ritual performance. By negating her past self and destroying its house—the body, Jessie gives existential value to her life and realizes her dream of being a free autonomous individual. The self she once lost, tried to be but never made it during her lifetime, has been realized through her ritual performance and fulfilled in her last act of shooting.

Ⅲ. A Whore's Elevation to Spiritual Guide in Initiating a Few Rituals

Different from *Getting Out* and *'night, Mother*, *The Holdup*① goes beyond domestic space and tackles the American frontier myth, a typical masculine genre. It is regarded as atypical of Norman's works yet also her most ambitious play because of her "use of American mythology, her development of symbolic characters, and her conscientious manipulation of history"(Cooperman 95). There is only one female character—Lily, a frontier beauty who once was a whore but now a rich hotel owner. Although Lily has suffered from the same patriarchal oppression as Arlene and Jessie do, she is not portrayed as an entrapped victim or sacrifice but a successful survivor. Those entrapped in this play are three male characters: the Outlaw, "a worn, grizzled, desperado"(107) who holds to his past glory and unable to integrate into the modern age; Henry Tucker, a thirty-year-old rancher who is hooked by the Old West legends and daydreams of becoming an old-fashioned outlaw, and Archie, a seventeen-year-old boy who is "held back by his mother and his age and his fear"(107). The three disoriented men need somebody to guide them out of their varied traps.

---

① *The Holdup* was developed in a 1980 Actors Theater of Louisville workshop directed by the author, and then as part of Circle Repertory Company's 1982 summer residency at Saratoga, New York, in a production directed by Rod Marriott. Under the direction of Edward Hastings, the play officially premiered at San Francisco's American Conservatory Theater in April 1983.

Though met with harsh critical response when it was staged, *The Holdup* is taken as an important play by Norman because "it was the first play in which I contained the action"(Savran, Their Own Words 184). Responding to critical attacks, Norman claims, "There are serious things to be said about stories and how they operate on our minds" ("Norman's Pulitzer" 16). Regardless of Norman's indication that Archie is the protagonist or the center of the play, Wang Li argues that this play is about the Outlaw who undergoes a transitional adaption from nostalgia for the western outlaw era to a new era (93). Believing that the play is about "characters who are trapped by history and by their own self-image", Bigsby points out that "each, in fact or fancy, is the protagonist of a story, performing roles which carry ever less conviction" ("Contemporary" 228). Cooperman focuses his analysis on the historical framework of the play, contending that the Outlaw and Henry embody the past, Archie stands for the future, and Lily "embodies the perfect balance of past and present" (104). Wattenberg's "Feminizing the Frontier Myth: Marsha Norman's *The Holdup*" examines the play in the tradition of frontier myth and illustrates the feminist ideology embodied in the role of Lily.

Indebted to Wattenberg's study, the present author argues that Lily is the pivotal character among the four, functioning as a connection of all males and a catalytic agent of their transformations. Although Lily does not undergo ritual death like Arlene and Jessie, she guides and participates in a few rituals, especially the funeral of Henry, the dying and resurrection of the Outlaw, and the initiation rite of Archie, in which Lily plays a key role in accelerating their change. She directs, organizes and participates in these rituals on the one hand, and urges, inspires and leads the Outlaw and Archie to a new stage of life on the other hand. They cannot achieve their

Chapter One Destruction and Resurrection   107

rebirth without Lily's help. Lily performs as a sweet lover, a supportive mother as well as a spiritual guide for the two men, reversing the traditional image of women. Norman inserts Lily's self-realization in the transformative process of the males' identity and elevates her from an object of male desire to a subject who owns economic independence, life wisdom, and spiritual power. In this play, Norman's female character finally becomes a woman who has an autonomous self and has all say in life.

Setting her drama in specific time and place, "northern New Mexico in the fall of 1914"(107), Norman works within the tradition of western holdup play, a dramatic genre introduced by Robert E. Sherwood with his *The Petrified Forest*. Rudolf Erben summarizes the features of western holdup play as follows,

> Structurally, the western holdup play builds on an old dramatic convention, known by such diverse names as the "lifeboat" or the "snowbound" genre. Though obviously contrived and conductive more to thought and talk than action and plot, the formula ensures dramatic unity and brings together characters who would not otherwise have met. Imprisoned by forces beyond their control, strangers start questioning themselves and one another under the pressure of confinement. When they are finally released, they have not only gained existential insights, but their lives are changed. (311)

According to this definition, Norman's *The Holdup* is a typical holdup play. Encountering each other accidentally at a cookshack which is miles from nowhere at a cold midnight, the four characters are all confined to their past experiences and present problems. Norman (also her characters) plays on the pun "holdup" which means a robbery carried out at gunpoint on the one hand, and a state of stoppage, bottleneck and stagnation on the other. Both happen simultaneously in the play. The Outlaw breaks into the cookshack of Henry and Archie, threatening them to provide him some eggs with a gun. Henry and the Outlaw turn a game of holdup into a real one, resulting in Henry's death. Beneath the apparent flow of conflicts is a dead end, which is expressed clearly by Henry's words: "She won't go on a horse, and he won't go in car! Is that the holdup, pop?" (121) A horse symbolizes the past that the Outlaw comes from and clings to, while a car symbolizes the present that Lily lives in and the progress of history. The Outlaw and Lily arrive at a crossroad, so do Henry and Archie, and so does the West of America. Taking place in one night and at one place, the play unfolds the liminal moments of the characters' life.

Norman chooses the year of 1914 as background of her story not only because it is the year when the First World War broke out, but also it is "a year of milestone advances in science, technology, and business"(Cooperman 97), which distinguishes it from other eras of the past in American history. At this turning point of history, some people welcome and embrace the progress of civilization enthusiastically, but some people are mired in the past, resisting new things and incapable of adapting to new life. Lily and Archie belong to the first type, while the Outlaw and Henry fall into the second category. Though with different reasons, all of them meet at the intersection of their life and will go through a transformation like the age they live in.

As what she does in *Getting Out* and *'night, Mother*, Norman again resorts to the ritual pattern of dying and resurrection to symbolize the change of people as well as history. Cooperman correctly points out, "Act 2 of *The Holdup* is actually an enactment of a ritual in which the myth, and the mythic figure embodied by the

Chapter One Destruction and Resurrection

Outlaw, die and are resurrected in a new form."(102) In fact, Act 2 contains not only the ritual of dying and resurrection of the Outlaw, but also the funeral of Henry and the initiation rite of Archie, which symbolizes the death of Old West myth and the victory of modern civilization. The confrontation and conflicts between man and woman, old and young, past and present, civilization and savagery, are all represented in the ritual performance of Lily, the Outlaw and Archie, who constantly challenge each other and negotiate their power relations.

Norman stages Henry's impromptu informal funeral as a comic scene with an elegiac mood. The Outlaw's casual attitude, inappropriate joke and ridiculous pray constitute sharp contrast to the seriousness, grief and anger of Archie and Lily. When Lily and Archie are stunned and angered by the Outlaw's brutal murdering of Henry, the Outlaw himself just takes it simple as a fair fight, expressing no regret or sadness, even making jokes to boast how skilled and swift he is. This suggests that the Outlaw still lives in the delusion of violent past and defines his existence by the ridiculous outlaw codes. As a wily survivor of the Hole-in-the-Wall era[①], the Outlaw incarnates the savagery that is no longer socially acceptable and the Old West which is fading away from history. Fearless and mean-tempered, he is still committed to violence. He pulls his gun to ask for eggs, which is unnecessary since Archie and Henry have agreed to give him. He makes fun of Henry by playing a holdup game and then shows his incredible marksmanship by shooting Henry to death in their duel. The problem is that such Wild West Show has died out in people's life. As Lily points out, "They don't play this

---

[①] The Hole-in-the-Wall was a gang in the American West, which took its name from the Hole-in-the-Wall Pass in Johnson County, Wyoming, where several outlaw gangs had their hideouts from the 1860s to the early 20th century.

kind of game even in bars anymore." (153) The Outlaw has not updated his thought and behavior although the West has moved forward as the result of scientific and technological progress. He has to change himself if he wants to reenter the present society.

It is Lily who instructs what the Outlaw should do in the funeral and impels him to introspect and adjust himself. As a punishment for the Outlaw's murder of Henry, Archie demands him to dig Henry's grave and preach Henry's funeral, but the Outlaw refuses to do anything because he does not feel sorrow or sorry for what he did. At these moments, Lily's attitude determines the Outlaws' choice. Norman highlights Lily's important status by giving a detailed description of the Outlaw's change.

> Archie: We'll bury him. (*To the Outlaw*) But you're gonna dig this grave, "outlaw."
> Outlaw (*Fiercely*): I never dug a grave in my life! (*Sees Lily's commanding look*) But I don't have to go just yet. I could help, I guess.
> Archie: You're not going to help. You're going to do it.
> Outlaw(*Still looking at Lily*): That's what I said.
> Lily: That's what I thought you said.
> Outlaw(*After a moment*): Good. Ready. Good idea, Kid. That's just what I'll do. (132)

Their dialogue is a negotiating process. Lily's commanding look and assertive words are performative. Semantically, they express Lily's attitude that the Outlaw should dig Henry's grave. Her illocutionary act is to require the Outlaw to do the work. Its perlocution is obvious. The Outlaw finally agrees to dig Henry's grave. Similar to this scene, the Outlaw also rejects Archie's demand that he should preach Henry's funeral at the beginning, and then accepts the suggestion when Lily intervenes although he thinks it is not proper. The Outlaw's unwilling conformity partly results from his love to Lily and partly from the frustrated and desperate situation he is entrapped in. When he appears on the stage, his first action is to shoot his horse to death because she is too old and ill to walk further. Horse is the trademark of Western outlaws, on which they build their business and life. The death of the horse symbolizes the degradation of the Outlaw's life and the dying away of the Western outlaw era. The questions the Outlaw raises as he arrives at the cookshack reveal his worries and fears vividly: "Think she's here? Think she's as old as you are? Think she's gonna show up at all? What do you do if she don't, huh?"(109) His doubt shows that he has no other people to ask for help except Lily. He owns nothing but a gun, which always causes violent death, and a satchel, which is full of "old wanted pictures, newspapers articles, books about his friends, books with his name in them"(127). He has visited Hole-in-the-Wall before his appointment with Lily, finding that he did not know anybody there and fences were set up everywhere that he even could not find a suitable place to commit suicide. Without gangs and their hideouts, he becomes the homeless last outlaw. Therefore, the Outlaw's only hope now is Lily's love.

With Lily's direction and sad requiem, the Outlaw preaches over Henry's funeral, which turns to be a farce because the Outlaw knows nothing of Henry's life and has to stop frequently during his sermon to wait for Archie to fill in the blanks, which makes the funeral funny and absurd. Contrary to the usual eulogy that praises the dead soul, the Outlaw summarizes Henry's life as "wasting""bored" and "hating", being good at nothing but lying, cheating and stealing. As for where to go, he thinks that Henry's place should be Hell, "being with a bunch of ranch hands that never amounted to nuthin' and died mad"(136). In his opinion, Henry's life is fruitless and worthless. Such summary of and comment on Henry's life can be used to describe the Outlaw's own life and most outlaws' lives too because as the heir of the outlaw culture in Old West, Henry can be interpreted as a younger alter ego of the Outlaw.

Intoxicated with the outlaw myth created by popular magazines, films and music, Henry imitates the outlaws' manners in daily life and performs a false outlaw identity. He cheats in egg hunts, draws his gun in a card game, bullies his younger brother ruthlessly, and lies that he is good at riding, roping and shooting. He is fascinated with the masculinities embodied by outlaws and takes "the outlaw territory as the ideal and desirable state of being"(Blatanis 165). Though having never seen any real outlaw or doing any real holdup, Henry regards himself as an expert of outlaw methods and dreams of running away from his present life to become a real outlaw one day. The accidental confrontation with the real outlaw ignites the fire in his heart. He tries his best to please the Outlaw with a hope of joining his gang. But the Outlaw's identity becomes ambiguous and unreal as he refuses to be any outlaw that Henry names out and insists that Tom McCarty is dead, which implies that the myth of the Old West that Henry relishes and mythologizes in fact does not exist. Despaired and disillusioned, Henry goes extreme to challenge the Outlaw with a gunfight by taunting him as a "coward" repeatedly. Cooperman argues that Henry's death is "a suicide brought about by the existential angst that accompanies a shattering of belief"(101). Blatanis reaches the similar conclusion, contending, "Henry is a simulacrum of an outlaw" and "he is in effect shooting at himself when aiming at the Outlaw"(167). He is a shadow of the Outlaw.

In this sense, Henry's death has two symbolic implications: the death of the Outlaw's former self and the disappearance of Old West outlaw culture. Therefore, the funeral is not only a mourning ritual for Henry, it is also a commemoration of the dying of the Outlaw and the Old West. Norman implies this by making the Outlaw the grave digger and funeral preacher. This is more explicit when the Outlaw expresses his death wish with a bitter and personal tone, "But you were lucky. You had help. Unlike me. Yes, sir, Henry Tucker, things are pretty bad when you can't count on somebody else to kill you."(136) Similar to Henry, the Outlaw hates himself and wants to die because the Old West they embody and belong to has died out. The death of Henry, his last admirer, in fact takes away his outlaw spirit, his past glory and his former self. To some extent, Henry's funeral is also the funeral of the Outlaw's dead earlier self and the dying Old West. The Outlaw's lament is also his own reflection and confession.

The last rite of the funeral, reading from the Bible and praying, exposes the large gap between Lily and the Outlaw, one as the civilized and the other as the uncivilized. When Lily and Archie pray, the Outlaw is shocked by what Lily says because he never expects that Lily could speak such things from the Bible. Urged by Lily, the Outlaw tries to say something, but only utters "Dust to dust, an eye for a tooth"(137), which reveals his ignorance and savagery. Angry and disappointed, Lily asks the Outlaw to express sadness or to pray, but he murmurs, "I don't know anything to say ... I don't know how." (137) Isolated from the outside world and wandering alone in the wildness for twenty years, the Outlaw is unable to express compassion or remorse to the dead, nor could he integrate into the normal life. However, even until this moment, he still holds to his outlaw image. The death of Henry does not wake up him from his illusion. When Archie tells him that he could say what he wants to say at his own funeral, he replies, "How 'bout, Okay boys, reload?"(137) This joke seems humorous for him but ridiculous and cruel for Lily. Norman dramatizes this small joke to emphasize the barbarous and hypocritical nature of the Outlaw. He cannot value others' life. The way he defines his existence is just killing. Even when he is entrapped in dead end, he still feels proud of his past and believes that Lily would not want him if he changes. He is unwilling to face the reality and wants everything to be like what it was. That is why he performs a holdup show in front of Henry, Archie and Lily, in which he thinks he can regain his power and glory as an outlaw. But it is a ridiculous misunderstanding since that's exactly what Lily hates now.

The Outlaw has performed his fake masculinity in order to maintain his self-dignity and win Lily's heart again at the first minute he meets her. As Lily's old lover, the Outlaw still regards Lily as a whore who would serve any man and the "old gal" who is weak and dependent. When Archie shows his admiration to Lily, the Outlaw attempts to humiliate Lily by telling Archie that he could sleep with this pretty lady all day and all night for a solid month if he gives his twenty-eight dollars to her. Archie says "no" to express his respect to Lily, and Lily defies the Outlaw by asking, "Do you know what year this is? I'm not a whore. It's not a whorehouse. It's a hotel now and I own it."(117) Annoyed by Archie and Lily's response, the Outlaw goes on to maintain his former role as Lily's protector. He behaves rudely and roughly, grabbing her and pushing her back down on the bench. Pretending that he has a lot of money and big business to do, he asks Lily to go with him to Bolivia impatiently and arrogantly. He can not accept the new image of Lily, a girl who "is driving a car and talking hard"(126). He wants to bring Lily back to the old days and be his "gal" again. However, Lily's big black Buick, shining costume and confident manner suggest that she has changed to be a mature modern woman who has her own property and life. The Outlaw's old-fashioned masculinity is not attractive but disgusting for Lily now.

Lily is the person who inaugurates the Outlaw's ritual of dying and resurrection and catalyzes his transformation. The Outlaw's silly performance and indifferent attitude on Henry's funeral make Lily very angry and disappointed. She says to the Outlaw, "I wasted so much time waiting for you. Well no more! This is the end. I am free of you for good and praise the Lord for it."(137) This typical speech act expresses Lily's letdown, declares Lily's decision to end their love relationship, and triggers the Outlaw's suicide. Lily's words smash the Outlaw's last hope of living. In order to prove that he is sorry for killing Henry, he shouts "I am sorry" six times with more and more loud voice and genuine attitude. Then he swallows the morphine hidden in his pocket and tells Lily, "There! How's that for sorry! I've killed myself." (137) He identifies with Henry as family and decides to die with the Old West like Henry.

Norman prolongs the Outlaw's dying and resurrection ritual in order to display the difficult transformative process and the battle between the past and the present. Lily performs the critical role in saving the Outlaw from death. After the Outlaw's announcement of swallowing morphine, Archie does not believe and doubts the Outlaw's intention sarcastically. He is reluctant to save the Outlaw because he kills his brother. It is Lily who lungs at the Outlaw and forces him to throw up by getting her finger down his throat. When the Outlaw drifts off and becomes slurred in speaking, Lily and Archie are convinced that he has really taken the morphine and will die soon if they do not take actions. The stage direction describes Archie's hesitation vividly, "Archie looks at her, then back at the Outlaw, and then to Henry's grave." (137) It is a very difficult decision to make because the Outlaw had killed many people, just killed Henry, and perhaps will kill more in the future if he is saved. At this moment, Lily turns to Archie, "There is no pleading, there is simply a decision to be made."(139) She demands Archie to save the Outlaw with her and tells him what actions they should take.

Regardless of Archie's reluctance, Lily rushes into the cookshack to look for water and anything that can help and urges Archie to give a hand. They force the Outlaw to swallow some tomato juice to throw up the morphine and keep him moving by kicking, slapping, and walking. They try all means to stimulate the Outlaw's desire of living. Lily's love becomes the best medicine. When Lily asks the Outlaw to look at her, he responds with "pretty". As Lily assures him that "we can save you if you'll help us"(141), he suddenly changes his mind and says, "I don't want to die. Don't let me die."(141) Archie also imposes a series of questions on the Outlaw for him to think over. "Why shouldn't we let you die? You killed my brother and who knows who else? You're obviously being thinking about it. Yes or No? Die or not?" (141) The Outlaw insists that he wants to live because Lily is pretty, which seems unreasonable but genuine. Norman dramatizes the Outlaw's mental change with the comic but meaningful dialogue to emphasize his reflections on "to be or not to be", which is the key for his redemption and rebirth. She foregrounds Lily's importance not only in awaking the Outlaw's desire for life but also in the action of saving him.

There are four turning points during the long process of the Outlaw's dying and resurrection ritual and each one is marked by a small rite which is full of symbolic meanings. The first rite is the Outlaw's reliving his past with Lily's help. When the Outlaw loses his consciousness, Lily and Archie have to shoulder him between them to walk. Lily's accidental mention of the word "sheriff" stimulates the

Outlaw who, to everyone's surprise, breaks away from them and charges around, shouting "Sheriff! God. It's Hazen! I can smell him he's so close! Reload!"(143) This dramatic effect inspires Lily. She starts a fight game with the Outlaw. As if they were in a battle, Lily shouts, "There is no way out. There must be twenty"(143), which excites the Outlaw again. As the Outlaw slumps into unconsciousness again, Lily slaps him and mentions a few Regulators' names, which awakens and recharges him repeatedly. Lily continues to say names of policemen and outlaws in the past to keep the Outlaw conscious. He relives his past life until Lily uses up all the names from her memory. In this funny game performance, Lily brings the Outlaw back to his past life and fulfills his heroic dreams once more. After this, the Outlaw comes to life by himself and survives as a new man. By putting the past on the present stage and letting the Outlaw integrating his past life into the present, Norman seems to argue that the myth of the Old West cannot and should not be put to rest although history has to move forward, and that the past is useful resources for the present and the future.

The second rite is the Outlaw's proposal to Lily, which symbolizes his first step to a new life. As the Outlaw wakes up from coma and learns that Lily and Archie have saved him, he begins to embrace reality and admits that there is no money in his satchel, which shocks Archie and arouses his sympathy to the Outlaw. Knowing that the Outlaw needs Lily's love but feels ashamed to ask her to marry him, Archie puts forward a suggestion that he should propose to Lily. Pretending that he is forced by Archie, the Outlaw asks Lily, "I've always loved you. I'm not much anymore. Will you have me? Will you marry me?"(148) Lily accepts the proposal on the condition that the Outlaw must marry her the next day, which is a wise term since she knows that the Outlaw is likely to break his promise in the next morning, which proves to be true. When the Outlaw wakes again in the morning, he returns to his old manner, denying his proposal to Lily and threatening to leave immediately. Lily shows no surprise or anger at his changed attitude. On the contrary, she remains calm and provides the Outlaw with eggs and peaches, which are his favorite food. As the symbol of fertility, eggs imply the continuation of life in the face of death. Eating eggs arouses the Outlaw's desire for living. After a comic debate about what animals there will be on their future farm, the Outlaw gradually accepts Archie's argument that violent killing is backward and totally wrong, and that people should abandon the Old West way. However, the Outlaw still has a feeling of nostalgia to his past glory and harbors a fear that Lily will not love him if he changes to a new person. Uncertain about the future, he hesitates and wavers, rejecting the civilized domesticity that Lily embodies.

In order to change the Outlaw completely and force him to start all over, Lily and Archie perform another rite: the burning of the Outlaw's old belongings. Norman has indicated that the Outlaw has nothing but a saddle, a gun and a leather satchel. Since his horse is shot dead, the saddle is only a symbol of his past. All his belongings are in the satchel, which is kept as a mysterious secret because he does not allow others to touch it. This satchel is not only a tool that contains all what he has but also a memento that reveals his identity. When Henry explores who the Outlaw is and suspects that he is Tom McCarty, the Outlaw insists that he killed McCarty and got his satchel. Then Lily asks Henry whether there is "Forget-me-not, LTK" on its back and proves that it is a gift she gave to Tom McCarty. This detail implies that the Outlaw is Tom McCarty himself. What is in the case is not money but "the newspaper articles, wanted posters and other bits of evidence of the Outlaw's exploits"(154). He keeps all these things in order to show who he was and upholds his status as an outlaw. Therefore, to burn them symbolizes the destruction of his old self and the absolute break from his past. Norman ritualizes this scene by letting Archie pulls one wanted post, crumples it up and throws it in the fire at the beginning, and then upends the satchel and dumps all on the fire. At the same time, Archie announces very formally, "All the outlaws are dead. McCarty was an outlaw. McCarty must be dead."(154) These words are performative, declaring the death of McCarty as an outlaw and all West outlaws. By performing the burning rite, they "metaphorically murder his savage outlaw identity" (Wattenberg 513). At the same time, it also marks the rebirth of the Outlaw. Different from the former one, the new person puts his gun away, accepts Lily's invitation to her farm and embraces the new civilized age by agreeing to take Lily's car.

The last rite is to give a new name to the reborn Outlaw to identify his new identity. When Lily asks the Outlaw to pick up a new name since Tom McCarty is dead, the Outlaw chooses "Doc", the nickname of Archie. He even simulates the tone of Archie and repeats the joke that Archie told them earlier. With Lily's agreement that "Doc is good", the Outlaw confirms with "Doc it is". Such a simple rite is significant and symbolic too. It marks the starting point of the Outlaw's new life. With a new name, he will be accepted by the town as a legal citizen and lead a normal life with Lily. His identification with Archie, a young man with great potentials and ideals, suggests that he finally discards the past, accepts the present and welcomes a bright future.

Lily not only plays a key role in transforming the Outlaw into a new person, she also performs the role of spiritual guide and ritual instructor in Archie's initiation rite and changes him from a "mama's boy" to a self-sufficient human being. Archie is regarded as the center of the play by Norman. She once said, "Archie is not threatening to kill himself, he's simply threatening to grow up. It's a simple matter of what is at stake." (Savran, *In Their Own Words* 184) Archie's coming of age is one of the most important motifs of the play. In this play, the frontier experience is embodied in a rite of puberty or initiation during which the adolescent protagonist learns to embrace an uncertain future.

Initiation is a common rite of passage in which a boy or a girl is transformed into an adult. According to *Encyclopedia of Religious Rites, Rituals and Festivals*, both female and male initiations prepare the novices for adult life and the hardships that they may encounter as an adult, giving special emphasis to their respective duties and responsibilities in family and society. Usually, boys and girls will be separated from their community firstly, then go through a suffering liminal period, and are reincorporated into society finally but with a different spiritual, social, biological, and political status. During the liminal stage, the novice symbolically dies in order to be reborn as an adult. The rite is usually guided by someone who has special knowledge or power. After a thorough analysis on male initiations, Joseph Campbell concludes that an initiation signifies the point when "the child outgrows the popular idyll of the mother breast and turns to face the world of specialized adult action"(136). They pass into "the sphere of the father who becomes, for his son, the sign of the future task, and for his daughter, of the future husband"(Campbell 136). In traditional initiations for boys, it is a male adult who performs the role of the initiator or the guide. He leads the boy to manhood and gives them instructions about sexual activities, customs and taboos of the community which are important in the adulthood.

Archie's initiation rite starts from the moment when the Outlaw appears in their cookshack with a gun pointing at the two brothers who are secluded from their mates. He is trapped in a desperate situation and encounters all kinds of dangers, troubles and hardships. At a young age and with a naïve mind, Archie is bullied by Henry frequently and is called "priss" "runt coward" "Diddly" by him. Terrified by the Outlaw, he tries to do whatever the Outlaw commands in order to survive. He becomes their laughingstock for his inexperience in both holdup and sex. When he reveals Henry's cheats and lies, he is slapped and insulted violently by Henry. He is grabbed by Henry as a shield as the Outlaw is going to shoot at them. What is the worst is that Henry trips him down and ties him up with a rope in order to fawn on the Outlaw. Being tied up and unable to do anything, Archie witnesses Henry's ugly performance and unexpected sudden death. Although Archie himself does not die, he has experienced death through his brother. The post-Henry Archie begins to question the country and people's behaviors. He loses his boyish idealism for technological progress and childlike enthusiasm for fighting in the World War. Freed from Henry's protection as well as manipulation, Archie has to face the world by himself.

However, boys cannot grow up without outside help. Archie needs someone to instruct him to find a way out and initiates him into a new phase of life. Contrary to conventions, Norman does not arrange a father-like male figure to be Archie's instructor, but offers him a mother-like female guide. Lily plays the role of mother by offering Archie a blanket and a drink when he was tied by Henry and by cutting the ropes to release him after Henry's death. She supports Archie's decision to have a funeral for Henry and joins him in praying from the Bible. It is Lily who pushes and urges Archie to save the Outlaw's life when he shows hesitation and reluctance. By witnessing the Outlaw's suicide and helping save his life, Archie becomes strong, confident and mature. He cannot hide his pride and ecstasy when the Outlaw recovers. He shouts, "I feel great! I never saved anybody's life before. The way I feel, I could thresh this whole field myself before they get back ... We did it! We saved his life!"(148) Archie finds his dignity and value in acting positively during a moment of crisis, which is significant for his growth. During the hours they walk the Outlaw, Lily tells her past life to Archie tenderly and listens to his stories with patience. She encourages him to leave home to try a different life and assures him that his mother will get along without him. This mother image is more prominent when Lily comes out with a quilt of Archie's mother around her shoulders at dawn.

The culmination of Archie's initiation comes with Lily and Archie's making love—a union or "marriage" in which Lily functions more like a teacher than a lover. Since all the characters are to some degree symbolic, the sexual relation between Lily and Archie cannot be interpreted as physical or secular. It should be understood as spiritual and sacred. Norman juxtaposes Lily's maturity and Archie's innocence in a sharp contrast and endows Lily a strong sense of responsibility to teach Archie what life really is. When she learns that Archie is still a virgin, she tells him, "saving yourself for some church girl could be a real mistake."(147) She even challenges male authority by assuring Archie that his dad is wrong as Archie defends that his father says "there is nothing to it"(147). In fact, it is Archie that requests Lily to tell him something about lovemaking to get him started. Norman foregrounds the seriousness and ritualization of their action,

   Lily: How old are you, Archie?
   Archie: Seventeen.

Chapter One Destruction and Resurrection

> Lily: (*Standing up*) That's old enough. I need a favor.
> Archie: Well you name it! I done all I could for both of them and they neither one deserved it probably. So you just tell me what it is and I'll do it.
> Lily: I want you to take me in the cookshack or wherever your bed is, someplace warm where—
> Archie: God, yes. You must be exhausted.
> Lily: We can lie down. I want you to take off all these hotel clothes I've got on and I want you to make love with me. And if you'd like to dance first, that's all right. Or if you want to have a drink of whisky, that's fine too. The only thing you can't do is say no. Don't say anything. (149)

As the older and the experienced, Lily first of all makes sure that the boy has been old enough and physiological mature for making love. Then she takes it as seriously business as possible, asking Archie not to show rejection, doubt or question. Her purposefulness and firmness send enough message to Archie. He takes the message quickly and accepts her invitation. In order to avoid any incestuous implication, Norman underlines the absurdity of life and the existential significance of their action through Lily's short speech about why she decides to do this. In Lily's opinion, this is the only chance for her and Archie because she is not sure what is going to happen in the morning: the Outlaw could wake up and kill them, could leave her and disappear for another ten years, could marry her as Archie suggests. Whatever happens, "this is just a little waiting time ... It's free clear time"(149). In other words, it is transitional or liminal time for all of them. They will depart for their different destinies in the morning and perhaps will never meet. Lily's speech has effected a considerable change in Archie. Hearing Lily's words, the playwright emphasizes, Archie "seems taller, more poised" (149). Archie takes Lily's head in his hands, kisses her and steps into the cookshack with her in a warm and sacred light. Under Lily's instruction, Archie loses his virginity and innocence, being changed from a boy to a man. Though temporary, the genuine love and ritual "marriage" provides Archie with power and bravery to go east and start a totally new life. Their union could be read as a celebration of Archie's newly-born sense of responsibility for his own life.

Lily welcomes her two men with nutritious breakfast as well as tender love in the early morning after this darkest night. However, Norman makes Lily much more than the embodiment of all traditional women. Her performance in the discussed rituals demonstrates that she is a perfect combination of traditional and modern woman. On the one hand, she respects the traditional feminine traits and values: wearing fashionable clothes, being loyal to her outlaw lover, cooking and offering food to men, dreaming of a normal family life, and so on. On the other hand, she is modern enough to manage a hotel, to drive a car and to install telephones at home. To everyone's surprise, Lily even saw an airplane once at St. Louis, which is so amazing that Archie regards it as "the best story I ever heard"(150). Cooperman is correct when he points out that Lily is "the agent who links the past and the present and is therefore responsible for 'linking' the minds of the Outlaw and Archie; it is through Lily that these men are able to come to an agreement to accept the future"(104).

Ostensibly, the play focuses on the transformation of the Outlaw and Archie: one represents the past and gets rebirth from self-destruction, the other represents the future and comes of age out of "death of childhood". However, under the superficial structure is another more significant motif that Norman intends to explore: What women can contribute to the progress of history? And how do they constitute their self through their body performance in various rituals? This study illustrates that Norman has positioned her female character Lily in the leading role in the rituals of redeeming and initiating men. Lily realizes her own transformation from a whore to a spiritual guide and constitutes a new identity by her performative acts in the ritual process. Compared to the males who are fallen behind or too idealistic, Lily has achieved a perfect balance by treasuring the past, loving the present and embracing the future. As an embodiment of progress, she not only devotes to but also benefits from the historical progress. She has become an active nurturer as well as a nation-builder. Through reversing and redefining the traditional rites of initiation by substituting the father figure with a mother figure, Norman also feminizes the western holdup play.

Epilogue

The female protagonists in Norman's *Getting Out*, *'night, Mother* and *The Holdup* are invisible and marginalized women. Arlene, Jessie and Lily have been confined to their female body which is gazed, manipulated and abused by patriarchal institutions represented by men. Constructed by the oppressive and exploitative gender norms, they are poor, dependent, voiceless and humble, never having a "self", who, according to humanism, is rational, autonomous and integrated, and who is capable of making choices and controlling her actions and destinies. Their earlier identities, a former prostitute and secondary murderer(Arlie), a useless and failed epileptic (Jessie) and a cheap whore (Lily), are the result of patriarchal oppression and sexist discourse. They have to abandon or destroy the old identity in order to acquire a new one.

In performing the rite of affliction, Arlie/Arlene exorcises her past evil self and declares the birth of her new good self by destroying her body that had been objectified and battered by men, and in renaming herself as Arlene rather than Arlie repeatedly, she initiates a battle of power to defend her new identity and becomes a woman of dignity, freedom and independence. *'night, Mother* is read not as an event of suicide but an event of ritual—the Requiem Mass that Jessie designs, instructs and performs for herself, and through which she transforms herself from a voiceless victim of patriarchy to a determined, autonomous and powerful individual. Jessie's speeches, gestures and actions are performative, constituting her new identity. The plot of *The Holdup* is based on three rituals: the funeral of Henry, the dying and resurrection ritual of the Outlaw and the initiation rite of Archie, in which Lily plays a role of instructor and initiator. Her performance of the rituals changes her from men's desired object to their life nurturer as well as spiritual guide who embodies both female and feminist consciousness. All the female characters have reconstructed their identities after having undergone some kind of death and rebirth during the ritual performance. Norman displays the transformative process of her heroines by situating them in rituals that are both destructive and creative and moving them from the margin to the center of her stage.

Ritual can be used as a device for individuals to deal with life crises. It also can be employed as a strategy or mechanism by institutions to perpetuate ideology and impose social control. Individuals will be constrained by rituals if they conform to the traditions, conventions and prescriptions, yet they still are able to escape from and rebel against such manipulation by subverting ritual rules and re-signifying ritual meanings. In the next chapter, the study will turn to a group of educated and professional women in Wendy

Chapter One　Destruction and Resurrection   127

Wasserstein's comedy to examine how they are shaped by conflicting discourses embodied by college, social and religious rituals, how they challenge them through performing or mis-performing these rituals, and how Wasserstein uses rituals to structure her plays and convey her feminist motifs.

Chapter Two

Compliance and Resistance:
Educated Women Redefined
by (Mis)performing Rituals

Wendy Wasserstein, though also committed to staging women's experiences like Marsha Norman, does not represent the lower-class female life with tragic form. She has been fascinated with comedy and "consistently interested in the traps of being a well-educated woman"(Murphy 215). Placing upper-middle-class women at the center of her drama, she writes about the confusion, dilemma, achievement, and disillusionment of the intelligent, independent, and modern women who "are struggling toward self-definition amid ever-changing societal imperatives" (Hubbard 101). As Ciociola points out, "Wasserstein does not pretend to speak for all women ... Her main characters are not every woman, but college-educated and career-driven 'uncommon women' determined to 'fulfill their potential' even when they have not reached certainty about the direction of that potential."(3-4) Being an observer and chronicler of American culture at a transitional time for women, Wasserstein believes that "people are products of the time in which they came of age"(Balakian 1). Most of Wasserstein heroines are bewildered and lost in a world that continually changes the rules and expectations for women. On the one hand, they are constrained by patriarchal values that society imposes on them. On the other hand, they are influenced by the women's movement and armed with a rebellious and subversive spirit. Their life is a constant resistance to the sex-determined destiny as wife and mother. Wandering like a flying Dutch (wo)man, they cannot hold on to a firm sense of identity and are always on the road of self-search, self-formation and self-realization.

One thing that Wasserstein shares with Norman is that she also deploys ritual performance as an important dramatic device to demonstrate the conflicting social forces and the changing female identities. There are various rituals in Wasserstein's plays, such as Fall Tea, Milk 'n Crackers, Gracious Living, Father-Daughter Weekend, and Commencement in *Uncommon Women and Others*, consciousness-raising (CR) ritual, wedding ceremony and baby shower in *The Heidi Chronicles*, the Sabbath Sundown ritual and Birthday Celebration in *The Sisters Rosensweig*, the rite of sacrifice in *Psyche in Love*, Jewish Tashlich in *An American Daughter*. Some of them are special rituals designed for girls in women's college, some are common rites of passage in daily life, and others are religious rituals. CR is a particular ritual of the feminist movement popular in America in the 1970s. Whatever categories they belong to, these rituals share the features that have been discussed in "Introduction": symbolic, performative and political, providing arenas where social values are conveyed and social conflicts are unfolded.

As cultural practice, ritual functions to inculcate and naturalize political, religious and ideological norms and values by "repetitively employing a limited pool of powerful symbols, often associated with emotional fervor"(Kertzer 95). By doing so, ritual can control, mold and define the participants. However, as Catherine Bell argues,

> A participant, as a ritualized agent and social body, naturally brings to such activities a self-constituting history that is a patchwork of compliance, resistance, misunderstanding, and a redemptive personal appropriation of the hegemonic order. ("Ritual Theory" 208)

Chapter Two Compliance and Resistance   133

In other words, the participants can conform to rituals and embody the values they enact. They also can negotiate, resist, even subvert what rituals impose upon them by performing them differently. No matter what attitude the participants hold, their engagement in the ritual are constitutive of who they are. Not all women in Wasserstein's plays are obedient conformists. As some of them comply with ritual norms and conventions, others are skeptical of, resistant to and even rebellious against the rituals they are forced to perform. In this way, they change the structure of power relations and constantly re-mold and re-define themselves.

This chapter explores the constitutive and dynamic relation between ritual and female characters' identity in Wasserstein's three representative comedies. College rituals such as Gracious Living and Father-Daughter Weekend which are aimed at cultivating college girl's femininity to help her become a perfect wife for her future husband in *Uncommon Women and Others* are challenged and subverted by girls like Holly and Rita who carnivalize the ritual performance with their bawdy words, funny gestures, improper clothes and sexual jokes. They prove to be "uncommon women" in deconstructing the dominant patriarchal discourse and enacting feminist ideals. In *The Heidi Chronicles*, Heidi is inspired by a group of radical feminists who organize a consciousness-raising rap and is converted from a humanist to a feminist by spectating and participating in the consciousness-raising ritual. When Gorgeous demonstrates her Jewish identity in performing the ritual of Sabbath Sundown in *The Sisters Rosensweig*, her older sister Sara tries to erase her Jewishness by resisting it, which exposes their opposite attitudes toward traditional Jewish values and triggers Sara's transformation. Together with the youngest sister Pfeni, the three sisters overcome their identity crisis and get rejuvenation by reestablishing their Jewish bond and sisterhood.

I. Becoming "Uncommon Women" by Carnivalizing College Rituals

Named after the inaugural speech "A Plea for the Uncommon Women" delivered by the president of Mount Holyoke College in 1957, *Uncommon Women and Others*[①] demonstrates the bitter-sweet college life of a group of white, upper-middle-class women who were caught in conflicting expectations of conventional marriage and motherhood versus meaningful public work and ambitious professional careers. The play begins and ends with a reunion luncheon of five women who graduated from Mount Holyoke College six years ago and meet at a New York restaurant now to revive their sisterhood. Between the reunion scenes are fifteen episodic flashbacks of their senior year in college. Although most of the vignettes happen in these girls' dormitory, revealing their private joys and tears with dialogues and monologues, five scenes take place in public space where communal rituals are performed and patriarchal authorities subverted.

He Anfang (2015) argues that the all-female campus is like a utopian "green world" which is permeated with atmosphere of freedom and carnival (7 - 8). She is correct to point out that the college girls' carnivalesque spirit is embodied in their funny games, amusing drag performance and bawdy sexual jokes in dormitory.

[①] *Uncommon Women and Others* was written originally as Wasserstein's Master's thesis at Yale School of Drama in 1975. In the summer of 1977, it was selected by the O'Neill Theater Center's National Playwrights Conference to be performed on the workshop. It was presented by The Phoenix Theater in New York City on November 21, 1977. Since then, it has been produced in regional and university theaters across the country.

However, she neglects the more carnival-like ritual performance enacted in the dining hall, the dance hall and the living room. Four collective rituals are performed one after another in the play. They are Fall Tea and Gracious Living at the beginning of the academic year, Father-Daughter Weekend during the semester, and Commencement Tea on graduation.

Balakian has discussed the above college rituals like tea hours and Gracious Living. He argues, "The play documents a disconnect between these feminist ideals and some of the anachronistic rituals of the college." ("Reading" 28) But he just provides some historical materials concerning these rituals without making any further interpretation. Reading Rita as "Lord of Misrule", Chiroco has noticed "the subversive interventions" of Rita's whisper (97). However, he focuses on its comic effect rather than political potential. Without giving any convincing explanation, Craig concludes, "The teas and other rituals of gracious living promoted by their women's college do not prepare them for the options and obstacles they face."(189) He is right, but he does not pay adequate attention to the subversive power in the college girls' carnivalesque performance.

Different from the abstract educational ideas expressed in the Man's voice hanging over each scene, the college rituals are thought in action, embodying the social values and gender norms that the college tries to inculcate in the young women. However, Wasserstein does not transplant the real ritual performance in Mount Holyoke directly into her comedy. She deflects it with carnival spirit and appropriates it to accommodate feminist ideals. When girls like Susie Friend and Samantha follow ritual conventions and perform stereotypical femininity, other girls such as Rita and Holly deliberately break ritual etiquettes, deliver obscene speeches and mock the authorities to express their different understanding of being a woman. Also, there are girls like Muffet who fluctuate between the two poles. Together, they sing, dance, eat, drink, chat, quarrel, even make lewd sexual jokes, changing the college rituals into their carnival-like parties. Their performance and mis-performance of the college rituals demonstrate the conflicting discourses concerning women's education and constitute their different gender identities.

Carnival festivities have not only played an important role in the everyday life in the West but also prevailed in its literature. Comedy originates from Greek word *kōmōidia*. *kōmos* means village festival and *idia* (*aeidein*) refers to sing and revel. Both parts connote the spirit of carnival which, according to Mikhail Bakhtin, is the free and powerful human vitality which "liberates the world from all that is dark and terrifying … It takes away all fears and is therefore completely gay and bright"(47). The spirit of carnival also connotes subversive, "to invert or 'carnivalize' given meanings and hierarchies, temporarily disturbing hegemonic values, behaviors and narratives"(Melo 95). Based on his insightful observations of folk culture and comedy in the Middle Ages and the Renaissance, Bakhtin asserts, "Comic literature was infused with the carnival spirit and made wide use of carnival forms and images."(13) He finds that the medieval comic theater is most closely related to carnival. The first medieval comic play, *The Play in the Bower* by Adam de la Halle, is a good example of a carnivalesque vision and conception of the world. The miracle and morality plays acquire to a certain extent a carnivalesque nature. There are various fascinating carnivalesque elements in early modern and modern literature as well. When discussing Shakespeare, Bakhtin points out, "Shakespeare's drama has many outward carnivalesque elements: images of the material body lower stratum, of ambivalent obscenities, and of popular banquet scenes." (275) Carnivalesque elements include collective participation, the comic, the grotesque, profanation, dual image, crowning and decrowning, and so on.

As a typical Wassersteinian comedy, *Uncommon Women and Other* permeates with the spirit of carnival from the beginning to the end, which, in effect, breaks the rigid convention of the college rituals and challenge the social values they embody. The scene of drinking and eating, the obscene sexual jokes, the crowning and decrowning of Rita, the dual image of Mrs. Plumm as both the "benevolent grandfather" and a feminist are all characteristics of carnivalization. With their subversive language and acts, the college girls satirize and deconstruct the patriarchal discourse and become "uncommon women" in the dynamic process of ritual performance.

The Man's voice uttered before each scene represents the dominant discourse at that time. As the cultural background, it explains the history, educational ideals and social contribution of this elite women's college. According to the Man's voice of Act 1 Scene 1, "uncommon women" refers to women "who as individuals have the personal dignity that comes with intelligence, competence, flexibility, maturity, and a sense of responsibility" (9). Then the Man's voice points out that "this can happen without loss of gaiety, charm or femininity" (9). This definition of "uncommon women" suggests that gaiety, charm or femininity are usually at odds with intelligence and competence, and that the traditional feminine qualities must be maintained. Such double standard sends a mixed message to the college girls.

Though serious and authoritative, the Man's voice hanging through the drama is always confusing and contradictory. On the one hand, it says, "the school was to do for young women what Yale and Harvard were doing for young men" (40) and "students at college are expected to encounter a wide range of opportunities"(40). Women should have the same intellectual curiosity, adventurous spirit and professional pursuit as men, "Go where no one else will go. Do what no one else will do"(22). On the other hand, it underlines women's "responsibilities to others" "capacity for giving" "compassionate understanding", and "serving their family"(21). It reveals the fact that "by the time a class has been out ten years, more than nine-tenths of its members are married and many of them devote a number of years exclusively to bringing up family"(50). This reflects the conflicting requirements of women and the huge gap between educational ideals and social demands. Young women who enter college with high aspirations are bewildered by what colleges propagandize and what they do in practice. As Salamon describes, when Wendy Wasserstein arrived at Mount Holyoke, she "didn't find the all-female intellectual citadel they had anticipated, and certainly not a campus fomenting radical thought. Instead they encountered a hothouse of girlieness, stuck in the 1950s, filled with bright women who seemed desperate to land a husband"(67). College girls are all busy with dating Yale/Harvard boys, knitting sweaters for their boyfriends or taking sports that would be good for their husbands' business. What college girls care about is not their own study but how to find an ideal boyfriend and be "pinned" with an engagement ring. The aim of women's college is to prepare "perfect" wives for Harvard and Yale graduates.

However, time has progressed and the outside world has changed. The girls who enrolled in the late 1960s and the early 1970s had been greatly influenced by the new women's movement sweeping through America in the 1960s. They had read or were reading feminist books such as *Feminine Mystique* (Betty Friedan 1963), *Sexual Politics* (Kate Millett 1969), *The Female Eunuch* (Germaine

Greer 1970) and *Woman in Sexist Society* (Vivian Gornick 1971). These feminists books revealed women's predicament, expressed sexual repression of women and exposed the inequality and unfairness that impeded women's development in career. Girls in the play like Muffet, Rita and Holly even have chosen to learn lessons like Women's History. They not only read books, but also know what are happening outside Mount Holyoke, such as the founding of National Organization for Women and other women's associations, the "great media blitz" for the second wave of feminism, the strike for equality, and the protest against Vietnam War, and so on. At this transitional moment in American history, young people begin to question everything, including sexism. In short, these girls at Mount Holyoke have picked up the feminist message. They have been influenced by feminist ideas and would act on them.

The above ideological ambiguity and contradiction is well demonstrated in the performance of the college rituals of Gracious Living, Father-Daughter Weekend and Commencement Tea. Shaped by the two different ideologies, these college girls have to negotiate among various social values and forces. Their growth is a dynamic negotiating process. On the one hand, they have to perform the traditional college rituals which confine their role within marriage and family. On the other hand, they have accepted feminist conceptions and developed a strong sense of self-realization. They are curious and eager to go out of family and compete in academic and professional areas to prove their competence and value. Oscillating between the two conflicting ideologies, they cannot perform these outdated rituals without challenge and resistance. This conflict constitutes the basic plot of the play.

Gracious Living is a special college ritual to display and reinforce lady-like manners and feminine features. It was first mentioned in the freshman handbook of Mount Holyoke College in 1950—51. By the 1969—70 academic year, the tradition was most often called Gracious Dining. The freshman handbook at that time offered incoming students a guide to the rules and customs that Mount Holyoke "girls" were meant to respect. Among them Gracious Living was described in the following way,

> On Wednesday evening and Sunday noon, the scene is set .... For these two meals, girls dress up more than usual and wear stockings and heels. "Gracious" provides a break in the everyday routine—gives you a chance to discard those Levi's and sweatshirts in favor of a paisley hostess skirt or a knit suit. Dinner is by candlelight, and coffee is served in the living room afterwards. (Salamon 68)

Clearly, this ritual is designed especially for girls, training them to be a qualified hostess. The strictly required clothes like stockings, heels, hostess skirt and knit suit are symbols of traditional femininity. Balakian points out that "historically, it belongs to the era of the feminine mystique" (30). "The Feminine Mystique", the title of Betty Friedan's 1963 book, refers to the stereotypical image of women as devoted wife and mother in America after World War II. This mindset tells women that their destinies are as wives and mothers, and that having careers and independence is unfeminine. Their chief concern should be getting and keeping a husband rather than pursuing intellectual and professional achievements. Gracious Living epitomizes this mindset and reinforces patriarchal ideology. It "in effect sought to prepare young women for the more genteel activities and social graces they might need to manage the home of a successful Ivy League husband"(Ciociola 27).

Feminine social codes are enacted repeatedly on Gracious Living

Chapter Two Compliance and Resistance

in the play. It is performed in the girls' living room with candlelight, tea service and various food. As the ritual instructor, Mrs. Plumm represents the college authority and carries out its policies and regulations. She organizes the activity and supervises the girls' behaviors. All the girls are required to wear skirts. They have to stand up and sing grace together before Mrs. Plumm comes in. When Mrs. Plumm enters and sits behind the tea service, they must sit down in unison. When tea is ready, all the girls will pick up their cups and form a line in front of Mrs. Plumm to get tea one by one. They can drink tea, eat food and talk with each other. Any of them could stand up to make announcements in front of the group if they like. All other girls will applause and click each other's tea-cup to show their respect. After the Gracious Living, each girl must fold her napkin neatly and put it into her own napkin cubbyhole with graceful manner.

Among the girls, Susie is a loyal supporter of Gracious Living and an active practitioner of the feminine mystique. As one of the little organizers in women's college, Susie behaves as a self-appointed assistant of Mrs. Plumm on Gracious Living, leading the grace singing, maintaining disciplines, and even admonishing other girls to attend this ritual more often. She is officious, ingratiating and saccharine. She grasps every chance to flatter Mrs. Plumm. When Mrs. Plumm pours tea for her, Susie not only says "thank you" as others do but also exclaims "Mrs. Plumm is my favorite housemother. And Earl Grey! I love Earl Grey!" with an exaggerated tone (16).

Described as a "comic cartoon" by Richard Eder (48), Susie performs traditional femininity wholeheartedly. She represents the college girls who prioritize marriage over career. Wasserstein highlights the tasteful Villager turquoise and engagement ring Susie wears when introducing her. Susie is so proud of her engagement with a Harvard student that she flaunts this to everyone she talks to. She offers Kate a ride to Cambridge on weekend in order to let Kate know that she is dating a Harvard. She emphasizes to Carter that the Snoopy calendar on her door is a present from Kenny at Harvard. Her repeated pet phrase is, "I used to date Wharton but that was before I knew what I wanted."(20) Whenever she says this sentence to others, she laughs at her own charm or winks mysteriously, which seems to show that she has mastered a secret wisdom and is a real super-achiever. Wasserstein portrays Susie as an "ideal" product of the time and the Mount Holyoke education. She lives for and is controlled by an absent man, the "Male Long Distance Caller", who frequently interrupts the all-female fantastic land.

As a "one-dimensional stock character"(Carlson 571), Susie embodies the college's fading social tradition and functions as a contrasting measure to other girls. Wasserstein once explains, "If you see *Uncommon Women* as a spectrum of women: on one end, there's Susie Friend, and on the other, there's Carter, the intellectual ... lots of women I know have grown up with Susie Friend."(Betsko & Koeing 422) Carter is on the opposite end and symbolizes the intellectual and professional orientation. Between Susie and Carter on the spectrum are Samantha, Muffet, Holly, Rita, Leilah, and Kate who are oscillating between the feminine mystique and the feminist ideals. Their attitudes to and behaviors on Gracious Living tell a lot about their personalities and orientations. Samantha, Muffet and Kate just follow the tradition and do as they are required though with reluctance. Leilah expresses her rebellion by refusing to attend tea or dinner. When Mrs. Plumm asks her whether she would stay for tea or not, Leilah replies, "No, I have more reading to do." (16) Holly and Rita serve as the dissenters and the *primum mobile* of protest among this group of women. When this ritual for genteel femininity is performed by this complicated group of girls, everything turns out to be ridiculous and absurd. The performance becomes not only a platform on which girls with different mindsets display themselves but also a political arena where two conflicting forces confront and negotiate with each other.

The solemnity and purity of the ritual is challenged when it begins. The girls' first act of the ritual is to sing grace together, which is supposed to be serious and solemn. But Wasserstein undermines its solemnity by pointing out that they "perfunctorily sing grace" and "the attitude towards grace varies"(15). At the end of this prelude, Carter pulls out her chair to sit down but is stopped by Susie who tells her the rule that "you can't sit down 'til Mrs. Plumm comes"(15). Susie's action suggests that Mrs. Plumm embodies order and authority. Mrs. Plumm works as the deputy of the college to practice and transmit the feminine codes that the ritual conveys. She should be a good model of virtues for these girls to follow. However, when Susie tells the puzzled Carter that Mrs. Plumm is the housemother, Rita whispers to them that "she [Mrs. Plumm] has syphilis"(15), which shocks the innocent freshman. Although it is proved to be Rita's mischievous rumor later, the name of the sexually transmitted infection, similar to the debasing jokes and insulting words in medieval carnivals, has contaminated the purity of the ritual and demeaned the image of Mrs. Plumm. Even if comically, it undercuts the educational effect of the ritual she hosts.

The carnival-like atmosphere degrades the genteel Gracious Living to a coarse banquet. Wasserstein does not display the romantic candlelight or the elegant manners of the girls on the stage. Instead, she exhibits a tumultuous scenario of mayonnaise, finger sandwich, tea, honey, milk, sugar and brandy, together with noisy glasses clinking, announcing, quarreling and toasting. Contrary to the ideal of pursuing the harmony of mind and heart that Emily Dickson's poem advocates, these girls indulge themselves in food and drink, talking about men and sex openly. According to Bakhtin, degradation from the spiritual and abstract to the material and bodily level is a typical carnivalesque feature. In their lighthearted chat, the girls exaggerate their love for food and drink, exclaiming "I love finger sandwiches" and singing "drink and never think" (18 – 19). Susie boasts of her love affairs with Wharton and Cambridge boys. Rita, impersonating Susie, announces how long hours she would allow men to violate her body according to which university they study at. The girls' indulgence in the bodily desires of food, drink and sexual life deviates from the genteel codes of Gracious Living.

The rule and procedure of Gracious Living are violated by rebellious Holly and ignorant Carter. Instead of wearing hostess gowns or skirts, Holly attends the Gracious Living in pants, which breaches its etiquettes. What should be noticed is that it is not the first time for Holly to do so. Mrs. Plumm complains,

> Holly, dear, I told you I can't permit you to come to tea in pants. It's not fair to other girls ... Let's not see it happen again. I know you can do it, you looked very pretty at "Gracious Living" once. (16)

Samantha concurs that Holly is very pretty in pink. Words like "skirt" "pink" "pretty" are common signs that describe women and denote feminine features, while pants are socially-accepted marks of men, signifying masculinity. Forcing women to wear traditional feminine clothes is to reinforce the patriarchal ideology, since, as Judith Butler argues, bodies are gendered by "political forces with strategic interests in keeping that body bounded and constituted by the markers of sex" ("Gender Trouble" 164). Holly's breach is not an

Chapter Two Compliance and Resistance

accident but a deliberate political gesture to demonstrate her rebellion against patriarchal constraints. As a freshman who attends the Gracious Living for the first time, Carter plays the role of ignorant fool, being frail, dumb and lost. Knowing nothing about the ritual, she applauds at wrong time, raises improper comments and questions, and stares blankly when others sing and dance. Her awkward and funny performance disturbs the ritual's harmonious rhythm and weakens its authority.

The more subversive act on the ritual takes place after Mrs. Plumm leaves the living room. Without her supervision, the girls feel free to express their ideas. They start a debate on Holly's rebellious behavior. Muffet is upset by Holly. She blames her, "You're not sorry. You loved every minute of it."(16) Kate wonders why Holly wastes time to torment Mrs. Plumm. Although neither of them likes Gracious Living, they do not bother to take actions to fight against it. Supporting Holly's act, Rita jokes that Holly is very metaphysical. Regarding Holly as a negative example, Susie persuades these girls to attend Gracious Living more often and take the ritual more seriously. Facing the misunderstanding and reproach, Holly lays bare her opinion about Gracious Living in a humorous way,

> I think "Gracious" is a cultural excess. When I get out of here, I'm never going to have dinner by candlelight in the wildness with 38 girls in hostess gowns. Unless, of course, I train for Amazon guerrilla warfare at the Junior League. Also I can't stomach the way Mrs. Plumm's neck shakes when she pours the sherry. (*The girls all shake their necks*)(16)

Holly's comment is an absolute negation of Gracious Living. By calling it "cultural excess", she reveals that Mount Holyoke is not the only college that requires students to attend rituals like Gracious Living. Such kind of social activities are very popular and prevalent in all colleges across the country, which, in Holly's opinion, is abnormal, unnecessary and even dangerous. Holly's words arouses a heated debate among the girls. They begin to compare Gracious Living in different colleges like Smith, Vassar, Connecticut, Conn, Wellesley, Bryn Mawr and Radcliffe, and find that all of the colleges pay much more attention to social activities than academic ones. They educate their girls for marriage market rather than job market. With a strong feminist consciousness, Holly has realized that Gracious Living perpetuates and reinforces the feminine mystique through college girls' repetitive performance of feminine acts. That is why she refuses to wear skirts on it.

Holly in fact is a mouthpiece of Wendy Wasserstein who once admitted that Holly was a recognizably autobiographical character. She told Bestsko in an interview, "Holly was the hardest to write because I thought, 'that's Wendy' or people will think, 'THAT'S WENDY!'" (424) Holly's words are in typical Wasserstein style: humorous, ironic and full of implications. With the Amazon guerrilla joke, Holly expresses her uncompromised rejection to Gracious Living vividly. Her reference to Junior League, a women's volunteer organization founded in 1901 by social activist Mary Harriman, suggests that she is concerned about women's issues and familiar with feminist activities. By declaring that she "can't stomach the way Mrs. Plumm's neck shakes when she pours the sherry", Holly derides the so-called graceful feminine etiquettes and challenges the authority of Mrs. Plumm. The funny imitation of Mrs. Plumm's neck shaking by all the girls are not only comic but also subversive, resisting the patriarchal power that Mrs. Plumm represents.

The most subversive act is crowning and decrowning of Rita as the "the Lord[or Lady]of Misrule". According to Chirico, Rita's function is similar to the Lord of Misrule, "the person chosen in medieval carnival practice to lead the festivities and incite the rebellious behavior"(89). She is the one "who embraces a feminist sensibility unequivocally" among these uncommon girls (Ciociola 31). Being called "outrageous Ms." by Beaufort (140), she performs as the principal agent of feminist discourse and wages relentless revenge on male-centered social system through her hilarious language and mischievous action.

Rita's first sacrilegious act on Gracious Living is to tell Carter that Mrs. Plumm has syphilis before Mrs. Plumm's arrival. Her more preposterous act is to make an announcement in impersonation of Susie when Mrs. Plumm leaves for a few minutes. Making an announcement is one of the routines of Gracious Living. The one who is going to announce something will click her glasses with her spoon and all other girls will click their glasses to welcome and call attention. Susie is the most active participant who makes announcements frequently, while Samantha, dependent and lacking self-confidence, has never made one during her four years in Mount Holyoke. Other girls tend to keep silent when Mrs. Plumm and Susie are present. Rita is bold, willful and extremely imaginative. She is never afraid to disturb the ritual and stir up debate and turmoil among the girls. When Mrs. Plumm exits and Susie runs out to answer her "Male Long Distance", Rita stands up and crowns herself as "the Lord of Misrule". Pretending to be Susie Friend, she makes a lewd sarcastic speech.

> Hi, I'm Susie Friend. I love finger sandwiches, Earl Grey, and Cambridge. I'm a psychology major, head of freshmen in North Stimson Hall, and I wax my legs. I'd let a Harvard man, especially from the Business or Law

Schools violate my body for three hours; Princeton, for two hours and fifty minutes, because you have to take a bus and a train to get there; Yale, for two hours and forty-five minutes because my Dad went there and it makes me feel guilty; Dartmouth, for two hours and thirty minutes because it takes them time to warm up; Columbia, I just don't know, because of the radical politics and the neighborhood. I learned that in psychology. Now, if I could have a Wellesley girl, or Mrs. Plumm, that would be different. (18)

Rita's speech and role-play are performative. It first of all derides Susie and that kind of college girls she represents who just care about food, drinks and boyfriends. Their thoughts have been twisted by the social values which encourage women to judge a man's worth only through the college he attends and to judge themselves only through the man she marries. Secondly, it mocks the snobbish hierarchic system of American colleges. The status of the college determines the value of its students in marriage market. Only men educated at prestigious, Ivy League schools are deemed as worthy of love and marriage.

More importantly, Rita shatters the traditional female image of being demure and decent. By playing jokes on sexual intercourse in public and making smutty comments on female-male relations, she reverses the gender identification associated with bawdy humor which is believed as the domain of men. Sigmund Freud writes in *Jokes and Their Relation to the Unconscious*, "Smut was originally directed towards women and may be equated with attempts to seduction."(97) Women have been constructed as a demure creature which would avoid bawdy language and sexual topics, while men have been free to use smut to harass women throughout the long history. However, Rita is never bound by such sexual limitations. She often plays the role of man in dormitory and starts discussions on sex. For example,

Chapter Two Compliance and Resistance

Rita once initiates a role play game with Samantha as if they were two boys. She asks, "Hey, man wanna go out and cruise for pussy?" She curses with "Fucking 'A' man" and kids that "I'd sure like to get into a hole"(42). She announces one night that she has tasted her menstrual blood and suggests forcing all men to menstruate, which arouses her roommates' interest in discussing topics like masturbation. She tells her roommates that "the entire society is based on cocks"(42), and that she has left "Johnny Cabot lying there after she had an orgasm and he hadn't"(42). She takes sex as her conquest on man rather than man's manipulation of her. In their single-sex environment, Rita revels in a lock-room discourse usually identified with men and claims power by directing smut towards men rather than women.

Rita's sarcastic performance here also encourages the girls around her to view their world differently. Salamone contends that the ribald and disrespectful behaviors in ritual can be interpreted as asserting the heterogeneity of ritual participants and their resistance to official authority (69). Chirico also points out that clowning figures not only can disrupt the social order, they are able to unite disparate individuals (91). Attracting the spectators' attention, they "constantly work to include, interest, and amuse the spectators" (Koenig 120). After listening to Rita, all the girls are amused and excited. They gather around Rita as a union and let out their various comments. Their solid sisterhood forms a countervailing force against patriarchal oppression embodied by women like Susie and Mrs. Plumm. In this sense, Rita serves as a role model for her friends and can be regarded as a "comic hero"(Chen Lin 104).

With Rita's inspiration, Holly also impersonates Susie Friend and announces a toast, which gets warm response from other girls. They stand up, toast their tea-ups and begin to sing a song together.

The Gracious Living turns to be a real carnival at this moment. The irony is that the song they sing is a sarcastic attack to Gracious Living itself and a humorous request for equal drinking. The first stanza sings, "Tired of books and boring classes/ Drop your books, fill up your glasses"(19), which incites the girls to drop their books and drink Manhattan, a kind of cocktail. The second stanza lists the famous bars in Amherst, Yale and Harvard, complaining that "it's dull adding lemon to your tea"(19) when boys drink to college joys. In the last stanza, the girls claim their right to drink the same thing with men's college by singing "Smith may have their Ice Tea Hours, we prefer our whisky sours"(19). It means boys in men's college should have tea hours like Gracious Living and girls in women's college should be allowed to drink alcohol in bars. The song reveals the inequality between men and women in a comic way and calls on to break the rules set by the patriarchy. Although it looks ridiculous, the song expresses their feminist spirit strongly and wittily.

However, Rita's role of Misrule is decrowned as soon as Mrs. Plumm comes back to the group. Study shows that carnival "celebrated temporary liberation from the prevailing truth and from the established order; it marked the suspension of all hierarchical rank, privileges, norms, and prohibitions"(Bakhtin 9-10). During the liminal time, people are liberated from norms of etiquette and decency imposed at other times. They can challenge, bend, subvert, and even nullify the sociopolitical structures. But such subversion is temporary and seasonal. The established order will be restored at the end of the carnival. Wasserstein carnivalizes the Gracious Living through the girls' subversive language, acts and spirit, but she does not let it go too far. The return of Mrs. Plumm and Susie brings all back to the normal order. The Gracious Living ends with each girl exiting one by one, "folds her napkin and puts it into a box"(42), leaving the freshman Carter struggling behind. As Susie tells Carter the etiquettes of Gracious Living and teaches her how to fold and put her napkin into a separate cubby compartment, the social norms and values that are derided and subverted by Leilah, Holly and Rita come back to throne and take dominant position again.

Although Wasserstein creates a closed single-sex environment for her female characters, their life has never been free from male gaze and patriarchal rules. Men, though physically absent from the play, infiltrate their world frequently and exert profound influence on their life. Most of the girls in fact view their lives with respect to male counterparts. Their uncommon features are defined by male voice-over, their conversations are interrupted by male long-distance callers and their lessons are taught by male teachers like Mr. Chip Knowles who imparts feminist ideas in class but espouses to his students the doctrine of penis envy in practice. Most of the girls' dialogues are concerned about their confusion and trouble caused by male-female relation in the male-dominated world. Theoretically, they are subjects in their own rights and uncommon women with unlimited potentials. But in real life, they are still confined by their sex and objectified as goods waiting to be sold in marriage market. Such paradoxical situation is demonstrated in the college's Father-Daughter Weekend, another special ritual at women's college.

Father-Daughter Weekend is established for fathers to visit their daughters on weekends. It usually consists of students' performance, welcome address, tea hour and dance. This is an occasion for the college to show its educational fruits and for fathers to know what their daughters learn and do at school. Julie Salamon gives a detailed description of one Father-Daughter Weekend that Wendy Wasserstein attended at the end of April in 1968 in the playwright's autobiography. At that weekend, the Mount Holyoke College

Dramatic Club staged a production of *Lysistrata*, the ancient Greek antiwar farce by Aristophanes, in which women refuse to have sex with their husbands until they end the Peloponnesian War with Sparta. The consulter Philippa Goold, a Latin and Greek professor with feminist consciousness, suggested that the male actors brought in from Amherst wear balloon phalluses for comic effect, which she believed would be greeted with enthusiasm. However, the result was totally out of her expectation. The sexual issues and the burlesque humor in the performance aroused puritanical response among the audience. Some of the fathers were so upset and angry that they even requested their daughters leave Mount Holyoke. One letter in *Choragos*[1] from an undergraduate student exposed the real purpose and function of Father-Daughter Weekend. The student says, "As I see it, the weekend was intended to please fathers and show them their annual $3,000 is going for a good purpose."(Salamon 77). The disputes caused by this performance shows that women's college like Mount Holyoke can not educate their students independently. Patriarchal power is always there to supervise these girls' education. The college girls are shaped not only by the progressive thoughts represented by professor Goold, but also by the traditional values represented by their fathers.

Wasserstein presents a Father-Daughter Weekend in Act 2. Scene 1 is the girls' singing performance in front of fathers, Scene 2 is Mrs. Plumm's welcome speech, and Scene 3 is about the influence of this weekend ritual on the girls' conceptions and lives. Both the girls' performance and Mrs. Plumm's speech send mixed messages,

---

[1] Choragos is the new name of *Mount Holyoke News*, the campus newspaper. In February 1968 a new editorial board had taken over the *Mount Holyoke News* and changed the name to Choragos, the leader of the chorus in Greek drama who asks questions and provokes discussion, in order to emphasize its pioneering spirit.

Chapter Two Compliance and Resistance

conveying patriarchal constraints on women and displaying women's rebellion concurrently. The song the girls sing on the ritual is called, "We're Saving Ourselves for Yale", a traditional song handed down by generation upon generation of Mount Holyoke women. It musingly relates tales of women who hold onto their virginity long enough to catch a Yale graduate to marry. The first stanza of the song portrays a group of girls who are sitting at the Taft hotel near Yale campus and working on a plan to catch a man to brighten up their lives a spell. Then the song reveals that these girls have rejected all boys from other colleges during the past thirty years in order to catch husbands from Yale. As the song goes on, their purpose is more explicit:

> Though we have had our chances
> With over night romances
> With the Harvard and the Dartmouth male
>
> And though we've had a bunch in
> Tow from Princeton Junction
> We're saving ourselves for Yale
>
> For thirty years and then some
> We've been showing men some
> Tricks that make their motors fail
>
> And tho' we've all had squeezes
> From lots of Phdses
> We're saving ourselves for Yale. (36)

Echoing with the "good purpose" in the letter written by the Mount

Holyoke undergraduate, this song exposes the popular social belief that the purpose for women to get high education is to catch a male graduate from a privileged university and get a good marriage. In the song, the girls promise that they would not let themselves be sold off "cheaply" but to "hold out" long enough for Yale men, which will please their fathers who hope that their money would get high reward. The girls' performance under male gaze reinforces the patriarchal marital values and the economic system behind them.

However, the meaning of the song is challenged and undercut by the girls' parodied performance and subversive interruptions. As the song sings, "Mildred, Maud and Mabel were sitting at their table down at the Taft Hotel"(35), Muffet whispers to her friends, "I slept with a Whiffenpool at the Taft Hotel."(35) Her words break the virgin myth the song constructs. When the girls in the song express their pride in keeping their virginity for thirty years, Rita whispers, "these women should have been in therapy"(35), which satirizes the outdated sexual conception and reverses the textual meaning of the song. The most subversive comment comes from Kate. After she sings her solo "And as they downed their pousse café", Kate murmurs, "I've been here four years and I still don't know what pousse café is." (35) Kate's ignorance of pousse café negates the meaning of the song completely because it suggests that the content of the song is so outdated and strange for these young girls that they never take it seriously or try to understand it, let alone believe what it says. Besides Samantha's yelling and Rita's winking during the performance, Carter also ridicules the song by raising her hand and shouting "I knew we had a purpose"(36) at the moment the song stops. "Purpose" in this context could be interpreted in different ways. According to the Male's Voice, the purpose of Mount Holyoke is to overcome the gender constraints imposed on women and to cultivate uncommon women with characteristics of the intellectual curiosity, hard work and the spirit of adventure. But the song demonstrates that the girls' single purpose is to marry Yale men. Therefore, the performance itself is an irony. Carter's farcical gesture strengthens the carnival and comic mood of the performance. As the individual voices of Muffet, Rita, Kate and Carter rise in opposition to the harmonious singing voices, they mock the traditional song and undermine the message it transmits and perpetuates.

Even Mrs. Plumm, the ritual organizer, is portrayed as a dual image. After the song performance, Mrs. Plumm addresses the daughters and fathers, which sends contradictory mixed message. On the one hand, she reveals that her father stopped attending Father-Daughter Weekend in her junior year because she insisted on buying a rifle regardless of her father's disapproval. Her father thought firearms did not provide an appropriate pastime for young women. But she was so rebellious that she set up a firing range on Upper Lake and acted a war-like shooting practice with her birder classmate Ada Grudder. On the other hand, Mrs. Plumm emphasizes that she was a dutiful daughter. After getting notes from home for two years saying "Please marry Hoyt Plumm, and can't you teach bird watching at the High School"(37), she gave in to her father and did what he wished her to do: got married and became a teacher. In laying bare her predicament and final decision to the college girls and their fathers, Mrs. Plumm implies that women have always been entrapped in the dilemma of being loyal to themselves or obeying their fathers, and that they should learn how to compromise and make a sensible choice. She also suggests that even though they still continue the college's Father-Daughter tradition, the world has changed and these girls have more choices than she had. Then Mrs. Plumm ends her speech and guides her audience to the date parlour to begin the dance party.

Although the dancing scene is not performed on stage, its performative effect as a carnival party and a male-dominated social activity is demonstrated clearly in the dialogues between Leilah and Muffet after the Father-Daughter Weekend. Leilah carried a package for Muffet and thought it was from Susie Friend, but Muffet revealed that it was a chocolate bunny sent by Susie's father, Mr. Lovens E. Friend, who was behind Muffet in the bunny hop game at the Father-Daughter Weekend. With the gift, Mr. Friend wrote a note to Muffet, saying: "For my Muffet, I can't bluff it. An Easter Bunny for my pixie honey."(38) It is a typical love letter to woo a girl, in which Mr. Friend has regarded Muffet as his lover. His diction expresses his intention explicitly. "Bunny" is a child word for a rabbit; "pixie" refers to an imaginary little creature like a fairy which is mischievous and has magic powers; and "honey" is an intimate way of addressing someone you love. By calling Muffet "my pixie honey", Mr. Friend belittled and objectified Muffet as his sexual pet. Although Muffet expressed her shock and bewilderment, she was nearly tempted by Mr. Friend to consider it as a possible choice to marry him upon her graduation. Feeling angry and disappointed, Leilah told Muffet that she had asked her father not to come up Father-Daughter Weekend because her father kept dancing with Kate and flattered her on the dance party in their freshman year.

The two cases suggest that the well-intentioned Father-Daughter Weekend has been abused by the fathers. They take it as a chance to hunt young girls as sexual objects, which is a big satire to the college's educational goal. As new women who have been awakened by feminist movement, Leilah and Muffet feel disgusted at these fathers' indecent behaviors and decide to fight back. After thinking twice, Muffet changes her mind and gives the chocolate bunny to Holly to eat it, which defeats Mr. Friend's desire. Leilah also makes her determination to go to Iraq and study anthropology. Both of them think that they are uncommon women and prefer to be alone. Muffet even invites Leilah to go to a bar and drink two Brandy Alexanders without any outside attention at night. They try to throw off the shackles of patriarchal system and act according to the feminist perception of uncommon women.

The last college ritual—Commencement tea—is also the final scene in college campus. Commencement is a ceremony at which students formally receive their degrees or diplomas. Tea party is a ritual held by the housemother in the living room of their dormitory to celebrate students' graduation. An extraordinary coincidence is that these girls' graduation take place at the same time with Mrs. Plumm's retirement and the abolishment of Gracious Living.

The ritual seems formal and serious at the beginning. The girls march in and form a line behind Mrs. Plumm's tea service accompanied by pomp and circumstance music. As the girls walk up to Mrs. Plumm to get tea, Mrs. Plumm asks each one the same question, "What are your plans?" (50) The girls' replies reflect the spectrum that Wasserstein designs. Kate and Leilah, the two career-oriented top students choose to study further as postgraduates. Samantha is the one who decides to get married. As a "prefeminist prototype whose cheerful disposition and unassuming manner seem so suited for the traditional role of good wife"(Ciociola 29), Samantha has never doubted the feminine mystique. She has embraced it with enthusiasm and announces her marriage intention very early. Called a "born homebody" by Douglas Watt (27), Samantha is gently attractive, quiet and tasteful in nature, knowing what she is good at and what she really wants. As the playwright comically points out, Samantha is the woman who secures Holyoke's claim that "Smith is to bed and Holyoke is to wed"(6).

The atmosphere of the Commencement tea changes dramatically when it is Holly, Muffet and Rita's turn to take the tea. Holly, usually a talkative and humorous girl, says nothing and leaves the cup when Mrs. Plumm asks her "Have you thought about Katie Kundert-Gibbs? It's an excellent business school" (50). Holly's silence and rejection could be interpreted as a gesture to express her confusion and protest. As the daughter of a Jewish velveteen manufacturer, Holly faces a far more intense identity crisis than her female friends. She suffers much pressure from family: pressure of marrying to a doctor from her mother and pressure of becoming an academic success from her brother. At the same time, Holly lives in the shadow of her female friends and suffers from peer pressure. Holly is not so excellent as Kate, Leilah or Rita in academic achievements, nor is she attractive to man as Samantha or Muffet. She admires Kate and Rita and wish to be them sometimes, and she envies Samantha and Muffet other times because they have set up secure relationship with men. Feeling extremely frustrated and lonely, Holly is eager to have a romantic relationship and attempts to connect secretly Dr. Mark Silverstein by phone for many times. However, she is so frightened to be looked down upon by him that she leaves a message to him, "Respect me. I'm a respectable grown up. My name is Simone de Beauvoir."(34)

Having been nurtured by feminist ideas, Holly wants to have a whole self and fulfill her life goals. She is afraid to be attached to or dependent on a man. She once told Kate, "If I fall in love it would be because I thought someone was better than me. And if I really thought someone was better than me, I'd give them everything and

Chapter Two Compliance and Resistance 159

I'd hate them for my living through them."(31) She does not want to compromise her independence for marriage. Therefore, Holly is still disoriented and uncertain about her future when she graduates. Mrs. Plumm's question is like a dagger stabbing into Holly's heart because business school is not Holly's interest but a choice that her family and teachers think the best. She is hurt but she does not want to offend the well-meaning housemother. She has to use silence as a weapon to protect her self-esteem. Her rejection of tea is her means to show her dissent.

Muffet takes a different strategy to confront Mrs. Plumm's question. Similar to Holly, Muffet has no concrete plan at the time of graduation either. But she does not refuse her graduation tea. When Mrs. Plumm raises the same question for her, she just giggles foolishly and tells Mrs. Plumm, "I'm assuming something is going to happen to me. I figure I have two months left."(51) This ambiguous yet confident reply incites Mrs. Plumm's giggle. Their giggles together get rid of the embarrassment caused by Holly's rejection and bring carnivalesque elements to the serious tea party.

Such carnivalesque spirit culminates in Rita's uninvited speech. As Muffet sits down, Rita stands up immediately and starts talking to all the audience without being invited. Once again, she performs as a self-crowned "Lord [or Lady] of Misrule".

> God knows there is no security in marriage. You give up your anatomy, economic self-support, spontaneous creativity and a helluva lot of energy trying to convert a male(half person) into a whole person who will eventually stop draining you, so you can do your own work. And the alternative—hopping onto the corporate or professional ladder is just as self-destructive. If you spend your life proving yourself, then you just become a man, which is where the whole problem began and continues. (51)

Like a clown in comedy or the Lord of Misrule in carnival, Rita tells "truth-in-foolery". She points out the possible dangers of both choices in front of these college girls. She sees the traps of patriarchal marriage in which women will be drained by their husbands. At the same time, she recognizes the pitfalls of unbridled career advancement to which the women's movement has invited them. For her, neither choice is satisfying because women will either live for men or live as men, losing themselves in both cases. Rita declares that what she wants is a room of her own so that she can get into her writing. She then comically reverses the power dynamics of sexual relation by announcing that she has changed her mind to marry Clark because he had become "damaged goods" by advertising himself as a houseboy in *The Village Voice* (51). By negating both the career orientation represented by Kate and the marriage orientation represented by Samantha, Rita has waged a war to the entire society which, in her opinion, is "based on cocks"(28).

Rita's subversive act is cut off by Mrs. Plumm who decrowns Rita and regains the normal order of the tea party. Chirico argues that Mrs. Plumm functions as the figure of the benevolent grandfather who, "begins the action of the play by withdrawing from it and ends the play by returning"(94). In fact, Mrs. Plumm plays a more important role than the traditional benevolent grandfather. Although she does not appear in the first and last scene of the play, she initiates these girls' college life with a fall tea speech and concludes it with a graduation tea address. She also hosts Gracious Living and Father-Daughter Weekend as the college housemother and a teacher. As the representative of the previous generation and the organizer of college rituals, she is a contradictory figure who performs as the link between the past and the present, the college and the students, and the traditional ideas and feminist ideology.

Chapter Two Compliance and Resistance

As a dual image, Mrs. Plumm has an ambivalent personality and performs double roles in the rituals. She is both conservative and radical. As the housemother, Mrs. Plumm is responsible to teach the college girls the traditional manners and behaviors for women and perpetuate the patriarchal values. However, her own experiences demonstrate that she had also suffered similar confusion and crisis when she was a college student. Her rebellion against her father and her sisterhood with Ada Grudder proves that she had accepted feminist conceptions and wanted to make her own life choice without male's intervention. Therefore, she is both strict and generous to the college girls. On the one hand, she forces them to wear feminine gowns and observe ritual rules. On the other hand, she resides quietly besides them as a chaperone, serving tea and sherry, giving advice, encouraging their choice, and tolerating their mischievous behaviors.

Mrs. Plumm's ambivalence and duality end with her retirement. Instead of blaming Holly and Rita, Mrs. Plumm declares her retirement, the abolishment of Gracious Living and her decision to restart her adventurous dream in her final speech, which responds not only to the change of her personal life but also to the social and historical transformation of their age. After congratulating on the girls' graduation and declaring her retirement, Mrs. Plumm begins to share her recent new thoughts, in which she relates,

> At my last Milk 'n Crackers at the college I had an interesting talk with Kate Quin, an articulate young woman, who told me somewhat wistfully that she thought my retirement and the recent student vote to abolish "Gracious Living" marked the end of an era. I have seen the world confronting Kate and her classmates expand—the realm of choices can be overwhelming. (51)

Gracious Living, starting at the beginning of 1950s, had dominated the women's colleges for a long time as a social practice to advocate traditional femininity and promote the feminine mystique. Influenced by the second-wave of women's movement in 1960s, Mount Holyoke abolished it in 1972 according to students' vote, which marked a turning point in the college history. Wasserstein cleverly inserts this historic event in Mrs. Plumm's speech and makes it take place at the same time with her retirement. This coincidence is significant. The abolishment of the outdated ritual means the victory of feminist ideology. To be specific, it is the winning of the uncommon women like Kate, Leilah, Holly, Muffet and Rita in the play. The retirement of Mrs. Plumm embodies the fall of her generation and the dying of the social values she represents. The two events mark the end of the feminine mystique era and anticipate the coming of a new era simultaneously.

Mrs. Plumm's speech is not only informative but also performative. It reverses her dual image and constitutes her identity as a feminist. Without regret or sadness, Mrs. Plumm is happy and optimistic. She believes that her young girls will have a more expansive world and more choices than her generation. With a short review of her life as a dutiful daughter, wife and housemother, Mrs. Plumm then surprises her audience by telling them that she will travel to Bolivia with her life-long friend Ada and her trusty trifle to have more adventures after retirement. She finally determines to pursue her dream after completing her duty as a daughter and a wife. She declares proudly that "I do not fear the change for my girls, nor myself" and "so you see, girls, perhaps, even I am in a transition period"(51). Different from Rita's negation of marriage and career, Mrs. Plumm attempts to make a reconciliation between women's family duty and personal fulfillment. She values her job of hosting the college rituals yet welcomes the abolishment of them too. She accepts the young generation's feminist notions and embraces the new era with enthusiasm. She at last shakes off all shackles and becomes her free and true self.

When talking about *Uncommon Women and Others*, Wasserstein said, "The play asks: why are they confused? I want to show you their confusion. But it's not saying I have answers."("Interview with Kathleen" 420) The carnivalized performance of the college rituals vividly demonstrates the conflicts between patriarchal values and feminist ideals, which is the root of the college girls' confusion. It also shows that being uncommon does not mean to be intelligent enough to achieve high academic scores like Kate, nor means to be lovely enough to anchor a marriage like Susie. The college girls' uncommonness lies in their rebellious, subversive and creative spirit, which is embodied in Holly, Muffet and Rita's deliberate mischiefs, bawdy languages and ridiculous behaviors on college rituals. Although the rituals are aimed at reinforcing patriarchal norms and restraining women within the role of homemaker originally, they are challenged and deconstructed by these young feminists. For Wasserstein as well as for these college girls, "uncommon women" means women who are always challenging and redefining themselves with the change of time and social values. What Wasserstein does in the play is not to give answers to the problems that the college girls confront but to depict their struggles to search for and realize themselves vis-à-vis the confusions and contradictions of the times.

II. A Humanist's Conversion to Feminist by Participating in a CR Ritual

Wendy Wasserstein continues to record the pulse of the women's movement and its impact upon women's life in her 1989 Pulitzer

Prize-winning drama *The Heidi Chronicles*. Spanning a quarter century, the play begins with Heidi's high school dance scene in 1965 and ends with the middle-aged Heidi rocking her adopted baby girl in 1989. As a "minor epic"(Stearns 5D), it interweaves Heidi's self-search and self-realization with "the history of the women's movement from its early days in the 1960s through the consciousness-raising groups of the 1970s to the myth of the 'superwoman' who can 'have it all' in the 1980s"(Moritz 612). With the ups and downs of the women's movement, Heidi grows up from a romantic, witty school girl into an unmarried art history professor at Columbia University. At the same time, she also transforms from a humanist to a feminist who participates in radical feminist activities, reflects upon the movement's gains and losses and feels disillusioned when the wave ebbs away.

Like what she does in *Uncommon Women and Others*, Wasserstein again employs ritual as a device to display the transformative process of her heroine. Among the eleven loosely connected episodic scenes, three are set at rituals: Scene 3 in Act 1 is an important feminist ritual: consciousness-raising(CR) rap, Scene 5 in Act 1 is Scoop's wedding ceremony, and Scene 1 in Act 2 is Lisa's baby shower. By inserting these rituals between public lectures, rally, protests and TV programs, Wasserstein draws a sketch of Heidi's personal development: her conversion to feminism, her complete breakup with Scoop, and the dissolution of sisterhood and solidarity she trusts. The one that occupies the central position and plays the turning point in the play is the ritual of consciousness-raising.

The CR ritual has attracted some critical attention. Balakian situates the scene in the background of feminist movement in the 1970s and discusses its progressive significance in promoting women's

Chapter Two   Compliance and Resistance

awareness (90 – 91). Focusing on the radical feminist images, Iska Alter argues that Wasserstein reduces the consciousness-raising group to parody(23). Similarly, Bigsby contends that Wasserstein depicts the ritual in order to mercilessly satirize the radical feminism ("Contemporary" 348). Gold also points out, the scene "re-creates the euphoric spirit of the time even as it lampoons its inane, huggy rituals" (A13). According to Carolyn Craig, "the ritual is funny in its effusiveness" and "Wasserstein draws it with a blend of comic satire, nostalgia, and respect"(198).

This author argues that it is a misunderstanding to interpret the CR ritual as an "inane parody" or Wasserstein's satire to the feminist movement. In fact, the scene is based on Wasserstein's own first consciousness-raising session in 1970. Although she flavors the recapitulated experience with comic elements, she never denies the passion, high spirit and feminist ideas it conveys, nor demeans the strong bond of sisterhood that these women form in the ritual. Wasserstein takes this scene and the entire play as seriously as possible. Growing out of Wasserstein's strong feminist sentiments, the play is "funny and touching and serious, it had all the elements of a sort of American Important Play" (Salamon 255). Also, Wasserstein warns in the Author's Note, "the key to the play is not in mounting nostalgic accoutrements, but in moving the chronicles forward as swiftly and simply as possible." (6) It suggests that the playwright wants to highlight Heidi's growing process rather than blame or regret what she had done at young age. Nostalgia is what she tries to avoid. Therefore, the ritual scene should not be understood as parody, satire or nostalgia. Wasserstein portrays it as it were at that time: optimistic, euphoric, powerful, yet idealistic.

Some critics mistakenly argue that Heidi is not a feminist. She "gets in trouble because basically she's not a feminist. She throws her hat into the ring of feminism, but basically she's a humanist" (Rothstein 28). Such argument in fact misses the point. Wasserstein uses a whole scene to re-present the CR ritual in order to highlight Heidi's transformative process from a humanist to a feminist and CR's historical significance in the women's movement. When the play became a mainstream commercial success, Wasserstein expressed her pride, commenting that, "that rap scene was on Broadway and commercial, that it won not only the Tony but the Pulitzer, says that the ideology—in the best possible way—influences society. So I feel very much a beneficiary of that."(Craig 193) According to Ciociola, Heidi is "not only one of feminism's true believers but also the only one of Wasserstein's heroines to make that fact absolutely clear in both theory and practice"(59).

Heidi's conversion to feminism is vividly demonstrated in the CR ritual scene. It separates the dramatic plot into two parts: Heidi's life before and after she becomes a feminist. It is the play's most crucial scene, "the one that pinpoints the moment at which she [Heidi] leaps from the personal to the political—from her private vision of feminism to the communal one"(Ciociola 62). The CR performed by this group of revolutionary women enacts their feminist thoughts and ideals, which is the same as all other rituals. The songs they sing, the words they articulate, the gestures they make and the procedure they follow are both symbolic and performative, expressing their political pursuit and simultaneously constituting their feminist identity. This ritual event transforms Heidi's identity from a humanist to a feminist. Heidi's faithfulness to and other women's betrayal of the feminist ideals embodied in the CR ritual constitute two narrative lines of the plot after this scene.

Consciousness Raising originates with early Marxist and socialist feminisms, which recognize the need to create a forum for women to become aware of their existential conditions. It adopts its name from the Old Left. CR groups were pioneered by New York Radical Women, an early women's liberation group in New York City. Similar to the forum to raise class consciousness among the proletariat, CR groups were established to awaken women's political consciousness and enhance feminist solidarity by bringing women together to discuss and analyze their lives without interference from men. In practice, CR ritual acts as a materialist strategy for "obtaining reliable knowledge and for correcting the distortions of patriarchal ideology"(Jaggar 356). It is also a cultural strategy for radical feminists to bond women together and preach their values in the group. According to Jaggar, CR groups in America are collective and dialogic. Without a formal, appointed leader, women could share their oppressive experiences freely and find power to disassociate themselves both from external and internalized models of oppression. Group members are equal, supportive and collaborative. Every woman could join in and share her personal experience without regard to status. The aim of such groups is praxis, which leads to new actions.

The CR group that Wasserstein depicts in her play is a typical one. Hosted by Jill, a forty-year-old mother of four daughters, the Ann Arbor CR group consists of a broad spectrum of women— preppy, feminine, lesbian, tomboy, young and middle-aged. Fran, thirty, in army fatigues, is a gifted physicist and a lesbian. Becky is a helpless seventeen-year-old high school student whose parents split up and whose boyfriend makes her feel suffocated and inferior. Susan is an active feminist lawyer who decides to "work within the male establishment power base to change the system"(20). Heidi is a New Haven graduate student who studies images of women from the Renaissance Madonna to the present. Regardless of age, education and social status, these women gather in the basement and tell their various female experiences openly and honestly. Inspired by feminist spirit, they unite hand in hand as sisters and give each other care and support.

   The song "Respect" that blares in the background at the beginning of the CR ritual is not a simple pop song but a symbol of the radical feminist activism. It is not an accident for Wasserstein to choose it as the accompanying music for this special occasion. The song was released in 1967 and quickly became popular among disenchanted lovers, bitter employees and anyone who ever felt they had been taken for granted. Then it was adopted as an anthem by the civil rights and feminist movements. For those who suffered from racial or gender oppression, it was much more than just a catchy tune. It articulated the true voice of the oppressed and gave them raw energy and a sense of triumphant elation. The chant that "all I'm asking (hooo) is for a little respect" is the basic thing that women demand to get from their men and the patriarchal society. It echoes with Jessie's anger at her brother and husband in 'night, Mother and Holly's wish to "clean up my desk and go out and say, respect me, I'm a respectable grownup" in Uncommon Women and Others(29). Just as Malawey points out, it "functioned as a song of empowerment for those who have been marginalized"(18). The music is historically significant. It could bring the audience back to the heyday of the women's movement in the 1970s when CR groups spread quickly throughout the United States. It is also politically powerful since it symbolizes the feminist spirit. It not only creates an exciting atmosphere for the ritual but also expresses the theme and purpose of the activity. Singing along and dancing, Jill and Fran prepare food, drink and chairs for the ritual and gradually get into the mood.

   Heidi is not a feminist but a humanist, as she declares, before

Chapter Two Compliance and Resistance   169

she comes to participate in the Ann Arbor CR Rap Group. She has been confined within her personal interests and struggling against patriarchal oppression alone. Heidi's attitude towards feminism is ambiguous and hesitant. As a rebellious young girl, Heidi, like Holly and Rita, covets her independence in front of men and insists, "all people deserve to fulfill their potential" (17). She rejects any man's subjugation bravely and embraces feminist ideology happily. However, she is also eager to be loved by man and dreaming of romantic relation like Samantha and Muffet.

Heidi's hesitant and confusing state is demonstrated vividly in the first scene. She attends a high school dance party with her girlfriend Susan but feels uncomfortable with the crude sexuality of this teenage ceremony. Heidi refuses to cater to male's gaze. When Susan unbuttons her sweater and rolls up her skirt to attract a boy, Heidi just sits on a chair silently to read a book. The dance party ends with Heidi's self-consciously conversation with a young man called Peter Patrone, who can appreciate her intellect and humor.

Her ambivalence is further embodied in her attitude to Scoop Rosenbaum, a sexist, arrogant yet smart Jew. Scoop assaults Heidi's dignity, devalues her intelligence and dismisses her aspirations. At the same time, he praises her uniqueness, admires her attractiveness and seduces her to go to bed with him directly. At the beginning, Heidi defends her independent position, argues against Scoop and expresses her disgust explicitly. However, she can not resist his charisma. At the end of Scene 2, Heidi follows Scoop after he kisses her passionately. As Watermeier asserts, Heidi is "both drawn to Scoop and repulsed by him" (353). The whole scene is characterized by "a contradictory tendency towards both submission and aggression, dependence and independence; she wants to/ does not want to lose her virginity" (Watermeier 353). As a quasi-feminist,

Heidi holds that well-educated women should not waste their life making tuna fish sandwiches for men and their children. But as a girl who grows up in a male-centered culture that defines women in their relation to men, Heidi has internalized some patriarchal values unconsciously and surrenders to Scoop's masculine chauvinism.

Heidi's doubt about feminism continues till her attendance of CR ritual. Even when she sits in the meeting of Ann Arbor CR Rap Group, Heidi still holds a prudent attitude and keeps a distance from the group. She deliberately moves her chair away and sits slightly outside of the circle when the rap begins. Heidi's manner shows that she wants to be a spectator rather than a participant. She just listens attentively and keeps silent when others tell their stories. As Fran asks Heidi whether she supports her choice to sleep with women, Heidi's answer is neither yes nor no, but "I'm just visiting"(20). She refuses to take a stand or make a judgement. Heidi insists that she interprets images of women from humanist rather than feminist perspective on her graduate program. As a self-declared visitor whose "inherent reserve manifests itself as causticity"(Richards E6), Heidi is reluctant to get involved in the activity. She prefers to remain her identity as a humanist.

However, CR is a political activity, aiming at raising women's awareness and changing their attitudes. Therefore, Heidi's status as a spectator has been constantly challenged by other group members. Since the CR group Heidi attends is named the Huron Street Ann Arbor Consciousness Raising Rap Group by Jill, rap or talking is their major means to communicate and work. They trust the power of language and narrative. Just as Fran tells Heidi, "Nothing's going to change until we really start talking to each other."(23) There is no formal procedure or strict rules for the CR ritual. All the women just sit in a circle at the conversation nook. Each one could tell their stories or report their headway in turn with others listening and giving different responses. Although there is no appointed leader to force somebody to speak or to impose her ideas, every group member is expected to have a clear political standpoint. Heidi's silence and reluctance is unacceptable for Fran, who actually performs as the spiritual leader of the CR group. When Heidi says that she is just visiting, Fran declares immediately, "I have to say right now that I don't feel comfortable with a 'just visiting' in the room. I need to be able to come here and reach out to you as my sisters."(20) In Fran's opinion, they must have a definite political commitment, "either you shave your legs or you don't"(21). There is no compromise or middle road. Feeling embarrassed, Heidi accepts Fran's opinion and agrees to get more involved in the activity.

The women's raps on this CR are typical speech acts which have multiple meanings and create various perlocutionary effects. First of all, the group members' raps express their oppressed experiences and expose their inferior status. Jill, a mother of four daughters, confesses that she is "a fuckin' Hostess cupcake"(20) because she takes care of everybody in her life including her husband and children, but completely forgets to take care of herself. Becky is a high school student whose father abandons her and her mother. She has to ask her boyfriend Bobby to live with her. However, their relationship is disastrous. Although Becky tries to be super nice to Bobby, making all his meals and never disagreeing with him, Bobby gets angry at her easily. Confused and suffocated, Becky often cries secretly in her bathroom. Similar to Jill and Becky, all the women share their troubles and bewilderment with regard to their status in the male dominant society.

Secondly, their raps arouse resonation, sympathy and indignation among the group. Jill's confession gets active responses from other women. Becky says she also feels that way sometimes. Susan concurs and complains that all women serve for men and feel invisible in their life. Fran, foul-mouthed and militant, shouts angrily, "we grow up on fuckin' 'Father Knows Best' and we think we have rights."(20) After listening to Becky's miserable story, all the women try to comfort her. Fran assures Becky that no one here is ever going to hate her for her servility. Jill invites Becky to stay with her family for a while. They also go beyond personal experiences and extend their problems to cultural ones with a long history. Fran points out that men have taken for granted that women should be subservient and servile to them since centuries ago. Jill calls on them to learn to give to those who appreciate it instead of to those who expect it. All the women are infected with strong emotion and burning passion.

Furthermore, their raps and communication lead to their collective actions of love and solidarity. Just as Jaggar discusses, CR group emphasizes non-judgmental behavior. Any experience, as long as it is owned by someone, is worthy of subject matter. Whatever story they hear, they would respond with supportive, collaborative comment or critical reflection(366). Their aim is not to provide answers to others' problems, but to unite them with sisterhood and feminist spirit. Ann Arbor CR Rap Group also works in this way. Jill's rap stimulates anger among the group, especially Fran's militant and rude shout, "You think Jane Wyatt demanded clitoral stimulation from Robert Young? No fuckin' way."(20) This frightens and disgusts Heidi, so she moves her chair further away from the circle. But other group members do not care about Fran's straightforwardness. They say "I love you, Fran" in turn to support her personal choice. This small rite repeats after Fran and Susan's quarrel on Susan's political decision to "work within the male establishment power base to

Chapter Two Compliance and Resistance

change the system"(20). This happens again when Jill invites Becky to live with her. Both Fran and Susan say "I love you, Jill" wholeheartedly. They even embrace each other to celebrate their sisterhood. In spite of disagreement and quarrel, all the women unite as one group with happiness and feel a sense of belonging. They well illustrate the meaning and power of solidarity and sisterhood.

Heidi has been moved and attracted by the honest rap, warm sisterhood and revolutionary spirit that Ann Arbor CR ritual conveys and displays. However, conversion is a difficult and suffering process. As a half-spectator-half-participant, Heidi sits out of the circle which functions as the threshold that separates her from other women as well as from the real rap. She listens to their raps silently and observes their enthusiastic even crazy performance thoughtfully. At the same time, she reflects upon her own stance and choice with a self-conscious mind. Wandering at the periphery of CR rap group, she is still confined to her small personal space and oscillates between a humanist and a feminist. In this sense, Heidi is a novice who is in a liminal state and needs someone to initiate her and catalyze her transformation.

Jill and Fran have performed the role of Heidi's initiator. They enlighten and instruct Heidi by both words and actions. Though being touched by the way Jill and Fran respond to Becky's story, Heidi is still reluctant to share her painful love experiences that have troubled her for a long time because she insists it is personal. At this moment, Jill tells her, "'Personal' has kept us apart for so many years. 'Personal' means I know what I'm doing is wrong, but I have so little faith in myself, I'm going to keep it as a secret and go right on doing it." (22 - 23) These words are powerful speech acts. Semantically, they describe a problem that has infected and afflicted many females and a reality that the feminists attempt to change. In terms of illocution, Jill performs two acts by saying them. First, she propagates a popular feminist belief on which CR rap groups were set up by women organizations. The early radical feminists believed that women were isolated from each other, and that many problems in women's lives were misunderstood as "personal", as the results of conflicts between the personalities of individual men and women rather than as systematic forms of oppression. Therefore, it was necessary and important to bring women together and share their experiences so that they could help each other to better understand the oppression they suffered. Jill explains the feminist thought to the newcomers clearly although in a brief way. Second, Jill persuades Heidi to get out of her narrow private space and share her troubles confidently with her sisters since it is wrong to obsess herself in the destructive unequal male-female relationship. In Jill's opinion, Heidi should trust her sisters and have faith in their feminist cause. Jill's words produce immediate effect on Heidi. Her feminist consciousness is successfully stimulated. When Jill says, "we shouldn't force her. Maybe Heidi isn't at the same place we are" (23), Heidi replies immediately and determinedly, "I *am* at the same place you are" (23), which is the perlocutionary efficacy of Jill's speech act.

Heidi's conversion does not come until Fran preaches her feminist ideology upon Heidi directly. Following Jill and Heidi's dialogue, Fran challenges Heidi deliberately by asking her, "How are you at the same place we are?" (23) Like a teacher who encourages her pupil to think deeply and search for her own correct answers, Fran pushes Heidi further to the core of feminism. As Heidi gives her reply, "I think all people deserve to fulfill their potential" (23), Fran shows her disagreement directly, which dumbfounds Heidi so much that she just exclaims "what?" This short dialogue suggests that Heidi's understanding of feminism is superficial and naive. She just focuses on "I", the personal development of an individual, rather than "we", the collective interests of all women as a class. She is, as Jill Dolan points out, "a confused might-be feminist tagalong" ("Wendy Wasserstein" 57). Seeing Heidi's shock and bewilderment, Fran delivers her powerful speech in an assertive tone.

> Heidi, every woman in this room has been taught that the desire and dreams of her husband, her son, or her boss are much more important than her own. Now the only way to turn that around, is for us, right here, to try to make what *we* want, what *we* desire, to be as vital to us as it would undoubtedly be to any man. And then we can go out there and really make a difference! (23)

As the spokesperson against patriarchal subjugation, Fran sums up the oppressed experiences of women in this rap group, who represent all women in the patriarchal social system. She tells them it is wrong for women to let men make decisions and speak for them. She also encourages her sisters to take actions to change this unfair system. Fran uses "we" to take the place of "I", which underlines the communal spirit that could bond all women as sisters.

Fran's feminist rhetoric awakens Heidi's feminist consciousness. Gaining strength from Fran's words and inspired by the promise of sisterhood, Heidi finally starts to talk. She admits that she has been seeing Scoop off and on since three years ago. Calling Scoop a "charismatic creep"(23), she exposes that Scoop dates a few other women and he is aloof when she needs him but unbelievably attentive when she decides to leave him. She now realizes that the real problem lies not in Scoop but in her, "I keep allowing this guy to account for so much of what I think of myself. I allow him to make me feel valuable."(24) This awareness resonates with both Jill's selfless devotion to her family and Becky's total submission to her boyfriend. It reveals the essential problem that has inflicted all women who judge their value through the eyes of men. Heidi's epiphany empowers her to end her relationship with Scoop and change her self-evaluation. It is the turning point of her romantic love, political stance as well as life choice.

With the help of Jill and Fran, Heidi goes out of her private space to embrace the sisterhood solidarity at last. Imitating Fran's feminist rhetoric, Heidi says, "The bottom line is I know that's wrong. I would tell any friend of mine that's wrong. You either shave your legs or you don't." (24) This can be regarded as Heidi's declaration of feminism. Heidi not only expresses her political awareness but also constitutes her feminist identity by citing Fran's feminist acts deliberately. At this moment, Heidi realizes she is not alone and women could unite to work together. As Richards argues, "Sisterhood strikes Heidi as the path of the future: women supporting and celebrating one another in communal solidarity." (E6) Heidi determines to teach other women her lessons and work as a feminist activist like Fran. She could integrate her once-private life into the fold of the women's movement and into a sisterhood of feminist allies. Now into the spirit of the CR, Heidi unfurls an emotional appeal that echoes the thrust of the movement: "I hope our daughters never feel like us. I hope our daughters feel so fucking worthwhile." (24)

Heidi's dramatic change brings the ritual to its climax. All the group members are inspired and excited. They embrace Heidi and say "I love you" one by one to welcome her new membership warmly and passionately. Ciociola points out correctly, "When Fran answers with a hug, Heidi's conversion is complete." (66) Heidi accomplishes her transformation from an isolated girl to a socialized woman, from a

Chapter Two Compliance and Resistance 177

hesitant spectator to an active participant, and from a humanist to a true feminist. As Heidi's friend who introduces her to the CR group, Susan happily declares she has "a feeling of completion"(24) because she changes their relationship from "*girl* friends" to "*women* friends" which, for her, is more important. In order to celebrate Heidi's conversion and their sisterhood, they perform another small rite. Everyone claps all other women's hands in turn and say "all right" and their names to each other. Then with Jill's suggestion and instruction, they get into a circle, join hands and begin to sway, singing "Friends, friends, friends, we will always be, whether in hail or in dark stormy weather"(25). This performance well embodies an upbeat image of solidarity and high spirits among the CR group women.

The last act of their CR is also symbolic and political. Echoing its beginning, their ritual ends with Aretha's song "Respect", which is put back by Fran. All of the group women sing along "R-E-S-P-E-C-T, find out what it means to me"(25) and dance with each other. As the anthem of feminist movement, the song not only expresses these women's personal needs but also reinforces the political goal of their activity. In order to show their determination and power, Fran leads the women making a fist salute on "*a little respect*" each time it is played. This militant gesture symbolizes the empowerment of the CR group women. Although it seems hilarious and silly, it represents the sisterhood and solidarity that are real for them at that moment. Their passion represents a short fever of the women's movement. Just as Craig describes, "arms linked, courage up, they capture the energy and zeal of the whole movement as they belt out together, R-E-S-P-E-C-T."(199)

As one rite of passage that appears and exists during the second-wave of women's movement, CR functions the same as other rites of passage that transform people permanently. Ann Arbor CR ritual changes Heidi forever. It marks her rupture with the old humanist self and her inauguration as a new feminist activist. Heidi becomes a true believer and a firm practitioner of the feminist idealism, "a woman who has internalized all of the values of the women's movement" and a representative of "a generation for whom friends are their family"(Horwitz 23). This change determines Heidi's future life as well as the development of the drama.

Though the playwright gives no detailed description of Heidi' life after the CR, her life choice clearly shows that she is faithful to this ritual event. In the following scene, Heidi leads a march of the Chicago Women's Art Coalition to picket for equal representation of female artists in 1974. Her conversation with Peter reveals that she has kept contact with Fran and Susan and has participated in many political activities. It is explicit that she has devoted herself to the feminist movement, especially in the field of art. In the two prologues of the play, Heidi gives two lectures on art history, introducing women artists who are excluded from art history textbooks and reevaluating female artistic works from the feminist perspective. As a professional feminist art historian, Heidi reinterprets earlier icons created by male artists and praises highly of women's contributions to the field. All the work she does is concerned about women. The books she writes are on topics such as Women and Art, Women and Madness, Woman and Bran, and so on. She becomes a director of Women's Art, a group dedicated to the recognition of American women artists. Even the speech she delivers at Miss Crain's School as a distinguished alumna is named "Women, Where Are We Going"(59). Just as Karen Lipson suggests, "one of the more clever conceits of this clever play is Heidi's choice to become a historian of women in art"(12), which supplants the humanist potential with a feminist one.

Heidi has also applied the feminist ideology into practice in her personal life. As Jaggar discussed, the aim of CR groups is praxis, so feminists are called on to apply their theory to life. At the Ann Arbor CR rap, Heidi lays bare that she has a strong emotional attachment to Scoop, an "irresistibly smug cad" (Gerard 38) and a "flippant womanizer" (Kissel 35), who offers Heidi no choice but subjugation to his will, either as his mistress or as a traditional wife who makes him a home. After the CR ritual, Heidi makes up her mind to change their status in the relationship. In the scene following the CR, Heidi admits to Peter that she is still in touch with Scoop but then she adds, "I'm not involved with him anymore, I just like sleeping with him" (27). It suggests that Heidi now is able to separate sexual needs from emotional dependencies and take the dominant position in their relationship. She would never allow the man to judge or determine her value as before. Unlike Wasserstein's earlier heroines who do not know how to choose between career and marriage, Heidi never compromises her career for marriage. The reason that she does not get married to Scoop is not because they do not love each other but because she would not sacrifice her life to him. As Scoop points out directly, Heidi would not devote her ten years to "making me a home and a family and a life so secure that I could with confidence to go out into the world each day and attempt to get an 'A'" (38). Heidi herself also wants to get an "A" and "self-fulfillment, self-determination, self-exaggeration" (38). In another scene, Heidi admits that she almost got married in England when she wrote her book there, but they parted because "I got this job at Columbia and he wanted to stay in London" (45). Insisting that women have equal right and power to fulfill their potentials, Heidi has placed career before marriage like Scoop. She would rather remain single than marry someone who does not want women to achieve and fulfill their best.

The CR ritual is not only the turning point of the character development, but also the climax of the drama's emotional structure. Wasserstein once revealed that her original feeling of writing *The Heidi Chronicles* was sadness and anger,

> I wrote this play because I had this image of a woman standing up at a women's meeting saying, 'I've never been so unhappy in my life' ... The more angry it made me that these feelings weren't being expressed, the more anger I put into that play. (Balakian 82)

Not only the playwright herself, many other feminists of her generation have such kind of feeling. Wasserstein said, "I heard a lot of feminists saying they were not happy, and that was the impetus for this play."(Barney 53) As a reflective comedy, the play examines both the joy and—especially—the pain of feminism's impact. Its atmosphere changes with the evolution of the feminist movement, and Heidi's feeling is quite different before and after the Ann Arbor CR rap scene.

As a quasi-feminist, Heidi is happy, optimistic and passionate in the first two scenes. The play begins with mid-1960s idealism. The popular songs like "The Shoop Shoop Song" "Hully Gully" and "Playing with Fire" provide it with a light-hearted romantic atmosphere. Heidi, young and energetic, is burning with what Wasserstein calls passion. Inspired by the feminist ideals, she is confident, ambitious and optimistic, enjoying the opportunities that the women's movement offers to her generation and believing that "she could be whatever she wanted to be. It didn't matter that she was a woman"(Rothstein C2). With the similar mood and spirit, the play moves to a dance party in 1968 which was organized for Eugene McCarthy's president campaign. Heidi's sharp sparring with Scoop suggests that she is in a radical's high spirit, ready to stand up for herself and fight for women's rights at any moment. Wasserstein does not set the scene in 1968 by accident. In fact, as Balakian illustrates, 1968 witnessed a few important events in feminist movement history. New York feminists buried a dummy of "Traditional Womanhood" at the all-women's demonstration against the Vietnam War. Feminists used the slogan "Sisterhood is Powerful" for the first time. The First National Women's Conference met in Chicago and two leagues, the National Abortion Rights Action League and the Women's Equity Action League, were established(85 - 86). These achievements have encouraged and empowered young women like Heidi, who believes that the future of women's movement is bright.

Such euphoric and celebratory mood reaches its peak at the CR ritual scene. With a high spirit, Jill and Fran give every group member an enthusiastic welcome by embracing each other and saying "it's *so* good to see you"(19) exaggeratedly. With a strong sense of sisterhood and solidarity, they believe that their collective activism can make a difference and change the world. As discussed above, the CR ritual scene is filled with exaggerated enthusiasm, excitement and rapture. All the women are immersed in their happiness of being together. The Ann Arbor church basement becomes a temporary utopia for them. Affected by dreamlike atmosphere, Heidi also becomes ecstatic and militant, singing, dancing and making fist salutes with the rap group. Empowered by collective spirit, Heidi holds high expectations for their friendship and sisterhood. Their excessive optimism in fact represents the early moment in a certain strand of American feminist history. As Bette Mandl points out, the CR scene "evokes the images of sisterhood that had prevailed during what is now recognizable as a particular phase of feminism"(124).

The mood of the play turns to be melancholic after the CR ritual scene. Although Heidi is active in feminist activities, she becomes more and more lonely. Heidi's friendship with the CR Rap group dissolves as the women's movement suffers the backlash from American mainstream. Except for Susan, the rap group women never re-surface in Heidi's life. The problem is that Heidi is a "serious good person" and a true believer "who didn't understand it was just a phase" (17). She still holds fast to the feminist idealism that the female community once shared when others begin to vacillate or move into "the system". The discrepancy between ideal and reality and the betrayal of their sisterhood throw Heidi into disappointment and sadness.

The most devastating setback to Heidi's sense of sisterhood comes from Susan who has been Heidi's bosom friend since high school. It is Susan who brings Heidi to the dance party, McCarthy rally, and especially the Ann Arbor CR Rap. She once was a radical feminist like Fran and caught in the same fever of idealism as Heidi. She not only attended political protests, joined CR Rap group, but also gave up life as a law clerk to live "on a Women's Health and Legal Collective in Montana" as a "radical-shepherdess-counselor" (28). Susan once performed as Heidi's arbiter of feminism and exemplified for Heidi the meaning of total commitment to the feminist principles. However, as time entered into the 1980s, Susan transformed herself "from a mountain radical to a Hollywood sharpie"(Winer 11). She accepted a job in L.A as executive V.P. for a new production company and moved fluidly into the Hollywood power set. Being called Heidi's "chameleon friend"(Weales 574), Susan was swept away by the materialistic spirit of the Me Decade. In their private lunch meeting in 1984, Susan failed to understand

Heidi's vulnerability and disillusionment. She even took their meeting as an opportunity to recruit Heidi and exploit her personal stories. She told Heidi, "I'm not political anymore. I mean, equal right is one thing, equal pay is one thing, but blaming everything on being a woman is just passé."(57) Susan even denied their early feminist cause by saying that their generation was funny and foolish and the current generation would not "want to make the same mistakes we did"(57). Susan "has left behind all that Heidi still believes in. She has moved into 'the system'"(Mandl 124). She betrayed not only their friendship but also their feminist ideals.

The dissolution of women's sisterhood and solidarity is embodied more clearly in another ritual, Lisa's baby shower, which "acts as a counterpoint to the consciousness raising scene in terms of both structure and character development"(Ciociola 69). On this ritual, the euphoric atmosphere disappears. Instead, all the women are unsatisfied and complaining about this or that. Betsy and Lisa, heavily pregnant now, sigh that they are worried about their future children and "get tired all the time"(46). Denise and Betsy grumble that it is unfair for women like Heidi and Susan who are such fabulous attractive to remain single. Heidi feels she has been unfamiliar to the real American life since she has been living out of the country for too long. Unlike the activist women who gathered in Ann Arbor CR Rap as a support group, these women do not have a sense of collective spirit. They are well on their ways to various life goals and have little interest in honest group dynamics. When Lisa goes out to answer Scoop's phone, the others discuss Scoop's cheating and infidelity. As Lisa crumbles and openly weeps after the phone call, her women friends circle her to console. Their huddle forms a sharp contrast to the earlier rap scene. Instead of high-spirited celebration, they toast a farewell to John Lennon and the dissolved

Beatles sadly, which functions as a metaphor of the collapse of women's solidarity.

Heidi's sadness and alienation reach a climax during her luncheon speech "Women, Where Are We Going" in Scene 4 Act 2. Heidi gives a satiric description of an exemplary superwoman who has a tight schedule everyday, which exposes the ridiculous and impossible standards of superwoman that imposed upon females. Then Heidi tells the truth that she in fact is unmarried and childless. What she really did before the speech was attending an exercise class where she met a group of women. Busy with their individual problems, each of them denotes an aspect of the superwoman model. All of them are trying their best to follow the materialist tidal wave. Standing among them, Heidi feels both "worthless" and "superior", "I'm embarrassed, no, humiliated in front of every women in that room"(46). On the one hand, Heidi "wants to be included in the group, but can't find any peace or comfort in relating to any of them"(Rothstein 28). On the other hand, she feels upset for their shallow materialism and soulless life style. The most important is that Heidi cannot find the spirit of sisterhood with them. She comes to feel alienated and moans, "It's just that I feel stranded. And I thought the whole point was that we wouldn't feel stranded. I thought the point was we were all in this together."(62) It's explicit that the most blameful source of Heidi's alienation is the disintegrated sisterhood. Her sadness comes not from personal failures but from the loss of the feminist values.

For Heidi as well as Wasserstein, feminism has made options available to women that previous generations could not imagine. But with the "feminist ideals of the 1960s faded into the greed of the 80s and into a liberation that ultimately became empty when it abandoned its communal spirit for self-glorification" (Stearns 5D),

Chapter Two Compliance and Resistance 185

the old solidarity has been replaced by the new individualism. Heidi, the true believer, feels that she is betrayed, abandoned and isolated. In Wasserstein's opinion, self-glorification is not the goal of feminist movement, "That's personal pursuit. That is not 'We' ... What's missing is the 'We'". (Rothstein 28) Distressed and disillusioned, Heidi chooses to escape to Midwest and start life again. She tells Peter that "I've been sad for a long time. I don't want to be sad anymore"(65). Her escapism is challenged by Peter who has lost a lot of friends who are infected with AIDS. Shocked by Peter's sadness and moved by his genuine friendship, Heidi decides to stay and reestablish their solidarity. She assures Peter that "I promise you won't lose this member of your family" (66). Holding each and crying, they re-enact their melodrama long ago and repeat the same line "if we can't marry, let's be great friends"(68).

Heidi not only reestablishes her bond with Peter, but also adopts a daughter who represents "a heroine for the twenty-first"(75). In the final scene, when the unexpected visitor Scoop asks Heidi whether she is happy, she replies,

> I have a daughter. There is a chance. That Pierre Rosenbaum and Judy Holland will meet ... And he'll never tell her it's either/or, baby. And she'll never think she's worthless unless he lets her have it all. And maybe, things will be a little better. And yes, that does make me happy. (74)

This echoes Scoop's ultimatum to her "it's either/or" during their conversation at Scoop's wedding ceremony. Also, it is reminiscent of her words spoken at Ann Arbor CR Rap, "I hope our daughters never feel like us. I hope all our daughters feel so fucking worthwhile" (24). In this way, Heidi reconstructs a feminist vision of possibility. She wishes that her daughter's generation will realize the feminist idealism that narrowly missed her own lifetime. With such a hope, Heidi becomes happy and optimistic again. She finally sits in the rocker and begins to sing her favorite song *You Send Me* softly. This end gives credence to Heidi's lifelong commitment as a true believer of feminism and links the past, present and future of the feminist movement. As the play ends with a slide of Heidi triumphantly holding Judy in front of a museum banner for a Georgia O'Keefe retrospective, it seems that the passionate Heidi that sings and dances with her CR Rap sisters comes back to life again.

As a play to tell the history of contemporary American Feminism, *The Heidi Chronicles* offers one of the first representations of a consciousness-raising group ever seen on the Broadway stage. According to Jill Dolan's observation, the CR scene has been performed as a "parody" "satire", being "superficial and facile" and "silly" for a long time. In Daniel Sullivan's version of *The Heidi Chronicles* in 1989, the CR scene was felt too cruelly satirical and the group's members seemed belittled. Heidi literally sat outside the circle with chilly antipathy for the proceedings, which urged the audience to see themselves as superior to these silly, striving women. At that time, the backlash against feminist activism was filling the mass media. The CR groups were dismissed as white women kvetching together rather than acknowledging their work as motivating, inspiring occasions for political awakening. It was particularly painful for feminists to witness the Ann Arbor CR scene being performed as a parody or satire (Dolan, "Wasserstein" 68 – 76).

When *The Heidi Chronicles* was revived on Broadway in 2006 and 2015, the director and actors made new interpretation of the CR ritual, the character of Heidi as well as the value of the play. The revival was acclaimed as successful and timely. MacKinnon said, "I don't think it' a dated play in any way, shape or form. "(Purcell) Isherwood argued that the play's questions did still "resonate today as strongly, and at times as painfully" (78) as in 1989. In the 2015 version, Elisabeth Moss performed Heidi as essentially a warm, strong and thoughtful character. When it came to the CR rap scene, Moss's Heidi deliberately committed wholeheartedly, joining the women proudly in their collective rendition of Aretha Franklin's song *Respect*. The scene was staged with positive and genuine manner. Dolan comments agreeably, "Even though the women might say 'I love you' a bit too freely to everyone and anyone, MacKinnon and Moss and the other actors played the scene with affection and intelligence that honored, instead of demeaning, the history of consciousness-raising"("Wasserstein" 76 – 77). The ritual of CR is recognized as a special social practice in feminist history and a special dramatic device of Wendy Wasserstein.

Ⅲ. Three Sisters' Self-Renewal after a Jewish Ritual of Sabbath Sundown

In her next play *The Sisters Rosensweig*, Wasserstein turns from rebellious college girls and reflective feminists to three super-achieved Jewish women over forty years old who have reached crossroads in their lives and suffered from identity crisis as the previous heroines do. Similar to her earlier works, the play also records women's lives at the transformative moments, although at later life stage. Its central issue, according to Wasserstein, is identity. She says, "Despite their maturity, most of the characters in the play are struggling with who they are." (xi) However, in contrast to *Uncommon Women and Others* and *The Heidi Chronicles*, *The Sisters Rosensweig* is not set against the women's movement but on the eve of a momentous historical event when the Soviet Union collapsed and Lithuanians tore down the statue of Lenin in Vilnius. This "created an atmosphere in real and stage life for ethnic reassessment"(Barnes 24). Though with comedic style, its structure is not episodic but a more traditionally one with unities of time, place and action. The problems that entrap the heroines are not limited to making choices between marriage and career, rather, it concerns a number of identity issues, "about being American, Jewish, and woman" (Barney 52).

The Sisters Rosensweig has been studied from ethnic, biographical, feminist and some other perspectives since it was first performed in 1992. Balakian gives a nuanced analysis on its female characters, regarding the three sisters as "the self-loathing Jew, the practicing Jew, and the wandering Jew"(113-137). Salamon provides extensive information of its life sources from Wasserstein family and compares the fictional and real three sisters in *Wendy and the Lost Boys*. Reading it in the context of Wasserstein's woman-conscious works, Ciociola argues that the play is "a middle-aged vision with a feminist slant" and its "Jewish elements just act as a sparring partner for Wasserstein's retrospective and feminist objectives" (82). Dolan reviews its feminist theme as well as Jewish ethnicity again in her 2017 new book on Wasserstein. Both He Anfang and Chen Lin approach the play from its comic characters and feminist spirit.

Though the Jewish ritual of Sabbath Sundown performed by Gorgeous in Scene 2 Act 1 has been discussed with reference to the issue of Jewish identity, its symbolic meaning, performative force and aesthetic function have not received adequate attention. As the single visible sign of Jewish culture in the play, the Jewish Sabbath Sundown ritual not only reveals Gorgeous's identity as a devout Judaist but also revives the past Jewish memories buried in Sara's

Chapter Two Compliance and Resistance

heart. On the surface, it looks precipitate, simplified, and even farcical, bringing chaos to Sara's house and the confrontation of the three sisters. It functions as the link between the three sisters and women of different generations. Therefore, the key to understand the play is to examine the scene of Jewish Sabbath ritual and the role it plays in changing the three sisters' identities.

The Sisters Rosensweig originates from Wasserstein's feeling of being "very much American and very much Jewish and ethnic" when she was writing *The Heidi Chronicles* in London (Balakian, "Speaking on Stage" 384). Since then she was eager to address directly her lifelong search for identity as a Jewish girl. The result is this one-set, non-episodic play, in which she tells a story about three Jewish sisters named Sara, Gorgeous and Pfeni who were originally from Brooklyn and reunite now in London to celebrate Sara's fifty-fourth birthday, a year after their mother's death. Beginning with the title, *The Sisters Rosensweig* is Wasserstein's most deliberately Jewish play and her own version of Chekhov's *Three Sisters*. The director of the play Daniel Sullivan says, "The idea of coming home and a sense of rootlessness was a reason she wrote the play. Jewishness became a very important thing in it."(Salamon 293) The Rosensweigs, similar to their counterparts in *Three Sisters*, are at a turning point of their lives. They "need to find Chekhov's Moscow of the spirit, to find their place in the world"(Barnes 24).

The other motivation of the play comes from Wasserstein's consistent concern about uncommon women's fate under different social conditions. Moving from young girls who carnivalize college rituals and the feverish feminists who attend CR rap, Wasserstein turns her eyes to three middle-aged women and examines the choices they have made, the problems they are confronted with, and the possibilities they could have. For Wasserstein, it was important to write a play about three uncommon women who are not 23 because "three middle-aged women on a stage who are accomplished and successful and not caricatures in our culture is still a surprise"(Miller H8). Different from the prevalent middle-aged female images that are "sketchily drawn as harridans, mindless ditherers, nags or dangerously unbalanced Medeas" (Hodgins 8), Wasserstein's three sisters are portrayed as intelligent, humorous, and thoughtful achievers who "begin seriously asking themselves significant questions about their past" (Richards, "School of Life" H5). Combining ethnicity and feminism, the play is "a captivating look at three uncommon women and their quest for love, self-definition, and fulfillment"(Gussow C3). The two identities, being Jew and being woman, are equally important for the three sisters.

Observant Jews perform all kinds of rituals to accompany major life events since they believe that all of life is sacred. For example, *brit milah* is a ritual to welcome a baby boy into the covenant of circumcision; *bar mitzvah* and *bat mitzvah* are rituals to mark people's coming-of-age; the marriage canopy(*khupah*) and the ritual smashing of a glass are used to recall the destruction of the temple at the wedding ceremony. There are a set of complicated rituals surrounding death and mourning such as *burial*, *cremation* and *shivah*. Among the Jewish rituals, Sabbath is a weekly commemoration of the resurrection in early days. The weekly observance of Sabbath is considered a most holy obligation prescribed in Exodus in the Decalogue. Keeping Sabbath involves rich home-based rituals and synagogue services. From sundown Friday to sundown Saturday all work ceases. The festive Friday evening meal involves special prayers for lighting the candles, blessing the wine, and blessing the two loaves of challah bread. A similar sequence of prayers occurs during specified Saturday meals. In the synagogue,

Chapter Two Compliance and Resistance

Sabbath services generally follow the structure of the daily morning, afternoon, and evening services.

Different from Gracious Living in *Uncommon Women and Others* and CR ritual in *The Heidi Chronicles*, the service of Sabbath Sundown in *The Sisters Rosensweig* is a religious ritual which is regarded as holy by Jews and should be performed solemnly. However, what happens in the play seems neither holy nor solemn, it looks rather ridiculous and funny. When Gorgeous arrives at Sara's house, she babbles a lot about her life in America and blames both Sara and Pfeni for their life styles, which angers Sara and triggers their bitter quarrel. In order to end their unhappy conversation, Gorgeous slips her shoes off and lies on the couch to complain about her fatigue journey and cheap shoes. Suddenly, she realizes that the sun is just going down. She puts on her shoes quickly and shouts, "Oh, my God! We have to light the candles," which surprises Sara who rebuts her, "Why? We have electricity" (36). Regardless of Sara's objection, Gorgeous starts to look for candles and a tichkel for the ritual. However, Sara is very indifferent to this and tells Gorgeous that she has two Asprey candelabras in the dining room, but no ordinary candles for Sabbath. Finally, Gorgeous finds the two candles on the mantelpiece and lights them. However, she cannot find a tichkel, the special cloth for her head in the ritual. Their dialogue demonstrates Gorgeous's insistence on performing the ritual and Sara's resistance to it.

>Gorgeous: I need a tichkel for my head.
>Sara: I doubt I have that.
>Gorgeous: All right. Just a napkin.
>Sara: Cloth or paper?
>Gorgeous: Sara, the sun's going down.

Sara: Here, take this. (*Gives her a cloth from India that Pfeni left on the couch.*)

Gorgeous: Matches?

Sara: Can't we wait for my birthday cake?

Gorgeous: Sara, remember the Sabbath Day and keep it holy. (*Lights the candles.*)

Sara: I can't tell you how many Sabbath Sundowns have come and gone here without lighting candles. And guess what? The next morning the sun comes right back up again.

Gorgeous: (*Prays over the candles*) Baruch ahtah adonai! Elohenu! Melech ha-olam! (37)

With the cloth from India on her head, Gorgeous looks very weird and ridiculous, but her piety becomes more prominent by contrast with Sara's indifference and satire. It is explicit that Sara and Gorgeous hold opposite attitudes towards the ritual although both of them were born and brought up in a traditional Jewish family in Brooklyn New York. The scene shows that Gorgeous keeps the Sabbath holy and performs the rituals regularly and devoutly, while Sara knows nothing about the ritual procedure or ritual utensils. She denies the significance of the ritual and never observes it at home.

As one important part of Jewish tradition, the ritual of Sabbath Sundown in this scene symbolizes Jewish culture and values. The candle-lighting, tichkel-wearing and Yiddish praying are cultural signs that reveal and mark the Jewish root of Rosensweig sisters. In contrast, the Asprey candelabras in Sara's dining room and the Victorian Majolica candles on the mantelpiece are both famous British luxury brands that symbolize the owner's high social status and WASP taste. Sara's manner suggests that she does not remember the Sabbath Day or keep it holy. She does not believe in Judaism, nor

Chapter Two   Compliance and Resistance   193

follow the Jewish way of life as Gorgeous does. Gorgeous's piety and Sara's defiance reflect their disputes over Jewish tradition and values, which in fact has determined their life path. Their confrontation on Sabbath Sundown ritual in fact reflects the conflicts between two different identities and two different cultural values.

　　Rituals are performative, forming or reinforcing one's identity. Gorgeous's performance of Sabbath Sundown is one of the continuous acts that constitute her identity as a "nice Jewish girl". As the sister who "wears her Brooklyn-Jewish roots on her frilly pink sleeves" (Stuart 77), Gorgeous is the embodiment of Jewish traditional values and the spokesperson of their mother Rita Rosensweig, who was not only committed to Judaism but also trying to impose Jewish traditional values upon her daughters. In Ciociola's words, Gorgeous "represents everything Sara has rejected" (83). In contrast to Sara and Pfeni, Gorgeous married to the attorney Henry, had four children and lived in the suburbs of Boston as a "happy" housewife. As she boasts, "we have a very comfortable lifestyle ... everything was going just great."(30) In her opinion, the only normal life for women is to get married and to devote their life to family. As soon as Gorgeous arrives at Sara's house, she begins to talk like their mother and plays a matchmaker for the other two. She insists that Sara is a hard woman who needs a man to make her soft again. Within seconds after meeting Merv, Gorgeous tells him, "Maybe you should marry her [Sara]."(28) When he rebuts, "I've only spent five minutes with her", Gorgeous responds, "So what? Some people know at first sight."(28) She is curious about Sara and Merv's sex after their one-night love and urges Sara to grasp him. As for her younger sister Pfeni, Gorgeous believes that she is simply wasting her time with Geoffrey because he is a bisexual and unwilling to settle down. She warns Pfeni that men are not interested in eccentric women in their forties and "you are just wandering yourself right out of the marketplace"(72). She imposes the question upon Pfeni, "Don't you want what any normal woman wants?"(72) In a word, Gorgeous is the most religious as well as the most conventional sister among the three. She, like Merv's former wife, performs the traditional "supporting role—enabling their husbands to study and work, transmitting Yiddishkeit to their children, helping their children rise to an even higher station in life than they expected to achieve" (Balakian 131). This is the only choice that Jewish traditional culture offers to women and the best life that their mother Rita wants them to have. Performing the Sabbath Sundown ritual is just one Jewish norm that shape Gorgeous's identity.

Sara's rejection of the Sabbath Sundown ritual is one of her acts to efface her Jewishness and to highlight her WASP identity. As a successful top corporate bank executive who once appeared on *Fortune*, Sara has done her best to erase her Jewish identity for a long time. She moves to London and decorates her room "with cozy, comfy, but expensive chintz couches, chairs and window treatments" (1). She acquires a British accent and an English last name from her second ex-husband. She names her daughter as Tess after Thomas Hardy's heroine in his famous novel *Tess of the D'Urbervilles* and sends her to Westminster school. She even dates "a socially acceptable, racist, sexist, and more than likely anti-Semitic" Englishman called Nicholas Pym just because he is a Thatcher M. P. (10). As Pfeni arrives at Sara's London home and uses a "New York tone" in their conversation, Sara is irritated and tries to stop her, which arouses Tess's interest in their life in New York. When Pfeni tells Tess a story about a Jewish man who visited their home every morning, Sara is angered so much that she declares, "New York in a way that has very little to do with us ... Pfeni's the one who's

Chapter Two Compliance and Resistance   195

romanticized a world we never belonged to." (9) Regarding her Jewish background as a symptom of Old World values and a liability to her international business affairs, Sara has "done everything short of converting to repudiate her Jewish roots in Brooklyn"(Stuart 63). When Merv tells her, "You are the first Jewish woman I've met to run a Hong Kong bank"(23), Sara corrects him immediately, "I'm the first woman to run a Hong Kong bank"(23), deleting "Jewish" deliberately. For Sara, Jewishness is undesirable. She has tried all means to assimilate into the mainstream culture. As Wasserstein puts it, Sara is "WASPier than a WASP"(Balakian 123).

Sara's repudiation of her Jewish identity leads to her double faces and split self. In his book *Portrait of American Jews*, Samuel C. Heilman describes the two faces of American Jewry by using Max Ferguson's double portrait called *Ralph Lauren's Worst Nightmare*, which represents two alternative Jews: one is the clean-shaven, assimilated American Jew, the other is bearded Jew wearing a fedora, wrapped in tallis. Viewers can see two different faces from different directions. The double portrait exposes the conflicted identity of American Jews. Such assimilated Jews have fooled themselves into thinking that they have successfully escaped who they are.

Sara is a typical double-faced Jew who has repressed her Jewish culture and run away from her past. She lives in an illusion that, like what Tess's thesis attempts to prove, "my early years have no bearing on my present life"(13). But the fact is just the contrary. Her past experiences have never really disappeared from her life. They linger in her mind and still impose influence upon her present. When Sara listens to a recording of her 1959 choral group singing a cappella version of "*McNamara's Band*", she suddenly begins to sing a different verse which points to the historic territorial conflict between Palestine and Israel and reveals the Jewish identity of the narrator. As she comes to the line "I'm the only Yiddish girl in McNamara's Band", the stage direction reads, "her voice cracks" (83). Sara cannot help crying. Her emotional collapse suggests that she cannot forget the suffering experiences caused by the marginalized status as the only Jew in an Irish band.

Oscillating between Jewishness and Americanness, Sara is split into two: on the surface, she is a well-assimilated successful American, yet in her heart, she is a Polish-Jewish woman who is haunted by Holocaust history. That is the reason for Merv to feel that Sara is "warm and cold all at the same time ... so familiar and so distant" (79). Merv sums up Sara's confused identity as follows, "You're an American, Jewish woman, living in London, working for a Chinese Hong Kong bank, and taking weekends at a Polish resort with a daughter who is running off to Lithuania."(81)

Wasserstein portrays the Sabbath Sundown ritual as an arena in which the three sisters display their attitudes and power. As Gorgeous continues her pray over candles with the Indian cloth on her head, Sara expresses her disgust explicitly by calling it "an ancient tribal ritual"(38) and interrupts it rudely by talking to Tom and Pfeni. When Gorgeous goes up stairs with her suitcase angrily and Tess complains of Sara's disrespect, Sara becomes more impatient, ordering Pfeni to "blow out the god-damned candles"(38). In Sara's eyes, the Sabbath Sundown ritual is primitive and intimidating. Gorgeous's ritual performance is an offense to her dignity and an intrusion into her space. Different from Sara, Pfeni does not object to Gorgeous's religious practice. She says sorry to Gorgeous when she realizes that her entering may interrupt Gorgeous's praying. When Sara asks her to blow out the candles, Pfeni expresses her dissent by pointing out that "Gorgeous just lit them"(38), which enrages Sara who shouts that "stop being the good little sister" (38). Under pressure, Pfeni has to blow out the candles. If Gorgeous is too Jewish, Sara is too WASP, then Pfeni is just wandering between the two extremes.

The three sisters' conflicts are not only caused by their religious problems, but also closely connected to their feminist ideology. Both Sara and Pfeni have stubbornly rebelled against their parents and fought traditional Jewish values that subordinate women. Sara chose to study finance and became the first woman who ran a Hong Kong bank just because her father taught his daughters that "girls weren't supposed to know about money"(36). Born in 1937 and coming of age in the fifties, Sara challenged male hegemony by entering a male-dominated profession and gaining the reputation of having the biggest balls at the Hong Kong/Shanghai Bank worldwide. Sara's career successfully defies the expectations of the women of her time and class. Her appearance on the cover of *Fortune* magazine shatters the glass ceiling inherent in traditional Judaism. Even after two divorces, Sara does not compromise in her feminist pursuit. She has no plan to marry Merv and tells him, "I didn't have a 'you' in my life at sixteen. I'm certainly not going to have a 'you' in my life now."(82) As Gorgeous argues that she should marry and settle, she replies firmly, "Gorgeous, trust me, I'm settled." (74) When Gorgeous blames Sara that she never grew up to be the woman their mother expected them to be, Sara assures her, "We are happy, Gorgeous, It's just not our mother's kind of happiness."(36) For Gorgeous and their mother, only marriage can bring women happiness, but Sara has other things to pursue.

Similar to Sara, Pfeni is not a "nice Jewish girl" like Gorgeous either. She also has conflict with her mother. In her own words, "I'm not every mother's dream daughter." (72) Pfeni has always traveled with shopping bags and made it her personal signature ever since their mother told her that "only crazy people travel with shopping bags"(7). At forty, she still remains single and wanders around the world, first as anthropological writer and then as travel journalist. She is part of group of young, contemporary Jewish American female protagonists growing up in Brooklyn, rejecting marriage and committing themselves to becoming writers.

Both Sara and Pfeni, like other feminists,

> Feared the constraints experienced by the adult women around them ... Fear of becoming an "ordinary housewife"... They rejected the world of their mothers and searched for an identity based on something besides marriage and motherhood. (Rosen 39)

Although their mother has been dead for a year, the Jewish traditional values she represents have remained powerful and the conflicts between her and her daughters have not been resolved. When Gorgeous reminds Sara of the good feeling they enjoyed as their mother stroked their hair, Sara denies it and complains that what she remembers is her mother's shrieking at her "where's the other point"(36) when she got 99 in exams. Even when her mother was in dead bed, Sara did not visit her, nor did she go back to attend the funeral because, according to Gorgeous, Sara suffered from Ovarian abscess and hysterectomy. However, as Gorgeous tells Sara, "mother really missed saying good-bye to you"(36), Sara does not appear to feel regret or guilty, instead, she replies, "mother and I had a Female Trouble conflict"(36), which seems to imply that Sara's absence owes less to her disease than to their past conflicts. In this case, Wasserstein demonstrates how matriarchal influence still troubles Sara's life. Pfeni has the similar problem. She implies that

Chapter Two   Compliance and Resistance

she dates Geoffrey partly because he is not "mother's dream date for their daughter"(72). To this absurd reason, Gorgeous warns Pfeni, "Don't waste your time rebelling against mother anymore. She's not even here to enjoy it. It's just us now."(72) Both Sara and Pfeni's rebellion against their mother actually is their way to fight against the limited destiny that patriarchal Jewish traditions impose upon them. Gorgeous's words suggest it is time for them to reconcile with their mother, their Jewishness as well as their past.

Gorgeous's arrival and performance of the Sabbath Sundown ritual disrupt the "WASP Disneyland" set up by Sara at Queen Anne's gate in London and bring Jewish heritage to the next generation. When Gorgeous is praying, Tess and her boyfriend Tom come back home and witness the ritual. As a British working-class young man, Tom knows nothing about Jewish ritual. His first response to Gorgeous's behavior is that she is "having a séance"(37), which is a meeting in which a spiritualist attempts to communicate with the spirits of the dead. He then equals it with Stonehenge and wonders why Gorgeous wears a "dishtowel" on her head, which reveals his ignorance of Jewish culture. Contrary to Tom's rash questions and rude interruption, Tess expresses her respect to the ritual by silencing Tom and telling Sara, "This is important to Aunt Gorgeous."(38) Tess's tolerance to Jewish ritual, together with her exploration of Sara's early life and her plan of going to Lithuania, reflects her identity confusion, which is caused by her mother's ambiguous attitude toward their Jewish root. On the one hand, Tess is curious about her family history and Jewish heritage. On the other hand, she feels disconnected from both Jewishness and Americanness. She cannot find any sense of belonging. Just as she wonders, "If I've never really been Jewish, and I'm not actually American anymore, and I'm not English or European, then who am I?"(106) Gorgeous's ritual performance displays Jewish culture in front of Tom and Tess. Her in-your-face ethnicity connects Tess to their Jewish root for the first time.

The three sisters' reunion in London after their mother's death is not just for Sara's fifty-fourth birthday celebration, it is more importantly an opportunity for them to confront each other's crisis, reconnect their family bond, and reestablish their intimate sisterhood. Despite of their apparent success, none of the three sisters is free of confusion, trouble and pain. They are entrapped in various crises and filled with what Wasserstein calls "yearning and melancholy"(Grossberg D1) As Lee Barney points out, "in her own way, each sister in the play struggles with identity crisis, trying to rationalize the choices she has made in her life."(51) All the three sisters' lives are stuck and need to be recharged and renewed. Only when they find who they are in their family root and get reconciliation with their past could they be empowered to survive the crises and move on.

Beyond depressing, Sara now is a vulnerable woman who is filled with rage and loneliness after two divorces and a fatal disease ovarian abscess. Having given up on love, Sara describes herself as "old and bitter" and "threatening" to man. With the death of her mother and the rebellion of her daughter, Sara begins to reflect on her own life choices. As a double-faced split American Jew, Sara likes Merv and enjoys being with him on the one hand, but on the other hand she pushes him away because he is "a little too Jewish" and "remind you [her]too much of home"(82). Standing at the crossroad of middle age as well as cultural conflicts, Sara is "in desperate need of hope and rebirth"(7).

Pfeni, wandering around the world as a funky writer and loosely dating with a bisexual director, meets her professional and emotional dilemmas at the same time. As she says at the outset, "Oh, my God, my life is stuck."(17) Her principal crisis comes from her career. As her well-known book *Life in the Afghan Village* illustrates, Pfeni formerly worked as a "journalistic voice of the oppressed masses" (Kissel 47). However, when she went back to the Afghan village to visit the women she had written about, she found that half of them were dead and the rest refugees. Being shocked and feeling guilty, Pfeni has undergone her most unsettling time and given up political writing. She now wanders from one hotel to another, just writing superficial travel articles. She has an ambitious project to write a book about gender and class on women in Tajikistan but unable to move on because she thinks "it's wrong for me to use these women" (78). Entrapped in the moral dilemma, she is avoiding the serious writing she should be doing, which makes her much guiltier. The other crisis of Pfeni is from her relationship with Geoffrey, a bisexual director who charms everyone with high spirits and bitchy anecdotes. They have been together as lovers for a few years and discussed to get married soon. But just at the moment when Pfeni thinks of ending her fabulous career to stay with him, Geoffrey suddenly deserts her and returns to his former gay lover Jordan because, in his words, "I have no other choice. I miss men"(88). In fact, Geoffrey is a gay. He pretends to love Pfeni because he had been frightened by AIDS and horrified by the death of his gay friends. After a few years' struggle, he has to face his real self and admits that he loves man more than woman. Geoffrey's betrayal is a terrible blow to Pfeni who already feels that her life is stuck.

Gorgeous seems less troubled than her two sisters and flaunts her "perfect" marriage to anyone she meets. However, the truth is that her husband has been unemployed for two years and unwilling to look for a job. He just writes mysteries in the basement and prows around the bars like a ghost. Gorgeous has to find a job at middle age and works extremely hard to support her family. In spite of her ostensible happiness and motor-mouthed optimism, Gorgeous is the most restless and vulnerable one among the three sisters. First, Gorgeous feels acutely left behind in the luster of her two sisters' enormously successful and challenging careers. In order to avoid being belittled, she has to boast of her husband, her kids and her job in a radio show, which gives an impression that she is "a superficial, unsophisticated suburban ... retro specimen"(Stearns 4D). Second, she has to conceal her husband's problem and pretend to be happy before others although her marriage has collapsed. Even her trip to London is not as enjoyable as it seems. In her words, "I've spent two days schlepping around London with the sisterhood and two nights having my own sisters tell me everything I do is wrong."(91) When her four-hundred-dollar new shoes are broken at Kensington Station and her embarrassment is witnessed by people along the way, Gorgeous cannot bear the stress anymore and bursts into tears in front of Sara and Pfeni.

Though the Sabbath Sundown ritual ends with Sara's hysterical shout, Gorgeous's angry complaint and Pfeni's innocent puzzlement, it has changed the pure WASP atmosphere at Sara's home and brought Sara's Jewish memories back. It provides a chance for the three sisters to experience Jewish culture and face their ethnic root again. As a ritual event, it uncovers Sara's WASP veil and triggers her transformation. Sara begins to reconcile with her past experiences and family heritage with the help of Gorgeous and Merv, a faux furrier who "sifts all discourse through his Jewish identity" and "always comes back to his roots"(Winer 76).

Merv awakens Sara's Jewish past purposefully. In the following scene after the Sabbath Sundown ritual, Sara joins the debate among

Tess, Nick and Merv about the political situation in Lithuania, in which Merv argues that Vilnius was home to about 65,000 Jews before the Holocaust and what always goes hand in hand with European nationalism is anti-Semitism. As an American who is traveling in Europe with the American Jewish Congress, Merv has a lot common with Gorgeous and multiplies her power of transforming Sara. He tries his best to connect Sara to her home in the Brooklyn, the place she is "working so hard to make it go away"(82). As Sara breaks down and cries suddenly after her birthday party, Merv hugs her and calls her "Sadie" gently, which reminds Sara of her grandfather. They then have an intimate talk about their middle school life and find they once studied at the same school, and even know the same people. Such warm chat softens Sara's heart and brings her back to the long forgotten past. With his wit, wisdom and patience, Merv convinces Sara that she is intelligent and attractive, and "there can be happiness in life. Brief but a moment or two"(58). When Merv addresses Sara as "Sara Rosensweig," Sara does not resist or get angry as before, rather, she laughs and exclaims, "Jesus. No one has called me that in thirty years."(58) This indicates that Sara has gradually relinks her present with her past.

Merv not only connects Sara to Jewish culture through reliving her past life as a Jewish girl, he also attempts to bridge her to all Jewish women and the Holocaust history. He tells Sara, "Sometimes I look at you and see all my mother's photographs of her mother and her mother's entire family."(79) Merv introduces his family history to Sara and discovers the sameness among all Jewish women in the following dialogue.

> My mother's family had a villa in a spa resort in Poland called Ciechocinek. And the pictures we had were of the family gathered at a picnic

... The women in their too-large dresses with their arms folded all had your brilliant eyes—they sparked even from those curled and faded photographs. Unfortunately, most of them and their families didn't survive. But Sara, when I look into your eyes, I see those women's strength and their intelligence. To me you are a beautiful and most remarkable woman. (79)

In Merv's eyes, Sara has inherited the Jewish traits and spirit that have passed on from one generation to another. Such Jewishness is rooted in their blood. Merv's authentic presentation arouses sympathy and positive response from Sara who reveals that she once was sent by the Hong Kong/Shanghai Bank to Ciechocinek to loan the local government to renovate the resort. She sees it as a triumph for her to decide how to put bread on the tables of those who had driven her grandparents out of the country. Their common Jewish experiences awake Sara's Jewish consciousness. After Merv leaves, Sara picks up the Cliffe Clef album and listens to the record, from which we hear her voice, "Hi, I'm Sara Rosensweig of Brooklyn, New York and we're the Cliffe Clef of 1959."(83) The album records her early life in Brooklyn as the only Yiddish girl in the singing group. This memory is both pleasant and bitter for Sara. Therefore, she cannot help singing along and crying. The record opens her closed heart and lets out her repressed feelings.

However, Wasserstein does not portray Merv as Sara's redeemer. Although Sara returns gradually to her true self as a Jewish woman after Gorgeous and Merv's influence and intervention. She still feels alienated from her earlier life and difficult to reconcile with her Jewish background. So when the too Jewish Merv attempts to go closer and proposes to live together with her, Sara pushes him away coldly by calling him "Mervyn" and telling him, "your world is very different from mine"(81). As an empowered feminist, Sara refuses

Chapter Two   Compliance and Resistance   205

to be protected by a conventional Jewish man who wants to be her "knight in shining armor"(81). Just as Howard Stein points out, Sara makes "her position clear: I don't want you to be the answer for me. And she means it"(25). Wasserstein creates Merv just as the foil of Sara. He, like Geoffrey, functions as the catalyst of dramatic action rather than the savior of the heroine.

What transforms Sara and rejuvenates Pfeni and Gorgeous from their crises is not man's love but the solid sisterhood that is based on their shared childhood memories and common Jewish heritage. Like the girls' dormitory in *Uncommon Women and Other* and the church basement in *The Heidi Chronicles*, Sara's house becomes an all-women space when the male characters leave for different reasons in the later afternoon Saturday. Circling in Sara's sitting room, the three sisters not only tell each other their pain and offer comfort, but also push each other further to reflect upon their choices and encourage each other to pursue their dreams persistently. It seems that Wasserstein creates a special family consciousness-raising for the sisters. In this private pure female space, the three sisters eventually face their troubles bravely, lay bare their true feelings clearly, and reconcile with their mother Rita as well as their own self peacefully. All of them are enlightened and empowered whereby get rebirth during the process.

The three sisters gather in the sitting room and rap about their troubles like the women group in *The Heidi Chronicles*, getting console and encouragement from their sisters. Pfeni tells Sara and Gorgeous that Geoffrey misses man and leaves her. Sara listens to her baby sister's murmur and embraces her gently, rubbing her tears off and assuring her that all will be fine by praying in Yiddish. Gorgeous holds a practical view about Pfeni's problem and asks her not to take it personally. When both of them learn that Pfeni responds to

Geoffrey's "I miss men" with "I miss them too", they burst into laugh together and praises her as a good brilliant girl, which helps Pfeni rebound from the pain.

Gorgeous does not reveal her problems until she returns to Sara's home with drenched clothes, a broken shoe and a bare foot. Bearing the stress no more, Gorgeous narrates what happened to her London trip, her terrible new shoes and her unemployed crazy husband, which shocks Sara and Pfeni. Sara tries to give a hand by recommending a cobbler and providing a few suggestions to solve Henry's problem. At this moment, Sara becomes Gorgeous's good big sister again rather than the harsh cold hostess who always criticizes Gorgeous.

Influenced by both her younger sisters, Sara at last admits that she also suffers from losing Merv, the symbolic character of Jewish culture. She has driven him away although she has a good time with him. Putting their own troubles aside, both Gorgeous and Pfeni start to help Sara and urge her to call Merv to tell him her true feeling. Their relaxed talk and sincere sympathy bring them back to the early home in Brooklyn and reset the sisterhood that have broken for a long time. Holding hand in hand and kissing each other, they enjoy "a moment of pure, unadulterated happiness" and play their childhood games again, "laughing and giggling like children"(98).

Referring to their Jewish mother Rita frequently in their conversation, the three sisters get reconciliation with Rita and restore her motherly image in their hearts. Pfeni is hurt so much by Geoffrey's abandonment that she recalls an anecdote of her mother. One night when she was about nine years old, Pfeni asked Rita what a broken heart felt like. Rita misunderstood her and thought she meant heartburn. So Rita told her to take Brioschi, a kind of medicine. Now Pfeni's heart is broken, she misses her mother and

Chapter Two Compliance and Resistance

sings "eat too much, drink too much, take Brioschi, take Brioschi" (89), the song that symbolizes Mama's care and love. As Sara wonders why Pfeni remembers these things, Pfeni cries, "I don't want to lose Geoffrey and Mommy at the same time."(90) Pfeni welcomes her mother back after her long time rebellion. Similarly, Gorgeous and Sara also recall their mother's goodness. When Pfeni blames herself for being stupid, Gorgeous assures her that none of Rita Rosensweig's daughters are stupid. Sara praises Rita for teaching her daughters to express thanks properly. With sweet memories of their mother and the Jewish humor they inherit from her, the three sisters gradually recover from their depression. They change from tea to wine and drink a toast to Rita. Wasserstein emphasizes this process through a small ritual,

> Gorgeous: Good girl!
> Sara: Brilliant girl! Maybe Rita Rosensweig didn't do so badly by us after all.
> Pfeni (*lifts her glass*): To Rita!
> Gorgeous (*lifts her glass*): To Rita!
> Sara (*lifts her glass*): To Rita! And her stunningly brilliant daughters.
> Gorgeous & Pfeni: And her stunningly brilliant daughters. (95)

They finally have resolved the "Female Trouble conflict" that has inflicted the mother-daughter relationship for a long time and reached reconciliation with Rita after one year of her death. At the same time, they stop self-blaming and begin to accept themselves as good, brilliant and gifted Rosensweig daughters, regaining the family bond through their love to mother. When Gorgeous tells Sara, "Mama always say you were a shtarker. Maybe you should take care of us now"(95), Sara agrees to play the role of mother to Gorgeous and Pfeni. With both Gorgeous and Pfeni lying down on Sara and being stroke by her on their foreheads, the three sisters share their family happiness and have a "special rejuvenation treatment"(98).

The three sisters are renewed by their solid sisterhood and common Jewishness. Encouraged by Sara and Gorgeous, Pfeni comes out of her career dilemma and decides to go back to a crock pot in Tajikistan to write her long-delayed book about gender and class there. She has recovered from Geoffrey's betrayal and finds out the right path she should choose. As she tells Gorgeous,

> If you only write "Bombay by Night" and you make sure to fall in love with men who can never really love you back, one morning you wake up at forty in your big sister's house, and where you should be seems sort of clear. (101)

As a representative wandering Jew, Pfeni has transcended her self-doubt and middle-aged depression, realizing that her "true calling" is in her powerful writing and that she must continue her job in Tajikistan. Pfeni has a real compassion to suffering women in the war-battered region and her writing about them is meaningful and significant. As Howard Kissel correctly felt, "Pfeni had secularized her Jewish idealism in radical journalism."(9) Her place in the world is not the warm arms of man, nor the country kitchen for kids, but the larger world where she travels around and writes about for political cause.

Gorgeous, impressing audience and critics as a "ditzy, motor-mouthed Jewish matron" at the beginning of the play(Barney 49), finally earns respect and reputation through hard and excellent work. She is given a real Chanel suit as a gift from Mrs. Hershkovitz and the ladies to express their gratitude for her help. Though being crazy

Chapter Two　Compliance and Resistance　　　　　　　　　　　　　　209

about luxurious fashionable clothes and dreaming of owning one Chanel by herself for a long time, Gorgeous determines to return every last piece of the suit to the House of Chanel because she knows that "somebody's got to pay for [her children's] tuition this fall" (103). This subverts her cliché status by denying her materialist pleasure and undertaking her family burden bravely. She is not just an "upside-down-cake-of-a-Jewish-princess" (Kraft B7), she is the one who follows Jewish tradition to get married and have a large family in past, but now she becomes a popular radio personality and provides both financial and domestic security for her family. In the end, she has proved herself to be a "special blend of philosopher and fool"(Simon 100) and a person of dignity.

　　Sara's transformation is more dramatic and significant. Urged by her two sisters, Sara finally calls Merv secretly and reveals her true feeling to him. Though with no plan of remarriage, Sara rebounds from her two failed marriages as well as terrible female disease and believes in love again. Also, Sara's acceptance of a post-industrial Zionist as a potential lover suggests that she has changed her radical prejudice against Jewish culture and embraced her Jewishness seriously. This change is demonstrated explicitly by Sara and Tess's dialogue at the end of the play. When Tess appears on the stage with Gorgeous's original pink ensemble and declares that she would not attend Lithuanian resistance, Sara feels a relief and tells her a story about Rita. She assures that Tess is just like Rita, "So if Rita could make the Cossacks run away, you are smart enough, and brave enough, and certainly beautiful enough to find your place in the world."(106) In this symbolic way, Tess is linked to their Jewish family and inherits the Jewishness through Gorgeous and Rita. Echoing the beginning of the play, Tess turns on her tape recorder and interviews Sara who, totally different from before, replies her daughter's questions pleasantly. Sara says, "My name is Sara Rosensweig. I am the daughter of Rita and Maury Rosensweig. I was born in Brooklyn, New York, August 23, 1937."(107) By using her original name and recognizing her past life in Brooklyn, Sara completes her journey back to home and forges a new self. She at last reaches a reconciliation with her Jewish root and combines the WASPness and Jewishness harmoniously.

As Wasserstein's most autobiographical play, *The sisters Rosensweig* expresses her ambivalence about Jewish ethnicity and her vison of middle-aged life of uncommon women. Based on her own sisters' life, Wasserstein charts three Jewish women's self-search and self-renewal wandering between the conflicting Jewish traditions and feminist pursuits. In order to link all the characters to the central ethnic issue, she depicts a typical Jewish ritual—the Sabbath Sundown, which, although performed in some sense comically and ironically, is an effective device to unfold the narrative, structure the dramatic action and develop characters. The three sisters confront each other on the ritual and reflect upon their past life after it. After their painful confrontation, heartfelt communication and serious self-reflection, each sister reconciles with their past self and gains empowerment, renewing their mindset as well as identity. Their final reconciliation and rejuvenation demonstrate that there are real possibilities in life for uncommon women even at middle-age and that Jewish heritage could be integrated into feminist discourse.

Epilogue

The college-educated and career-driven women in Wasserstein's drama have been shaped by two contradictory ideologies, constrained by traditional feminine roles as devoted wife and mother on the one hand, and liberated by feminist ideals which encourage them to pursue self-fulfillment on the other. Such conflicts are vividly demonstrated in the rituals performed or mis-performed by these women who are constantly in search of their true self.

College rituals such as Gracious Living and Father-Daughter Weekend which promote feminine gender norms and patriarchal marital values are carnivalized and subverted by the rebellious girls like Holly, Rita, Muffet and Kate with their bawdy languages, obscene jokes, sarcastic role-play and funny gestures. By re-orienting and re-signifying these traditional rituals, the college girls overturn gender stereotypes and constitute their "uncommon women" identity. With its symbolic signs, political commitment and performative power, the feminist ritual of consciousness-raising transforms Heidi, a humanist girl trapped in a suffocating love and confined to her personal interests, into a revolutionary feminist who values sisterhood highly and devotes her whole life to feminist cause. As an optimistic, euphoric and serious ritual event, the CR Rap in Ann Arbor functions as the turning point of the play in terms of both character development and emotional structure. The Jewish ritual Sabbath Sundown is performed devoutly by Gorgeous, but resisted coldly by Sara, and spectated curiously by Pfeni, Tess and Tom, which reveals their different attitudes toward the family's Jewish and American root. As the symbol of Jewish culture, the ritual works as the bond of the three sisters, the link of Sara's past and present as well as the bridge between Jewish tradition and feminist ideas. The three sisters reestablish their intimate sisterhood, recover from their life crises and renew their split self after the ritual performance.

Ritual can be performed genuinely, yet it also can be imitated or parodied. In his PhD dissertation "Parodied Ritual in the Plays of Edward Albee", Kathleen M. Sullivan argues, "Albee parodies the symbolic codes central to a ritual" and "distorts the intrinsic value of the ritual" (2). Through parodied rituals, Albee dramatizes the spiritual bankruptcy of his characters and the deterioration of family and society. In her play *And Baby Makes Seven*, Paula Vogel makes a dialogue with Albee by parodying rituals and re-imagining family structure. However, Vogel's use of parodied ritual is different from that of Albee's. In the next chapter, this project will focus on the parodied rituals performed by the transgressive women in Vogel's plays to examine how they reverse power relations, subvert traditional gender norms and reconstruct their female identities.

Chapter Three

Subversion and Reconstruction: Transgressive Women Empowered Through Parodied Rituals

Similar to Norman and Wasserstein, Paula Vogel also positions women at the center of her plays. However, Vogel, as a self-declared feminist and lesbian, is more sensitive to power politics between men and women. She has never performed a "good" girl in life, nor does she write "good" girls in her plays. She deliberately dramatizes female characters who are transgressive and subversive, such as the promiscuous Desdemona, the pregnant lesbian, the old-aged prostitutes and the masculinized sexual abuse victim. What she wants to do, in her own words, is to "give [women] three dimensionality, and the major focus is that—complicating and problematizing female characters"(Bigsby, "Contemporary" 292). These female characters are not exemplary feminist heroines but conflicted characters who both enact and resist the discourses that constitute their bodies and identities. They struggle desperately to escape their predetermined destinies in the tough male-dominated world and subvert the traditional guiding assumptions of gender, sexuality, love and family by transgressing various boundaries and limits. According to A. Susan Owen et al, "Eve serves as the primordial Christian sign for the culturally inscribed transgressiveness of women" and woman, "embodied existence as 'other'" is transgressive ontologically (5). Besides the ontological sense, women's transgression in Vogel's plays also conveys cultural and social signification. Transgression for them is willful and conscious acts to break rules and fight against social and cultural oppression.

In contrast to Norman's serious tragedy and Wasserstein's ironic comedy, Vogel's theater is satirical and campy revision of canonical plays by William Shakespeare, Thornton Wilder, Edward Albee, Sam Shepard and David Mamet. Mansbridge designates Vogel's dramaturgical strategy as a "performative burlesque", a parody of a high culture literary or dramatic work, in which Vogel juxtaposes "broad comedy and serious drama, high and low culture, sex and gender, language and sensation" (Mansbridge, "Paula Vogel" 7). Vogel drafts absurd collage-like play worlds where the boundaries between past and present, femininity and masculinity, and fantasy and reality are blurred. In this way, she makes an authentic dialogue with the history of theater as well as contemporary American culture. Vogel not only parodies classic works, but also popular movies, political discourses and social conventions.

Vogel's deployment of ritual is different from that of Norman and Wasserstein too. Ritual, for Vogel, is both symbolic structure to imitate and cultural codes to parody and challenge. On the one hand, most of Vogel's plays are ritualistic in form, tone and language. *The Oldest Profession* consists of six scenes dimming with blackouts. Each scene begins with a group of old prostitutes' ritual talk and ends with a prostitute's death, forming a repetitive structure. *And Baby Makes Seven*, *The Baltimore Waltz* and *Hot 'N' Throbbing* are all circular in their organization. Their ends in fact return and repeat the beginning scenes, signifying that everything has remained the same yet simultaneously changed radically, which imitates the process of many rituals. *The Long Christmas Ride Home* revolves around cultural rituals such as Christmas Mass and Christmas dinner. In *How I Learned to Drive*, Vogel ritualizes Peck's seducing process and Li'l

Chapter Three   Subversion and Reconstruction   217

Bit's coming of age by inserting the repetitive driving lessons in her fragmented memories. On the other hand, Vogel's characters parody and deconstruct rituals that are traditionally performed by and for men or between heterosexual couples. The courtship rituals initiated by Desdemona, Anna and Li'l Bit subvert the traditional gender structure. The parodied death scenes and service of the three imaginary children express two lesbians' emotional turmoil and reconstruct their gender roles. Waltzing, the mating ritual, is danced between two men whose bodily gestures suggest their homosexuality. Analysis on these parodied rituals will provide illuminating insights into Vogel's dramatic world.

This chapter elaborates the symbolic meaning, performative power and political signification of the rituals of "dying" and service in *And Baby Makes Seven*, the rite of remembrance and loving exorcism in *The Baltimore Waltz*, and the rites of initiation and courtship in *How I Learned to Drive* and explores the sexual and gender power politics embodied in the ritual performance. It is argued that all the female protagonists have parodied and subverted traditional sexual and gender discourses in one way or another by transgressing the boundaries of femininity/masculinity, paternity/maternity, heterosexuality/homosexuality, and fantasy/reality. In this way, they empower themselves into active subjects and reconstruct their identities.

Ⅰ. Negotiating Gender Roles in Playacting Rituals of "Dying" and "Service"

Written and produced in 1984, *And Baby Makes Seven* is "a traditional burlesque of Edward Albee's *Who's Afraid of Virginia Woolf*" (Mansbridge, "Paula Vogel" 204). Similar to George and

Martha in *Woolf*, the lesbian couple Ruth and Anna in *And Baby Makes Seven* create their sons in imagination to animate their childless life and then "kill" them in order to welcome the flesh-and-blood child of Anna and Peter, their gay friend who donates his sperm. What is different is that Vogel inverses the central premise that false illusions have destructive effects on real life in *Woolf*. Instead, she demonstrates that life is greatly enhanced by the creative potential of fantasy, and that a vivid imagination fosters the relationship between family members. The imaginary sons in *Baby* are not used as a discursive weapon by their parents to attack and hurt each other. They are embodied and performed by Ruth and Anna vividly as a means of entertainment and a strategy to deal with life crisis. Basically, *Baby* is a play about the crisis that queer family confronts and deals with. It is "a journey that a lot of people face at some point in their lives ... that kind of insane crisis period just before you have a child, when you know your entire life will change but you're not sure how"(Bilowit 5F).

Baby suffered an ill-fated production history and had not attracted much critical attention until its rejuvenation in 2014. The reason is perhaps that its queer family vision "was on the bleeding edge of that cultural wave"(Purcell 3) and "a trio of gay parents was so poorly received" in the 1980s (Hagan 7). Its revival in the twenty-first century arouses both negative and positive comments. Some scholars criticize that its "central conceit is reductive, repetitive and extremely off-putting"(Grode), and that it is "a simple-minded feel-good piece of fluff"(Shirley). Others consider it as a hilarious yet prescient work with serious motifs. Carey Purcell acclaims, it is a "hysterically funny and deeply touching play about what means to be a family" and "Paula explores it in a way that is funny, edgy, and very honest"(2). Jeremy Gerard argues that its theme resonates in today's society and Vogel proves "even her lesser work has a theatrical, emotional punch"(1). Taking *And Baby Makes Seven* as one of Vogel's representative works, Joanna Mansbridge, Vanessa Campagna and Jin Lili have explored the performative power of embodied performance, the Brechtian and feminist concerns and the role reversal in the play. [1]

The present author continues the above efforts to celebrate and clarify this controversial play by analyzing the rituals of "dying" and "service" of the three imaginary children playacted by Ruth, Anna and Peter from Scene 6 to 12. When discussing the traits of absurd theater, Nelvin Vos points out, "The act of dying is dramatized most frequently and most powerfully in the Theater of the Absurd as a ritual where the action is often both of the levels of seriousness and of parody."(83) According to Mansbridge, Scene 6 to 12 are "the play's most effective scenes, animated by a complex affective structure that weaves broad comedy with loss and also a sense of genuine panic at the finality of the children's 'death'"("Paula Vogel" 60). Different from the parodied game rituals which are evil and destructive in *Woolf*, the rituals of "dying" and "service" in *Baby* are well-meant, heart touching and life-giving. Though absurd and farcical, these rituals address some serious issues such as the characters' suppressed desires, identity crisis and gender war. The parodied performance of ritual is a constant negotiation of authority and power as well as a process of reconstructing gender roles.

In terms of gender politics in family, the central question is what gender roles husband and wife should take respectively. Gender role

---

[1] Mansbridge, "Camp, the Canon, and a Performative Burlesque: Paula Vogel's Plays as Literary and Cultural Revision"(2010); Campagna, "Gesturing toward Queer Utopia: The Children's World of Paula Vogel's *And Baby Makes Seven*"(2017); Jin Lili, *Through Female Eyes: A Study of Paula Vogel's Plays in the Context of Dramatic Tradition* (2013).

is a slippery term which has evolved and changed with the development of history, especially the history of feminism. Janice Lee defines it in the following way,

> Gender roles are the traits, expectations and behaviors associated with men and women and what it means to be "masculine" or "feminine", [and they are] learned through gender socialization that begins shortly after birth and transmits culturally-shared beliefs and values associated with masculinity and femininity to children and adolescents. (6)

This definition aligns man with masculinity and woman with femininity. In patriarchal society, the dominant ideology advocates the biology-is-destiny notion and the gender roles of men and woman are predetermined and fixed. Such binary division implicates a hierarchical power regime in which men and the masculine are dominant or central, and women and the femininity are understood as marginal or subordinate. This mindset influences the status of husband and wife in heterosexual family where husband is supposed to be masculine and wife feminine. Representing authority, truth and power, husband is superior to wife and has all say in family life.

With the development of the women's liberation movement and the gay rights movement, the binary oppositions concerning sex, gender and sexuality, namely, male/female, masculinity/femininity and heterosexuality/homosexuality, have been challenged and deconstructed by feminist philosophers and sociologists such as Kate Millett, Julia Kristeva, Luce Irigaray, Helene Cixous, Eve Kosofsky Sedgwick, and Judith Bulter. Among them, Butler's theory of performativity is very influential. She argues that there is no stable and coherent unity of sex, gender and sexuality and gender is "an identity tenuously constituted in time, instituted in an exterior space through a *stylized repetition of acts*" ("Gender Trouble" 179). The attributes of masculinity or femininity are not natural or confined to male or female body. In her view, "gender itself becomes a free-floating artifice, with the consequence that man and masculine might just as easily signify a female body as male one, and woman and femininity a male body as easily as a female one" ("Gender Trouble" 10). In light of this theory, gender roles should be changeable and fluid, free from the bounds of biological sex. Consequently, the hierarchy of man/woman and masculinity/femininity is broken and the dominant or central position of husband/father in family is subverted.

However, many gays or lesbians in queer family choose to imitate the traditional roles of husband or wife in heterosexual family, which is designated as the "butch-femme aesthetic" by Sue-Ellen Case. Case (1989) champions the butch-femme couple as "playfully inhabiting the camp space of irony and wit, free from biological determinism, elitist essentialism, and the heterosexist cleavage of sexual difference" ("Butch-femme Aesthetic" 298). Though revealing masculine and feminine roles as roles, the "butch-femme" pattern does not break the spell of gender warfare originated in heterosexual family. Conflict and power struggle are still prevalent in queer family.

Vogel's representation of gender roles in *And Baby Makes Seven* is different from that of both heterosexual and "butch-femme" family. She envisions a threesome gender relationship which is both similar to and different from the husband-wife gender warfare that haunts the traditional heterosexual couples such as Helmer and Nora in *A Doll's House*, Zhou Puyuan and Fan Yi in *Thunderstorm*, and George and Martha in *Who's Afraid of Virginia Woolf*. In *And Baby Makes Seven*, the threesome relationship is more complicated and delicate. The three characters are entrapped in both "battle of sexes" and "gender trouble". Despite the fact that Anna and Ruth are the primary couple, marriage is never mentioned. Neither is any kind of formal, sanctioned commitment. As an integral part of the family, Peter signs a contract with Anna and Ruth, promising to raise their real baby together. But he has additional gay relationships outside of the threesome. This three-partner, open arrangement is so queer that it departs from the traditional nuclear family centered on a couple who has made a legal/public/spiritual commitment. The first Act of the play demonstrates that their conflicts are unavoidable and the utopian threesome family mode might not work.

The triangle wrestle of authority and power among the three characters is exposed as soon as the curtain goes up. The play opens with Peter's assertive line, "I think they have to go. That's all I'm saying"(67), which evidently expresses Peter's attempts to claim his central and authoritative status in the family as a traditional father does. "They" refers to Ruth and Anna's imaginary sons, Orphan, Henri and Cecil, who are embodied and performed—in triplicate—by Ruth and Anna. Annoyed by Ruth' frequent naughty role-play, Peter demands that the three imaginary boys must be sent away in order to prepare a healthy environment for their flesh-and-blood child. Peter, as the newcomer with conventional patriarchal ideology, intends to perform the traditional father role that is closely related to the qualities of masculinity such as tough, powerful, aggressive, intelligent, creative and rational.

However, as the fruit of "Women Creating"(71), the three imaginary boys belong to Ruth and Anna, who obviously prefer to keep them and retain their lifestyle. In Ruth's eyes, she is the "father" of the imaginary children and should have right to decide their fate. Peter's patriarchal manner provokes Ruth. She defies his

Chapter Three Subversion and Reconstruction   223

proposal firmly by threatening that "If they go, I go" (67). When Peter insists that the imaginary children must be eliminated during their debate, Ruth teases Peter by singing a nursery rhyme "You are a big, fat wee-wee head" (68) in the role of Henri, and then bites Peter savagely in the role of Orphan. Ruth's extreme behaviors intensify their conflicts and create an antagonistic atmosphere. Anna, standing between Peter and Ruth, tries to mediate and soothe both. As the quarrel scene ends with Peter's angry "storm[ing] out of the room" (71), the playwright unfolds a different picture of "the battle of sexes" which concerns not one man and one woman but one man and two women.

The rituals of "dying" and "service" is the result of Ruth's compromise with Peter. After a few rounds of discussion and quarrel, Peter becomes very confused and upset by Ruth's obsessive role-playing. At the same time, Ruth gradually realizes that she has to readjust her life if she wants to keep the threesome family moving on. She makes a concession and announces to Peter and Anna that she decides to give up their imaginary children, "We're going to kill them. One by one. First Orphan. Then Henri. Cecil will be the last to go" (84). Nevertheless, Ruth admits that she cannot stop her fantasy suddenly. She is "going to tidy up the plots" so that she can "get [her] last inch of fantasy out of them" (84). Her decision gets support and cooperation from both Anna and Peter. Anna joins the game ritual in the role of Cecil, while Peter becomes the facilitator and spectator behind the curtain.

Vogel's trick is that she gives the stage to Ruth and Anna, letting them plot how to kill their imaginary children and perform the dying scenes in their house, which occupies half of the play. This in fact reverses the direction of their power struggle in favor of Ruth and Anna. As soon as Ruth starts the "killing" process, the characters break away from their ordinary daily life and enter into what Bruce Kapferer calls the virtual reality of ritual, "a self-contained imaginal space ... that enables participants to break free from the constraints or determinations of everyday life"(47). Moving freely in and out of reality and fantasy and slipping seamlessly from feminine to masculine personas, from adults to children, Ruth and Anna take the center stage, empowering themselves and dislocating our understanding of gender roles through their creative performances.

In designing and performing the rituals, Ruth "steals" the authoritative position and becomes a "double father". When introducing the play, David Savran argues, "*Baby* is really a play about narrative, about the stories that people make up to construct their identities, to deal with the people they love, and to divert themselves."("Loose Screws" xiv) At the beginning of the play, Vogel emphasizes that Ruth creates the three imaginary children and she is their legal parent. But with Peter's intrusion, Ruth's position is challenged and undermined. She has to concede in order to keep peace. It seems that Peter would seize power and take the place of Ruth in the family. However, as the "dying" scene of Orphan gets started, Ruth turns out to be the most active figure on the stage. By plotting, directing and performing the "dying" rituals, Ruth establishes herself as a performative authority. Like a playwright, Ruth devises the plot of Orphan, Henri, and Cecil's "death" and composes scripts for these scenes by piecing together various dramatic fragments from *Macbeth*, *King Lear*, *Romeo and Juliet*, *Ghosts*, *A Streetcar Named Desire* and *Julius Caesar*. Like a director, she instructs Anna how to play along with her and how to weave their story with wild imagination. Like an actress, she performs the roles of Orphan and Henri in the "death" and "service" scenes and articulate her desires and opinions in their names. Being creative and

Chapter Three Subversion and Reconstruction   225

assertive, Ruth, rather than Peter, becomes the one who says what will happen and what is right to do. Peter is excluded from Orphan and Henri's death ritual and is arranged to participate in Cecil's without being notified in advance. In this way, Ruth in fact upholds and reinforces her former status as the "father" of the three imaginary children. In other words, Ruth gets self-empowered during the ritual performance.

Strategically, Ruth negotiates with Anna on the question of who is the "father" to her real child by making full use of the power of narrative and performance. After the "death" and "service" of Orphan, Ruth has a bedtime chat with Anna in the role of Henri, which looks like a comical scene between "mother" and wheedling "child" at the beginning. But it shifts to an intense and uncomfortable argument as Henri/Ruth confronts Anna with the "truth" of the parentage of Anna's child:

> Henri (Ruth): Peter still thinks he is the father to your child. You have led him to think so.
>
> Anna: He most certainly is! I should know. Why are you—
>
> Henri (Ruth): I have reason to think otherwise. We both have reason to think otherwise. ...
>
> Anna: What are you implying?
>
> Henri (Ruth): That I am the father to your child.
>
> Anna: Whoa. Time out, Ruthie. We agreed never to—
>
> Henri (Ruth): It was late in November. All the leaves had fallen. Ruse was out of town. We had seen that film which had made you so sad.
>
> Anna: (*Starting to understand*) Are we feeling a little bit jealous?
>
> ...
>
> Henri (Ruth): But who will Peter believe if I tell him I am the father? (102)

By imposing the question "who is the father of their real child" on Anna and reminding her of their common memories, Henri/Ruth first expresses his/her jealousy and insecurity caused by the presence of Peter. Then he/she declares his/her desire to supplant Peter as the father of Anna's child. Vogel's use of character-doubling is not merely for comedic effect, it has distinct feminist implications. Ruth of course cannot "father" Anna's child biologically since she is a woman. But as Anna's lover, she believes she can occupy the position of the "father" in the family. It means she would undertake the responsibilities that are conventionally assumed by a father. As Ruth through Henri urges Anna to re-examine and re-define their sexual roles, asking Anna to question the paternity of their child, Vogel, through Ruth/Henri, asks the audience to re-examine and re-define their own ideas of normative sexual relationships as well as question what should truly characterize masculinity and femininity. During this conversation, Henri/Ruth does not calm down until Anna promises, "Nothing will ... hurt you. You're my ... treasure. And nothing ever will, nothing ever could, replace you." (103) Anna's promise not only proves her faithful love to Henri/Ruth but also acquiesces Ruth's insistent demand of being the "father" of her child. Ruth wins Anna's heart back and succeeds in gaining the "father" status, which is confirmed by Peter and Ruth's shared "fatherhood" after the birth of their real son, Nathan. Both of them take care of Anna and Nathan at home and go out to work to earn bread.

This reconfiguration of father role deconstructs the traditional male-father-masculinity/female-mother-femininity matrix. Vogel seems to imply that a female body is able to undertake the traditional father duties in the family and the so-called gender role is nothing but a social construct. Though occupying the "father" status, Ruth is not portrayed as a masculinized or demonized woman like Martha in

Chapter Three　Subversion and Reconstruction

Woolf. Marsha is harsh, wicked and demonic in Albee's play. She drinks alcohol, seduces their male guest and uses abusive language and their imaginary son as a weapon to bully, manipulate and emasculate her husband George, assuming a dominant masculine position through their parodied game rituals. Describing Ruth as "short, dark, intense" (iii), Vogel portrays Ruth as a more complicated woman who has a fluid gender identity.

Ruth performs femininity by parodying feminine languages and manners on the children's "service" for Orphan. When Cecil (played by Anna) and Henri (played by Ruth) hold a children's service for Orphan in the kitchen, Henri/Ruth is so teary and lost that he/she asks Cecil/Anna, "So ... so now what do we do" (90). He/she is dependent on Cecil/Anna who is more coolheaded and mature. With Cecil/Anna's instruction, they hold hands and sing Orphan's favorite song in a sweet, high boy's soprano. After Cecil/Anna delivers a short eulogy for Orphan, Henri/Ruth quavers and bursts into heart-rendering cries on Cecil/Anna's shoulder. Cecil/Anna comforts Henri/Ruth ardently and swears fiercely to protect him/her. In this ritual, Cecil/Anna performs the role of a strong dependable man, while Henri/Ruth behaves more feminine and childish. Similar to drag in camp, their performance exposes the discontinuity of body and gender and destabilizes the distinctions between masculinity and femininity. Here, two female bodies perform two male roles, but one male displays masculine traits, the other exhibits feminine traits.

Such gender fluidity is further demonstrated in the send-off ritual of Henri. Ruth, in cowboy pajamas, is herself at the beginning, begging Anna sadly to change her mind and not let Henri go. When Anna rejects her request, Ruth moves into the role of Henri without hesitation and becomes falsely cheerful. Realizing that his/her fate cannot be reversed, Henri/Ruth becomes gloomy and melancholy like

Hamlet, quoting "do not ask for whom the bell tolls"(106) from Hemingway, sighing that "grown-ups do not know everything"(107), and insisting that *Le Ballon Rouge* is not a movie but his life(108). He/she parodies the fictional male heroes in novels or movies and performs masculine gestures. But when the last moment is coming, Henri/Ruth attempts to change the agreed plot, which complicates the situation by blurring the boundary between the narrative and the fact, the imaginary and the real.

> Henri/Ruth: I've changed my mind. I don't want to go. I love you, Anna. Please, please, let me stay—
> Anna: Wait a minute, Ruth—
> Henri/Ruth: You could hide me. In the closet. I'll be good. Hide me from Ruth and Peter, they're trying to k—
> Anna: This is not what we agreed—
> Henri/Ruth: Ruth is going to kill me. You don't understand. She'll throw me off the fire escape—
> Anna: Ruth, that's not fair—
> Henri/Ruth: Please, Anna, please, I don't want to die—
> Anna: (*Crying out*) Ruth! STOP IT! You're hurting him!! (*There is silence*)
> Anna: For God's sake, don't hurt him.
> Ruth: (*Quiet*) I'm sorry. (108-109)

Just as they create Henri through narrative, Ruth is trying to change Henri's fate by changing the narrative in the middle of their playacting. This shocks and angers Anna so much that she addresses Ruth directly several times, but Ruth refuses to "break character". She continues her bargain in the guise of Henri, distancing herself from Anna as well as the reality.

Chapter Three Subversion and Reconstruction

This absurd scene highlights the double-identity of Ruth, who is both an adult woman and an eight-year-old boy, depending on what role she chooses to play. Her dizzying transition from one to the other transgresses the borders of sex, gender, age as well as the fictional and the real. Performing both roles of mother and son, Ruth demonstrates more feminine and motherly attributes. She implores Anna with tears to protect their imaginary son, shows great care and love to Anna as well as Henri, and submits to Anna's determination as soon as Anna gets angry. Ruth's femininity is embodied in "the deflated red balloon"(109) left in her hand after Henri is taken away, which symbolizes a mother's broken heart when her child is lost. By using the character/actor doubling, Vogel not only portrays the changeable gender traits of Ruth, but also reveals the performative nature of gender formation. This dramaturgy produces Brechtian Alienation Effect, allowing the actress who plays Ruth/Henri to step aside from her characters and observe their interchangeable roles. Also, it jars her audience into re-evaluating the problematic construction of sex, gender and reality.

Ruth destabilizes both gender role and sexuality by parodying famous characters in canonical plays in the dying scene of Orphan. Coming home after getting groceries, Anna discovers Ruth-as-Orphan bound and gagged. According to Ruth's narrative, Orphan had rabies and was in the last stages, only an hour or two left. As soon as Anna understands what is going on and plays along with the story, Ruth shifts to the role of Orphan and tells Anna how he petted a stray dog and was infected rabies. Then Orphan/Ruth goes crazy and articulates some strange fragmentary sentences, for example, "Fuck Me, Jesus!" "A p-p-plague o-o-o' both your houres!! —z-z-zounds, a d-d-dog, a rrratt, a m-mouse, a k-k-k-kcat, to scratch a m-man to death!!!!" "W-washed, I said, are they washed? Arggh, that unwashed gggggrrr-grape has transported her soul" "Da-da-Damien! W-w-why you d-do this to me?" and "Good night, ladies; good n-night, GooGooGooJoob,—O UNTIMELY Death?!" (88). This polyvocal quotations seem irrelevant, illogical and unintelligible at first sight. However, close reading reveals that all the sentences are taken from classic and popular dramatic texts, including *The Exorcist*, *Macbeth*, *King Lear*, *Romeo and Juliet*, *Ghosts*, *A Streetcar Named Desire*, and *Lassie*. They are spoken by male, female, and even dog protagonists who are mad or going to die, constituting an intertextual montage that works as a parody of popular and highbrow representations of possession, death and madness.

Taking it as "the most meta-theatrical—and the most humorous—scene" (221) in the play, Mansbridge argues, its polyvocality "emphasizes the ways in which the voice can articulate the divergent aspects within an individual person" and Ruth's ventriloquism of classic and popular texts works as "a comic dramatization of what it means to be possessed by cultural narratives" ("Camp" 222). Ruth's meta-theatrical performance exposes the rupture between language and the speaking body, and comically reveals the fact that our identities are a patchwork of internalized identifications and gender is a kind of cultural trope. On the female body of the actress who plays Ruth, Vogel inscribes multiple layers of identities: Ruth—a young lesbian, Orphan—a boy raised by stray dogs, and other diverse fictional figures from literary works.

Orphan/Ruth's mad words and acts are both expressive and performative. First of all, they express Orphan's primal fear of death and the psychosis that emerges in the liminal moments between life and death. Secondly, they demonstrate Ruth's chaotic mental state: her sadness, anger, puzzlement and reluctance to say farewell to

Orphan and to "kill off" her own fantasy. Finally, it constitutes Ruth's multiple identity. Her quotations are not chosen arbitrarily but meaningfully since behind each of them stands a well-known fictional character, no matter it is Hamlet or Blanche. Regardless of their sex, gender or sexual orientation, they represent different aspects of Ruth's identity. In this way, Ruth, a performer par excellence, displays the hybridity of her identity by citing from them.

Among all the above quotations, the sentence "that unwashed gggggrrr-grape has transported her soul" is spoken by Blanche Dubois in Tennessee Williams's *A Streetcar Named Desire* when she is being taken away from her sister's house to the psychiatric hospital by the doctors. Ruth's parody of Blanche serves a few functions. First, it reveals her identification with Blanche. In *Streetcar*, Blanche's marriage to a gay and her reputed sexual promiscuity characterize her sexuality as deviant. She is subjugated and defined as insane by Stanley, the hyper masculinized antagonist. In *Baby*, Ruth is the one who frequently transgresses gender boundaries by wearing both Peter's and Anna's clothes, by her personification of two young boys and by her sexual seduction of and erotic attachment to Peter in the role of Henri. Similar to Blanche, Ruth also indulges in role-playing and clings to a belief in the reality of fantasy. Ruth's unconventional behaviors have been criticized as unhealthy and insane by Peter too. Second, Ruth satirizes and defies the ridiculous heterosexual discourse that suppresses any unconventional sexuality, homosexual or bisexual, which has been stigmatized as a form of psychosis. Third, Vogel pays tribute to the canonical plays by master playwrights, implying that identity is in fact the product of historical texts and one's self could be constituted through citation and imitation.

When discussing the gender roles of Ruth, Anna and Peter, Joanna Mansbridge compares them to Blanche, Stella and Stanley in *Streetcar* and argues, "Anna and Stella, both pregnant, embody a conventional, maternal femininity."("Paula Vogel" 62) This idea is partially true but not complete because she just notices the superficial similarities between Anna and Stella while ignores their essential differences. In *Streetcar*, Stella is a marginalized other, weak and inferior. She submits totally to Stanley's masculine force and has no power to protect her sister. Aligned with what is real, true and sane, she performs hyper femininity and represents the traditional maternal role. While in *Baby*, Anna is an autonomous lesbian who lives happily with her female partner as well as their imaginary children. Her pregnancy is not the result of compulsory heterosexual marriage but her voluntary intercourse with a gay friend in order to have a baby of their own. Though confined to domestic space for her overweight pregnant body like Stella, Anna is not entrapped in her maternal role. Contrary to Stella's obedience and powerlessness, Anna is articulate and assertive, mediating and negotiating successfully between Ruth and Peter. Cooperating with Ruth, Anna takes an active role in performing the previously discussed rituals, displaying both feminine and masculine traits and functioning as both "mother" and "father" to the family member. She almost walks freely between femininity and masculinity, maternal role and paternal role, transgressing and transcending these binary oppositions.

That Mansbridge misreads Anna as a Stella-like figure is because she is portrayed as a dutiful housewife as well as a kind mother who embodies femininity in the realistic scenes of the play. Although with its distinctly absurdist bent, *Baby* is set in a loft apartment with kitchen, bedroom and fire escape in New York City. The three

Chapter Three Subversion and Reconstruction   233

characters are just ordinary people who are busy with everyday domestic routines. In this realistic setting, Anna is often seen working in the kitchen, making coffee, tidying the room, carrying shopping bags, nursing the new born baby or chatting with the family members. She is sweet and gentle to Ruth, showing a lot of care and love to her. She is patient and considerate to Peter. When Peter leaves home with anger and does not come back until midnight, Anna sits up, waiting for him like a kind mother. She is a reasonable judge and mediator between Ruth and Peter, solving their conflicts and maintaining peace and harmony in the family. She stays at home and takes care of their son as a responsible mother. All these suggest that Anna plays a typical conventional maternal role in the family, always ready to shoulder the responsibilities as a mother and a housewife.

However, Vogel, as a lesbian feminist playwright, has never believed in such a pure traditional feminine role. The female characters in her drama are constantly challenging and transgressing gender boundaries. Like Desdemona in *Desdemona: A Play about a Handkerchief* and Charlene in *Hot 'N' Throbbing*, Anna also feels suffocated by the maternal role she performs and suffers from a female "angst" or in Betty Friedan's term—The Feminine Mystique, which is clearly expressed in her furious dialogue with Peter and Ruth,

> Anna: Don't fucking condescend to me! Like I'm the one who's crazy ... like I'm a goddamn carton of eggs that has to be carried very carefully or
> Peter: We are not talking to you like that, Anna—
> Anna: Like hell you're not—
> Ruth: What do you want from us?
> Anna: Just some respect ... You two just traipse in and out at all hours of

the day while I sit here, bloated and tethered like some goddam Good Year blimp on Super Bowl day .... and I'm expected to be understanding of what Ruth wants, what Peter needs. —Who the fuck am I, some kind of knocked-up Miss Manners? ... I fucking hate New York ... I WANT TO KILL, MAIM, MOON THE NEIGHBORS! (96 – 97)

Anna's explosion first of all lets out her anger to Peter and Ruth's disrespectful behaviors. Secondly it gives vent to her own depression and angst caused by her pregnancy. Most importantly, it questions the maternal role she has performed. If Anna has repeatedly cited and performed traditional feminine acts, thereby forging a maternal identity before this moment, her explosion now marks a breach or a crisis in her identity. Anna begins to doubt and rebel against her former too-feminine self. She uses four-letter words deliberately and smashes her coffee cup violently, which are traditionally believed to be masculine traits. The sentence "you can both suck my imaginary dick" (97) shouted by Anna as she exits is more suggestive of masculinity.

The discontinuity of Anna's gender is demonstrated in her roleplaying Cecil in the "service" for Orphan and the "dying" ritual of Cecil. Although just at the age of nine, Cecil has a genius IQ and a philosophical mind. He acts like a rational, mature and authoritative man. For example, Cecil/Anna explains how babies are made to Orphan and Henri with clinical and assertive languages like a knowledgeable doctor. He/She often gives Orphan and Henri life advice and resolves their disputes. With a black armband, Cecil/Anna instructs a children's service for Orphan in their kitchen. He/she holds Henri/Ruth's hand and sings an elegy, imitating what adult men do on funeral service. He/she makes a short memorial speech to lament the death of Orphan and explains the eternality in terms of the Laws of Physics rather than the Devine Presence. He/she even performs the role of strong protector of Henri by promising that "I won't let anything happen to you. I swear it!"(91). Anna's parody of masculine acts in the fictional ritual seems funny and absurd, but it reveals the performativity of gender identity and displays the manly attributes on a female body.

Anna's father-like masculine performance culminates in her playacting Cecil's "dying" ritual, which parodies Act 5 of Shakespeare's *Julius Caesar*. In this scene, Ruth leaves the room secretly, forcing Peter to stay alone with Cecil/Anna and to get involved in "killing" Cecil. In the role of Cecil, Anna becomes very aggressive and angry. He/She interrogates Peter where Henri is and what Peter does to him. As Peter attempts to escape, he/she shouts firmly, "Nobody leaves this room." (111) Feeling hurt by the disappearance of Henri, Cecil/Anna accuses Peter of murder and suspects that Peter will kill him soon. Peter defends that he never means to hurt anybody, he just wants to prepare for the coming of his real child. Cecil/Anna quotes "For Brutus is an honorable man"(111) ironically, implying that Peter is a murderer rather than a father. He/she laughs wildly and speaks furiously, laying bare Peter's guilt in a sarcastic tone, which embarrasses and frightens Peter into "sweat" "silence" and "nervousness"(112). Contrary to her motherly image in front of Peter, Anna performs an image of the rough and furious man.

Peter and Cecil/Anna's "father-son" relationship is challenged and inverted in this poignant scene. When Peter expresses his anxieties about becoming a father and about repeating the patterns that he learned from his own father, Cecil/Anna changes his/her tone and talks to Peter like an experienced male adult. He/she reveals a lot of Peter's childhood stories and assures him that Ruth and Anna do not want a traditional father figure to father their child. He/she also encourages Peter to forget the traditional father mode and reconstruct father role by telling him "just make it up on your own, this father thing, okay" (113). Here, as Mansbridge argues, parenthood is demystified as the natural roles that men and women assume as a rite of passage into heterosexual adulthood. Rather, they are roles that we learn to play, and we are not locked into performing them the same way over and over(232). This gives Peter the power to think outside the Oedipal paradigm traditionally used to understand fatherhood and to devise his own father image creatively. Being consoled and inspired, Peter feels a lot better and changes his mind to get rid of the imaginary child. He even begs Cecil to "change the ending" and "stick around" (113), which is turned down. What is more suggestive is the words Cecil tells Peter before his death, "I think you're going to make a wonderful father" (114). Here, Cecil/Anna is like an old dying father, while Peter is like an unexperienced young man. Cecil's symbolic death prepares Peter for his new role as father. In this way, both the adult/child and father/son hierarchy is reversed.

The last act of the ritual is hyper masculine. Imitating the tragic suicide of Cassius in Act 5 of *Julius Caesar*, Cecil/Anna orders Peter to "hold then my sword, and turn away thy face", and then "runs" on the "sword", dying like "the noblest Roman of them all" (113 - 114). When the heavy pregnant lesbian body of Anna performs an extremely violent and brave act of "nobleman", all the binary oppositions concerning gender are subverted. At the same time, the father-mother hierarchy is also reversed since Cecil is role-played by Anna. Such comic dissonance, similar to other "dying" scenes, produces Alienation Effect on the stage, breaking the audience's gender expectation and highlighting the inherent fluidity of gender construction.

As a kind of performance, ritual is not only symbolic but also performative, bringing to its perlocutionary effect or impact to the participants. The effects of the "dying" rituals on Ruth and Anna are easy to see. First of all, both of them feel exhausted and devastated in emotion, suffering of loss and grief. Secondly, the performance helps them release fantasy, anxiety and anger and gives them kind of catharsis. Thirdly, their fluid and transgressive gender roles are constituted during the ritual process. The rituals' impact on Peter is out of expectation. He is changed from the "killer" of the imaginary boys to their "male role model" and "savior".

As the proposer of the "killing" action, Peter's original purpose is to exorcize the imaginary children from their life and usurp the father status in the family. Therefore, when Ruth and Anna take actions to "kill" their imaginary children, Peter becomes a curious eavesdropper and a close spectator, enquiring what is going on and showing concerns frequently. As an outsider, Peter is excluded from Orphan and Henri's "dying" rituals. His inquiry and urge sometimes irritate Anna and Ruth. When he asks, "When's it gonna happen?" Anna retorts, "Why? Want front-row seats?"(95) Peter is rejected and hated by Anna and Ruth as the real "killer" of their imaginary sons.

If Peter is like Stanley in *Streetcar*, as Mansbridge argues, "act as the masculine antagonistic force"(62) in the beginning of the play, he is influenced and won over gradually by Ruth and Anna. Invited by Ruth, Peter joins their mourning of Orphan. He wears the same black armband and takes Cecil and Henri to the zoo. Performing their "strong male role model"(98), Peter teaches them knowledge about animals and listens to Cecil's sad recitation of Darwin's theory of evolution attentively. As Cecil/Ruth recites "Let the Strongest Live, and the Weakest Die" (100), he/she cannot control his/her feeling and grips Peter and buries his/her head into Peter's side, weeping softly. At this moment, Peter does not stand antagonistic to Anna or Ruth. He cooperates with their roleplaying and gives his care and consolation to them. Shocked by Cecil/Anna's genuine grief, Peter feels kind of restless and guilty. He begins to understand the importance of the imaginary sons in Anna and Ruth's life.

Peter's traditional concept of fatherhood is changed by the "dying" ritual of Cecil. Peter was born and brought up in a broken family and had only a vague memory of his own father. Without a role model to learn from or imitate, he is very nervous and worried whether he could adapt to the role of a father. Confined to the traditional patriarchal paradigm, Peter is eager to dominate the central position and have all say in the family. Neither can he understand the lesbians' wild imagination nor accept the existence of the three imaginary children. He believes that fantasy is unhealthy for the real baby and it must be removed from their family. However, the angry accusation, intimate talk and tragic "suicide" on the "dying" ritual of Cecil/Anna shocks, moves and enlightens Peter. He begins to understand the meaning of fantasy for Anna and Ruth. At last, Peter shifts from an indifferent bystander of the ritual to an enthusiastic participator of it. He even changes his mind and attempts to stop Cecil's death in the middle of their performance. Especially, after Cecil/Anna's reveals, "We have a lot in common, Uncle Peter; Anna modeled me a little bit on you" (112), Peter realizes that killing Cecil in fact means killing part of himself. Cecil/Anna's last words "Don't ... be afraid ... to play with your child" (114) unveil a secret of being a good and successful father, that is, to be imaginative, creative and playful. Parenthood does not necessarily mean to give up one's fantasy and fun.

Peter's gender role is reconstructed after witnessing and participating in the above rituals. In the final scene, Vogel depicts a sweet picture of an ordinary family. Peter is cooking in the kitchen, Ruth is setting the table and Anna is nursing their son Nathan. They sit down to have supper and chat casually about the baby and their work. But Peter suddenly acts weirdly. He blanches and twitches slightly at first, then blows bubbles into his glass and stutters like Orphan, finally he falls from chair and rolls on the floor, shouting "Orphan! Revenge! Oorrrppphannn ... "(122). Imitating Ruth and Anna, Peter playacts Orphan and brings the three boys back to life, giving figurative birth to a newly reinvented Cecil, Orphan and Henri, who will coexist harmoniously with their real child, making the family as "seven". Peter is transformed from the "killer" of the imaginary children into the "savior" of them. Peter's voluntary acceptance of the imaginary children and identification with the "Woman Creating" means that Ruth and Anna have triumphed in their gender war. Peter has given up his previous patriarchal ideology and integrated successfully to the lesbian family.

When talking about her *Baby*, Vogel once said, "I think the structure of the play *is* the meaning of the play ... There is a sense of comic crisis in the structure of the play itself."(Bilowit 5f) She constructs the play aptly into a ritual-like structure in at least two dimensions. First, the dramatic action chronically stages the life of Ruth, Anna and Peter during the last weeks of Anna's pregnancy. It consists of three distinct phases: the threesome meet a crisis (Scene 1-5); they deal with the crisis by performing the imaginary children's "dying" rituals(Scene 6-12); they resolve the crisis by welcoming the birth of their real child and the rebirth of their imaginary children (Scene 13-14). This process constitutes what Arnold van Gennep defined "a rite of passage" and the three characters are in a liminal state during Scene 6 – 12. All of them, as liminal entities, are "neither here nor there; they are betwixt and between the positions assigned and arrayed by law, custom, convention, and ceremonial" (Turner, "Ritual Process" 95). They have to negotiate with each other and reconstruct their gender roles in order to overcome the crisis. In this sense, the play is realistic, representing a life crisis that a lesbian-gay family encounters and how they deal with the crisis by parodying "killing" and "dying" rituals.

Second, the successive "death" of Orphan, Henri and Cecil, the birth of the real child Nathan, and the resurrection of Orphan, Henri and Cecil form a cycle of death, birth and rebirth, which imitates the cyclical ritual of four seasons in nature and implies a feminine understanding of the circuitous nature of life. Opening the play with a Prologue in which Orphan, Henri and Cecil are discussing how babies are made in their "darkened" boy's room and concluding it with an Epilogue in which the reborn boys are talking about Peter's "tushy" in the same room, Vogel gives her play a perfect circular form, which again parodies the ritual of life-death-resurrection. In the prologue and epilogue of the play, it seems that nothing has changed, but the truth is that everything has changed. All these elements constitute the ritualistic feature of the play, in which both the comic spirit and the transformative power of the cyclical rituals of season and life are embodied.

Ⅱ. Identifying with the Other Through Fantasized "Rite of Loving Exorcism"

If fantasy and imagination take half of the stage in *And Baby Makes Seven*, they are given more space and significance in *The*

Chapter Three Subversion and Reconstruction 241

Baltimore Waltz. ① Similar to Ambrose Bierce's story "An Occurrence at Owl Creek Bridge", the entire action of *Waltz* takes place only in the heroine's mind at the shocked moment when she hears her brother's death. In the play, Anna is a schoolteacher who has been infected with a fatal disease —Acquired Toilet Disease(ATD), and travels through various European countries with her brother Carl in order to find a magic cure in black market. After going through the seven stages of terminal patient and encountering a series of absurd adventures, Anna is brought back to reality by a loud alarm clock, finding her brother dead in Baltimore hospital. She then dances the Baltimore Waltz with Carl's corpse in the "harsh, stark and white" stage lights(56). The audience do not realize that it is the brother rather than Anna who has a fatal disease, namely AIDS, until the last scene. In fact, Anna is the surrogate of Paula Vogel herself, and Carl in the play bears the same name with the playwright's homosexual brother Carl Vogel, who died of AIDS-related complications in 1988. Their journey to Europe, inspired by a trip the playwright failed to take with her brother, occurs just in Anna's imagination. It is "a fantasy trip, a mock quest which, like most quests, derives its meaning not from realizing its objective but from the journey itself"(Bigsby, "Contemporary" 307). The whole play, as Lloyd Rose points out, is "a hallucinatory, satirical, angry, fantastical outputting of her helpless grief"(C1). Combining painful tears and biting humor, the play touches on the themes of homophobia, homosexuality, feminine desire, sibling relationships

---

① *The Baltimore Waltz* was written in the summer of 1989, premiered October— November 1990 at the Perseverance Theater in Douglas, Alaska, and produced February 1992 at the Circle Repertory Company in New York City. It won the Obie Award in 1992. It has been reproduced in 1994, 1997, 2004 and 2011 respectively by different companies across America.

and discriminatory discourses surrounding AIDS.

  The Baltimore Waltz has been regarded as a ritual by the playwright as well as a few critics. On the front page of the play, Vogel writes, "To the memory of Carl—because I cannot sew"(3), which implies that this is Vogel's version of an AIDS quilt. AIDS Memorial Quilt is the largest ongoing community arts project designed by Cleve Jones in 1987 and joined by thousands of people in order to mourn the death and raise the awareness to prevent the disease. Sewing the quilt has become a communal ritual to honor the dead and bring healing to the person's loved ones. Besides this dedication, Vogel also prefaces the play with a letter written by Carl to her after Carl's first bout with pneumonia at Johns Hopkins Hospital, in which Carl gives a detailed description of his future funeral. First, concerning the choice between a religious ceremony and a memorial service, he prefers a traditional form and a woman cleric; second, he tells Paula the five-step rites to display his body at the funeral; third, he suggests some highbrow music as his funeral score; finally, he asks Paula to read A. E. Housman's poem "Loveliest of Trees" for him(4 – 5). With a flair for the theatrical and a bittersweet humor, Carl imagines his funeral as a performance that "everybody wants to direct" and his "role has been reduced involuntarily from player to prop"(4). Christopher Bigsby comments on Carl's expected memorial service as "an event that was to be part ceremony, part camp display, part celebration, an invitation to a continued friendship beyond the grave"("Contemporary" 307). In Playwright's Note, Vogel gives permission to all future production of *The Baltimore Waltz* to reprint the letter in the accompanying program in order to "let him speak to us in his own words"(4). By this way, Vogel ritualizes the play and immortalizes his brother since Carl's words will be read and his life will be relived every time the play is staged.

When *The Baltimore Waltz* premiered in 1992 at the Circle Repertory Company in New York City, Robert Brustein made a brief comment on the performance and concluded that the play was "a touching rite of loving exorcism, personal yet transcendent, tenderly written by Vogel" (29), emphasizing its sentimental effect and performative power. Joanna Mansbridge points out, "Vogel uses the theater as a public place of commemoration—a ceremony and celebration of personal and collective memories." ("Camp" 328) Performance studies scholar Peter Dickinson characterizes the play as a "queer ritual of remembrance" because it "challenges fundamentally the standard Freudian model of mourning" (201). Indeed, the play parodies psychoanalytic models of mourning and crafts the tragedy of death with comic humor and surreal fantasy.

Based on the previous discussion, this study argues that the play is both a ritual of exorcism to cast out Anna/Vogel's grief and a ritual of commemoration to mourn her brother Carl and other people who die of AIDS. It provides a liminal space and time for Anna as well as the playwright to translate her personal loss into public mourning, to recognize the homosexual other as the same human as the heterosexuals, and to reconstruct her female identity by incorporating Carl into her sense of self. Vogel makes full use of the transformative potentials of both mourning and fantasy by exchanging the roles of the mourner and the dead and parodying AIDS discourse and gender norms. As a typical feminist subversive gesture, Vogel places Anna firmly in charge of the audiences' gaze. Anna's point of view, for the most part, dominates the play, and her needs drive the action of the play. Anna gains the power to experience the suffering of the AIDS patients, to articulate their repressed desire, and to subvert the gendered stereotypes. At the same time, she empowers herself by performing the active subject in her sexual relationships with various men, subverting conventional stereotypes of female sexuality. Anna's identification and empowerment are realized through the symbolic signs, her performative languages and her subversive sexual acts.

When discussing the death caused by AIDS and the mourning for those lost lives, Judith Butler argues,

> One mourns when one accepts the fact that the loss one undergoes will be one that changes you, changes you possibly forever, and that mourning has to do with agreeing to undergo a transformation the full result of which you cannot know in advance. ("Undoing Gender" 18)

This notion resonates with Gennep and Turner's assertion that mourning is a complex transitional period for both the dead and the survivors. Similar to the situation in other rites of passage, the mourners go through three stages, namely, rites of separation, transition and incorporation, and are transformed permanently. The experience of mourning and grief, Butler further contends, reveals "who we are", delineates "the ties we have to others", and exposes "the constitutive sociality of the self" ("Undoing Gender" 20). The mourners suffer from a rupture of identity and are being dispossessed. In the history of the broad movement for sexual freedom, such dispossession has been realized through the notion of "ecstasy" which means "to be transported beyond oneself by a passion, but also to be *beside oneself* with rage or grief" ("Undoing Gender" 20). In *The Baltimore Waltz*, Anna, the mourner and the narrator, is overwhelmed by the grief of losing her brother and the rage over the stigmatization of homosexuals in American society. She falls into an "ec-static" state and lives out of her self temporarily, fantasizing that it is she, rather than her brother, that is dying. She is split and dispossessed. In order to reestablish the ties with her brother, Anna enters into her brother's world through the exchange of identity and finds out who her brother is and who she is.

Anna's identification with the other begins with her recognition of Carl's homosexual identity, which is not presented directly but implicated in a symbolic and closeted way in the play. There are a few signs that suggest Carl's homosexuality. The first one is the "pink triangle" Carl wears on his farewell to his students. Pink is a typical feminine color. It conveys ironically negative meaning when being used as an emblem for homosexuals. According to Richard Plant, "pink triangle" was originally designed to label homosexual prisoners in Nazi concentration camp during World War II with the connotation of shame and inferiority(175). However, its meaning was changed in the early 1980s by pioneers of the gay liberation movement. They wore the "pink triangle" deliberately to show their gay identity, which transformed the sign from a stigma of shame into a mark of gay pride. Before leaving his job as a librarian in the San Francisco Public Library, Carl teaches his pupils to cut out the "pink triangles" and asks the children to wear them during "Reading Hour with Uncle Carl". He even encourages the children to make pink triangles for their "Dad, Mom, brothers and sisters"(8). Without any preoccupied prejudice against this sign, the children enjoy making the "pink triangles" and wear them happily. Then they have a sing-along together. But their playful time is interrupted by Mrs. Bizio, who, according to Carl's reaction, asks Carl to leave immediately without waiting until Friday to collect unemployment. Although being absent from the stage, Mrs. Bizio represents the social authorities and regulations that expel the homosexuals as the other and punish them ruthlessly.

By staging Carl's rite of making and wearing "pink triangle", Vogel conveys several messages symbolically to the audience without mentioning any word like gay or homosexual. First of all, Carl is not only a gay but also an activist of gay movement. His last lesson is more than a playful entertainment, it is his preach to the young generation and to the adult audience as well, educating them to accept the "pink triangle"/homosexual as normal and beautiful. Secondly, Carl's expulsion from the library for his openly homosexuality and HIV positive status exposes the rampant homophobia and irrational fear concerning AIDS and calls the attention from the audience to the serious social persecution imposed on the homosexual other. Thirdly, by imagining Carl's farewell to job in this way, Anna expresses her understanding, sympathy and support to her brother's sexual orientation.

The most eye-catching, persistent and suggestive symbolic sign in the play is Carl's childhood rabbit named Jo-Jo, which, according to Vogel's production notes, should be "in every scene with Carl after Scene VI"(6). When they pack for their European trip, Carl grabs a stuffed rabbit and thrusts it in Anna's suitcase, which triggers a dialogue about the toy:

> Anna: What are you doing?
> Carl: We can't leave bunny behind.
> Anna: What is a grown man like you doing with a stuffed rabbit?
> Carl: I can't sleep without bunny.
> Anna: I didn't know you slept with ... stuffed animals.
> Carl: There's a lot you don't know about me. (15)

Carl's attachment to bunny is weird and unintelligible to Anna. His reply to Anna's questions suggests that there is a big gap between what Anna knows of him and what he really is. During the following trip, the stuffed rabbit appears more than ten times and becomes a dominant prop in the play, symbolizing something mysterious and secret that Carl conceals from Anna and all. Their travel turns out to be a hide-seek game: on the one hand, Anna is anxiously curious about the stuffed rabbit and wants some answers from her brother; on the other hand, Carl keeps his secret and insists that "there are some things you're better off not knowing"(30).

Anna's exploration of the meaning of the rabbit in fact is a process of her knowing and identifying with her brother. The process consists of three phases. In the first phase, Anna sees and feels Carl's extreme nervousness when they pass through airport security check and customs check. Every time, he takes the rabbit out of the bag and asks Anna to hold it. When Anna passes through smoothly with the stuffed rabbit in her hand, Carl sighs, relieved. But each time, the security guard looks at Carl suspiciously and almost strip-searches him. Anna is scared by Carl's abnormal behavior and asks why the rabbit is so special, Carl just tells her that "It's beyond measure. It's invaluable to me"(30).

In the second phase, Anna runs across Carl's secret dating with another man who wears the same clothes with Carl and holds the same stuffed rabbit. She also witnesses their intimate behavior— stroking the stuffed rabbits. Anna decides to get the truth from Carl since she believes that "whatever trouble he's in, he has to share it with me"(34). Then Carl makes a retrospective monologue, which reveals that he loved to play her sister's dolls when he was a child, but his parents believed that dolls were for girls, not boys, so they gave him the stuffed rabbit as an acceptable surrogate. In this way, a thin line is drawn by his parents to assure the "natural" gender of Carl.

According to Jin Lili, the parents are incarnation of the larger society which restricts people's sexual behaviors through constructed lines. The rabbit in their eyes symbolizes masculinity and heterosexuality. But Carl transgresses the conventional gender ideology by endowing the rabbit with sexual connotations different from what defined by his parents. In his monologue, Carl describes the rabbit in a sexual way, "He did not have the flaxen plastic hair of your sister's Betsey-Wetsy, but he had long, furry ears, soft white on one side, pink inside."(34) Jin contends that the stuffed rabbit represents "Carl's homosexual identity, a crucial composition of his individual" (134). Robert Post argues that the stuffed rabbit represents "lust, sexuality, or promiscuity"(47) because it has been displayed with Anna a few times when she makes love with different men. Both of them just see one side of the symbol but ignore its whole picture. In fact, the symbolic meaning of the stuffed rabbit changes with the course of the story. It belongs to Carl and represents his homosexuality at the beginning. Then it is transferred to Anna and becomes her rabbit too during the journey. In Scene 18, we see both Anna and Carl holding a stuffed rabbit after Carl narrates his childhood story about Jo-Jo and the Third Man sends the message that "he(Carl) is running out of time" (35). This is the moment that they identify with each other. Since then, the rabbit embodies all sexual desires that are repressed as "the other" in patriarchal society, no matter it is Anna's or Carl's, and no matter it is heterosexual or homosexual or bisexual.

In the final phase, as Anna awakes from her fantasy and returns to reality, she hugs the stuffed rabbit and realizes that Carl is dead. The rabbit, brought to the hospital by Anna to comfort Carl, becomes the embodiment of Carl himself. Anna discovers, recognizes and accepts her brother's homosexual identity through decoding the meaning of the stuffed rabbit. During the pursuing process, the audience follow Anna's eyes and find out the symbolic meaning of the stuffed rabbit and Carl's true sexual orientation gradually.

Historically, homosexual behaviors have long been regarded as sins and morally wicked. Homosexuality has been repressed, discriminated and persecuted as "the other" since the middle ages, which is demonstrated evidently in the "Wilde trials" in 1895. As "the love that dare not speak its name", it has been stigmatized as corruptive, morbid and evil. Neil Miller observes,

> One crucial factor was the biomedical conceptualization of homosexuality in an age that increasingly classified people by their sexual inclination—the heterosexual and the homosexual ... This new way of looking at homosexuality tended to stigmatize it, set it apart from the rest of society, and represent it as a medical condition or a symptom of degeneracy. (xxiii)

That is the reason that Carl tries his best to hide his true sexual orientation and Vogel presents homosexuality in such a suggestive and closeted way in *The Baltimore Waltz*. The stigmatization and otherness of homosexuals are worsened by the AIDS epidemic spread in the 1980s because the first two cases of AIDS happened to be discovered in gay men in New York and San Francisco in 1981. People consider AIDS as "gay cancer" or "Gay-Related Immune Deficiency" (Miller 440). As John Clum sums up, "AIDS is not disease, but retribution ... Therefore the person with AIDS should be isolated but not offered any of the benefit of society: compassion, government support for medical treatment" (41). In such social background, homosexuals who are infected with AIDS become the most marginalized "other" in the homophobia society. They are usually shunned and abandoned by their lovers and people around them. This serious issue has been depicted vividly in many AIDS dramas like Robert Chesley's *Night Sweat* (1984), William Hoffman's *As Is* (1985), Larry Kramer's *The Normal Heart* (1985), and Tony Kushner's *Angels in America: A Gay Fantasia on National Themes* (1992). Therefore, how to take AIDS homosexuals as they are and express their feelings faithfully thereby arouse audience's understanding and sympathy to them becomes a political issue.

In *The Baltimore Waltz*, as analyzed above, Vogel uses Anna's perspective to probe into the homosexual's world and reveals their anxiety, fear and anger in a symbolic way. However, it is not enough to just recognize Carl's homosexual identity since he is also an AIDS patient who has died of this epidemic. What is more significant is to feel what he feels and express the sufferings he undergoes during the illness. To achieve this aim, Vogel removes the AIDS virus and its attached, often homophobic stigmas and replaces it with the comic, somewhat silly "syndrome" of ATD, a virulent, hushed-up affliction that strikes down single schoolteachers who share the "johnny" with their young students (11). She then places Anna, the healthy one, in the position of Carl who suffers from AIDS, and lets her go through all the syndromes of ATD, which parodies that of AIDS. With this absurd transformation, Vogel changes the possible tear-jerking melodrama into a thought-provoking comedy, which is "profoundly feminist, profoundly personal and profoundly political " (Hammermeister 24).

Anna's second way to identify with "the other" is to be "the other" by herself. She imitates and performs the emotional terror, mental disorder and sexual lust that an AIDS patient is supposed to confront. As an ATD patient whose life is "cut down in the prime of youth by a toilet seat" (10), Anna experiences the terror, alienation and indifference caused by medical professionals as well as governmental institutions at first hand. Instead of explaining the disease in an intelligible language and slow speed, the Doctor bombards Anna and Carl with arcane medical jargon. He tells them, "There are exudative and proliferative inflammatory alternations of the endocardium, consisting of necrotic debris, fibrinoid material and disintegrating fibroblastic cells." (9) Overwhelmed by this nonsensical explanation, Anna and Carl are lost in the Doctor's language game and beg him to explain it slowly, which invites the Doctor's much longer and more difficult nonsense. Here, the Doctor's language is typical performative. The meaning of the words are not important, but the manner he articulates them and the effect they impose on Carl and Anna are more significant. They frighten and estrange Carl and Anna effectively. Carl and Anna, like two people drowned in deep water, struggle desperately and have to encourage each other by repeating "I'm right here, darling. Right here"(9). Anna finally exclaims in despair, "It's the language that terrifies me." (9) This sentence is the same line that she uses to describe her fear of going abroad. Similar to a foreign language, the Doctor's medical jargon is so strange to Anna that she feels a sense of helplessness and alienation.

In sharp contrast to the incomprehensible medical jargons, the Doctor shifts dramatically to naïve babyish language when talking about how to prevent the contract of ATD. He tells Anna, "I guess you should do what your mothers always told you. You know, wash your hands before and after going to the bathroom. And never lick paper or coins in any currency."(11) As for treatment, the Doctor knows nothing, and to Carl's question why nobody hears of this disease, he says it is kept as a secret in order to avoid political disaster. To some extent, the Doctor serves as the spokesman for the medical institution. Their indifferent attitude and irresponsible policy are further demonstrated in the comical Operation Squat announced by a Public Health official, in which single schoolteachers from twenty-four to forty are listed as high-risk and foolish instructions like "don't eat meals in public restrooms" are proclaimed. By parodying AIDS discourse in the absurd way, the play exposes the powerlessness and "otherness" of the AIDS patients in front of the medical and government authority and criticizes the institutional dysfunction in dealing with AIDS epidemic. Although ATD is coined ironically and the performance is astonishingly funny, Anna's pain and panic are real and obvious. Her terror and alienation re-present those of Carl and all other AIDS patients vividly.

Besides shock and alienation, Anna also experiences Carl's otherness through her enactment of the mental problems of a dying patient. In response to the dehumanized treatment of dying disease and in order to understand and help the terminally ill patients, Elizabeth Kubler Ross puts forward six psychological stages that they will travel through in the course of illness: "Denial and Isolation, Anger, Bargaining, Depression, Acceptance and Hope."(8) With the Third Man's introduction of each stage, Anna simulates and performs the six stages one by one sequentially in Scene 14. In the Denial and Isolation stage, Anna is seen sitting upright at night, sleepless, lonely and suspicious. She cannot believe she would die soon and suspects that the Doctor mixes her specimens up with others'. While in the stage of Anger, Anna interrogates "how could this happen to me" with roaring fury(27). Her long monologue reveals that she has been a faithful, responsible and innocent primary schoolteacher for the past ten years, doing nothing evil and giving her best years of life to those kids who, according to the Doctor, possibly transmit the virus to her. Literally, Anna's self-reflection expresses her anger to the unfair fate, but implicitly, her words mock and question the moralizing rhetoric surrounding AIDS discourse in the 1980s, which associates AIDS with immoral sexual activities among gay man. By taking a single, female, heterosexual schoolteacher as the victim of ATD, Vogel disables the moralizing impulse underlying debates about the illness. Vogel articulates her critique through Carl's mouth. When Anna worries that people would know her illness, he reminds her, "It's not a crime. It's an illness." (17) This is one of the most pointed and political line in the play. Anna's case shows that ATD/AIDS is just a disease rather than a form of retribution for the immoral "crime" of homosexual activity. By fantasizing the traumatic experience of ATD patients, Anna displays their pain and panic on stage.

What deserves special attention is that Vogel highlights Carl's response to Anna's performance. At the first stage, Carl pulls Anna down on the bed to him and strokes her brow when Anna says she cannot sleep. Then, "they change positions on the bed"(27). During the entire process, Carl sleeps on the same bed with Anna, accompanying her and offering comfort. They often hold each other's hands like children and express love and commitment to each other. They always "change positions" at the end of every stage. This ritualistic behavior implies that the siblings have merged with each other and become a symbiotic one. What Carl has done for Anna is exactly what Anna has dreamed of doing for Carl. Their innocent togetherness reveals the playwright's ideal that people should be kind and warm to AIDS patients, which lacks in reality. In the society as well as in some AIDS plays, people usually are cold and cruel to their loved ones who are diagnosed as HIV positive. For example, Rich in Hoffman's *As Is* is shunned by his lover and people around him. Louis in Kushner's *Angel's in America* leaves his lover Prior helpless and lonely in his sickbed. Vogel presents a different vision in this play, proposing a critique to society and a hope for correction. Carl's selfless love to Anna and Anna's identification with Carl indicate the possible inclusion of AIDS "other" into healthy "self".

In addition to the above six stages, Vogel adds Lust to Ross's paradigm as the seventh stage, believing that body, the carrier of disease, is also the weapon to combat disease. Driven by "a growing urge to fight the sickness of the body with the health of the body" (29), Anna starts her sexual adventure in Europe after being assured by the Doctor that she cannot infect anyone through love-making. Reversing her image as a "good girl" who lives up to the social norms and conventions in the past thirty years, Anna takes initiatives in seducing "every Thomas, Deiter und Heinrich" (42) and has sexual encounters with the French Garcon, the Little Dutch Boy at 50, the Munich Virgin, and the Radical Student Activist in succession during her journey.

However, Anna's promiscuity cannot be interpreted literally or realistically since Vogel applies Brechtian Alienation Effect to her depiction of Anna's sexual acts. For example, all the men that Anna makes love with are played by one single actor, which draws the actor out of the characters and turns the audience's attention from the individual man to the message their sexual acts convey. Also, Anna often distances herself from the action she is doing and narrates her own experience to the audience with a detached tone of a historian. Another A-Effect method is to place Carl in the position of observer and participator: sometimes watching and commenting on Anna's sexual behavior, and sometimes lying on the same bed with Anna and her lover. These A-Effect techniques not only astonish the audience thereby estrange them from these scenes, but also provoke them to re-see and re-think the male body and the female desiring subject in sexual relationships. In this sense, Anna's sexual adventure is her

Chapter Three   Subversion and Reconstruction   255

unique way to identify with Carl's desire for men and her subversive act to deconstruct the otherness in sexual politics through her body.

When being questioned as to why she portrays Anna as an initiator in the sexual relationship, Vogel replies,

> In my plays, I want to present women as desiring subjects, which means that men sometimes become the object of the female gaze ... [In *The Baltimore Waltz*] I wanted to pay homage to my brother's desire for men. In order to do that I used a woman subject desiring the male body. I wanted the audience to appreciate how beautiful the male body is. Some women automatically do that, so I used a woman, and through a female subject, straight men who are homophobic would go, yeah, I can see how she finds him beautiful. And if I've got them there, I've got the entire audience understanding that the male body can be a desired object. And then I am halfway there in terms of overcoming our homophobia towards men on stage. (Vogel, "Interview")

It is clear that Vogel's intention in choosing a woman as the protagonist is to invite all audience, male or female, straight or gay, to appreciate the beauty of male body and sympathize with the AIDS patients. Because of the deep-rooted social prejudice against homosexuality, man's desire for man or homoerotic desire has been excluded from the stage or presented in extremely implicit way in theatrical history. Male body in homosexual relationship is usually twisted as morbid and evil, seldom celebrated as beautiful and desirable. "Gay body" has long been stigmatized as some kind of 'third sex', neither male nor female (Clum 20). Homosexual intercourse is regarded as illicit, secretive, dirty, or deviant and male body is viewed as the uncanny other by audience. The AIDS epidemic further reinforces such discrimination and stigmatization. Therefore, it is difficult and risky to present male-male desire directly in the 1990s. Vogel's conceit here is to look at male body through Anna's eyes, transforming the focus from a homosexual, male perspective to a heterosexual, female one.

Anna begins her exploration of male body at the Left Bank in France while Carl enjoys the "phallic" art in this "haven for outcasts, foreigners and students"(19). Her first sexual adventure is to seduce the French Garcon, to make love with him in her hotel room, and to learn basic French vocabulary of body parts by touching his body from neck to phallus. Though all these acts are realized through Anna's body, Carl has never been absent from these scenes. In Scene 12, the instruction reads, "Anna and the Garcon are shapes beneath the covers of the bed; Carl clutches his stuffed rabbit."(22) Vogel juxtaposes Carl's introduction of Jean Baptiste Camille Corot with Anna and the Garcon's love-making, Carl's cold lecture being frequently interrupted by their hot exciting sounds. As Anna and her Parisian Garcon reach a climax of self-in-relation—shouting in unison "I-I-I-I- /Je! -Je! -Je! -Je"—Carl tells the audience, "In art, as in life, some things need no translation."(23) Indeed, as Mansbridge points out, "sex is the only literal thing in the play—nothing more and nothing less than what it is."("Paula Vogel" 156) Body pleasure in sex is a pure primitive language that both man and woman, both homosexuals and heterosexuals could share. Then in Scene 13 "Basic Vocabulary. Parts of Body", Carl "slightly out of the next scene, watches them"(23), which means all Anna sees will be seen by Carl and all Anna does with her body will be done by Carl through his mind. Under Anna and Carl's double views, the beauty of man's body is presented through Anna's narration,

> Lying here, watching him sleep, I look at his breast and remember the

Chapter Three Subversion and Reconstruction

rose with its single, pathetic thorn for protection. And here—his puckered red ripple, lying poor and vulnerable on top of his blustering breast plate. It's really so sweet about men. (24)

Anna touches and appreciates the Garcon's body in the same way as Carl appreciates David's painted body in Louvre.

Anna's sexual adventure with the Radical Student Activist in Germany is also under Carl's gaze. The stage direction of Scene 24 goes, "In the hotel room. Anna, awake, lies in the middle of the bed. To her left, Carl sleep, curled up. To her right, the Radical Student Activist, curled on her breast, slumbers." (45) This is a tranquil scene after a stormy sexual intimacy, in which two male bodies are displayed in front of Anna. Then Anna addresses the audience,

> In lovemaking, he's all fury and heat. His North Sea pounding against your Dreamer. And when you look up and see his face, red and huffing, it's hard to imagine him ever having been a newborn, tiny, wrinkled and seven pounds. That is, until afterwards. When he rises from sleep and he walks into the bathroom. And there he exposes his soft little derriere, and you can still see the soft baby flesh. (45)

Here, Anna uses the second person "you" instead of the first person "I" to comment on their love-making. This grammatical switch invites Carl as well as the audience to gaze at the male body with her together, reversing the gendered, traditionally masculine gaze of the theater. In Anna's eyes, the male body is as powerful as the North Sea and as pure and delicate as baby flesh. It is admirable and desirable, representing the vitality and force of nature. By using a woman as a desiring subject and presenting two male bodies unrealistically, Vogel achieves her original purpose: to get her entire audience, both women and men, understanding that male body can be a desired object and homosexuality is as healthy and pleasurable as heterosexuality. In this way, Anna/Vogel identifies with Carl's desire for man and includes him as an acceptable member of human community with Kristeva's "ethic of respect for the irreconcilable" ("Strangers" 182).

Anna's sexual acts are politically subversive not only in terms of male homosexuality but also in terms of female heterosexuality. In traditional heterosexual matrix, woman is the other, the inferior, and man usually occupies the position of desiring subject position and gazes at the objectified female body. By staging Anna as the desiring subject and endowing her the power to gaze at male body, the play reverses the conventional stereotypes of female sexuality. Anna is neither an innocent victim of a disease nor a stigmatized whore, she is a first-grade schoolteacher who rebels against her earlier self and decides to "fuck her brains out"(12) in order to make up for lost time. The "good girl" constructed by patriarchal ideology is meaningless for her now. She discards the traditional notions of femininity such as being passive, chaste and weak. Her virile sexuality is characterized in the play as active, inherent and spontaneous, the qualities that are traditionally attached to masculinity. Anna once argues with Carl that she goes out to "get fucked" rather than "to fuck" because "the passive voice is used to emphasize the subject, to indicate the truth of the generalization" (43). Anna's subjectivity is not only embodied in her torrid sexual encounters with various men, but also in the initiatives she takes in their sexual relationships.

During her tryst with the Munich Virgin, a very young bellhop, Anna assumes a position of ritual initiator. Similar to that of Lily

Chapter Three   Subversion and Reconstruction   259

who initiates Archie into adulthood in *The Holdup*, Anna's seduction of the Munich Virgin has a tender, almost maternal quality. After their loving-making, she tells the virgin,

> Anna: Is this your first time? You always remember your first time. (*pause*) I'm very honored. (*pause*) Listen. I'm a schoolteacher. May I tell you something? A little lesson? When you're a much older man, and you've loved many women, you'll be a wonderful lover if you're just a little bit nervous ... like you are right now. Because it will always be the first time.
> Munich Virgin: You are a very nice woman.
> Anna: The human body is a wonderful thing. Like yours. Like mine. The beauty of the body heals all sickness, all the bad things that happen to it. And I really want you to feel this because if you feel it, you'll remember it. And then maybe you'll remember me. (41)

Here, Anna plays a role of a teacher who gives lessons about sex and body. She transforms the Munich Virgin into a mature man, leading him from innocence to experience and teaching him how to feel the healing and life force of human body. For Anna, sex is a healing act that does not carry disease, but combats it, and body is a locus of beauty and love, where the memories of those we are connected to can be stored and will be reanimated through sensations in the future. Anna, like Li'l Bit in relation to the young man on the bus trip in *How I Learned to Drive*, turns to be the first, the translator and the teacher of the virgin.

In another scene, though ironically, Anna tells the Radical Student Activist, "You just committed a revolutionary act with a first-grade schoolteacher who lives in low-income housing."(46) This declaration suggests that Anna agrees with the Radical Student Activist on his ideas that fucking is revolutionary act and that sex by two complete strangers is something radical that exists outside of bourgeois conventions of love, capitalist system and patriarchal family ethics. For Anna, all her sexual encounters through the journey are like politically revolutionary acts to subvert patriarchal gender stereotypes. However, Anna goes much further than the Radical Student Activist by confessing her low marginalized status in the highly hierarchical society, expressing her will against social injustice towards the other. Before the student's departure, Anna points out his naivety and hypocrisy by telling him, "the missionary position does not a revolution make" (46), which again shows her subversive spirit in gender politics.

During mourning, the ritual subjects, usually the family members, have to understand the meaning of death, feel their loss fully and incorporate the sense of loss into their new self-hood before they could move on and reenter normal life. Mansbridge argues, "the erratic movements of Anna's fantasy journey is itself the work of mourning."("Camp" 335) In the play, Anna goes through the three mourning stages by learning foreign languages, animating childhood memories and dancing Waltz with Carl's ghost.

The ritualistic repetition of the new sentence structure "there is nothing (one) can do" denotes the difficulty for Anna to understand and accept Carl's death. The play begins with Anna practicing her language lessons in preparation for her imagined journey. The first words she says are: "Help me please. (*Recites from memory*) Dutch 'Kunt U mij Helpen, alstublieft?' 'There's nothing I can do.' French (*Searches in vain*) I have no memory."(7) "There's nothing I can do" relates back to the moment when the doctor at the John Hopkins Hospital in Baltimore says to Anna, "I'm sorry ... There was nothing we could do"(9), which announces the death of Carl. Anna's helplessness in memorizing the foreign languages resonates her powerlessness and desperation in hearing the Doctor's verdict. In her language lessons, Anna repeats this line in various possessive cases, "There is nothing I can do. There is nothing you can do. There is nothing he, she, or it can do. There is nothing we can do. There is nothing they can do."(14) On the surface, it shows how hard to learn a foreign language. However, its repetition is performative, confirming the truth of Carl's death, helping Anna to understand the news and releasing her anguish and grief. This ominous line echoes throughout the play and provides a point of return at the play's end. When the Doctor expresses his regret by saying "I, uh, if there's anything I can do", Anna responds calmly, "Thank you, but there is nothing you can do."(57) This dialogue suggests that Anna finally understands and accepts the finality of Carl's death. She has to face the permanent loss bravely.

The irreversible departing and losing are delayed and prolonged by Anna's memory and fantasy, which provides her more time to feel and assimilate the loss fully. Creating *The Baltimore Waltz* as a heartfelt elegy for her dead brother, Vogel weaves her traumatic feelings of loss into the recollections of her childhood shared with Carl. Alan Shepard and Mary Lamb argue, "Vogel makes her characters preoccupied with the topos of memory as well as the memories recollected on stage."(199) In the play, Anna's fantasy journey is often interrupted by her sweet or bitter memories when the siblings were together. One special memory narrated by the Third Man titled "The first separation—your first sense of loss" vividly depicts Anna's attachment to Carl and her unwillingness to sleep separately when their parents forced her to at the age of five. Anna would climb back to Carl's bed secretly and "fall to sleep, breathing in the scent of your own breath and his seven-year-old body"(17). Anna has felt the sense of loss and the scare of separation since at the very early age. The childhood memories she invokes link her sense of separation in the past to her feeling of loss at the present moment. Anna's memory is rooted in the body and she hopes to keep these memories through bodily touch. She tells Carl, "When I hold your hand, and I kiss it ... I try to memorize what it looks like, your hand ... I wonder if there's any memory in the grave?"(28) Their togetherness during the fantastical trip, which is always jeopardized by separation, is Anna's deliberate deferment to face Carl's death. Anna assimilates the loss of her brother by reconstructing pieces of her childhood memories and imagining their companionship during the surreal journey.

 The incorporation of the dead into the life of the mourner is embodied in Anna's Baltimore Waltz dance with Carl at the end of the play. After her long surreal fantasy and failed efforts to animate Carl's stiff dead body, Anna is seen to dance with Carl in the dreamy atmosphere. The stage direction writes, "Softly, the Strauss waltz begins. Carl, perfectly well, waits for Anna. He is dressed in Austrian military regalia. They waltz off as the lights dim."(57) With the changes of music, lighting and costume, Vogel presents a romantic harmonious heterosexual dancing scene. However, this waltz is danced with a partner who is dead and will forever be absent. Similar to the ghost of Orphan in *And Baby Makes Seven* and the ghost of Uncle Peck in *How I Learned to Drive*, the ghost of Carl also symbolizes a lost other, with which the ritual subject wants to identify. According to David Savran,

> Virtually every ghost in the contemporary theater signals a crisis in the construction of the subject, for whom the ghost represents an other who has

been lost and yet is imagined to inhere both inside and outside the self. ("Modernity's Haunted Houses" 121)

By dancing with the ghost of Carl, Anna opens herself to the lost brother and embraces Carl's absolute otherness as a dead man. The symbolic resurrection of Carl becomes a permanent gesture of commemoration.

The Baltimore Waltz is like an elaborate quilt that Paula Vogel sews for her brother. It repeats and suspends her personal moment of loss. She weaves all her memories of love, pain, grief, anger and helplessness into the art object and turns the theater into a public altar to commemorate Carl as well as all gay men who die of AIDS. At the same time, it transcends affective mourning and remembrance and expands to political domain. As Butler points out, maintaining the grief and staying with the sense of loss do not mean that we are left only passive and powerless. It can become a resource for politics ("Undoing Gender" 23). Vogel transforms the ritual of commemoration into a field of sexual and gender politics. Anna's fantasy trip gives her an opportunity to express and accomplish her sexual desire as a female subject. She is not a passive object who are gazed by males but an active subject who gazes at male body. Anna's journey with Carl is also "a journey into the strangeness of the other and of oneself, toward an ethics of respect for the irreconcilable" (Kristeva 182). Her experiences parody and criticize the ridiculous discourses concerning homosexuality and AIDS in the late 1980s and early 1990s. Her sympathy and identification with Carl, the exiled gay AIDS other, is a political act which overturns the conservative AIDS rhetoric and integrates the other into "I" and community. In her Pulitzer Prize play *How I Learned to Drive*, Vogel continues to take drama as a ritualistic journey to explore sexual and gender politics.

Ⅲ. Shifting Power Through Parodied Rites of Initiation and Courtship

How I Learned to Drive is Vogel's most celebrated play. Since its premiere in February 1997, the reviews of it have been almost unanimous in their praise of the playwright's keen sense of balance and the play's nuanced depiction of a controversial subject—child sexual abuse. However, critics hold opposite attitude towards Vogel's portrayal of Peck, the pedophilia, and his sexual relationship with Li'l Bit, the teenage girl. *New York Observer*'s John Heilpern, *Washington Post*'s Michael Toscano, London reviewer Paul Taylor, and many others criticize that the play is lack of moral judgment, that the blunt categories of victim and pedophile are not maintained, and that Vogel is unable to state who or what is right or wrong (Heilpern 1997; Taylor 1999; Toscano 2004). Kim Bowers blames that Vogel "perpetuates incest myths by creating sympathy for Peck" and "romanticizing the abuse Li'l Bit endures from Peck"(28). In contrast, some critics call it a "love story" and describe the abuse Li'l Bit suffers as "empowering" and "beneficial". Michael Feingold of *The Village Voice* praises the play for being "the sweetest and most forgiving play ever written about child abuse"("All for Love" 2). Jill Dolan feels that Peck's attraction towards and objectification of Li'l Bit empowers her in the midst of a bad family life (127). Laurie Stone of *The Nation* reduces the sexual abuse in the play to "a lousy deal" and suggests that Li'l Bit controls Peck and "likes the power" (2).

Such conflicting interpretations stem from both Vogel's deliberate ambiguity and the critics' neglect of the play's shifting patterns of power between Peck and Li'l Bit. In fact, Vogel, as she once expressed, has "no interest in a movie-of-the-week drama about child-molesting", she wants, rather, "to see if audiences will allow themselves to find this erotic; otherwise, they only see victimization without empowerment" (Druckman, "A Playwright on the Edge" H6). Female empowerment is one of the playwright's original intentions. Vogel has talked of her alarm at a victim culture in the United States. She said, "I hate the word victim. It's a buzz word people use these days." (Druckman, "A Playwright on the Edge" H6) She is disturbed by the feminist theater that portrays the woman as unequivocal victim without a way out. Vogel is not content simply to condemn or sentimentalise. She wants to "create a man who was, in a way, a love object to a woman as subject" and "wanted the arrows to reverse themselves in the course of the play" (Bigsby, "Contemporary" 320). As a feminist retaliation of Nabokov's *Lolita*, *How I Learned to Drive* puts a young woman in the driver's seat and gives her the narrative voice through which to direct the story. Critics who blame Vogel just see her sympathy to Peck but ignore her empowerment of Li'l Bit. Feminist critics like Dolan have recognized the empowering force hidden in the sexual relationship between Peck and Li'l Bit. However, they have not made any convincing analysis on the empowering mechanism or Vogel's dramatic technique to realize the transfer of power.

Without denying the pain and hurt that Li'l Bit suffers, Vogel has attempted to transcend the sentimental victimization and find out a way for the victim to move on. Just as Misako Koike argues, "Vogel is almost the first playwright who allows the central female character to survive sexual and other scandals."(101) Therefore, the key to understand this play is to know how the empowerment of Li'l Bit takes place. A few questions need to be explored: How does power shift from Peck to Li'l Bit? How Peck is objectified? And what female self Vogel has constructed in the transitional process of power? This study argues that Vogel has parodied a few patriarchal rituals and reverses the gender status and power pattern in the original ritual in order to disempower Peck and simultaneously empower Li'l Bit.

There are two different rituals that run through the entire play. The first one is Li'l Bit's learning to drive, which is "an essential rite of passage for any American teenager outside of New York City" (Whately 18). The other one is the sexual awakening of and exploration by the female protagonist Li'l Bit from age eleven to eighteen, which parodies the rite of initiation for boys. When discussing Li'l Bit's coming of age, C. Bigsby points out, "reverse the gender and you have an entirely familiar genre of novels and plays in which young boys are initiated into manhood by understanding women, accommodating prostitutes and even aggressive and sex-hungry matrons." ("Modern" 417) Vogel weaves the two ritual processes together and presents the gender power politics between a middle-aged married man and a sexually inexperienced girl.

Besides the two prolonged rituals, there are a few episodic rituals inserted between the driving lessons. However, none of the rituals is normal or genuine. The typical family dinner turns out to be sexual harassment of Li'l Bit from all family members who poke fun at her big breasts. The celebration dinner proves to be Peck's deliberate seduction of Li'l Bit in terms of both drinking and sex. "The Initiation into a Boy's First Love" is performed not for a boy but for a girl. Peck harbors a hope of changing Li'l Bit's eighteenth birthday celebration into his marriage proposal, but the rite of courtship in his eyes is mocked and subverted by Li'l Bit and the Female Greek Chorus, resulting in his objectification and degradation. Among them, the rites of initiation and courtship are the two turning points of Peck—Li'l Bit power structure.

The section titled as "The Initiation into a Boy's First Love" plays a decisive role in Li'l Bit's empowerment and self-formation. "Initiation" here is a pun with double meanings. Firstly, it means the act of starting something. The monologues spoken in turn by Peck and Li'l Bit at the beginning of the scene shows that "The Initiation into a Boy's First Love" refers to Peck's falling love with car when he was just a boy. As a country on wheel, America has always promoted the concept that owing a car means achieving a high status. Car has become the symbol of power, status and identity, especially for man. Katherine Parkin's study suggests, in America, "car ownership offered the wealthy an affirmation of their privileged status" and "offered people speed, ease, pleasure, and expediency" (3). Man's "love affair" with the automobile is illustrated vividly by Peck's obsession with luxury high-speed automobiles. He says, "my favorite car will always be the '56 Bel Air Sports Coupe ... went from zero to sixty miles per hour in 8.9 seconds."(32) Man's love to car happens at his adolescent age, in Li'l Bit's words, "long after a mother's tits, but before a woman's breasts ... after the milk but before the beer ... long after he's squeezed down the birth canal but before he's pushed his way back in" (32). During this period, car takes the place of mother and wife. In this sense, a boy's first love to car refers to Peck's initial experience of growing up and domineering something that is lovely and obedient. In men's eyes, car is like a woman, "someone who responds to your touch" and "the thing that bears his weight with speed"(33). Peck calls car a "baby" and a "she". Vogel highlights the analogy of car and woman by presenting slides of erotic photographs of women and cars on stage, "women posed over the hood, women draped along the sideboards"(32), which indicates the symbolic signification of car and the objectification of woman in

American culture.

"Initiation" also means a special ceremony by which a boy or a girl is officially accepted as a member of an organization or an adult. In this sense, "The Initiation into a Boy's First Love" refers to the rite for Li'l Bit's falling love with car—the man's toy, and her entry into the world of men, acquiring confidence and power that are traditionally considered as masculine. Although the rites of initiation vary in different regions and cultures, their social function is similar. Traditionally, female initiation rites usually are performed individually for girls and coincide with puberty, emphasizing womanhood and the girl's responsibility for her future marriage, her future husband and children, and duty to others in the community. Male initiation rites prepare boys for adulthood and manhood and emphasize male duties. Usually, female initiation is guided by female adults and male initiation by male adults (Salamone 7-9). However, Vogel does not follow any rule of traditional rites of initiation in *How I Learned to Drive*. The guide of Li'l Bit is not an older woman but a middle-aged man. What she learns is not womanhood or family duties that a girl should know but some personalities that only man could own traditionally. It seems that Vogel names Li'l Bit's first driving lesson deliberately as "The Initiation into a Boy's First Love" in order to foreground Li'l Bit's dramatic change from a "girl" into a "man". Vogel parodies and reverses the traditional rites of initiation for both males and females.

Before the initiation, Li'l Bit is a "typical girl": naive, curious, vulnerable and powerless, being sexualized and objectified by people around her. Li'l Bit is abandoned by her father at very early age and is eager to have an adult man to depend on, which exposes her to the danger of sexual harassment. As an adolescent girl, Li'l Bit is curious about sex, but her grandmother and mother provide her with totally opposite notions of loving-making, which confuses and frightens the little girl. Her precocious body attracts too much attention and malicious tease. Her grandpa, who believes that women are at best breeding machines, grasps every chance to sexualize Li'l Bit. He jokes, "if Li'l Bit gets any bigger, we're gonna haveta buy her wheelbarrow to carry in front of her [breasts]." (13) He even laughs at Li'l Bit's plan of going college by asking "what does she need a college degree for?" and mocks that "she's got all the credentials she'll need on her chest"(14). In school, Li'l Bit's male classmates pretend to be allergic and grab her breast to check whether it is made of foam rubber. Her female classmates peep at her body secretly in bathroom.

Growing up in such an over-sexualized environment, Li'l Bit feels angry, ashamed and helpless. Her body, especially the two developing breasts turn to be a heavy burden for her. She says, "I feel like these alien life forces, these two mounds of flesh have grafted themselves onto my chest ... they'll just keep growing ... until I collapse under their weight". (39) Although Peck behaves like a gentleman and takes care of Li'l Bit like a father, he is in fact a calculated and practiced seducer who occupies the dominant position in their relation. He molests Li'l Bit by sitting her between his legs during a mock driving lesson when she was just eleven years old and caresses her breasts once a week in his car in the following several years. When Li'l Bit is thirteen years old, Peck brings her to his basement and takes sexy pictures for her. David Savran considers that the photo shoot graphically represents Li'l Bit's objectification because she "has become an actor in a drama that has been scripted for her by an exploitative, if well-meaning spectator who is, in turn, the product of a society that values women for their allure" ("Playwright's Voice" 264). Kimbrough argues further, "When the audience focuses on Li'l Bit, they are in part unwittingly standing in Uncle Peck's shoes, gazing at her through the lens of the camera." (53) In a word, Li'l Bit is a sexualized object, a weak prey that Peck is "stalking"(15).

Exposed to Peck's sexual exploitation for years, Li'l Bit is always in a position of alertness and self-defense while they are together alone. When she gets into the driver's seat, she still behaves as an ignorant girl. Her reply to Peck's question "what's the first thing you're going to adjust" is "giggle" and "my bra strap"(33). As Peck tells her to lock the car doors, she jokes sarcastically that "but I'm locked in with you"(34). When Peck asks her to put her two hands on the wheel, she hesitates and worries, retorting "how do I defend myself" (34). On the one hand, Li'l Bit's psychology has been distorted so much that she is too conscious of her body and behaves too feminine. She even becomes frivolous. On the other hand, Li'l Bit does not take driving as a serious business. Her manner in the car is girlish and playful. However, Peck, as the mentor, is extraordinarily serious and strict. He commands Li'l Bit to turn off the radio and concentrate all her attention "with surprising firmness" (33). In order to remove Li'l Bit's anxieties and usher her into his lesson, Peck changes his tone and promises softly, "Now, listen. Listen up close. We're not going to fool around with this. This is a serious business. I will never touch you when you are driving a car." (34) Affected by Peck's words, Li'l Bit turns to be focused and earnest. Vogel ritualizes this scene by emphasizing Peck's consistent solemnity and the gradual change of Li'l Bit's attitude.

Both with a serious attitude, Peck and Li'l Bit enter into the initiation, which consists of three steps: gazing at hands, delivering a speech and taking a vow. The first step is brief but solemn. Being silent for a while, Peck instructs Li'l Bit "to lift your hands for a second and look at them"(34). Although feeling a bit silly, Li'l Bit raises her hands and gazes at them. Peck says to her simultaneously, "Those are your two hands. When you are driving, your life is in your hands. Understand?"(34) As a novice, Li'l Bit seems puzzled by this, but she feels its significance from Peck's seriousness and nods her head firmly.

Since driving in this play is both a fact and an extended metaphor, Peck's words could be interpreted literally as well as symbolically. On the one hand, Peck teaches Li'l Bit where to put her hands and how to control the wheel when driving a car and assures her that driving is a serious business. On the other hand, he offers her a lesson in responsibility for her own life. This ritual act is so effective that it changes Li'l Bit permanently because, as we learn from Li'l Bit later, it was the nine and three o'clock position and Peck's philosophy that saved her life when she sped on Maryland road alone at night with whiskey, desperation and suicidal impulse in 1970.

What constitutes the main part of the initiation is the second step—Peck's touching yet stern speech to Li'l Bit, which is a typical speech act that not only communicates something but also does something. It is easy to catch the semantic meaning of Peck's speech, but the illocutionary acts he performs and the perlocutionary effects he produces are far more complicated. In saying these words, Peck at least accomplishes three kinds of acts. First of all, he declares his genuine love to Li'l Bit by comparing her to his own son and offering her the most important thing he could give. He says, "I don't have any sons. You're the nearest to a son I'll never have—and I want to give you something. Something that really matters to me."(34) Although he has been an evil abuser in his darkest side since long time ago, Peck is "a loving and lovable figure—a caring complex man"

(Craig 220) and is sincerely attentive of his niece. Regardless of his intention, at the core of his speech is love. Secondly, he promises Li'l Bit that he will give her a sense of power behind the wheel of a car and teach her to drive like a man. As an instructor, Peck is dead serious about teaching Li'l Bit how to drive a car. He is fixed on conveying to his student the importance of power that comes with driving by affirming her "there's something about driving that nobody can take from you"(34). It is, he announces, "a power". "I feel more myself in my car than anywhere else. And that's what I want to give to you."(34) To him, men are taught to drive with confidence and aggression while women tend to be polite and hesitant, which can be fatal. He wants to train Li'l Bit like his son and change her into a masculine driver. The third act that Peck performs is to warn Li'l Bit that she must watch out for what the other guy is going to do before he does it. Only in this way could she survive car accidents and "be the only one to walk away"(35).

Peck's speech also performs several perlocutionary acts, which, according to J. L. Austin, are "what we bring about or achieve by saying something, such as convincing, persuading, deterring, and even, say, surprising or misleading" (108). The immediate perlocutional effect is that Li'l Bit is attracted and persuaded by Peck. As Peck asks her whether she is going to drive with him, Li'l Bit replies determinedly, "I will, Uncle Peck. I want you to teach me to drive"(35), which is her vow to follow Peck's driving creed and learn from him. This is the moment when Li'l Bit is initiated into a Boy's first love in terms of driving. She, as Peck once did, falls in love with car. She begins to know the car inside and out in the next four weeks and gets her driver's license after a few months. Peck is an excellent teacher, as Li'l Bit confirms later, "I never so much as got a ticket. He taught me well."(17) Li'l Bit is a good student too.

Chapter Three Subversion and Reconstruction

She responds quiet seriously to his instruction and finally gains a sensation "of flight in the body"(58) when she is driving.

The long-term and more important perlocution is that it empowers and masculinizes Li'l Bit. In Peck's speech, Vogel highlights gender differences in driving and affirms that the road belongs to men. She also lets Peck gender his car as female, which arouses Li'l Bit's curiosity. However, Li'l Bit decides not to change the gender after Peck explains his erotic feeling of touching and controlling a car. This implies that Li'l Bit has identified herself with masculinities. She wants to drive like a man, which, as Donald Lyons points out, "in this culture meant, we see, like a free person." Li'l Bit is enlightened to know that driving can give her the sense of strength and power that defines a man. She must "steal" them from Peck regardless of the risk of being molested by him. In this sense, power now is being shifted from Peck's hands to Li'l Bit's. She is initiated to a man's domain rather than a woman's world. Becoming confident and aggressive, she not only masters Peck's lessons on "power" and "control" of a car but also enjoys having them in her hands through her life. She learns to take a masculine position, both in the driver's seat and in broader social interactions. The metaphor of the driving lesson and Li'l Bit's experiences reinforce that gender is not something that is born, but something that is taught and constructed. Masculinity can be manifested in both male and female bodies.

Another perlocutional effect is that Peck has forged Li'l Bit into into a weapon against himself without knowing it. When he instructs her in the need to "think what the other guy is going to do before he does it"(35), he plants something more than a piece of road craft advice in her mind. On the literal level, he teaches Li'l Bit how to drive a car defensively on the road, which, he believes, will guarantee Li'l Bit to survive an impending disaster. However, to think ahead and take actions to avoid risk is also a useful survival strategy in social life, which equips Li'l Bit's mind. We later realize that it is a genuine warning against his own planned action. He prepares Li'l Bit with the survival skills that eventually allow her to surpass her teacher in the ability to withstand the shocks of living and keep going. Vogel believes that this is the gift that a victim can receive from an abuser. She says,

> The gift of the driving lessons, to me is a gift that is actually teaching Li'l Bit how to destroy him. It's telling her how to be a survivor: "You've gotta watch out for what the other guy's gonna do; stay five steps ahead." He's basically—not knowing it—but preparing her and giving her the ego formation to survive and destroy him. (Craig 165)

Vogel does not excuse the harm Uncle Peck does to his niece. But she wants her audience to see "the gifts we receive from people who hurt us"(ibid). For her, it is Peck who equips Li'l Bit with abilities to fight against him. When he counts down to Li'l Bit's eighteenth birthday, Li'l Bit understands his purpose in advance and tells him, "I know what you want to do five steps ahead of you doing it, Defensive Driving 101."(50) Therefore, she takes actions before he does it and rejects his desperate marriage proposal, which results in Peck's tragic demise. Craig points out, "in leading to Peck's demise, his own gift of the driving lessons to Li'l Bit becomes the most potent agent."(231)

However, what the rite of initiation does is just starting the process of Li'l Bit's empowerment and transformation. Li'l Bit at this moment is still an enlightened novice and a subject in becoming. Her awakened consciousness of power and autonomy has not yet developed full-fledged. Her self-formation will be a long and difficult journey. The moment of "the arrows to reverse themselves in the course of the play" does not come until the two sessions named "Shifting Forward from Second to Third Gear" and "Shifting Forward from Third to Fourth Gear". With the gear moving higher and Li'l Bit's eighteenth birthday coming nearer, Peck's love to her becomes so ardent and uncontrollable that he performs a few rites such as giving gifts, writing love letters, counting down days, toasting to her birthday, buying her a car, lying together on bed, and proposing marriage with a ring, in order to transform their immoral relationship into legal one. But Peck's exaggerated rite of courtship looks ridiculous in Li'l Bit's as well as the audience's eyes. Without Li'l Bit's cooperation and participation, it turns to be a parody rather than a real one. Vogel highlights the scene of the parodied rite of courtship, which is the climax of this episodic play, marking the fall of Peck and the reverse of power between him and Li'l Bit.

Courtship, the interactive behavior and ritual between two people who are emotionally and romantically engaged, has been "an abiding and compelling subject in human discourse from the most ancient times because it ritualizes elements that are fundamental to social existence: love, sex, marriage, and procreation" (Bates 6). Courtship rituals are not only universal social practices performed across the world and through the history, they are also interesting subjects of theater. Ann Cook argues that every Shakespeare's play includes "at least some reference to wooing or wedding, and in most plots it is a crucial element, frequently dominating the entire action" (7). She reconstructs the system of courtship that is familiar to Shakespeare and his audience and decodes the courtship rituals in his plays in *Making a Match: Courtship in Shakespeare and His Society*, which provides an insightful interpretation of Shakespearian drama.

The rite of courtship also plays a very important role in modern dramas like *The Glass Menagerie*, *A Streetcar Named Desire*, *Isn't Romantic*, *Devotees in the Garden of Love*, and so on. According to the studies of Nancy Forand, Catherine Bates and Ann Cook, the performance of courtship ritual is not only a living and ever-changing exchange of sexual desires but also a power negotiation between two individuals, two families and even two countries if the suitor and the beloved are royal. It is an intricate process of success and failure, domination and subordination, and obedience and subversion.

Peck imposes his abnormal love upon Li'l Bit aggressively by the ritual of gift-exchange and countdown. When Li'l Bit enters college, Peck sends her all kinds of gifts with ardent love letters and mysterious numbers. Vogel ritualizes Peck's crazy actions by letting Female Greek Chorus, Male Greek Chorus and Teenage Greek Chorus read the scripts in turn, showering Li'l Bit with gifts like tape cassettes, roses, chocolates, books, perfume, and a series of numbers such as "only ninety days to go""sixty-nine days""47""only two weeks more""nine days and counting"(48). As the Greek Chorus increase their speed and the number changes smaller, the atmosphere becomes more and more intense and the power of Peck is more and more forceful. As usual, Peck is confident and patient. It seems that he still occupies the dominant position in their relationship. However, the same as other rituals, gift-exchange is also haunted by its intrinsic structural ambivalence, "allow[ing] for the fact that each of these inaugural acts may misfire, and that it receives its meaning, in any case, from the response it triggers off, even if the response is a failure to reply"(Bourdieu 5). Its meaning and effects depend on the understanding and responses of the recipient rather than the giver's intention. It is not an irreversible, mechanical process but a complex interplay of giving and receiving, offering and responding, and

Chapter Three Subversion and Reconstruction   277

asking and replying. Peck's gifts and love letters do not please Li'l Bit as he has expected. On the contrary, they anger and scare her, "I am so pissed off at you, Uncle Peck,"(49) Li'l Bit says. "You scared the holy crap out of me."(49) For Li'l Bit, the numbers that Peck writes in the mails are intimidating, "like some serial killer"(50), although in Peck's mind, they just represent the days to her eighteenth birthday. He wants to express his excitement and thrills Li'l Bit, "trying to pick up your spirits, trying to celebrate your birthday" (50). Li'l Bit's misrecognition does not derive from her ignorance of the semantic and symbolic meaning of the numbers. In fact, she has penetrated Peck's secret intention behind the gifts and numbers because she has grown up with both his sexual abuse and driving lessons. She knows that "statutory rape is not in effect when a young woman turns eighteen"(47) and Peck cannot wait to go over the line that she has drawn. She has to stop him before he takes action. She has learned, as Peck teaches her, to think what Peck is going to do before he does it. Li'l Bit's negative response has cancelled the effect of the ritual of gift-exchange and countdown and challenged Peck's authority.

As the beloved, Li'l Bit undermines Peck's power gradually by refusing to cooperate with him on the courtship rituals he initiates. When Peck opens the champagne to celebrate Li'l Bit's eighteenth birthday, he "makes a big show of it"(50), trying his best to behave like a decent gentleman and wanting to perform their drinking as a formal ritual. But Li'l Bit does not care Peck's feeling or follow any etiquette. She just drains the first glass of champagne without waiting for him and pours herself another two glasses, ignoring Peck's tentative manner and warm toast to her. With the failure of his first attempt, Peck tries another one. He offers a new car, a Cadillac El Dorado, the best gift in his eyes, to Li'l Bit to mark her entry into adulthood. Again, he imposes his powerful, articulate will upon Li'l Bit, which not only confuses her but also arouses her resistance. Li'l Bit refuses the gift and tells Peck, "I don't want us to 'see' each other anymore."(52) Since both of them love car and all their past stories happen in cars, car functions as the essential bond between them and symbolizes the power Peck wishes to exercise over Li'l Bit. Li'l Bit's refusal not only means her decision to cut ties with him but also her act of rebellion against his manipulation.

When the parodic young lover's courtship rituals have failed to win over Li'l Bit, Peck resorts to sex and body. He assures Li'l Bit that lovemaking is just like breathing and "it won't hurt you if the man you go to bed with really loves you"(52). But his words could not persuade Li'l Bit. Instead, she is more scared, insisting that "I can't see you anymore"(52). In a desperate attempt to plea for her affection, Peck entreats Li'l Bit to lie down on the bed with him and just hold one another like a man and a woman, only feeling each other through body, because he believes that "the body knows things that the mind isn't listening to" (52). This of course could be interpreted as Peck's cunning trick to seduce Li'l Bit, and the scene could be staged as a disturbing sexual exploitation. However, Vogel ritualizes this scene and makes it as sacred as possible by setting it in a tranquil atmosphere. She describes in stage directions, "Peck lies down on the bed and holds his arms out to her"(52). Li'l Bit, "half wanting to run, half wanting to get it over with, half wanting to be held by him"(52), lies beside him, putting her head on his chest. As always, Peck keeps his promise not to cross the line. They lie silently and motionlessly. "He looks as if he's trying to soak her into his pores by osmosis. He strokes her hair, and she lies very still."(53) This intimate behavior parodies the consummation of bride and bridegroom, the final stage of marriage ritual. In order to give it more ritualistic sense, Vogel inserts a long chorus titled "Recipe for a Southern Boy" into the scene. While Peck lies motionless with his eyes closed, the Male Greek Chorus and the Female Greek Chorus as Aunt Mary, Peck's wife, come into the room and narrate the chorus in turn. Rising in the bed and responding to her aunt, Li'l Bit joins in the chorus and relates her fragmented, sensual memories of her love for Peck. Similar to the mime in the first scene and the split of Li'l Bit's body and voice in the last scene, this non-realistic intervention creates Alienation Effect, distancing the audience from emotional involvement and forcing them to think critically.

The parodied lovemaking or consummation between Peck and Li'l Bit has attracted some critics' attention. Liang Chaoqun and Zhang E contend that the chorus is like the hero requiem in ancient Greek tragedy and this scene is the most moving yet tragic one in the play (79). Mansbridge points out, "There is a devastating desperation in Peck's desire in this scene". ("Paula Vogel" 140). Both of them have seen the pain and desperation of Peck and shown their "negative empathy" to Peck, "the feeling-with-the-other" or "the identification with those we might rather disavow"(Mansbridge 127). Such sympathetic response is one effect that Vogel tries to achieve through her dramaturgy since she wants to draw Li'l Bit and Peck with equal skill and sympathy.

However, *How I Learned to Drive* is not an Aristotelian but a Brechtian drama. Its non-chronological narration and non-natrualistic acting in fact interrupt and even defy conventional spectatorship and identification. The combination of realistic depiction of Peck and non-realistic performance of the Choruses in this scene provokes more complicated responses than pity and empathy. Since Vogel intends to switch the hierarchical power structure between male and female and change man into "objects" in writing *How I Learned to Drive*, gender power politics has been the most important issue it deals with. The present author argues that Vogel accomplishes a few "reverses" she avows to make in this parodied consummation.

First of all, the original power structure between Peck and Li'l Bit is reversed. Since the first molestation when Li'l Bit was just eleven years old, Peck has enjoyed having power in his hands. Although he always shows her courtesy, promising her "nothing is going to happen between us till you want it to"(23), he has in fact violated both her body and heart by force at the beginning. Vogel shows this explicitly though very late: Peck cheats Li'l Bit that she can drive a car by sitting on his lap, then he puts her between his legs in the driving seat, and, uninvited, caresses her breasts until he gets sexual gratification. Li'l Bit is so shocked and scared that she tells the audience many years later, "That day was the last day I lived in my body. I retreated above the neck, and I've lived inside the 'fire' in my head ever since"(58). So Peck was lying. Something had already happened between them long time ago. During the seven years, Peck has played a father-mentor-lover role in Li'l Bit's life, taking advantage of the little girl's innocence, curiosity and compliance to seduce her. He is the "driver" who controls the direction of their relationship. Li'l Bit is the weak and dependent one. When Li'l Bit replies "I don't know" to Peck's question "Do you want something to happen"(23), Peck responds, "Then I'll wait. I am a very patient man. I've been waiting for a long time. I don't mind waiting."(23) In using the words "till" and "wait", he shows his confidence and certainty, "the certainty that her full acquiescence is merely a matter of time"(Whately). Being obsessed with his control of Li'l Bit, Peck never expects the possibility of her refusal, rebellion or escape. He dreams of changing Li'l Bit's eighteenth birthday celebration into his marriage proposal ritual and fulfilling their consummation.

However, Li'l Bit has grown old enough to free herself from Peck's manipulation. Her constant rejection to Peck's gifts and proposal crushes his dream and throws him into darkness. Peck turns to be the dependent and vulnerable one. He tells Li'l Bit, "Your going away has just made me realize how much I miss you. Talking to you and being alone with you. I've really come to depend on you." (51) Peck's vulnerability is exposed more clearly in their parodied consummation. He holds Li'l Bit with desperate love and tenderness, hoping that his body could awaken Li'l Bit's sexual desire and keep her with him forever. When Li'l Bit gets up to leave, Peck asks her eagerly, "Did you ... feel nothing?" Her reply is "No. Nothing". Then Peck continues to press upon Li'l Bit, "Do you—do you think of me?" Her answer is still "No"(54). Contrary to her earlier hesitation and obedience, Li'l Bit at last says "no" to Peck's sexual harassment and emotional domination. Vogel highlights Peck's disappointment and powerlessness when Li'l Bit tells him firmly, "I am leaving. Now. I am not seeing you. Again."(54) He lies down on the bed for a moment, "trying to absorb the terrible news. For a moment, he almost curls into a fetal position"(54). Peck now is as weak and helpless as a baby. He loses control over Li'l Bit forever. Li'l Bit becomes the "driver" who decides where their relationship should go towards.

Secondly, the subject-object position of Peck and Li'l Bit is reversed in the parodied consummation. Li'l Bit has been gazed by Peck as an object of sexual desire even since her birth. It is Peck who holds the one-day old baby girl and nicknames her as "Li'l Bit"—just a little bit—which is a euphemism for her genitalia. "I have loved you every day since the day you were born"(44), Peck confesses to Li'l Bit after he takes nude photos for her. David Savran considers "The Photo Shoot" as the center of the play because it demonstrates Li'l

Bit's objectification. He argues, "It is in this scene that Li'l Bit most graphically becomes an object for her Uncle Peck, and more ominously, for herself as well."("Queer Sorte of Materialism" 197) In this scene, Li'l Bit moves swiftly through the performative gestures of feminine embodiment: self-consciousness, shame and compliance. She performs all kinds of classic *Playboy* or *Vargas* poses under Peck's instruction and pleases him with her body and its postures. With a desire for command over Li'l Bit's body, Peck gazes her from behind his camera and appreciates her beautiful body lasciviously. Vogel reveals the sexualization and objectification of female body in American visual arts and media by interspersing Li'l Bit's images with those of *Playboy* bunnies, popular celebrities and even Alice Liddell.

But Vogel is not content to just expose the problem. She goes further to subvert the patriarchal gender pattern. In the inserted chorus of the parodied consummation scene, Peck is gazed as an object of sexual desire by Aunt Mary and Li'l Bit. In their eyes, the way he speaks is like "a drawl of molasses," his skin is like cream with a taste of "gumbo of red and brown" and his eyes are "warm brown", with the allure of bedroom and the spirit of "Southern Baptist Fire and Brimstone" (53). Connecting Peck's body with delicious food, the female characters articulate their desires for male body directly. They watch, touch, smell and taste, using all sensory perceptions to appreciate the beauty of Peck's body and admitting its allure. Attracted by his "closely shaven beard" and "sweat of cypress and sand," they are eager to reach out to "hold him in your hand" (54). Different from the spectatorship in the "Photo Shoot" scene, the positions of Peck and Li'l Bit are exchanged: Peck now is a passive sexual object while Li'l Bit becomes an active subject. As a political act of retaliation, Vogel unites Li'l Bit, Aunt Mary, Male Greek Chorus as well as her audience into a communal one to gaze at a male body, objectifying and sexualizing it. This reverses the theatrical mode that usually puts female body under male gaze and interrupts conventions of spectatorship and identification.

The third reverse that Vogel accomplishes is that the original abuser turns to be the victim while the original victim survives. Li'l Bit has not only learned how to desire, she has also learned how to occupy a controlling position in their relation as well as in her future life. Resisting Peck's allure, she "wrenches herself free" and "gets up from the bed"(54) after the chorus. When Peck opens a ring box to ask her to marry him, she calms down and retains her rational and ethical sense, telling Peck that "Family is family" and "You should go home to Aunt Mary"(54). Then Li'l Bit leaves Peck who "sits rigid" and says "I need a real drink"(54). Peck's lifeline is cut and he is finally lost. He brokenheartedly turns to alcohol and eventually dies. As Li'l Bit explains, "It took my uncle seven years to drink himself to death. First he lost his job, then his wife, and finally his driver's license. He retreated to his house, and had his bottles delivered." (55) The loss of his driver's license is simultaneously a fact and a symbol as he loses that power over his direction, that command of his life. Their unusual love "finds its apotheosis not in consummation but sacrifice"(Bigsby, "Contemporary" 319). Peck, as the abuser, gets his poetic justice for what he did, while Li'l Bit escapes from the disaster and moves on. She is, as he had urged her to be, the only one to survive the accident. This ending confirms that while Li'l Bit is certainly a victim, she is also a survivor. There is a clear political message in this ending. It signifies Vogel's desire to create a more hopeful alternative for her female protagonist and her audiences. She once said,

> I am paying more attention these days to endings. The fact that Peck doesn't get out of it doesn't mean that she doesn't. I think that the ending of

> *How I Leaned to Drive* came very much as a response to some of my students being crushed by the ending of *Hot 'N' Throbbing*. *How I Learned to Drive* was a response to this young woman who just sat and cried in my office. (Linden 249)

As a feminist playwright, Vogel dislikes the victimization of women in American culture. She believes that "great harm can be inflicted by well-intentioned therapists, social workers, and talk show hosts who encourage people to dwell in their identity as victim" (Vogel, "Interview"). In order to reverse this tendency, she provides the abused woman a way out in this play and gives hope to the young generation.

With its recursive structure and non-chronological narrative, *How I Learned to Drive* is neither a psychological portrait of the past trauma, nor a moral accusation of pedophilia, it is concerned with a girl's self-formation in an over-sexualized culture and through an abusive yet genuine love. In learning how to drive a car, Li'l Bit has learned how to desire, how to transgress gender border, and most importantly, how to win the game of power in gender politics. She not only survives in a world that constructs her as an object, but also gains the power to drive like a man, to assume a masculine position in sexual relation, and to take control of her past, present and future. When the play opens, Li'l Bit has been a forty-something woman. With "softer-looking" (9) and adult wisdom, she looks back on her adolescence and, specifically, her relationship with her Uncle Peck with both righteous authority and big-hearted generosity about her abuser. She is not trapped in the orbit of post-traumatic stress disorder. On the contrary, she is now the dominant agent and the playwright of her life, re-ordering what was once a crippling disorder and re-writing a history of oppression with both understanding and forgiveness. As the narrator-protagonist, Li'l Bit has actively reclaimed control over her experiences by reprocessing them dramaturgically. On one occasion, she met a teenage boy on a bus and seduced him when she was twenty-seven years old. She took the initiatives, directed the "plot" and experienced the same thrill that Peck once must have felt. She becomes the older, the first, "the translator, the teacher, the epicure, the already jaded" (29), and finally understands the allure of innocence, the seductiveness of seduction, and the compelling nature of power. In one sense, it is ironic that Li'l Bit becomes the abuser from the abused. But the reversed status gives her a masculine perspective to see sexual relationship and understand gender politics. The transgressive experiences provide her necessary nutrition to forge a complete self that combines both traditional masculinity and femininity. As the curtain falls, Li'l Bit tells her audience that she finds herself "believing in things that a younger self vowed never to believe in. Things like family and forgiveness" (58). Then she floors her car and starts her long journey with the spirit of Uncle Peck sitting in the back seat. This time, it is Li'l Bit who takes the driver's seat and controls the direction. Power finally falls in her hands and will be there forever.

Epilogue

With absurd and burlesque features, the parodied rituals in Vogel's drama are more subversive and performative. Ritual is employed by female characters as an effective strategy to deal with psychological problems, gain power and reshape self-identity. As a result, the ritual subjects deconstruct a few patriarchal binary oppositions, realize the transition of power from man's hands to woman's, and constitute their fluid androgynous gender identity.

The lesbian couple Ruth and Anna release their anxiety of becoming newly parents, defend their authority in the family and constitute their fluid gender identity in enacting the successive "dying" rituals of their imaginary sons and the funeral service for Orphan. Their ritual performance transgresses the boundary of masculinity/femininity, heterosexuality/homosexuality, and paternity/maternity.

The female protagonist (Anna) in *The Baltimore Waltz* identifies with the homosexual other (Carl) in her fantasized ritual, reversing the hierarchy of man and woman, heterosexual and homosexual, self and the other, and becoming an active subject by taking initiatives in making love with a few men, which could also be interpreted as sexual rituals. She finally accepts the death of Carl and incorporates her sense of loss into her new selfhood.

How I Learned to Drive parodies the rite of initiation for boys and the traditional courtship rituals. During the ritual performance, Li'l Bit is empowered, becoming a mature, active and independent subject, while Peck is disempowered, changing to be women's desire object and losing his masculinity and life. In this way, the hierarchical power relation between them is reversed.

Chapter Four

The Performativity of Ritual and Identity in Contemporary American Women's Drama

The close reading of the dramatic texts of Norman, Wasserstein and Vogel in the foregoing chapters demonstrates that ritual plays a key role in the formation and transformation of the female self as well as in the power politics between patriarchal and feminist discourses, which provokes further thinking on the interrelationship of ritual and female identity outside of the fictional world. This chapter shifts its focus from textual analysis to social and theoretical exploration of ritual, drama and female identity through the lens of performativity. In section one, the author investigates rituals in the women's movement and the feminist ritual theater during the 1970s and the 1980s, contexutualizing rituals in Norman, Wasserstein and Vogel's plays in the specific social and cultural background. Regarding literary text as action and ritual as the central performative textual element, the author explores the performative efficacy of rituals within dramatic texts and what they bring to the real world. Based on the practice of ritual performance and self-transformation in both real life and dramatic works, section three discusses the performativity of female self in light of Beauvoir and Butler's feminist theories.

Ⅰ. Ritual in the Women's Movement and the Feminist Ritual Theater

The plays of Marsha Norman, Wendy Wasserstein and Paula Vogel are written and staged in the contexts of the second wave of women's movement and the feminist ritual theater. Different from the earlier women's movement, the second wave beginning from the mid-1960s gives priority to action/experience over history and memory, aimed at changing the patriarchal culture through female writing and feminist activities. One of the popular and effective strategies of women's struggle is to perform rituals, which, according to Sue-Ellen Case and Charlotte Canning, has enhanced the communal bond among all women and concomitantly empowered the female individuals (Case, "Feminism and Theater" 24; Canning, "Feminist Theaters" 110). At the same time, feminist theater groups are eager to find forms that would enable them to express the experience and vision of the women's movement onstage. To do this, they also find ritual, "the type of performance that demonstrated the bonds and fabric of a community through its history, conventions and myths"(Canning 120). Their efforts develop into a special form of drama—the feminist ritual theater. Performance of rituals in feminist activities and theatrical practice are inextricably linked, inspiring and nurturing each other.

A variety of rituals have been created and performed by radical feminists in order to protest against patriarchal oppression and enact feminist ideas. The most influential one is the (CR) ritual which is advocated and organized by the women's consciousness-raising groups, the early units of radical-feminist thought and practice. Realizing that the patriarchy is the primary cause of the oppression of women and that women, as the oppressed gender, need to unite and fight together, these CR groups are open to all women regardless of their economic status, race, color and religion, providing women with a voice to articulate what it feels like to be a woman and giving them an opportunity to enter into a dialogue with other women. Women, for the first time, feel free to express their relationship to the workplace and the family unit, as well as their dreams, memories, fantasies and hopes. As was discussed in Chapter Two, CR ritual, performed in all-women communities and in an interactive form, is practical, political and performative, awakening feminist consciousness, enhancing communal sisterhood and converting many women to feminists. Other communal political rituals in the women's movement are aimed at different social problems. For example, "the Bra-Burnings" is performed by women to reclaim their bodies from the sexualizing elements of patriarchal culture; "They Take Back the Night March" "Three Weeks in May" "In Mourning and in Rage" and "We Fight Back" are collective rituals to fight against violence, primarily rape, and reclaims women's rights and power.

Ritual is highly valued by spiritual feminists who believe that women can discover their own power and spirituality through creating their own symbols and events. In *Beyond God the Father: Toward a Philosophy of Women's Liberation*, *Gyn/Ecology: The Metaethics of Radical Feminism*, and *Women and Nature: The Roaring inside Her*, Mary Daly and Susan Griffin deconstruct the symbols, metaphors, rituals and experiences of the patriarchal religions and construct the feminist sense of spirituality which emphasizes the intimate bond between women and nature and highlights the privileged position of the female gender. For the spiritual feminists, the exploration and development of rituals is the spiritual equivalent to the material struggle for legal, political and economic gains for women. They encourage and guide women to produce the rituals peculiar to their gender. Usually performed in a separatist environment of women, their rituals commonly celebrate women's biological cycles, intuition, fertility and bonding or resist patriarchal oppression.

Inspired by the feminist spirituality movement, many women have invented their personal rituals around their biological features. For example, a few rituals celebrate the beginning of menstruation for young girls and the spiritual powers of the menstrual cycles. Some women taste their menstrual blood to prove that they are truly liberated. They could prepare a wand in the way "to dig out a little from one end and stuff it with a piece of cotton and a drop of your menstrual blood" (Budapest 11), which, they believe, can protect them from rape, "the patriarchal weapon that directly wounded or violated women"(Case, "Feminism and Theater" 66).

More emphasis is given to collective rituals that strengthen the commonalities and connections among women. The feminist ritualists often identify themselves as witches or goddess-worshippers. They combine the mythical goddess/witches' rituals with feminist politics to illustrate the tie between women's biological, spiritual selves and the social issues such as rape. Sue-Ellen Case describes a few such rituals in her *Feminism and Theater*. One ritual performed by Hallie Iglehart and Barbry My Own is to renew and empower women.

> Women simulated a birth canal and birthed each other into their circle. They raised power by placing their hands on each other's bellies and chanting together. Finally, they marked each other's faces with rich, dark menstrual blood saying "This is the blood that promises renewal". (Spretnak 80)

Many women performed a ritual in June 1980 at the top of Mount Tamalpais, outside San Francisco, to mourn the women who were raped and murdered at this site and to "send their pain and anger into the Earth, asking that it be changed into energy for action"(Spretnak 469). Another ritual is to hex a rapist—a girl could take a black penis candle, write on it her curse to the rapist, anoint it with Double-Cross oil and urine, then place it on the altar with incense and chanting. When the candle burns, she/they can imagine what could happen to the rapist, knowing that "rape is the foundation for patriarchy"(Budapest 67 – 68).

As a kind of cultural performance rich in symbolic signs and acts, ritual is performed by women not just for expressing feelings like anger and hatred, but also for changing the reality. Women have achieved a few performative effects by performing these rituals. Ritual heals their trauma in two aspects. For individual victims of rape and domestic violence, performing rituals repeatedly could alleviate their pain, exorcise their fear and rebuild their self-confidence. For women as a community, rituals that highlight women's cultural signs and embrace female attributes could heal their cultural trauma that has haunted women of all generations. Also, collective rituals like CR unite women together and reinforce their common bond. Inspired and encouraged by feminist rituals, a lot of women join feminist groups and organize feminist activities to help more sisters. In addition, ritual empowers the participants. Feminist activists gain spiritual power from ancient mythologies on the one hand, and discover physical power of women from nature on the other hand. They create new rituals that combine myth, nature and feminist ideals. In performing such rituals, women could link themselves to their ancestors, to their body and to other women, which empowers them and changes their lives.

The women's movement, especially the ritual performance of radical feminists, provide rich inspirations and resources for feminist theaters. Many of the earliest feminist theaters are devoted to integrating ritual into their productions. Based on the feminist theatrical practice in the 1970s, Batya Podos theorized the feminist ritual theater in 1981, arguing that it linked the feminist thought and belief with the spiritual realm and resisted the separation imposed by the patriarchy of public and private, mind and body, spiritual and quotidian. Podos stated firmly,

> Not only must ritual theater seek to provide a transformative spiritual experience, it must educate an audience whose spiritual experiences, self-definitions, and world perceptions have been taught and nurtured by a misogynist society—an audience that has been denied knowledge of its own history and power. (306)

Believing that the origins of theater were in "spiritual and ritual magic" and "pageants, festivals, ceremonies, and seasonal celebrations were all parts of early theater" (306), Podos proposed to combine ritual with theater to integrate women's daily life into theatrical performance in order to effect transformation of all the participants. She posited ritual theater as the medium through which women could recapture the connections with their power that have been destroyed by the patriarchy.

The most influential and well-known feminist ritual theater groups in America include: It's All Right to Be Woman Theater (1970), The Circle of the Witch (1973), Rhode Island Feminist Theater (1973), At the Foot of the Mountain (1974), The Cutting Edge (1975), The Women's Experimental Theater (1977), The New Cycle Theater (1977), and so on. In its published statements, At the Foot of the Mountain declared that one of its goals was "to create new rituals for our time" in order to "renew hope and celebrate the healing power of women by recreating life-giving cultural myths" (Canning 126). With such feminist aspiration, these theaters produced a lot of plays that used the methods of ritual. The ritualistic characteristics of their dramatic works are embodied in the theme, image and form of their productions.

Some of the feminist ritual theaters imitate real life and stage feminist rituals directly in their theaters. For example, It's All Right to Be Woman Theater was influenced greatly by the consciousness-raising ritual. The group used CR techniques along with the movement and composed its products with material from the women's experiences that emerged in the CR process. Its productions could be perceived as dramatizations of the dynamics of the CR process: performed only to all-women audiences who act like a kind of extended CR group, creating a new kind of emotional intimacy between audience and performers that broke with the traditional concept of the "fourth wall" or aesthetic distance, and encouraging audience to speak out their personal stories and take action to change their lives.

The ritual theater practitioners also explore mythic and religious rituals to reinterpret the andro-centric biases of Greek based myths, celebrate the matriarchal power and link the past with the present and the future of women. The New Cycle Theater, taking its name from the cycles of the female body, the seasons, the birth and rebirth, bases its productions on spiritual-mythological themes. Its work *A Monster Has Stolen the Sun* (1981) contains a few elements of feminist rituals: a Celtic tribe, an invocation to the sun and a child entering through a cervexlike opening in the scenery, connoting birth. *Persephone's Return*, first performed by Rhode Island Feminist Theater in 1974, is a ritual piece that infuses the mythic tale of Demeter and Persephone into modern life, exploring how the matriarchy was supplanted by patriarchy and how patriarchy still exploits women through rape, marriage and control in contemporary time. The play begins with a ritual dance titled the "People's Dance" and continues to the "Woman's Dance" which is followed by alternating scenes between modern heterosexual couples and mythic ones among the Greek pantheon. It ends with a communal "Future Dance", in which all the women performers gather together to build a fire and dance for an androgynous, nonhierarchical future. As Canning points out, the play emphasizes the cyclical nature of ritual, while at the same time it also "offers the notion that rituals can be a part of change and break a cycle"(132).

Another technique of feminist ritual theater is to create new rituals that reinforce the links between mother and daughter, audience and performer, and individual and community. The trilogy *The Daughters Cycle*, created by The Women's Experimental Theater, is a ritual celebration of and lament for the power and oppression women experience within the family unit. The first play, *Daughters*, is defined by WET as "a ritual exploration of the mother/daughter relationship" (Canning 127), in which the ritual of Matrilineage was first used. The performance begins with the cast's recitation of their own matrilineage,

> I am Sondra
> daughter of Lille
> daughter of Sarah Rebecca
> who came to this country when she was sixteen
> and never saw her mother again
> daughter of Tzivia
> daughter of a woman from Austria. (Coss 234)

At the end of the play, the cast would invite the audience onstage to recite their own lines of maternal descent, which breaks the boundary of performers and spectators. The Matrilineage affected women profoundly and became a signature ritual in the two subsequent plays. Clare Coss remembered quite clearly how effective the device was, "women would come back with their mothers, their daughters, their sisters ... It was thrilling to have generations come back"(Canning 127). The feminist historian Bettina Aptheker was so moved by the experience of reciting her foremothers that she even used it as the introduction to her book on women's history (vi). Another play *The Story of a Mother*, produced by At the Foot of the Mountain, consists of five sections and each section includes an opportunity for the audience to participate in "open-ended ritual segments"(Boesing 44), that enable them to perceive the world as their mothers. For example, during the first ritual moment "Calling Forth the Mothers", a performer instructs the audience to imagine that each of them enters her mother's body and recites a "litany" in her mother's voice. At the end of the play, the performers offer bread to the audience and sing together. Martha Boesing comments, "It's both very personal and very ritualized at the same time. But the audience is no longer a witness, they literally participate in the event."(Canning 128) Depending on audience participation, all of the plays are organized in a nonlinear repetitive structure, with ritual segments alternating with other written units.

The plays of Norman, Wasserstein and Vogel are not products of the mentioned feminist ritual theater groups. They do not belong to the post-dramatic theater coined by Hans-Thies Lehmann either since dramatic texts still occupy the central position, full characters are portrayed and complete actions are staged. However, they are invested with a few characteristics of the ritual or post-dramatic theater. Wasserstein re-presents the CR ritual she attended as a college student in 1969 in *The Heidi Chronicles*, which captures the high spirit and radical action of the event without overlooking the serious frustration of women at that time. Besides this, the all-women gathering of Lisa's baby shower(*The Heidi Chronicles*), the college girls' dormitory conversations (*Uncommon Women and Others*) and the three sisters' heartfelt talk (*The Sisters Rosensweig*), are CR-like activities, by which women exchange personal problems, encourage each other and strengthen their sisterhood. Even the conversation between Arlene and Ruby in *Getting Out* has some features of CR ritual and achieves similar effects. Wasserstein also stages a few real rituals that are popular in women's colleges in the 1970s to mock them with a comic spirit in *Uncommon Women and Others*. When Norman, Wasserstein and Vogel use rituals that are traditionally patriarchal or religious, such as funeral, service, the Sabbath Sundown and courtship, they feminize them by replacing the male guide with a woman or reversing the original male-female power pattern in order to accommodate feminist issues. At the same time, they create new rituals for their female characters. Arlene's self-affliction and renaming in *Getting Out*, Jessie's "Requiem Mass" in *'night, Mother* and Ruth's parody of "killing" and "dying" of fictional children in *And Baby Makes Seven* are invented and performed by themselves in order to release pressure, survive crisis and get self-autonomy.

Norman, Wasserstein and Vogel all lay emphasis on audience's involvement in the ritual event on stage, which breaks the "fourth wall" and transgresses the boundary of fiction and reality. Norman includes her audience as the participants of Jessie's ritual by starting the dramatic action at 8:15 in the evening and placing two clocks which run through the performance on the stage. Wasserstein uses collective singing, dancing and chorus to affect her spectators in the theater. The male speaker in *Uncommon Women and Others* addresses not just to the girls on stage but also to the audience in theater, so does Heidi's luncheon speech "Women, Where Are We Going". Vogel regards each performance of *The Baltimore Waltz* as a remembrance event for her brother and "uses the theater as a public place of commemoration"(Mansbridge, "Camp" 328). Therefore, all the audience have to join in the events. Li'l Bit in *How I Learned to Drive* is both the protagonist and the narrator of the story. She often walks out of the fictional world and talks directly to the audience, commenting on what is taking place on stage and forcing the audience to think critically. In addition, most of their plays (except for *'night, Mother* and *The Sisters Rosensweig*) employ nonlinear narrative and episodic structure, the typical Brechtian feminist model of drama which reveals the repetitive and cyclical nature of life and embodies the philosophical views that "social being determines thought and man is alterable and is able to alter"(Chen 56).

Evidently, ritual is not only a practical tool for feminist activists to organize political events but also a poetic device for feminist playwrights to produce artistic works. Being aware of and attracted by the performative power of ritual, both activists and playwrights have deployed it as a strategy to achieve their political goals. The performative effects produced by the rituals in feminist activities have been demonstrated and confirmed by the history of the women's movement. Women who perform private rituals in real life heal their traumas and build up self-confidence. They set up sisterhood tie with other women and feel the power of female community by participating in collective rituals. At the same time, their performance of rituals enacts their feminist beliefs and displays their new images in front of the public, which have redefined what a woman is and brought about social, political and cultural change to reality.

However, the performativie effects of ritual in feminist theater remain to be explored. How to evaluate the function of the ritual performance within the dramatic text and outside it? To be more specific, what women playwrights like Norman, Wasserstein and Vogel want to do and have done by writing and staging ritual in their dramas? In the next section, these questions will be discussed by invoking the performative theories of Jonathan Culler and Terry Eagleton and the critical practice of J. Hillis Miller, He Chengzhou and Eva Hettner Aurelius.

Ⅱ. The Performativity of Ritual

The theory of performativity conceives of literature as an action or event, paying more attention to what literature does than what it says. Culler argues, "Literature is not frivolous pseudo-statements but takes its place among the acts of language that transform the world, bringing into being the things that they name."(96) Literary texts, especially those connected to religious or political practices, can perform something, such as constituting identity and constructing fantasy. J. Hillis Miller regards literature as conduct or speech that acts, which can be observed in three dimensions: the author's act of writing, the speech acts that the narrators and characters utter in a work of fiction, and the reader's act of reading, with each act doing other things in its turn ("Literature as Conduct" 2). The acts of writing, speaking, reading and performing literary texts are forms of doing things in the world, which can exert change to the reality.

In this sense, the performativity of Norman, Wasserstein and Vogel's dramas can be interpreted at least in three facets. Their playwriting is first of all the political and artistic acts they perform to articulate female voice in response to American social and theatrical reality during and after the second wave of feminist movement, as this author has illustrated in Introduction, which constitutes their identity as feminist playwright. Secondly, it brings into being their dramatic works, in which new female images are created, new feminist ideas and concepts are formed, and new dramatic techniques are invented. These dramatic works, as symbolic actions within a given cultural context, will do something in turn, which will be discussed in details later. Thirdly, when these dramatic works are read in privacy or performed in public, they will affect the readers/audience, and even bring about change to their thought and action. This process of reception, although very important, is too complicated and difficult for this study to handle, so it will be left aside for further study in the future. In this section, the author mainly focuses on what their dramatic works do.

When discussing the methodology of the theory of performativity in literary studies, Aurelius and He Chengzhou give emphasis to textuality, arguing, "since the text is the central medium here, the analyzing of the text is still crucial" ("Performativity in Literature" 19). However, they point out that the focus of textual analysis in performativity study is different from the traditional one (semantic, structuralist, etc.). Since the text is considered as an action and event situated in its historical, cultural and social contexts, more attention should be given to "such textual elements that connect the text to its cultural settings, its audience, its aims" (ibid). That includes: 1) the textual elements that can be interpreted as act; 2) the textual elements that Irmgard Maassen calls the structural performativity of the text, such as those textual strategies that convey participation, closeness, orality, the simulation of bodies, presence, fictions that produce authenticity, self-fashioning and audience-fashioning, and so on ("Performativity in Literature" 19).

Accordingly, this author argues that ritual is the central element of Norman, Wasserstein and Vogel's dramas because it is not only a performative act itself but also one significant textual element that connects the dramatic texts to their cultural settings, audience and aims. Therefore, analysis on ritual is the key to disclose what Norman, Wasserstein and Vogel's dramas do to the world. To understand the performativity of ritual in Norman, Wasserstein and Vogel's dramas, two questions should be answered: What does ritual do as an act of the female character within the text? And what does ritual do to the real world as the dramatic device of the women playwrights? Study in the first three chapters has provided a nuanced analysis on what ritual does within the text, which can be summarized as follows.

The most important efficacy of ritual performance is the constitution of new identity. All the female characters discussed have been shaped by patriarchal ideology and confined to the traditional roles of daughter, mother, wife, prostitute or sexual abuse victim when the curtain rises. Similar to Arlie/Arlene in *Getting Out*, they have to break the old prison, physical, psychological, sexual, relational or social, that have suffocated them for a long time, and become the person they want to be. Ritual, as human practice that enacts thought, belief and value, is deployed by the female characters to embody their feminist consciousness and ideals. During the ritual process, such as the affliction and renaming of Arlie/Arlene, the Requiem Mass of Jessie, the consciousness-raising ritual of Heidi, the parodied rite of initiation of Li'l Bit, these female characters free themselves from their previous self, undergo tremendous change and constitute a new identity through the performative languages, gestures and acts that embrace feminist ideas. The transforming and becoming of the female identity are fully embodied in these liminal ritual events.

The second efficacy that ritual brings about in Norman, Wasserstein and Vogel's dramas are the realization of women's empowerment. According to ritual theory, ritual practices are themselves the very production and negotiation of power relations and ritualization is a strategic arena for the embodiment of power relations. Ritual actuates power and "constitutes a particular dynamic of social empowerment"(Bell, "Ritual Theory" 181). Not only those who control or regulate ritual could be empowered, but also "those seen as controlled by ritual authority are not simply able to resist or limit this power; they are also empowered by virtue of being participants in a relationship of power"(Bell, "Ritual Theory" 214). In *Getting Out*, Arlie/Arlene obtains the power of controlling her body and deciding her future life by insisting on renaming herself repeatedly. Jessie in *'night, Mother* becomes, for the first time, the owner and master of her two houses, the real house controlled by her mother and her body controlled by disease and men, through performing her own "Requiem Mass". Lily in *The Holdup*, Ruth in *And Baby Makes Seven*, Anna in *The Baltimore Waltz*, and Li'l Bit in *How I Learned to Drive*, are all entrapped in the power struggles between two genders. Power is in men's hands at the beginning, but these women gains the upper hand gradually in the power relation by using ritual as their strategy. Although girls in *Uncommon Women and Others* are forced to perform the college rituals that objectify them, they take it as an opportunity to resist patriarchal oppression and express their feminist ideas by carnivalizing the ritual performance, resulting in the abolition of the rituals and the victory of feminist discourse. Heidi, who is a hesitant participant of CR ritual, is empowered and converted by other feminists who believe in the magic of ritual. For these women, to perform ritual is to negotiate power with men and get self-empowered.

Furthermore, ritual unites women as a community and consolidates sisterhood. This point is well illustrated by the collective ritual performance in Chapter Two. When college girls such as Holly and Rita act rebelliously in Gracious Living and other rituals, they share common feeling and spirit, fighting against the oppressive gender norms together and supporting each other to pursue their different dreams. Such ritual spirit even extends to their dormitory life, in which they continue to discuss, sing and dance in one group, forming a strong female community. The aim of the CR ritual in *The Heidi Chronicles* is to unite women from all walks of life as sisters and fight patriarchy as one class. Their rap about personal troubles and the sympathetic response from other women heal their trauma and awake their feminist consciousness. When the group are singing "Respect", dancing in circle and slapping each other's hands, especially when they are making a fist salute leading by Fran, they enter what V. Turner designates communitas, "a relationship between concrete, historical, idiosyncratic individuals" who are "not segmentalized into roles and statues but confront one another rather in the manner of Martin Buber's 'I and Thou'" ("Ritual Process" 131-132). All of the women, regardless of their social status, are considered as equal sisters. Although the three Rosensweig sisters hold different attitudes to Sabbath Sundown, they are united by the Jewish culture the ritual symbolizes and renewed by the sisterly love manifested in the ritual event. Ritual brings women together and reinforces their sense of belonging.

The rituals in Norman, Wasserstein and Vogel's dramatic works, although fictional, do not come from vacuum. They have their roots in reality, especially the practice of the feminist movement and feminist ritual theater in America. Their function is not limited to the fictional world within the text but extends to the outside real world. Eagleton-argues that performative acts in fiction can also be "powerful interventions in the world, accomplishing momentous changes and producing tangible effects" (128). As the central performative act in the plays under consideration, ritual performance does not stand aloof from the historical and cultural settings that give birth to them. It intervenes, changes and reshapes reality, which are manifested in the following four aspects.

The ritual performance records and bears witness to women's struggle against patriarchal oppression and gender discrimination from the 1960s to the 1980s in American society. As baby-boomer generation, Marsha Norman, Wendy Wasserstein and Paula Vogel came to age in the 1960s. They have experienced the conspicuous double standards for boys and girls in family and school, the apparent marginalization of women in society, the sexism and homophobia in profession and the tumultuous women's movement in the 1970s. All these experiences push and inspire them to write stories of their own. With her realistic style, Norman depicts the genuine life of low-class figures who are modelled on real people in her life. The prototype of Arlene is a wild girl murder Norman encountered at Central State Hospital in Louisville, the detached and suffocating mother-daughter relationship in *'night, Mother* is based on her own feeling about her mother, and even the frontier beauty Lily is a combination of past whore and contemporary feminist. The rituals they perform demonstrate their shackles, pain and angst on the one hand, and display their awaking, struggle and achievements on the other hand, paralleling the real situation of women during the second wave of feminism.

Being called a social historian and chronicler, Wasserstein sets all her plays in contemporary cultural, political and feminist history and honestly tracks social change and women's personal development during and after the women's movement. The college rituals in *Uncommon Women and Others* and the CR ritual in *The Heidi Chronicles* are authentic events taking place in the playwright's life. They truthfully record young feminists' confusion, aspiration and transformation, bridging fictional and real worlds. With the collapse of the Soviet Union as its backdrop, the Sabbath Sundown reveals the political, racial as well as feminist problems that trouble the Rosensweig sisters who, in fact, are created according to the real-life experiences of Wasserstein and her two sisters.

As a feminist playwright with a deep political sense, Vogel insists on exposing social problems that entrap and oppress women and envisioning the possible ways for her victims to survive. All her plays are rooted in American reality and address contemporary issues directly. The prolonged rituals of "dying" and "service" playacted by Ruth and Anna deal with emotional and psychological turbulence that lesbian family encounter. *The Baltimore Waltz*, written for her brother as a ritual of exorcism and commemoration, heals Vogel's personal trauma and addresses homophobia and AIDS fear directly. The parodied rites of initiation and courtship in *How I Learned to Drive* illustrate how child sexual abuse happens and how the victim reverses power relation to survive the abuser. In a word, ritual performance is not only the action of female protagonists within the text but also the action of the playwrights to represent and intervene reality outside.

By using ritual in their plays, Norman, Wasserstein and Vogel create new women images that are distinctly different from the previous ones in American women's theater. According to *American*

Women Playwrights edited by Brenda Murphy, the earliest woman image in American theater is "republican mother", who is free, active, loyal, courageous and patriotic, representing the national ideals of freedom, happiness and hope (3-18). By 1845, however, a more conservative vision of American womanhood becomes evident and women are confined to domestic scenes and feminine passivity. During the Progressive Era, women images shaped by women playwrights such as Zona Gale, Rachel Crothers, and Marion Craig Wentworth could be categorized into two kinds: those who are entrapped in domestic roles and plights like Miss Lulu Bett, and those who enter into workforce and become the so-called "New Women", the sexless, single, strong, free, unafraid and independent career women who "take the values of home and care and attempts to infuse them into society at large" (Murphy 39). These two images are further explored and developed in the dramatic works of Susan Glaspell, Sophie Treadwell and Lillian Hellman who expose women's struggle and impasse in patriarchal society. Some women are "caged bird" imprisoned in kitchen (like Minnie Wright in *Trifle*), others become money hunger in work market (like Regina in *The Little Foxes*), and there are also those who are entrapped and lost between motherhood and career (like Young Woman in *Machinal*). Being victims of patriarchy, they cannot find a way out and end with a tragic destiny. Whatever images they are portrayed as, positive or negative, kitchen-confined or career-oriented, these women characters are usually static, that is, their personality and identity do not change through dramatic action.

Different from the previous one-dimensional and stereotyped women images, all the female characters in Norman, Wasserstein and Vogel's plays undergo change and development during the ritual process and transcend their predetermined destinies. When the curtain rises, all the women, including Arlene, Jessie, Lily, college girls, Heidi, Rosensweig sisters, Ruth, Anna, and Li'l Bit, are victims of patriarchal system and entrapped in this or that prison and crisis. In this sense, the dramatic texts are representational, reflecting social problems authentically and giving voice to silenced women. However, the main purpose of these texts is not to expose the pain and victimization of the women but to explore the possibilities of survival, metamorphosis and prosperity of them. Ritual, as the central event, provides an arena for destroying as well as creating. These women undergo a transformative process by performing rituals. They change from victim to survivor, from silence to articulation, from dependence to autonomy, from object to subject, from margin to center, and from powerlessness to powerfulness. Such women images in creating and becoming are typical of and unique to Norman, Wasserstein and Vogel's dramas, which brings new feature to American feminist theater. In this sense, their dramatic texts are performative, reshaping the outlook of women on stage.

New feminist ideas and spirits are enacted through the performance of ritual. By portraying women as active, creative and self-constructive ritual body, Norman, Wasserstein and Vogel deconstruct oppressive gender norms, reimagine what women should be and explore new possibilities for mother-daughter, man-woman and woman-woman relationships according to their feminist ideals. Traditional masculinity is challenged, mocked and replaced in Arlene's renaming ritual, Henry's funeral, Father-Daughter Weekend, Ruth's performance of Henri and Orphan, and especially in Li'l Bit's parodied initiation. While conventional femininity is discarded by these female characters, they begin to embrace and acquire the strong personalities that have been conceived as masculine, such as independent, brave, aggressive, heroic, and so on. The mother-daughter relationship is not intimate or mutually supportive. Instead, it is indifferent, alienated and even damaging, which exposes the rupture between two generations. All the mothers, Arlene's, Jessie's, Rosensweig sisters' and Li'l Bit's, are victims of patriarchal system themselves, but with their internalization of patriarchal norms, they become accomplices in discriminating against and repressing their daughters who have to take extreme measures to rebel and cut off their bond. The mother-daughter conflicts and hatred and the daughters' revolt are unprecedented, which embodies the feminist spirit of the young generation. Such a spirit is also reflected in the new pattern of man-woman relationship. In the rituals such as Arlene's renaming, Henry's funeral, Archie's initiation, three imaginary boys' dying and Li'l Bit's parodied initiation, power is negotiated and shifted from men to women, which conveys the playwrights' feminist visions clearly. A new woman-woman relationship is established too. Ruby's voluntary help saves Arlene and encourages her to start a new life. The friendship and sisterhood among the college girls, the Ann Arbor CR Group and Rosensweig sisters are warm, supportive and powerful. Especially, Vogel portrays a lesbian couple who imagine three boys and invite a man to have a real baby with them, therefore, they have a family of seven, which, as Vanessa Campagna argues, "gestures toward Queer Utopia"(107). Such new visions about family and gender relation challenge patriarchal traditions and provide feminist alternatives to the world.

Ritual, as an effective dramaturgic device of Norman, Wasserstein and Vogel, constitutes a new woman's aesthetic in contemporary American theater. When discussing whether good art is genderless or not, Carolyn Cope argues, "To say that good art(or good theater) is genderless ignores important issues of representation, experience, sensibility, and viewpoint." (2) She quotes from Wendy Wasserstein, Maria Irene Fornes, Marsha Norman and other women playwrights to show that "plays written by women, like plays written by men, begin with a gender-derived set of assumptions about how the world works"(Norman, "Introduction" Vii). Her study proves that there is an identified woman's aesthetic which consists of particular themes, structures and dramatic devices, and that ritual is one of the dramatic devices that are effectively used by some women playwrights. The critical efforts made by feminist scholars such as Lynda Hart, Janet Brown, Sue-Ellen Case and Jill Dolan have explored the special aesthetic that belongs to women playwrights.

Norman, Wasserstein and Vogel have feminized the rituals that are traditionally designed, directed and manipulated by men to address women's issues and convey feminist ideology. Women are placed at the center of ritual. There is no male participant in Arlene's rite of affliction, Jessie's Requiem Mass, college girls' Gracious Living and the three sisters' Sabbath Sundown. It is women who design and carry out these rituals, and it is the female identity that is transformed during the ritual process. When men are included in the rituals such as renaming, funeral, initiation, courtship and the dying and resurrection, they are not the person who guides or controls the ritual. On the contrary, they are emasculated and disempowered, losing their original dominant position. Bennie yields to Arlene's strong will of changing her name. The Outlaw turns out to be incapable of preaching a funeral and has to accept Lily's instruction. Peter loses the traditional father role he attempts to take in the family and agrees to welcome Ruth and Anna's imaginary sons back. Peck's dominant status as the teacher, the father and the initiator is challenged and reversed by Li'l Bit who herself grows up and becomes a teacher and an initiator of a young man.

Norman, Wasserstein and Vogel reinterpret and reformulate some traditional rites from a feminist perspective. For example, the rite of initiation is traditionally performed by male adults for boys. According to Joseph Campbell, "the mystagogue (father or father-substitute) is to entrust the symbols of office only to a son who has been effectually purged of all inappropriate infantile cathexes"(135). However, In *The Holdup*, Archie's initiator, the "father-substitute", is the mother figure, Lily. It is Lily who leads Archie to a full understanding of adulthood and initiates him into the mysteries of sexual love. As Richard Wattenberg argues, "Norman 'feminizes' the traditional initiation rite and, consequently, escapes the danger of restructuring the male-centered frontier myth into a new male-centered initiation rite."(515) In *How I Learned to Drive*, the novice of initiation rite is not a boy but a girl. The initiator is not a wise and kind father who helps the novice understand the cosmos and life but a sexual abuser and a life destroyer. The girl is transformed into a woman with traditional masculine attributes rather than feminine ones. Vogel reverses all the conventions of the rite completely. She also feminizes the typical masculine ritual—courtship, in which man usually takes initiatives and gazes at female body as a sexual object. In Peck and Li'l Bit's courtship, Peck loses his dominant status gradually and Li'l Bit becomes the stronger one. When Peck is lying in the hotel bed to beg for Li'l Bit's love, his body is gazed by Li'l Bit and Aunt Mary as a sexual object, which changes the male-female relation in the traditional courtship.

Ritual helps to organize the dramatic action in terms of space, emotion and rhythm no matter whether the play is structured as linear or non-linear. In *Getting Out*, the rite of renaming recurs in the conversations between Arlene and other four characters and goes through the entire plot as Arlene's persistent gesture, forming the basic structure of the play. Regarding the whole play as a ritual, Norman arranges stage time and space in a ritualistic way and composes Jessie's action according to the repetitive rhythm of music. A few different rituals are inserted in *The Holdup*, *Uncommon Women and Others*, *And Baby Makes Seven* and *How I Learned to Drive*. They mark the rise and fall of the dramatic rhythm and constitute the keynote of the dramatic emotion. CR ritual in *The Heidi Chronicles* is the central event of the play, functioning as the turning point of character development as well as emotional structure. Sabbath Sundown in *The Sisters Rosensweig* triggers the dramatic conflicts and unites the family as one emotionally. All in all, rituals in Norman, Wasserstein and Vogel's dramas are female-centered and feminized. They serve effectively for their feminist commission and become a characteristic of their theater.

The central issue of both the feminist ritual theater and the plays of Norman, Wasserstein and Vogel is the female identity, which is also the primary problem that feminist theorists and activists are confronted at the emergence of feminism[①]. When feminist activists perform all kinds of female rituals to propagate feminist ideas and reshape female images in life, feminist playwrights create and stage new woman characters who transform their selves through

---

① See Linda Ginter-Brown, "Toward a More Cohesive Self: Women in the Works of Lillian Hellman and Marsha Norman" (1991); James Frieze, *The Interpretation of Difference: Staging Identity in the United States* (2002); Li Li, "Identity Politics in Contemporary American Theater" (2017); Zhu Xiaoying, "Men's Theater and Women's Drama: Contemporary American Women Playwrights' Encounter with Pulitzer Prize" (2012); Han Xi, "From Realism to Feminism: A Study on American Women Playwrights" (2014); Chen Yilei and Chen Aimin, "Identity Trouble: The Core Theme of American Theater in 20th–21st Century" (2015).

performing feminized rituals in theater. All the women, in reality or fiction, are searching for a true self that belongs to them, which means they try to know what a woman is, should be and could be according to feminist ideology rather patriarchal gender norms. The performativity of ritual in both the women's movement and feminist theater demonstrates that women are able to question, change and redefine their self-identities. They are always in a process of change. Their self-transformation process provides a theoretical insight into the question of what a woman is, which has aroused a lot of debates among feminists and philosophers. In the next section, the author attempts to discuss the question of female self in light of feminist theories of Simone de Beauvoir, Toril Moi, and especially Judith Butler.

Ⅲ. The Performativity of Female Self

According to Western humanist ideology, the individual is at the center of meaning and action, and there exists something called "self", the rational, autonomous, coherent and unique entity, who is capable of making choices and controlling its own actions and destiny. The problem is that this centered, privileged self has exclusively identified with man since Plato, through Descartes and Kant, to Freud. Female self has been systematically denied, diminished, subordinated, belittled and reduced to invisibility. As Luce Irigaray points out, "this centered self is in fact a phallic self, constructed on the model of the self-contained powerful phallus." (43) Female self used to be designated as irrational, passive, weak, dependent and immoral, essentially construed as an object that is defined and controlled by men. Simone de Beauvoir exposes this oppressive hierarchy trenchantly, "He is the Subject, he is the

Absolute—she is the Other."(8) Women as the Other are inferior, second and subservient to men who represent the Law, the Universal and the Essential.

The androcentric, sexist and masculine conception of men and women is based on the earlier natural philosophy and the Middle Ages theology (God's plan for mankind). Then it is reinforced by Freudian psychological theory and biological science in modern time. At the time that modern feminism is born, biological determinism has been pervasive and dominant. Some biological determinists claim, "Men's brains enable them to grasp the unknown: discoveries, science, the highest artistic and philosophical insights are reserved for them. Women's brains can deal with the known, the ordinary, and the everyday ... The ovum is conservative, the male cell progressive."(Brooks 258) "It is generally true that the males are more active, energetic, eager, passionate and variable; the females more passive, conservative, sluggish, and stable."(Geddes & Arthur 270). In the pervasive picture of sex, Toril Moi finds, "A woman becomes a woman to her fingertips ... Pervasive sex saturates not only the person, but everything the person touches. If housework, childcare, and selfless devotion are female, heroic exploits are male, and so are science and philosophy."(12) Biological determinism reduces a man to an enormous sperm cell and a woman to a giant ovum, believing that biology grounds and justifies social norms. Gradually, the binary framework of sex-gender-desire is formed, by which a female body is aligned with that which is culturally feminine, and this woman, as a proper woman, naturally desires men. This biology-is-destiny formulation imprisons women in their subordinate position, confines them to limited gender attributes and denounces any transgression of gender norms as unnatural and pathological.

Therefore, the first and most urgent task of feminism is to

deconstruct the sexist and misogynist conception of the self and re-conceptualize what a woman or a female self is and should be. Generations of feminists have contributed to the cause of redefining women, and different feminist theories have provided various answers. Liberal feminism insists that women and men are the same, and female and male natures are identical. Following the traditional humanist conception of self, liberal feminists argue that women are also rational and independent subjects who are capable of reasoning, judging, defining and authoring, and who have the same needs, wishes and desires as men to realize their full human potentials and take full moral responsibilities. Advocating individual freedom and equality, they prefer an un-gendered and androgynous self.

Cultural feminism accepts gender differences and confirms female characteristics, which, they argue, have long been distorted and devalued by sexist culture. Therefore, cultural feminists devote their efforts to revalidating female attributes according to feminist framework and giving positive implications and new values to femaleness. In their opinion, what should be changed is not female attributes but the masculine culture that undervalues and distorts femaleness.

Another influential group is psychoanalytical feminists who are interested in the function of inner psychic nature in forming one's self. They believe that the self grows out of the interface between nature and culture, and each person's self is individual and unique. They hold that there is neither universal male self nor universal female self; instead, there are as many selves as there are people. Whatever they focus on, sameness, difference or psyche of men and women, all the three feminist schools are basically essentialist, assuming that there is some existing identity or a core self that constitutes the subject for whom political representation is pursued.

This essentialist concept of self/woman is challenged by some feminists, among whom Simone de Beauvoir and Judith Butler are two of the most well-known and revolutionary. In *The Second Sex*, Beauvoir refutes, "The biological facts establish for her a fixed and inevitable destiny."(71) She claims famously, "one is not born, but becomes a woman"(301), which means a woman is not a fixed reality and is always in the process of making herself what she is. Beauvoir accepts the sexing of the body as either male or female, but denies that such a binary division implies any necessary consequences for what it is to be a woman. The body, for Beauvoir, is not a thing or an object, but a situation, meaning that the body is engaged in a dialectical interaction with its surroundings. A woman defines herself through the way she lives her embodied situation in the world, or in other words, through the way in which she makes something of what the world makes of her. A woman is free but her freedom is not absolute but situated. She has agency and can make choices in the process of making and being made, which is open-ended and ongoing. Just as Judith Butler interprets, "It follows that woman itself is a term in process, a becoming, a construction that cannot rightfully be said to originate or to end."("Gender Trouble" 33)

Adhering to Beauvoir's theoretical legacy, Butler continues the discussion of the concept of woman in *Gender Trouble*, challenging the stable, abiding or common identity of woman and its foundational position as a feminist subject waiting to be represented. Butler argues,

> It is not enough to inquire into how women might become more fully represented in language and politics. Feminist critique ought also to understand how the category of "women", the subject of feminism, is produced and restrained by the very structures of power through which emancipation is sought. (5)

Denying both biological determinism and social or cultural determinism, Butler emphasizes the body's stylized performance of compulsory gender conventions and norms. By invoking the concept of performativity, Butler contends that gender attributes are not expressive but performative, and they effectively constitute the identity they are said to express or reveal. She argues,

> Gender ought not to be construed as a stable identity or locus of agency from which various acts follow; rather, gender is an identity tenuously constituted in time, instituted in an exterior space through a stylized repetition of acts. The effect of gender is produced through the stylization of the body and, hence, must be understood as the mundane way in which bodily gestures, movements, and styles of various kinds constitute the illusion of an abiding gendered self. ("Gender Trouble" 179)

According to Butler's formulation, the iteration of gender norms operates like a performative speech-act where the discursive repetition of norms acts to constitute or produce what it enunciates. The repetition of gender norms necessarily precedes the emergence of the subject and initiates the subject into the dominant social order. The performative norm is a form of compulsion. Bodies cannot perform freely or randomly. They suffer under the weight of the conventions that they are brought to repeat and thus are normalized. For example, under patriarchal system, a female body has to perform feminine attributes and play the limited female roles in order to be recognized as a "true" woman which, for Butler, does not exist before the performative gestures and acts. Gender performatives are normative, compulsory and repressive, producing the "proper" subjects and concomitantly excluding others who fail to perform them correctly. Three elements stand at the center of Butler's gender performativity: body, gender norms and power. Gender identity is constituted in the process of the body performing gender norms, in which power is anchored and perpetuated or challenged and shifted.

The political significance of Butler's gender performativity lies in that she not only sees the normalizing power of gender performatives, but also recognizes the possibility of their failure and breakdown. The threat first of all comes from those who fall outside of the norms, the abnormal, the abjected, and the discriminated. They always exist as the dissonant and disruptive force, such as homosexual to heterosexual. Secondly, the production of stable identities is understood as a work of identification that is constitutively incapable of being completed. As Butler says, "To the extent that gender is an assignment, it is an assignment which is never quite carried out according to expectation." ("Bodies That Matter" 231). No one can perform gender norms fully and ideally. Thirdly, gender performatives are vulnerable in their repetitive structure. They can only exist and work through being cited, repeated and reenacted, which provides chance of hollow parody and mis-performing. Acts repeat, but they can repeat differently. Thus, gender acts can be turned towards undermining their organizing norms even as they "cite" them. Butler designates this subversive strategy as resignification, by which the spell of norms can be broken.

All of the discussed conceptions of self/female self have been manifested and embodied in the plays of Norman, Wasserstein and Vogel. As the products of the second wave of feminist movement, they expose and critique the normative and oppressive nature of gender norms. Men and women are restrained by the normative, oppressive and destructive gender norms. Women are prisoned in their inferior, fixed and victimized self-identity, while homosexuals are deprived of basic human rights. Men are superior to women, occupying the central and dominant position and controlling women's life through sexualizing and objectifying them. The female bodies are gazed, manipulated and exploited by males. Both men and women perform the limited gender norms legitimated in patriarchal paradigm and constitute their self-identity. The male characters such as Father, Bennie and Carl in *Getting Out*, the Outlaw, Henry and Archie in *The Holdup*, Mr. Lovens Friend in *Uncommon Women and Others*, Scoop in *The Heidi Chronicles*, Peter in *And Baby Makes Seven*, and Uncle Peck in *How I Learned to Drive*, try their best to perform the traditional masculinity: strong, violent, active, dominating, showing arrogance and superiority before women and regarding female body as an exploitable object.

Women's destinies are determined by their sex. Raped by men at early age, Arlene and Lily are forced to work as prostitutes. Jessie has to be confined in kitchen because of her ill body and female sex. Although women in Wasserstein's plays have got high education and jobs, they are constantly discriminated and oppressed, being forced to choose between family and career. Anna in *The Baltimore Waltz* performs traditional femininity and becomes a "good" girl, but finds herself infected with a fatal disease and being prejudiced just because of her sex. Being sexually abused by her uncle and sexualized by people around her, Li'l Bit even has an illusion that her two breasts are alien life forces that keep growing until they suck all her nourishment and collapse her. The only path of life provided by the society for her is to satisfy the male's sexual gaze and desire.

The rigid sex-gender-sexuality matrix is strictly maintained. Regarded as unfeminine, Arlie's rebellious behaviors get repressed and punished. Jessie and her mother's economy is controlled by her father and then her brother because women are believed to be incapable of financial management. Lily's modern clothes, strong character and driving ability are denounced by the Outlaw as unwomanly. All the girls in Wasserstein's plays are required to learn feminine manners, desire male bodies and sacrifice their lives to their husbands. Heterosexuality is conceived as normal while singleness and homosexuality, as abnormal, are oppressed and exiled. Gays such as Peter in *The Heidi Chronicles* and Carl in *The Baltimore Waltz*, have to repress their sexual desire for a long time and face ruthless treatment after they come out of the closet. Geoffrey in *The Sisters Rosensweig*, although preferring to have a boy as his partner, is forced to live with a girl and conceals his true feelings. They not only are confronted with sexual discrimination but also haunted by homophobia and AIDS. Peter and Geoffrey are frightened by the death of their AIDS friends and Carl himself is fired for AIDS and dies of AIDS.

However, the female self that identifies with patriarchal gender norms is entrapped in troubles and crises. Each of the women in Norman, Wasserstein and Vogel's plays is confronted with a rupture of self-identity. Each has an old self that must be discarded or renewed. The old self, as the performative effect of patriarchal gender norms, is suffocated, oppressed, battered and lost. All of them are struggling for a new life and a different self. The rupture of self-identity opens the possibilities of change and reformulation. The dramatic actions display how women's new self-identities are constituted through their bodies which perform rituals that enact feminist ideology. Ritual becomes their strategy to struggle with antagonist force and realize their new selves.

Situated in different social strata, these female characters have various visions of being a woman. Growing up in poor families and struggling at the bottom of the heap, women in Norman's plays are more concerned about independence and self-dignity. With rich family background and high education, women in Wasserstein's plays care more about equal opportunity, self-value and self-fulfillment. Having a strong consciousness of politics, women in Vogel's plays defy gender norms and crave as much power as men possess. Therefore, the new female selves forged by ritual performance are concrete, historical and individual, embodying a mixture of liberal feminism, cultural feminism, psychoanalytical feminism and materialist feminism.

The self-transformation process of the marginalized women, the educated women and the transgressive women illuminate a few theoretical insights into gender, and more generally, self. First of all, it demonstrates that there is no universally shared concept of woman and that the female self is not stable, fixed or single, but mutable, developmental and pluralistic. Each female body is concrete and each woman is historical. They interact with the outside world through their bodies and constitute their different self-identities. There is no female self that is determined by anatomical body and expressed by feminine attributes. Instead, it is the performative acts that constitute the self in the process of the body's stylized performance of norms and regulations. The female self changes with the change of body performance.

It also indicates that there is no primarily interior, stable or integrated core of gender. Gender is the performative effect of acts, gestures and desire on the body through the work of corporal signs and other discursive means. It is an illusion that can be broken, a fabrication that can be subverted, changed and remanufactured. Since the sexist and patriarchal ideology have created the illusory inferior female gender through manipulating female body in order to maintain the male's superior status and control women, feminist ideology could work in the same way to create new female gender that serve for women's interests through different gender performatives. Feminist movements and feminist theater have made great efforts to achieve this goal in the past fifty years. Gender is a forever ongoing process of making and remaking.

It furtherly shows that the binary biological determinist formulation of sex-gender-sexuality cannot hold water. As the new female selves in Norman, Wasserstein and Vogel's dramas demonstrate, a female body can perform both femininity and masculinity, and can desire both male and female body. Rather than being silent, passive and dependent, these women become articulate, active and independent. The traditional masculine attributes, such as reason, intelligence, rationality, courage, humor and competitiveness, can be found in these women. They are not satisfied to just stay at home as wife and mother, serving their husband and children; instead, they enter college and career, becoming financially prosperous and professionally successful. When confronted with the danger of rape and sexual abuse, these women choose to fight against and reverse the power pattern rather than tolerate silently. Sexuality and bawdy language are not forbidden things in college girls' dormitory. They can talk about sex and use bawdy humor freely. In addition, women can choose to love men and get married like Susie, Samantha and Gorgeous, to stay single and devote to career like Heidi and Sara, and to love and live with women like Anna and Ruth. Homosexual family, as Vogel portrays, is as happy and troublesome as heterosexual family. Therefore, the presumed coherent gender is broken up and the stable binary divisions of male/female, masculinity/femininity, and heterosexuality/homosexuality are undone.

In this sense, Norman, Wasserstein and Vogel's plays resonate and confirm Judith Butler's theory of gender performativity. However, they also challenge Butler's theory by highlighting the subjectivity of free individuals. Different from Butler's stress on the decisive role of structural force in initiating resignification of cultural signs and transformation of identity, Norman, Wasserstein and Vogel give more emphasis on the agency of the female subjects. As Toril Moi criticizes, Butler makes discursive power sound like a God and regards the body as abstract and generic(47), which in effect belittles the agency of an individual person. In Norman, Wasserstein and Vogel's dramatic world, each woman, situated in different social strata and with various desires, experiences the world with their own body, "the concrete, historical body that loves, suffers, and dies" (Moi 49). Although all of them have been subjected to patriarchal oppression, sexual harassment, gender discrimination or heterosexism in one way or another, they never stop their efforts of resisting, defying and struggling. Their bodies are not passive objects totally subjugated by male power or gender norms. They enact new rituals or mis-perform old rituals to embody feminist spirit and ideas, thus, constitutes new self-identity. Their self-transformation depends on their subjectivity. This is close to Beauvoir's notion that "the body is not a thing; it is a situation, it is our grasp on the world and a sketch of our projects"(110). According to Beauvoir, the body is not just brute matter to the self; it is a fundamental kind of situation that founds one's experiences of oneself and the world. It encompasses both the objective and the subjective aspects of experience. Human consciousness is part of every human experience and one's subjectivity is always embodied. The meaning of a woman's body is bound up with the way she uses her freedom which will lead to social and individual transformation. Therefore, women are always in the process of making themselves what they are by interacting with the world through their bodies. For Norman, Wasserstein and Vogel, although the oppressive structural force is pervasive and powerful, it is not impossible to resist, subvert and reverse it. Change depends on the agency of the female body. Norman, Wasserstein and Vogel highlight the subjectivity of individual women by situating the female characters' bodily performance of rituals at the center of their stage.

Epilogue

Believing that ritual is an effective practice that enacts thought and power, feminist activists have created and performed various rituals to raise women's consciousness, consolidate sisterhood, resist sexism and empower women, establishing a symbolic ritual system special to women. Inspired by the ritual events in the women's movement, feminist playwrights have combined ritual with theatrical performance and invented what Batya Podos called the feminist ritual theater which have staged all kinds of female rituals from life and myth in order to provide transformative experiences to the audience and change their conceptions. Influenced by the women's movement and the feminist ritual theater, Norman, Wasserstein and Vogel stage feminist rituals directly and feminize traditional rituals to represent women's experiences and exert impact on their audience.

As the central performative element in the plays, ritual has done something within the fictional world and brought about something new to the real world. Its performative efficacies within text include the constitution of new identity, the realization of women's empowerment and the consolidation of female community and sisterhood. Its performativity in reality is manifested in bearing witness to women's struggle against patriarchy and sexism, creating new liminal women images in American theater, enacting new feminist ideals and forming a unique aesthetic of women playwrights.

The female character's self-transformation through performing rituals demonstrates that self-identity, especially gender identity, cannot be construed as essential or stable; it is the performative effect of norms, acts, gestures and desire enacted by the body. Self-identity is mutable and multiple, always in the process of construction, transformation and reconstruction. Although the discursive force of the dominant ideology is powerful, the agency of the subject can work to initiate resignification and transformation.

Conclusion

The plays of Marsha Norman, Wendy Wasserstein and Paula Vogel abound with various kinds of rituals, such as the rite of affliction, the rite of renaming, the Requiem Mass, funeral, the rite of dying and resurrection, the rite of initiation, Gracious Living, Father-Daughter Weekend, commencement tea, consciousness-raising ritual, the Sabbath Sundown, children's service, the rite of loving exorcism, and the rite of courtship. By performing, mis-performing or parodying these rituals, the female protagonists heal trauma, transform self-identity, negotiate power with men and embody feminist ideology. They negate or discard their old selves which are forged by patriarchal gender norms, and constitute their new selves with feminist thought and spirit, which illustrates that the female self is not a fixed identity, but the performative effect of stylized bodily acts of the female subject who interacts with the ever-changing social situations.

Female identity and gender politics are two central issues of the women's movement and feminist theater. As the baby boomer generation, Norman, Wasserstein and Vogel participate in actively and are influenced considerably by the second wave of the women's movement. All of them are devoted to staging women's experiences in the male-dominated American theater and reformulating female images which have been belittled, demonized and victimized. Women in their dramas are neither angels in the house nor mad women at the attic, they are rebellious and creative women who are trapped in identity crisis and undergo all kinds of ordeals before being renewed and empowered. They challenge male authorities, subvert patriarchal discourse and cast off constraining gender norms. At the same time, they express their needs and aspirations, gain control of their destinies and redefine who they are. Like Odysseus, they are in a liminal stage of life and are always on a journey of struggling and searching for a true self. This common theme threads most of the plays of Norman, Wasserstein and Vogel.

The other prominent feature shared by Norman, Wasserstein and Vogel's dramas is that all the three playwrights utilize ritual and ritualization to portray female image, organize dramatic plot and convey feminist theme. Ritual is a central performative textual element and serves vital functions in three dimensions. It is a strategic act performed by female protagonists to deal with crisis and empower themselves within fictional stories. It is also an effective dramatic device utilized by the playwrights to arrange time, space, emotion and rhythm of dramatic texts. In addition, ritual is a textual strategy that connects dramatic texts to their cultural settings, target audience and social functions. As both a cultural performance and a textual strategy, ritual not only expresses something but also does and creates something. Their performative effects are as significant as their semantic and symbolic meanings for understanding Norman, Wasserstein and Vogel's dramatic œuvres.

As the strategic acts of the female protagonists within dramatic texts, rituals in Norman, Wasserstein and Vogel's plays produce a few performative effects in the fictional world. New identities are constituted, male / female power hierarchy is reversed and female community is consolidated. Rituals in Norman's plays are both destructive and creative. Some of them are death rituals (the Requiem Mass and funeral), others contain symbolic death and rebirth (the rite of dying and resurrection and the rite of initiation), and still others are aimed at exorcism and replacement (the rite of affliction, the rite of renaming). The objects, signs and behaviors in the rituals are rich in symbolic meanings. The languages and gestures are full of performative power. By designing, directing and performing the rituals with tragic spirit, the female protagonists experience death and rebirth in one way or another, destroying their old selves and creating new self-identities. They also gain independence, autonomy and power during the ritual process.

Different from the somber, tragic death-rebirth rituals performed by individuals in Norman's plays, rituals in Wasserstein's dramatic works are euphoric, comic and collective, being performed in an exaggerated and funny manner but addressing serious issues. The ritual is a dynamic and dialectical process, in which compliance and resistance coexist and the tension between ritual structure and ritual body is highlighted. The participants who follow ritual codes are constrained, shaped and defined by the ritual while others who challenge and disobey ritual codes are constituted by their rebellious and subversive words and acts. Mis-performing ritual such as carnivalizing is used as a strategy to counter ritualization. The meaning, force and effect of ritual are not determined by the original ritual intention or structure but by the agency of the participants. For Wassserstein and her female characters, ritual is a political arena where various social forces encounter, negotiate and compromise and female selves are constantly shaped and reshaped.

Rituals in Vogel's plays are parodic, satirical and absurd. They are deployed by the playwright to mock rigid gender norms, deconstruct oppressive patriarchal and heterosexual discourses and reverse male-female power hierarchy. The female protagonists are presented as central ritual subjects who transgress the borders of masculinity and femininity, survive life crisis, negotiate power with men and constitute androgynous self-identities by improvising and parodying rituals from social life or literary works. Male bodies are gazed and appreciated by both women and men as desired objects and men are changed or disempowered during the parodied ritual process.

Rituals serve important functions in arranging dramatic events and structuring dramatic action. The plot of *Getting Out* is based on Arlene's renaming rite and reaches its climax at her rite of affliction. In *'night, Mother*, dramatic time is in line with ritual time, stage space is separated according to its ritual function, and the entire dramatic action parallels with Jessie's ritual performance. The reunion rite of Lily and the Outlaw, the funeral of Henry, the ritual of dying and resurrection of the Outlaw and the initiation rite of Archie constitute the plot of *The Holdup*. *Uncommon Women and Others* starts with a reunion dinner, moves on with a few college rituals and ends with the same reunion dinner, constituting a circular structure. Consciousness-raising ritual in *The Heidi Chronicles* marks the turning point of Heidi's identity and the tone of the narration, dividing the dramatic action into two distinct parts. The Sabbath Sundown ritual is used to trigger the conflicts of Sara and Gorgeous and connect all the characters in the play. Its narrative function is as important as its thematic function. The whole dramatic action of *And Baby Makes Seven* revolves around the three children's rituals of dying and rebirth. In *How I Learned to Drive*, two rites of passage, Li'l Bit's driving learning and sexual awakening function as the main narrative lines that run through the entire play.

As both a performative act itself and a textual strategy that links dramatic text to its cultural settings, audience and aims, ritual together with the dramtic text can be conceived as action which extends its performative power to the external real world. First, the ritual performance records and bears witness to women's struggles against gender oppression from the 1960s to the 1980s in the United States. Second, rituals create new liminal women images that are unprecedented in American theater. Third, New feminist vision and ideology are enacted and embodied by ritual subjects. Last, Norman, Wasserstein and Vogel not only create new rituals but also feminize conventional rituals to convey feminist themes and organize their dramatic works, which constitutes a new female dramatic aesthetic in American feminist theater.

The creative, constitutive and performative power of ritual has been recognized and utilized by radical feminist activists and other feminist playwrights. Collective rituals are organized by radical feminists to raise feminist awareness and protest against sexual violence. New rituals peculiar to female gender are created by spiritual feminists to celebrate women's sexual characteristics and enhance sisterhood. An innovative dramatic form—feminist ritual theater—is produced by women theater groups. Varied feminist rituals such as the ritual of Matrilineage are designed and performed in theater, linking women with their matriarchal ancestors and recapturing their lost power. Although performed by different people in different spaces and with different forms, rituals in both feminist movement and theater achieve similar performative effects. They heal women's personal as well as cultural trauma, raise feminist consciousness, transform and empower ritual participants, and reinforce women's solidarity.

The transformation and reconstitution of female identity through performance of rituals shed light on a primary and long-debated issue of feminism—what a woman is and how the subject of woman is produced. It challenges the biological essentialist concept of sex, gender and sexuality and illustrates that a woman is not a fixed or abiding reality, but a changeable and developmental construct. Women are compelled to perform limited gender roles and traditional femininity in patriarchal society, which result in their inferior, second sex identity. Equipped with feminist consciousness, women transgress gender boundaries, break the presumed coherence of sex-gender-sexuality, and deconstruct the binary opposites of masculinity/femininity and heterosexuality/homosexuality. Their languages and body gestures in the ritual constitute their new self-identities. This process illustrates that it is the iteration of gender norms and attributes that produce a woman and initiates it into the dominant social order. Gender is the performative effect of bodily gestures, movements and styles of various kinds in the constantly changing world. Although gender norms are normative and repressive, they can be subverted, mis-performed and re-signified. The individual agency plays a significant role in the making and remaking of the female self.

The dramatic works of Marsha Norman, Wendy Wasserstein and Paula Vogel can be conceived of as speech act or action, which are not only representational but also performative. Set against the feminist movement, gay right movement and other social movements in America from the 1960s to the 1990s, these plays penetrate into the lives of women from all social strata. They describe women's personal troubles, concerns, crises, desires, aspirations, pursuits, loss and gains, articulate their voices which have been silenced, repressed and marginalized for so long, and represent their protest, resistance, struggle and striving against discrimination, oppression and objectification in the male-dominated patriarchal society. Also, writing these works is Norman, Wasserstein and Vogel's conduct and act performed to express their political and artistic stances as women playwrights. Their plays bring a group of new female characters that embody feminist ideology to American literature. The female characters' personal journey of self-search, self-empowerment and self-realization runs parallel to the playwrights political quest and fight. Their personal pursuit in dramatic art is in conformity with their political cause—to change the invisibility and voicelessness of women in American theater. Their act of writing is their political act to engage in the feminist movement, which constitutes their identity as feminist playwrights. Another performative dimension lies in reading and performing their dramatic works, which, as events, could affect its readers and audience. Although it is very difficult to measure the influence of each reading and performing event, their performative power can be perceived from the debate they arouse, the popularity among readers and the endurance of performance. Since the 1970s, their plays have been read, performed and studied not only in America but also in many other countries. Their Pulitzer Prize works have been recognized as feminist classics.

As original, innovative and remarkable women playwrights, Marsha Norman, Wendy Wasserstein and Paula Vogel have worked persistently at the forefront of contemporary American drama and successfully enter mainstream market or win top prizes of drama. They make significant contributions to feminist theater in that they demonstrate the transformative and performative process of female identity and envisage what a woman should be and could be according to the creeds of feminism by employing ritual and ritualization as their dramatic device. Their ingenious deployment of ritual provides a new and effective form to unravel women's experiences and explore feminist themes, which constitutes one important aspect of a woman's aesthetic in the dramas of contemporary American women playwrights.

By exploring rituals' symbolic meaning, performative effect, political implication and poetic function in Norman, Wasserstein and Vogel's plays, the present study highlights the indispensable role of ritual in their dramatic works and provides a new perspective to analyze contemporary American feminist theater. It unprecedentedly reveals the strategic mechanism of identity transformation and female empowerment, which enriches the scholarship of these women playwrights. Also, it gains new insights into the theories of ritual, performativity and gender and paves the way for further research in the future.

References

[1] ALFORD R. Naming and identity: a cross-cultural study of personal naming practices [M]. New Haven: Harf Press, 1988.

[2] APTHEKER B. Women's legacy: essays on race, sex and class in American history [M]. Amherst: University of Massachusetts Press, 1982.

[3] AURELIUS E H, HE C Z, & HELGASON J. Performativity in literature [C]. Stockholm: KVHAA, 2016.

[4] AUSTIN J L. How to do things with words [M]. Beijing: Foreign Language Teaching and Research Press, 2002.

[5] BAKHTIN M. Rabelais and his world [M]. Bloomington: Indiana University Press, 1984.

[6] BALAKIAN J. Reading the plays of Wendy Wasserstein [M]. New York: Applause Theater Cinema Books, 2010.

[7] BARKO C C. Rediscovering female voice and authority: the revival of female artists in Wendy Wasserstein's *The Heidi Chronicles* [J]. Frontiers: a journal of women studies, 2008, 29(1):121-138.

[8] BARNES C. Wendy Wasserstein: a casebook [M]. New York & London: Garland Publishing, Inc., 1999.

[9] BARNEY L. Hot ticket [J]. Spotlight magazine, 1993(March): 48-54.

[10] BEARD S. An interview with Marsha Norman [C]//WOETZEL J R. (ed.). The southern California anthology. Los Angeles: University of

Southern California Press, 1986.

[11] BEAUFORT J. A wry reunion [N]. The Christian science monitor, 1977, (Nov. 30).

[12] BEAUVOIR S De. The second sex [M]. PARSHLEY H M. (trans.). New York: Vantage Book, 1989.

[13] BEGLEY V. Objects of realism: Bertolt Brecht, Roland Barthes, and Marsha Norman [J]. Theater journal, 2012, (64): 337-354.

[14] BELL C. Ritual: perspectives and dimensions [M]. Oxford: Oxford University Press, 1997.

[15] BELL C. Ritual theory, ritual practice [M]. Oxford: Oxford University Press, 2009.

[16] BENNETTS L. An uncommon dramatist prepares her New York [N]. The New York times, 1981, (May 24): Sec, 2-5.

[17] BETSKO K & KOENIG R. Interviews with contemporary Women Playwrights [C]. New York: Beech Tree Books, 1987.

[18] BETTINA A. Women's legacy: essays on race, sex, and class in American history [M]. Amherst: University of Massachusetts Press, 1982.

[19] BIGSBY C. Modern American drama 1945—2000 [M]. Cambridge: Cambridge University Press, 2001.

[20] BIGSBY C. Contemporary American playwrights [M]. Cambridge: Cambridge University Press, 2004.

[21] BILOWIT I J. Bringing up baby: Paula Vogel's newest born [N]. Back stage, 1993, (May): 5f.

[22] BLATANIS K. Popular culture icons in contemporary American drama [M]. Cranbury, NJ: Rosemont Publishing & Printing Corp., 2003.

[23] BOESING M. The story of a mother: a ritual drama [C]// CHINOY H K & JENKINS L W. (eds.). Women in American theater. New York: Theater Communications Group, 1987.

[24] BOWERS K. *How I Learned to Drive*: a critical look at the

acceptance of sexual abuse myths in the play and its reception [D]. The University of Arizona, 2000.

[25] BROOK B. Feminist perspectives on the body [M]. London & New York: Routledge, 2014.

[26] BROOKS W K. The law of heredity: a study of the cause of variation, and the origin of living organisms [M]. Baltimore: John Murphy, 1883.

[27] BROSIUS C. Ritual matters: dynamic dimensions in practice [M]. London: Routledge, 2010.

[28] BROWN J. Taking center stage: feminism in contemporary U. S. drama [M]. Metuchen, N. J. : Scarecrow Press, 1991.

[29] BROWN S. I thought you were mine: Marsha Norman's 'night, Mother[C]//PEARLMAN M. (ed.). Mother puzzles: daughters and mothers in contemporary American literature. New York: Greenwood Press, 1989: 109 - 113.

[30] BRUSTEIN R. What do women playwrights want [N]. The new republic, 1992, (April 13): 28 - 30.

[31] BRYER J R. The playwright's art: conversations with contemporary American dramatists [M]. New Brunswick, N.J: Rutgers University Press, 1995.

[32] BUDAPEST Z. The feminist book of lights and shadows [M]. Venice, Calif. : The Feminist Wicca, 1975.

[33] BURKMAN K. The Demeter myth and doubling in Marsha Norman's 'night, Mother [C]// SCHLUETER J. (ed.). Modern American drama: the female canon. Rutherford: Fairleigh Dickinson University Press, 1990.

[34] BUTLER J. Undoing gender [M]. New York: Routledge, 1990.

[35] BUTLER J. Excitable speech: a politics of the performative [M]. London & New York: Routledge, 1997.

[36] BUTLER J. Gender trouble: feminism and the subversion of identity [M]. London & New York: Routledge, 1999.

[37] BUTLER J. Bodies that matter [M]. London & New York: Routledge, 2011.

[38] CAMPAGNA V. Gesturing toward queer utopia: the children's world of Paula Vogel's *And Baby Makes Seven* [J]. Journal of dramatic theory and criticism, 2017, (1):107-126.

[39] CAMPBELL J. The hero with a thousand faces [M]. Princeton: Bollingen Series, 1997.

[40] CANNING C. Feminist theaters in the U. S. A.: staging women's experience [M]. London & New York: Routledge, 1996.

[41] CARLSON S. L. Comic textures and female communities 1937 and 1977: Clare Boothe and Wendy Wasserstein [C]//SCHLUETER J. (ed.). Modern American drama: the female canon. Rutherford: Fairleigh Dickinson University Press, 1990.

[42] CASE S E. The personal is not political [J]. Art & cinema, 1987, 1 (3):35-41.

[43] CASE S E. Feminism and theater [M]. New York: Routledge, 1988.

[44] CASE S E. Toward a butch-femme aesthetic [C]//HART L. (ed.). Making a spectacle: feminist essays on contemporary women's theater. Ann Arbor: University of Michigan Press, 1989: 282-299.

[45] CHARLES L H. Drama in first-naming ceremonies [J]. Journal of American folklore, 1981, (64):11-35.

[46] CHIRICO M M. Female laughter and comic possibilities: *Uncommon Women and Others* [C]// BARNET T C. (ed.). Wendy Wasserstein: a casebook. New York & London: Garland Publishing, Inc., 1999.

[47] CIOCIOLA G. Wendy Wasserstein: dramatizing women, their voices and their boundaries [M]. London: McFarland & Company, Inc., 1998.

[48] CLINE G. The impossibility of getting out: the psychopolitics of the family in Marsha Norman's *Getting Out* [C]// GINTER-BROWN L. (ed.). Marsha Norman: a casebook. New York: Garland

Publishing, Inc. 1996: 20-28.

[49] CLUM J M. Acting gay: male homosexuality in modern drama [M]. New York: Columbia University Press, 1994.

[50] COHEN E. Uncommon women: an interview with Wendy Wasserstein [C] // REGINA B (ed.), Last laughs: perspectives on women and comedy. New York: Gordon & Breach, 1998.

[51] COMAROFF J. Body of power, spirit of resistance [M]. Chicago: University of Chicago Press, 1985.

[52] COOK A. Making a match: courtship in Shakespeare and his society [M]. Princeton: Princeton University Press, 2014.

[53] COOPERMAN R. I don't know what's going to happen in the morning: visions of the past, present, and future in *The Holdup*[C] //GINTER-BROWN L. (ed.). Marsha Norman: a casebook. New York: Garland Publishing, Inc., 1996.

[54] COPE C. The women's aesthetic in selected plays of Maria Irene Fornes, Holly Hughes, Wendy Wasserstein, Marsha Norman and Suzan-Lori Parks [D]. Southern Illinois University, 2005.

[55] COSS C & SKLAR R. Separation and survival: mothers, daughters, sisters—the women's experimental theater[C]//EISENSTEIN H & JARDINE A. (eds.). The future of difference. Boston: G. K. Hall & Co., 1980.

[56] CRAIG C C. Women Pulitzer playwrights: biographical profiles and analyses of the plays[M]. North Carolina: McFarland Company, 2004.

[57] CULLER J. Literary theory: a very short introduction [M]. Oxford: Oxford University Press, 1997.

[58] CURB K R. Re/cognition, re/presentation, re/creation in woman-conscious drama: the seer, the seen, the scene, the obscene[J]. Theater journal, 1985,37(3): 302-316.

[59] CZEKAY A. Not having it all: Wendy Wasserstein's uncommon women [C]//HERRINGTON J. (ed.). The playwright's muse. New

York: Routledge, 2002.

[60] DALY M. Gyn/ecology: the metaethics of radical feminism[M]. Boston, Mass. : Beacon Press, 1978.

[61] DALY M. Beyond god the father: toward a philosophy of women's liberation[M]. Boston, Mass. : Beacon Press,1985.

[62] DAVIS-FLOYD R. Birth as an American rite of passage [M]. Berkeley: University of California Press, 1992.

[63] DEMASTES W W. Jessie and Thelma revisited: Marsh Norman's conceptual challenge in 'night, Mother[J]. Modern drama, 1993,36 (1): 120-9.

[64] DERRIDA J. Limited Inc [M]. Evanston: Chicago University Press, 1988.

[65] DESHAZER M K. Walls made out of paper: witnessing *Wit* and *How I Learned to Drive* [J]. Women performance: a journal of feminist theory, 2002,13(1): 107-120.

[66] DICKNSON P. World stages, local audience: essays on performance, place, and politics [M]. Manchester: University of Manchester Press, 2010.

[67] DOLAN J. Feminist performance criticism and the popular: reviewing Wendy Wasserstein [J]. Feminism and theater, 2008,(10): 433-457.

[68] DOLAN J. 'night, Mother [J]. Women & performance journal, 1983,1(1):102-104.

[69] DOLAN J. The feminist spectator as critic [M]. Ann Arbor: University of Michigan Press, 1988.

[70] DOLAN J. Performance review: *How I Learned to Drive* [J]. Theater journal, 1998,50(1):128.

[71] DOLAN J. Wendy Wasserstein [M]. Ann Arbor: University of Michigan Press, 2017.

[72] DONALDSON S. Outside, looking: female leadership in Wendy Wasserstein's *An American Daughter*[J]. Public integrity, 2006, 8 (3): 207-214.

[73] DOUGLAS M. Natural symbols [M]. New York: Random House, 1973.

[74] DREW A M. And the time for it was gone: Jessie's triumph in *'night, Mother* [C]//GINTER-BROWN L G. (ed.). Marsha Norman: a casebook. New York: Garland Publishing, Inc. ,1996.

[75] DRUCKMAN S. A playwright on the edge [N]. The New York times, 1997,(March 16):H6.

[76] EAGLETON T. The event of literature [M]. New Haven: Yale University Press, 2012.

[77] EDER R. Stage "*Getting out*" by Marsha Norman [N]. The New York times, 1979,(May 16).

[78] EPSTEIN G. At the intersection: configuring women's difference through narrative in Norman's *Third and Oak: the Laundromat* [C]// GINTER-BROWN L. (ed.). Marsha Norman: a casebook. New York: Garland Publishing, Inc. , 1996.

[79] ERBEN R. The western holdup play: the pilgrimage continues [J]. Western American literature, 1989,23(4 Winter):311-322.

[80] FEINGOLD M. All for love [J]. Village voice, 1997 (March 25):97.

[81] FEINGOLD M. Wendy Wasserstein, 1950—2006 [J/OL]. Village voice, 2006(Jan. 30):5. http://www.villagevoice.com.

[82] FISCHER L E. The transformative power of performance: a new aesthetics [M]. London: Routledge, 2008.

[83] FORTE J. Realism narrative, and the feminist playwright [J]. Modern drama, 1989,32: 115-127.

[84] FOSTER K. De-tangling the web: mother-daughter relationship in the plays of Marsha Norman, Lillian Hellman, Tina Howe, and Ntozake Shange [D]. University of Nebraska-Lincoln, 1994.

[85] FOSTER V A. After Chekhov: the three sisters of Beth Henley, Wendy Wasserstein, Timerlake Wertenbaker, and Blake Morrison [J]. Comparative drama, 2013,47(4): 451-472.

[86] FOUCAULT M. Discipline and punishment: the birth of the prison [M]. SHERIDAN A. (trans.). New York: Vintage Books, 1995.

[87] FREUD S. Jokes and their relation to the unconscious [M]. London: The Hogarth Press, 1960.

[88] FRIEDAN B. The feminine mystique [M]. New York: W. W. Norton & Company, 2001.

[89] FRIEDMAN S. Revisioning the woman's part: Paula Vogel's Desdemona [J]. New theatre quarterly, 1999, (15):131 - 141.

[90] FRIEZE J. The interpretation of difference: staging identity in the United States [D]. University of Wisconsin-Madison, 2002.

[91] GEDDES P & ARTHUR T J. The evolution of sex [M]. London: Walter Scott, 1998.

[92] GENNEP A V. The rites of passage [M]. London & New York: Routledge, 2010.

[93] GERARD J. Review of *And Baby Makes Seven* [J]. Variety, 1993, (May 11):1.

[94] GERARD J. Review of The Heidi Chronicles [J]. Variety, 1995, (Oct. 9 - 15): 216.

[95] GINTER-BROWN L. Toward a more cohesive self: women in works of Lillian Hellman and Marsha Norman [D]. The Ohio State University, 1991.

[96] GINTER-BROWN L. Marsha Norman: a casebook [C]. New York: Garland Publishing, Inc., 1996.

[97] GLENN A S. Female spectacle: the theatrical roots of modern feminism [M]. Cambridge: Harvard University Press, 2000.

[98] GOLD S. Circle pins to power lunches [J]. Wall Street Journal, 1988 (Dec. 16):A13.

[99] GRETCHEN C. The impossibility of getting out: the psychopolitics of the family in Marsha Norman's *Getting Out* [C]//GINTER-BROWN L. (ed.). Marsha Norman: a casebook. New York: Garland Publishing Inc.,1996.

[100] GRIFFIN S. Women and nature: the roaring inside her [M]. New York: Harper, 1980.

[101] GRIMES R L. Ritual, media, and conflict [M]. Oxford: Oxford University Press, 2011.

[102] GRIMES R L. The craft of ritual studies [M]. Oxford: Oxford University Press, 2014.

[103] GRODE E. The inner children of parents-to-be [N/OL]. The New York times, 2014, (Mar 25.) http://www.nytimes.com/2014/03/26/theater/paula-vogels-and-baby-makes-seve-is-revived.html? mcubz = 3.

[104] GROSSBERG M. Close to home [N]. Columbus dispatch, 1995, (April 23): D1.

[105] GROTOWSKI J. The theater's new testament [C]//SCHECHNER R & SCHUMAN M. (eds.). Ritual, play and performance. New York: Seabury Press,1976.

[106] GUSSOW M. Review of *Isn't It Romantic* [N]. The New York times, 1981,(June 15): C3.

[107] HAGAN M. BWW review: from the mouths of babes: Paula Vogel's *And Baby Makes Seven* at new Ohio theater, now through 4/12 [J/OL]. Broadway world, 2014, Mar 31. http://www.broadwayworld.com/offbroadway/article/BWW-Review-From-the-Mouths-of-Babes-Paula-Vogel's-AND-BABYMAKES-SEVEN-at-New-Ohio-Theater-Now-Through-412-20140331.

[108] HAMMERMEISTER S. Re-visionary bodies: feminist/Brechtian theory in the plays of Paula Vogel [D]. University of Nevada, Las Vega, 2000.

[109] HANSEN C M. Ritual speech acts and the Shakespearean stage [D]. University of Nebraska, 2005.

[110] HARRIOT E. Marsha Norman: *Getting out* [C]//JEFFERSON N C. (ed.). American voices: five contemporary playwrights in essays and interviews. London: McFarland & Company, Inc. , 1988.

[111] HEILMAN S. Portrait of American Jews: the last half of the 20th

century [M]. Seattle & London: University of Washington Press, 1995.

[112] HEILPERN J. Pedophiles, sock fetishists ... hey kids, it's Oprah drama [J]. New York observer, 1997, (Apr. 7):32-35.

[113] HERREN G. Narrating, witnessing, and healing: trauma in Paula Vogel's *How I Learned to Drive*[J]. Modern drama, 2010, 53(1): 103-113.

[114] HODGINS P. Southern California theatres host a new breed of female hero [N]. Orange county register, 1994, (Aug. 19):8.

[115] HOMES M A. Wendy Wasserstein [J]. Bomb, 2001, 75:34-39.

[116] HORWITZ S. The playwright as woman [N]. Theater week, 1991, (Aug. 26-Sept. 1).

[117] HUBBARD K. Wendy Wasserstein [J]. People weekly, 1990, (25):99.

[118] IRIGARAY L. Speculum of the other woman [M]. GILL G. (trans.). New York: Cornell University Press, 1985.

[119] ISHERWOOD C. Review of *The Heidi Chronicles* by Wendy Wasserstein [N]. The New York times, 2015, (March 19):24-26.

[120] JAGGAR A M. Feminist politics and human nature[M]. Totowa: Rowman & Allanheld, 1983.

[121] JANARDANAN D. Images of loss in Tennessee Williams's *The Glass Menagerie*, Arthur Miller's *Death of a Salesman*, Marsha Norman's *'night, Mother* and Paula Vogel's *How I Learned to Drive* [D]. Georgia State University, 2007.

[122] JONES C. Wendy Wasserstein, 1950—2006[J]. Chicago tribune, 2006, (Jan 31.):15-17.

[123] KANE L. The way out, the way in: paths to self in the plays of Marsha Norman [C]//BRATER E. (ed.), Feminine focus: the new women playwrights. New York: Oxford University Press, 1989.

[124] KAPFERER B. Ritual dynamics and virtual practice: beyond

representation and meaning [C]// HANDELMAN D & LINDQUIST G. (eds.). Ritual in its own right. New York: Berghahn Books, 2005.

[125] KEOHANE N O. ROSALDO M, & GELPI B C. Feminist theory: a critique of ideology [M]. Chicago: University of Chicago Press, 1982.

[126] KERTZER D. Ritual, politics and power [M]. New Haven: Yale University Press, 1988.

[127] KEYSSAR H. Feminist theater: an introduction to plays of contemporary British and American woman [M]. New York :Grove Press, Inc. , 1984.

[128] KIMBROUGH A. The pedophile in me: the ethics of *How I Learned to Drive* [J]. Journal of dramatic theory and criticism, 2002,16(2): 47-67.

[129] KIMBROUGH A & LIU Z G. Taking *The Heidi Chronicles* to China: a dramaturgical reflection [J]. Theater topics, 2008, 18 (12): 147-159.

[130] KISSEL H. Family circus: Wasserstein turns 'Sisters' into a jovial juggling act [N]. Daily news, 1992, (Oct. 23).

[131] KLEMESRUD J. She had her own "getting out" to do [N]. The New York times, 1979, (May 27).

[132] KNOWLES R. Shakespeare and carnival after Bakhtin [M]. London: Macmillan Press Ltd. , 1998.

[133] KOENIG S. Hopi clay, Hopi ceremony: an exhibition of Hopi art [M]. New York: Katonah, 1976.

[134] KOIKE M. Challenges and hopes for American theater in the twenty-first century [J]. The Japanese journal of American studies, 2000,(11):91-108.

[135] KRAFT D. Wasserstein's '*Sisters Rosensweig*': a pungent comedy [N]. North Jersey herald and news, 1993, (March 26): B7.

[136] KRAMER M. Portrait of a lady [N]. New Yorker, 1988, (Dec. 26).

[137] KRISTEVA J. Powers of horror: an essay on abjection [M]. New York: Columbia University Press, 1982.

[138] KRISTEVA J. Strangers to ourselves [M]. New York: Columbia University Press, 1991.

[139] KROLL J. Before and after meet in a girl [N]. Newsweek, 1979, (May 28).

[140] KUNDERT-GIBBS J. Revolving it all: mother-daughter Paris in Marsha Norman's *'night, Mother* and Samuel Beckett's *Footfalls* [C]//GINTER-BROWN L. (ed.). Marsha Norman: a casebook. New York: Garland Publishing Inc., 1996.

[141] LAWSON T & MCCAULEY R. Rethinking religion: connecting cognition and culture [M]. Cambridge: Cambridge University Press, 1990.

[142] LEE J. Gender roles [M]. New York: Nova Biomedical Books, 2005.

[143] LEE R & MORGAN D. Death rites: law and ethics at the end of life [C]. London & New York: Routledge, 2005.

[144] LEHMANN H T. Post-dramatic theater [M]. London & New York: Routledge, 2006.

[145] LINDEN A. Seducing the audience: politics in the plays of Paula Vogel [C] // HERRINGTON J. (ed.). The playwright's muse. London & New York: Routledge, 2002.

[146] LOXLEY J. Performativity [M]. London & New York: Routledge, 2006.

[147] MANDL B. Feminism, postmodernism, and *Heidi Chronicles* [J]. Studies in the humanities, 1990, (17): 120-128.

[148] MANSBRIDGE J. Popular bodies, canonical voices: Paula Vogel's *Hot 'N' Throbbing* as performative burlesque [J]. Modern drama, 2009, 52(4): 469-489.

[149] MANSBRIDGE J. Camp, the canon, and a performative burlesque:

Paula Vogel's plays as literary and cultural revision [D]. City University of New York, 2010.

[150] MANSBRIDGE J. Paula Vogel [M]. Ann Arbor: University of Michigan Press, 2014.

[151] MELO C. Carnivalizing carnival-land in the urban *Sertões* of Teatro Oficina[J]. Latin American theater review, 2010, 44, (1 Fall): 93 – 113.

[152] MILLER J H. Literature as conduct: speech acts in Henry James [M]. New York: Fordham University Press, 2005.

[153] MILLER N. Out of the past: gay and lesbian history from 1869 to the present [M]. New York: Vintage Books, 1995.

[154] MOI T. What is a woman? and other essays [C]. Oxford: Oxford University Press, 1999.

[155] MORGAN D & LEE R. Preface: law, ethics and death: silence and symbolism [C]// LEE R & MORGAN D. (eds.). Death rites: law and ethics at the end of life. London & New York: Routledge, 2005.

[156] MORITZ C. Wendy Wasserstein [C]// Current biography yearbook 1989. New York: H. W. Wilson, 1990.

[157] MURPHY B. The Cambridge companion to American women playwrights [C]. Shanghai: Shanghai Foreign Language Education Press, 2001.

[158] MURRAY G. Excursus on the ritual forms preserved in Greek tragedy [C]//HARRISON J E. (ed.). Themis: a study of the social origins of Greek religion. Cambridge: Cambridge University Press,1912.

[159] MURRAY T. Partriarchal panopticism, or the seduction of a bad "Getting Out" in theory [J]. Theater journal, 1983, 35 (3): 376 – 388.

[160] NEWTON E. Mother camp: female impersonators in America [M]. Chicago: University of Chicago Press, 1972.

[161] NIETZSCHE F. The birth of tragedy out of the spirit of music [M]. WHITESIDE S. (trans). London: Penguin Books, 1995.

[162] NORMAN M. In the wake of Norman's Pulitzer [N]. Los Angeles times, 1983, (April 22): C16.

[163] NORMAN M. *'night, Mother* [M]. New York: Hill and Wang, 1983.

[164] NORMAN M. Lillian Hellman's gift to a young playwright [N]. The New York times, 1984, (26 Aug).

[165] NORMAN M. Marsha Norman [C]// BETSKO K & RACHE L. (eds.). Interviews with contemporary women playwrights. New York: Beech Tree Books, 1987.

[166] NORMAN M. Four plays: Marsh Norman [M]. New York: Theater Communication Group, 1988.

[167] NORMAN M. Introduction [C]//SMITH M L. (ed.). Women playwrights: the best plays of 1997. NH: Smith and Kraus, 1998: vii - ix.

[168] NOTH P D. Marsha Norman on "the color purple" [J/OL]. Milwaukee Journal, 2014, 19(Sept.) http://urbanmilwaukee.com/2014/09/19/theater-marsha-norman.

[169] NOURYE H A. Flashing back: dramatizing the trauma of incest and child sexual abuse[J]. Theater symposium: a journal of the southeastern theater conference, 1999, (7): 49 - 63.

[170] NOVY M. Saving Desdemona and /or ourselves: plays by Ann-Marie MacDonald and Paula Vogel [C]//NOBY M. (ed.). Transforming Shakespeare: contemporary women's re-visions in literature and performance. New York: St. Martin's, 1999: 67 - 85.

[171] O' CONNOR J J. *Uncommon Women and Others* in TV tonight [N]. The New York times, 1978,(May 24): C24.

[172] OWEN A S, STEIN S R et al. Bad girls: cultural politics and media representations of transgressive woman [M]. New York: Peter

Lang, 2007.

[173] PAIGE L R. The "other" side of the looking glass: a feminist perspective on female suicide in Ibsen's *Hedda Gabler*, Heilman's *The Children's Hour*, and Norman's *'night, Mother* [D]. University of Tennessee, 1989.

[174] PARKIN K. Driving home class status: women and car advertising in the United States [J]. Advertising & society quarterly, 2019, 20 (2):15-21.

[175] PAVIS P. Dictionary of the theater: terms, concepts and analysis [M]. Toronto: University of Toronto Press, 1998.

[176] PELLEGRINI A. Repercussions and remainders in the plays of Paula Vogel: an essay in five moments [C]//KRASNER D. (ed.). A companion to twentieth century American drama. Oxford: Blackwell Publishing Ltd., 2007:473-485.

[177] PLANT R. The pink triangle: the Nazi war against homosexuals [M]. New York: H. Holt, 1986.

[178] PODOS B. Feeding the feminist psyche through ritual theater [C]// SPRETNAK C. (ed.). The politics of women's spirituality: essays on the rise of power within the feminist movement. New York: Doubleday, 1982.

[179] PORTER L. Contemporary playwrights/traditional forms [C]// MURPHY B. (ed.). The Cambridge companion to American women playwrights. Shanghai: Shanghai Foreign Language Education Press, 2001.

[180] POST R M. The sexual world of Paula Vogel [J]. Journal of American drama and theater, 2001, 13(3): 42-54.

[181] PURCELL C. New Ohio theater to present Paula Vogel's *And Baby Makes Seven* [N]. Playbill, 2013, (Nov. 19):11.

[182] PURCELL C. A Woman's world: Pam MacKinnon on the decision to restore Wasserstein's cut dialogue to *The Heidi Chronicles* [N]. Playbill, 2015, (Feb 28.):22.

[183] RAPPAPORT R. Ecology, meaning, and religion [M]. Richmond: North Atlantic Books, 1979.

[184] RAPPAPORT R. Ritual and religion in the making of humanity [M]. Cambridge: Cambridge University Press, 1999.

[185] REUNING S. Depression—the undiagnosed disability in Marsha Norman's 'night, Mother [C]//FAHY T R & KING K (eds.). Peering behind the curtain: disability, illness and the extraordinary. New York: Routledge, 2002:55-67.

[186] RICHARD S E. Dramatic wit and wisdom unite in *Uncommon Women and Others* [N]. The New York times, 1977, (Nov. 22).

[187] RICHARDSON B. Voice and narration in postmodern drama[J]. New literary history: a journal of theory and interpretation, 2001, 32(3): 681-694.

[188] RICH F. Suicide talk in 'night, Mother: Review of 'night, Mother by Marsha Norman [N]. The New York times, 1983, (Apr. 1).

[189] ROSE L. *The Baltimore Waltz*: dying in wonderland [N]. The Washington post, 1994, (May 17): C1.

[190] ROSEN R. The world split open: how the modern women's movement changed America [M]. New York: The Penguin Press, 2000.

[191] ROSS K E. On death and dying [M]. New York: Routledge, 1973.

[192] ROTHSTEIN M. After the revolution, what? the daughters of feminism [N]. The New York times, 1988, (Dec. 11):1-28.

[193] ROUDANE M. American drama since 1960: a critical history [M]. New York: Twayne Publishers, 1996.

[194] SALAMONE F A. Encyclopedia of religious rites, rituals, and festivals [M]. New York: Routledge, 2004.

[195] SALAMON J. Wendy and the lost boys [M]. New York: The Penguin Press, 2012.

[196] SAVRAN D. In their own words: contemporary American playwrights [M]. New York: Theater Communications Group, 1988.

[197] SAVRAN D. Loose screwsp: *The Baltimore Waltz and Other Plays* [M]. New York: Theater Communications Group, 1996.

[198] SAVRAN D. The Playwright's voice: American dramatic on memory, writing and the politics of culture [M]. New York: Theater Communications Group, 1999.

[199] SAVRAN D. A queer sort of materialism: recontextualizing American theater [M]. Ann Arbor: University of Michigan Press, 2003.

[200] SAVRAN D. The haunted houses of modernity [C]// KNOWLES R. (ed.). Modern drama: defining the field. Toronto: University of Toronto Press, 2003.

[201] SCHECHNER R. Performance studies: an introduction [M]. London & New York: Routledge, 2013.

[202] SCHROEDER P R. Locked behind the proscenium: feminist strategies in *Getting Out* and *My Sister in This House* [J]. Modern drama, 1989, 32: 104-174.

[203] SHEPARD A & LAMB M. The memory palace in Paula Vogel's plays [C]//MCDONALD R & PAIGE L R. (eds.). Southern women playwrights: new essays in literary history and criticism. Tuscaloosa: University of Alabama Press, 2002:198-217.

[204] SHIRLEY D. Stage review *And Baby Makes Seven*: amusing child's play [N/OL]. Los Angeles times, 1990,(Mar. 12). [2019-03-20] http://articles.latimes.com/1990-03-12/Entertainment /ca-103 _1_baby-makes-seven.

[205] SIMON J. The best so far [N]. New York, 1992 (Nov. 2): 100-101.

[206] SMITH J. When seduction's all in the family [N]. New York magazine, 1997, (Mar. 31):86.

[207] SMITH R H. *'night, Mother* and true west: mirror images of violence and gender [C]//REDMOND J. (ed.). Violence in drama. Cambridge: Cambridge University Press, 1991: 277-289.

[208] SNOEK J A M. Defining ritual [C]//KREINATH J, SNOEK J, & STAUSBERG M. (eds.). Theorizing rituals: issues, topics, approaches, concepts. Leiden: Koninklijke Brill NV, 2006.

[209] SPENCER J S. Norman's 'night, Mother, psycho-drama of the female identity [J]. Modern drama, 1987,(30): 364-375.

[210] SPENCER J S. Marsha Norman's she-tragedies [C]// HART L. (ed.). Making a spectacle: feminist essays on contemporary women's theater. Ann Arbor: University of Michigan Press, 1989: 147-65.

[211] SPRETNAK C. The politics of women's spirituality [M]. New York: Anchor Books, 1982.

[212] STEARNS P D. Lively, liberated artists [N]. USA today, 1989, (Mar. 10): 4D.

[213] STEWART Z. And Baby Makes Seven [J]. Theater mania, 2014 (Mar 23):18-22. www.theatermania.com/new-york-city-theater/reviews/03-2014/and-baby-makes seven_67961.html.

[214] STONE E. Playwright Marsha Norman: an optimist writes about suicide, confinement and despair [N]. Ms. 1983, 102 (July): 52-59.

[215] STONE L. Sex trials [N]. The nation, 1997, (July 28):3.

[216] SULLIVAN K M. Parodied ritual in the plays of Edward Albee [D]. University of Notre Dame, 1987.

[217] TAMBIAH J S. Culture, thought, and social action: an anthropological perspective [M]. Cambridge, Mass., and London: Harvard University Press, 1985.

[218] TAYLOR P. Theater: the misuse of abuse [N]. Independent, 1999, (Apr. 7).

[219] THOMPSON E R. Saving the southern sister: tracing the survivor narrative in southern women's modern and contemporary novels and plays [D]. The University of Memphis, 2010.

[220] TOSCANO M. Ambiguous "drive" takes audience on muddled ride [N]. Washington post, 2004, (Feb. 5).

[221] TURNER K. Contemporary feminist rituals [J]. Heresies special issue: the great goddess, 1978, 2(1):23-28.

[222] TURNER V. Frame, flow and reflection: ritual and drama as public liminality [J]. Japanese journal of religious studies,1979, 6,4 (Dec.):456-499.

[223] TURNER V. The ritual process: structure and anti-structure[M]. New York: Cornell University Press, 1987.

[224] TURNER V & TURNER E. Image and pilgrimage in Christian culture [M]. New York: Columbia University Press, 1978.

[225] VOGEL P. And Baby Makes Seven [M]//The Baltimore Waltz and other plays. New York: Theater Communications Group, Inc., 1996.

[226] VOGEL P. The Baltimore Waltz[M]//The Baltimore Waltz and Other Plays. New York: Theater Communications Group, 1996.

[227] VOGEL P. How I Learned to Drive [M]. New York: Dramatists Play Service Inc.,1998.

[228] VOGEL P. Women who write plays: interviews with American dramatists [C]//GREENE A. (ed.). NH: Smith and Kraus, 2001.

[229] VOGEL P. Through the eyes of Lolita: Pulitzer prize-winner playwright Paula Vogel is interviewed by Arthur Holmberg [EB/OL]. The American repertory theater, 〈http://www.amrep.org/past/drive/drive1.html〉, 2006.

[230] VOS N. The process of dying in the plays of Edward Albee[J]. Educational theater journal, 1973, XXV,(March 1):80-85.

[232] WASSERSTEIN W. Uncommon Women and Others [M]. New York: Dramatists Play Service Inc., 1978.

[232] WASSERSTEIN W. Interviews with contemporary women playwrights [C]//BETSKO K & KOENIG R. (eds.). New York: Beech Tree Books, 1987.

References

[233] WASSERSTEIN W. The Heidi Chronicles [M]. New York: Dramatists Play Service Inc., 1990.

[234] WASSERSTEIN W. Bachelor Girls [M]. New York: Vintage, 1991.

[235] WASSERSTEIN W. The Sisters Rosensweig [M]. New York, San Diego and London: Harcourt Brace & Company, 1993.

[236] WATERMEIER D J. The search for self: attachment, loss and recovery in The Heidi Chronicles [C]//MAUFORT M. (ed.). Staging difference: cultural pluralism in American theater and drama. New York: Peter Lang Press, 1995:351-362.

[237] WATT D. Holyoke hen sessions [N]. New York daily news, 1977, (Nov. 22):27.

[238] WATTENBERG R. Feminizing the frontier myth: Marsha Norman's The Holdup [J]. Modern drama, 1990,(33):507-517.

[239] WEALES G. American theater watch, 1988—1989 [J]. The Georgia review, 1989, (43): 573-585.

[240] WHATELY K. Abuse and ambiguity [N]. Financial times, London edition, 1998,(June 25):18.

[241] WIMMER L C. Slicing silences and hatchet words: operations of women's anger in twentieth's century plays by American women [D]. University of Maryland, 2001.

[242] WINDER L. Wendy Wasserstein: the art of theater XIII [N]. The Paris review, 1997, (142 Spring):177.

[243] ZUSSE M E. The encyclopedia of religion [M]. New York: Macmillan, 1987.

[244] ŽIŽEK S. Event: a philosophical journey through a concept [M]. New York: Melville House, 2014.

[245] 白锡汉. 论《晚安,妈妈》中的饮食符号意指[J]. 湖北第二师范学院学报,2014,(1):10-12.

BAI X H. Analysis of food symbolic meaning in 'night, Mother[J]. Journal of Hubei University of Education, 2014 (1): 10-12.

[246] 岑伟. 女性身份的嬗变:海尔曼和诺曼戏剧研究[D]. 济南:山东大学博士论文,2009.

CEN W. Evolution of female identity: a study on the plays by L. Hellman and M. Norman [D]. Jinan: Shandong University, 2009.

[247] 岑伟. 舞台魅影:玛莎·诺曼剧作中不在场的男性形象[J]. 四川戏剧,2010,(3):95-97.

CEN W. Ghosts on stage: the absent males in Marsha Norman's plays [J]. Sichuan drama, 2010 (3): 95-97.

[248] 陈琳. 温迪·华瑟斯汀女性意识戏剧研究[D]. 南京:南京大学博士论文,2011.

CHEN L. In search of comic possibilities: a study of Wendy Wasserstein's woman-conscious comedies [D]. Nanjing: Nanjing University, 2011.

[249] 陈一雷,陈爱敏. 身份的麻烦:20—21世纪美国戏剧核心主题探[J]. 四川戏剧,2015,(9):29-33.

CHEN Y L & CHEN A M. Identity trouble: the core theme of American theater in 20th-21st century [J]. Sichuan drama, 2015 (9): 29-33.

[250] 韩曦. 从现实主义到女性主义:美国女剧作家简论[J]. 戏剧(中央戏剧学院学报),2014,(6):51-61.

HAN X. From realism to feminism: a study on American women playwrights [J]. Theater (The journal of the Central Academy of Drama), 2014 (6):51-61.

[251] 贺安芳. 追寻自我:温迪·华瑟斯廷和她的女性人物[D]. 上海:华东师范大学博士论文,2006.

HE A F. In search of self: Wendy Wasserstein and her women[D]. Shanghai: East China Normal University, 2006.

[252] 贺安芳,费春放. 论温迪·华瑟斯廷剧作的喜剧精神[J]. 外国语文,2015,(2):5-11.

HE A F, FEI C F. On the comic spirit of Wendy Wasserstein's plays [J]. Foreign language and literature, 2015 (4): 5-11.

[253] 贺安芳. 论温迪·华瑟斯廷喜剧的忧伤情调[J]. 戏剧（中央戏剧学院学报），2015，（4）：36-46.

   HE A F. The atmosphere of sadness in Wendy Wasserstein's comedy [J]. Theater (The journal of the Central Academy of Drama), 2015 (4): 36-46.

[254] 贺安芳. 母女关系视角下的玛莎诺曼作品研究[J]. 宁波大学学报（人文科学版），2013，（5）：32-36.

   HE A F. Mother-daughter relationship in Marsha Norman's plays [J]. Journal of Ningbo University, 2013 (3): 32-36.

[255] 何成洲. 文学的事件[M]. 南京：南京大学出版社，2020年.

   HE C Z. Literature as event [M]. Nanjing: Nanjing University Press, 2020.

[256] 何成洲. 巴特勒与表演性理论[J]. 外国文学评论，2010（3）：132-143.

   HE C Z. Butler and the theory of performativity [J]. Foreign literature review, 2010(3): 132-143.

[257] 何成洲. 西方文论的操演性转向[J]. 文艺研究，2020，（8）：39-49.

   HE C Z. The performativity turn in western literary theory [J]. Literature and art studies, 2020 (8): 39-49.

[258] 金李俪. 透过女性视角：戏剧传统语境中的弗戈尔戏剧研究[M]. 上海：上海外语教育出版社，2013.

   JIN L L. Through female eyes: a study of Paula Vogel's plays in the context of dramatic tradition [M]. Shanghai: Shanghai Foreign Language Education Press, 2013.

[259] 李莉. 当代美国戏剧中的身份政治[J]. 世界文化，2017，（2）：39-41.

   LI L. Identity politics in contemporary American theater [J]. World culture, 2017 (2): 39-41.

[260] 李淑玲，李梦阳. "陌生化"的诱惑：《我如何学会驾驶》的叙事表演策略[J]. 四川戏剧，2016，（5）：13-16.

   LI S L & LI M Y. The seduction of defamiliarization: the narrative and performative techniques in *How I Learned to Drive*[J]. Sichuan drama, 2016 (5): 13-16.

[261] 梁超群,张锷. 话剧《我是怎么学会开车的》:一次成功的诱惑[J]. 戏剧艺术, 2014, (2): 78-84.
LIANG C Q & ZHANG E. *How I Learned to Drive*: a successful seduction [J]. Theatre arts, 2014 (2):78-84.

[262] 刘秀玉. 从《晚安,妈妈》看玛莎·诺曼的女性主义戏剧创作[J]. 辽宁大学学报(哲学社会科学版), 2008, (3): 59-62.
LIU X Y. On Marsha Norman's feminist play: a case study of *'night, Mother* [J]. Journal of Liaoning University, 2008 (3): 59-62.

[263] 王蕾. 论温迪·瓦瑟斯坦戏剧中的女性身份危机[J]. 南京工程学院学报(社科学版),2013, (4): 16-21.
WANG L. On the female identity crisis in Wendy Wasserstein's plays[J]. Journal of Nanjing Institute of Technology (Social science edition), 2013 (4): 16-21.

[264] 王莉. 论玛莎·诺曼戏剧中的过去和记忆[M]. 北京:中国社会科学出版社,2014.
WANG L. Past and memory in Marsh Norman's dramatic works [M]. Beijing: China Social Sciences Press, 2014.

[265] 汪晓云. 从仪式到艺术:中西戏剧发生学[M]. 桂林:广西师范大学出版社, 2016.
WANG X Y. From ritual to art: genesis of Chinese and western theater[M]. Guilin: Guangxi Normal University Press, 2016.

[266] 吴庆宏. 论温迪·瓦萨斯坦的女性主义戏剧创作[J]. 当代外国文学,2007, (1): 11-16.
WU Q H. On the feminist plays of Wendy Wasserstein [J]. Contemporary foreign literature, 2007(1): 11-16.

[267] 谢江南,何星莹. 性别与自我塑造:温迪·华森斯坦戏剧研究[J]. 戏剧(中央戏剧学院学报),2017, (2): 23-33.
XIE J N & HE X Y. Gender and self-fashioning: on plays by Wendy

Wasserstein[J]. Drama (The Journal of the Central Academy of Drama), 2017 (2): 23 - 33.

[268] 张金良. 语言视角:三位美国当代戏剧家研究[D]. 南京:南京大学博士论文,2007.

ZHANG J L. Language as a perspective: a study of three contemporary American dramatists [D]. Nanjing: Nanjing University, 2007.

[269] 张生珍. 在创伤中成长:保拉·沃格尔剧作《我如何学会驾驶》研究[J]. 戏剧文学,2012,(11):87 - 91.

ZHANG S Z. Growing up through trauma: a study on *How I Learned to Drive* by Paula Vogel[J]. Drama literature, 2012 (11): 87 - 91.

[270] 张生珍. 她们的舞台:当代美国妇女剧作家研究[M]. 北京:中国社会科学出版社,2014.

ZHANG S Z. Drama of their own: a study of contemporary American women playwrights[M]. Beijing: China Social Sciences Press, 2014.

[271] 朱晓映. "男人的剧院"与女人的戏:美国当代女剧作家与普利策奖的相遇[J]. 外国文学动态,2012,(3):8 - 10.

ZHU X Y. Men's theater and women's drama: contemporary American women playwrights' encounter with Pulitzer prize[J]. New perspectives on world literature, 2011 (3): 8 - 10.

[272] 左进. 二十世纪美国女剧作家自我书写的语用文体研究[D]. 上海:上海外国语大学博士论文,2010.

ZUO J. A pragmastylistic study of the self-writing of American women playwrights in the twentieth century [D]. Shanghai: Shanghai International Studies University, 2010.

图书在版编目(CIP)数据

仪式与女性自我：当代美国女剧作家研究：英文 / 李淑玲著. —— 南京：南京大学出版社，2022.10
ISBN 978 - 7 - 305 - 25846 - 6

Ⅰ.①仪… Ⅱ.①李… Ⅲ.①话剧-戏剧文学评论-美国-现代-英文 Ⅳ.①I712.073

中国版本图书馆 CIP 数据核字(2022)第 092241 号

出版发行　南京大学出版社
社　　址　南京市汉口路 22 号　　　邮　编　210093
出 版 人　金鑫荣

书　　名　仪式与女性自我——当代美国女剧作家研究
著　　者　李淑玲
责任编辑　张淑文

照　　排　南京南琳图文制作有限公司
印　　刷　江苏扬中印刷有限公司
开　　本　718 mm×960 mm　1/16 开　印张 23.25　字数 335 千
版　　次　2022 年 10 月第 1 版　2022 年 10 月第 1 次印刷
ISBN 978 - 7 - 305 - 25846 - 6
定　　价　85.00 元

网　　址　http://www.njupco.com
官方微博　http://weibo.com/njupco
官方微信　njupress
销售热线　(025) 83594756

* 版权所有，侵权必究
* 凡购买南大版图书，如有印装质量问题，请与所购
　图书销售部门联系调换